## Praise for the Nightkeepers Series

"This series goes right to your heart! Jessica Andersen is a must read for me!"
—#1 *New York Times* Bestselling Author J. R. Ward

### Demonkeepers

"Andersen ramps up the danger . . . mix[ing] action . . . with soul-searching, lust, and romance. Jade's inner journey is particularly engaging, and while the background makes more sense to returning fans, even new readers will find plenty to latch on to." —*Publishers Weekly*

"Destiny and free will are on a collision course in this high-stakes romantic drama. Andersen delivers another exhilarating entry!" —*Romantic Times*

"Intense . . . thrilling . . . a world that fans of any genre will enjoy." —The Romance Readers Connection

"Fabulous . . . will have the audience appreciating the skills of master magician Jessica Andersen."
—*Midwest Book Review*

### Skykeepers

"An exciting, romantic, and imaginative tale, *Skykeepers* is guaranteed to keep readers entertained and turning the pages." —Romance Reviews Today

"A gripping story that pulled this reader right into her Final Prophecy series."
—Romance Reader at Heart (top pick)

"The Final Prophecy is a well-written series that is as intricate as it is entertaining."
—The Romance Readers Connection

*continued . . .*

## The Novels of the Nightkeepers

# STORM KISSED

### A NOVEL OF THE NIGHTKEEPERS

## JESSICA ANDERSEN

A SIGNET ECLIPSE BOOK

SIGNET ECLIPSE
Published by New American Library, a division of
Penguin Group (USA) Inc., 375 Hudson Street,
New York, New York 10014, USA
Penguin Group (Canada), 90 Eglinton Avenue East, Suite 700, Toronto,
Ontario M4P 2Y3, Canada (a division of Pearson Penguin Canada Inc.)
Penguin Books Ltd., 80 Strand, London WC2R 0RL, England
Penguin Ireland, 25 St. Stephen's Green, Dublin 2,
Ireland (a division of Penguin Books Ltd.)
Penguin Group (Australia), 250 Camberwell Road, Camberwell, Victoria 3124,
Australia (a division of Pearson Australia Group Pty. Ltd.)
Penguin Books India Pvt. Ltd., 11 Community Centre, Panchsheel Park,
New Delhi - 110 017, India
Penguin Group (NZ), 67 Apollo Drive, Rosedale, Auckland 0632,
New Zealand (a division of Pearson New Zealand Ltd.)
Penguin Books (South Africa) (Pty.) Ltd., 24 Sturdee Avenue,
Rosebank, Johannesburg 2196, South Africa

Penguin Books Ltd., Registered Offices:
80 Strand, London WC2R 0RL, England

First published by Signet Eclipse, an imprint of New American Library,
a division of Penguin Group (USA) Inc.

First Printing, June 2011
10  9  8  7  6  5  4  3  2  1

Copyright © Jessica Andersen, 2011
All rights reserved

SIGNET ECLIPSE and logo are trademarks of Penguin Group (USA) Inc.

Printed in the United States of America

**PUBLISHER'S NOTE**
This is a work of fiction. Names, characters, places, and incidents either are the
product of the author's imagination or are used fictitiously, and any resem-
blance to actual persons, living or dead, business establishments, events, or
locales is entirely coincidental.
    The publisher does not have any control over and does not assume any re-
sponsibility for author or third-party Web sites or their content.

*This book is dedicated to strays, and to the generous hearts who bring them in from the cold.*

# AUTHOR'S NOTE AND ACKNOWLEDGMENTS

I don't know about you guys, but I love a bad boy, especially one who lives by his own code of honor. Dez is one of those guys—except he went off the rails a while back and broke the heart of the woman who was, and will always be, his soul mate. What's more, Reese Montana—a former bounty hunter who is a badass in her own right—isn't the kind to forgive and forget. So when they're reunited, major sparks fly.

Please join me now as these two butt heads, lock lips, and try to figure each other out while racing to discover the secret of the serpent bloodline, and kicking some serious ass in the process.

For new readers and fans alike, there's a glossary and list of characters at the back of the book. I hope you'll check it out.

To explore the Nightkeepers' online world and sign up for Nightkeeper News, please visit www.Jessica Andersen.com. Also, you can friend me on Facebook to get a look at my oh so Freudian typos and other authorial misadventures!

My heartfelt thanks to Deidre Knight, Claire Zion, Kara Welsh, Kerry Donovan, and others too numerous to name for helping me bring these books to life; to J. R. Ward for being my sounding board; to Suz Brockmann for being a mentor and an inspiration; to Sally

Hinkle Russell for reminding me to keep my eyes up and my heels down; and to my family, friends, and many e-friends for always being there for a laugh or (cyber) hug.

And thank you, dear reader, for picking up Reese and Dez's story. I hope you love it as much as I do—I'm not much of a weeper, but the ending of this one gets me every time.

Jessica (aka Doc Jess)

Bound by blood and magic, the Nightkeepers must defend mankind from the rise of terrible demons. In order to reach their full powers, they must find and bond with their gods-destined mates . . . who aren't always who or what they seem.

With their ancient enemy reincarnated in the form of a brutal mage named Iago, their gods trapped in the sky by the destruction of a critical Mayan ruin, and people disappearing mysteriously, the magi need all hands on deck. So when one of their own—a powerful and dangerous mage named Mendez—vanishes without a trace, the Nightkeepers' king does the only thing he can think of . . .

# CHAPTER ONE

Ten years ago
*Denver*

Reese Montana had survived her parents' divorce, a grabby-fingered stepfather, and hitting the gang-infested streets at fifteen. She had survived—barely—being targeted by the leader of one of those gangs, and had turned police informant to help bring him down. But now, at nineteen, she was sick of surviving. She wanted to *live*. And, damn it, she wanted to do it with the man who was squared off opposite her in the main room of their shared two-bedroom, looking like she'd just gut-shot him.

"Reese," he grated. "Don't do this."

Mendez meant it as an order, but it came out more like a plea. His pale hazel eyes slid from hers, but he didn't move, just stood there—six seven worth of wide-shouldered, rawboned energy wearing jeans and a leather jacket he shouldn't have been able to afford, with an angular face that hadn't been carded in years, though he'd only just turned twenty-one.

His big body vibrated with the same tension that ran through hers—the need to fight, to kick ass, to burn off the heat that had been growing between them for months now. But although he would fight for her, fight with her, he wouldn't fight *her*. His control, like his protection, had been his promise. And she was sick of both.

"Sorry. I've had it with your timetable." She kept her voice dead level, knowing that if she got shrill and snippy—or worse, let him sense her nerves—he would find a way to put her back in the "little sister" box inside his rock-hard head. But she wasn't his sister, hadn't ever been.

Closing the distance between them, she splayed her hand on his chest as she had often done in their early days together, when they had huddled in abandoned squats, sharing body heat and vigilance. His heartbeat was fast against her palm, his chest a solid wall of muscle.

Heat pooled alongside her nerves, and her stomach gave a little flutter. She knew his body completely, yet she didn't. The shared-warmth cuddles had ended a year ago when they'd finally started making enough to get into an official flop with actual utilities, a signed lease, and the locks he'd installed on the insides of both their bedroom doors. And she was sick of that, too. More, she was afraid that if she didn't do something, he was going to decompress. He'd been driving himself too hard lately, straying way too close to the line between right and wrong. The thought of him going all the way over that line scared her worse than the idea of being rejected.

Almost.

"Don't push me, Reese." His words vibrated against her palm, setting up resonant quivers inside her. "Not—" He bit it off, but she heard it anyway: *Not now.*

"Why not now?" She wasn't quite brave enough to wrap her arms around his neck, though she badly wanted to, had envisioned herself doing just that when she'd played it out over and over again in her head. Instead, she shifted to grip the edges of his leather, leaving a scant inch of space between their bodies. "We've got jobs and a place of our own."

Outside it was night-black and pissing rain, cold and hard-edged with the chill of early fall. The sharp drops hammered against the room's single window, but inside the apartment they were warm and dry.

He shook his head. "It's not enough."

"This is what we've got. This is our life." She tightened her fingers on his jacket, willing him to listen to her, to really *hear* her this time. "Maybe in a perfect world things would've been different. You wouldn't have been raised by your crazy-assed godfather. My dad wouldn't have left, or my mom would've believed me rather than Number Two. But that's not the way it happened. We got through it. We made *this*." Her gesture encompassed the two of them and the space around them. The three-room apartment, with its crappy flooring, Salvation Army decor, and Febreze-defying funky smell, still felt like heaven to her.

His look labeled it a dump. "You deserve better." But then his eyes softened and his voice dropped an octave. "Damn it, Reese, you deserve the dream. We both do."

But the fantasy of escaping to a place with wide-open skies had been just talk, a story she would tell when he fell silent. She hadn't grown up like him, didn't know the things he did, so she'd taken a picture that was burned into her brain and turned it into an imaginary world. For her, it had been a way to avoid the reality of growling stomachs, frozen toes, and constant vigilance. For him, it had become a goal. "Someday I'll give you a palace," he would say. But she wasn't a princess and she didn't want him to surround her with stone walls and armed guards. Which was exactly what he would do if he got the chance.

He'd been just three when his parents and baby sister died in a horrible fire, and he still had nightmares about being dragged away by his godfather, Keban, who had spent the next dozen years alternating between teaching him the history of warfare and subjecting him to bizarre, often bloody rituals. So she got why he didn't want to let his guard down—even with her—until they were far away from the gang that had made their lives, and the neighborhood, a living hell. He wanted to feel safe. More important, he wanted to know that *she* was safe, that he wouldn't lose her the way he lost his family. And having seen too many other street kids start with big dreams only to wind up with a kid or two of their own, stalled in a crappy apartment only a couple of streets away from where they started, he didn't want things to go any further between them until they were someplace better.

Stubborn ass that he was, he wouldn't talk about it. Boom, done, end of discussion.

But she didn't want to be on a pedestal, damn it. If she wanted something she'd earn it herself, and if she felt threatened, she could deadeye a rat across a cluttered warehouse with her .38. But she hadn't gotten anywhere with that logic, or with anything else. And the more she pushed him, the harder he pushed himself.

Something had to give, and she wanted it to be her.

"I've already got the dream, dumbass. *You're* my dream." Stomach fluttering like it was filled with crackhead moths, she shifted her grip to his collar, used it as leverage to pull herself up onto her toes. And kissed him.

She must've been taller in her fantasies, because she'd always pictured herself hitting his lips. She got the side of his throat instead, tasted the faint salty tang of his skin, and felt his quick indrawn breath when the move brought their bodies flush. Her heart drummed in her ears as he stiffened and grabbed her upper arms. But he didn't push her away. And the pulse beneath her lips throbbed hard and fast.

"Reese. Don't." His voice was a low growl of warning.

But she was done playing by his rules. So instead of backing off, she leaned in, grazed her teeth along the throbbing vessel and bit down, not hard enough to break the skin, but hard enough to say: *I want you, here and now.* Against his throat, she whispered, "I know you're working to get us someplace better, and I want that too. But don't you understand? We're safest when we're staying sharp and watching each other's backs. And if you think ignoring what's going on between us isn't a distraction, then you're a bigger idiot than I thought . . . unless you're not distracted, in which case *I'm* the idiot."

His answering laugh was part groan. "You're not an idiot." He got a hand on the back of her neck and pressed her face into the crook of his neck, though she wasn't sure if he was trying to hold her close or stop her from kissing him again. Beneath her ear, his words rumbled hollowly as he said, "But you know what happens when people pair off around here. They fucking *stay* here."

"Not us," she said firmly. "We're better than that. We won't let ourselves stall." But she would do her damnedest to slow him down a little before he crashed and burned. "We can be together and still have our dreams." She might not want a wide-open prairie anymore, but she hadn't stopped picturing tomorrow, didn't ever plan to.

He held himself still and silent for a long moment as thunder rumbled beneath the rattling raindrops. Then, softly, he said, "Do you really think so?"

For a second she thought that she had to have imagined the question. But there was no mistaking the way one of his hands slid from the back of her head to her nape, the other from her shoulder to her waist. Suddenly, he wasn't holding her captive against him anymore. He was simply holding her.

*Holy shit.* The air left her lungs in a rush as she realized that she was getting through to him. Or maybe he'd finally gotten to the end of his self-control—maybe, probably, a combination of the two. She didn't know, didn't care. Putting all her certainty into it, she said, "I know so. We're better together than apart, and that's a fact."

Together, they had waged war on the Cobras, had helped Detective Fallon's task force weaken the powerful gang and its reign of terror. They had watched each other's backs, watched each other grow up. And if he had been the boss of their joint ventures more often than not, she had been okay with following his lead . . . at least until now.

Now, she was taking the lead. And he'd better catch up.

"I don't want to get this wrong," he rasped. "It's too damn important." But his hand dropped to her hip and his fingers curved in a warm, possessive grip.

Her pulse hammered. A gust rattled the windows, making her feel as if the storm was inside her, inside him, racing between them. The beat of the rain was the rush of blood in her veins; the lightning was the searing electricity she saw in his eyes. "I don't want to make a mistake either," she said softly. "But I'm tired of waiting to start our lives. I want to live them instead."

Thunder rumbled as he tightened his grip on her. "Reese, there's something else I need to—"

"Love me," she interrupted, forcing the words past the weight of nerves because her gut said it was time to stop talking. "Please love me, because . . . Hell, because I love you."

She had never said the words before; neither of them had. Not, she suspected, to anyone. And the moment she did, lightning flashed hard, something went *zzzt* outside, and the electricity died.

Holy. Crap.

It wasn't the first time they had lost power during a storm—far from it—but it was the first time she'd been in Dez's arms when it happened, the first time the darkness had made her so vividly aware of her other senses. She smelled the newness of his leather and the stormy air that still clung to him. And when he said, "Damn it, Reese," she heard loud and clear the too-serious tone that meant a lecture was coming.

She tightened her grip on the collar. "Don't even think—"

He cut her off with a kiss that made her senses spin even as the reality froze her in place.

Dez. Was kissing. Her.

Nerves and heat collided and combined as she closed her eyes, memorizing the moment in her heart . . . and then threw herself headfirst into a kiss that was everything that she had hoped for and nothing like she had planned.

His lips were softer than she had expected, their press more a question than a demand, but the contact was electrifying. Warmth furled through her as he framed her face in his hands and kissed the corner of her mouth, her cheek, the point of her jaw, and back again. The difference in their heights meant that they weren't plastered together anymore, but she leaned into him, opened to him, and felt the electric jolt of con-

tact when their tongues met in an achingly soft caress.
Her heart shuddered with the restraint he was using to
show her how he felt, even if he hadn't said the words.

As he kept things soft and slow, though, her frustration built. She could sense his coiled tension, knew
it was costing him to be so gentle. But, damn it, she
wanted *him*—the stubborn, arrogant, know-it-all who
always had to be in charge—not this careful, watered-
down version that was still trying to protect her, still
saw her as some fragile-assed princess.

Hissing out a breath, she deepened the kiss, sliding
her tongue against his and adding a scrape of teeth that
had him groaning deep in his throat. "I won't break,"
she said against his lips. "Kiss me for real, or I'll find
someone who will."

It was an empty threat, but he froze, not even breathing. Lightning flashed, illuminating them in a starburst
of blue-white, and she saw raging heat in his eyes, a
barely leashed fury that was almost enough to make
her retreat. Almost. But this was Dez. This was what
she wanted. So she reached for the zipper tab of her
sleek black sweater and eased it down a few inches,
far enough that when the lightning flickered again, he
could see the edge of her bra beneath. And nothing
else.

He growled her name, followed by a succinct: "Fuck
it."

She laughed, because that was the man she knew,
the one she wanted. But the sound quickly turned to
a gasp as he spun them in a dizzying whirl that put
her up against the nearest wall. His lower body pinned

hers in a full-contact press that let her feel the hard lines of his thighs and the rigid bulge behind his fly, but she had only an instant to ride the slashing, adrenaline-charged sense of victory. After that, his lips slammed on hers, all hard edges, heat, and the frustration that had been building for far too long.

And then she couldn't think at all.

She sucked in a breath, floundering for a split second, and in that moment of hesitation, his tongue surged through her parted lips and his mouth clamped on hers, sealing them together. Wild heat lashed through her, and she let out a desperate moan as he boosted her up and urged her to twine her legs around his hips.

Their lips parted, then reconnected in a deeper, darker kiss as he ran his hands up her arms and then inward, to cup her aching breasts and drag his thumbs across her nipples, which were so hard they hurt. When he touched them, though, the pain became plea-sure, sharp and acute, and like nothing she'd ever felt before. All of a sudden, *none* of it was like anything she'd ever experienced—not the wildfire sizzle in her veins, the yearning ache in her core, or the sudden clawing need to be skin on skin with him, to have him surrounding her, filling her.

She had dated a rookie cop from the gang task force for a few months the year before, and had gone out a few times with a guy who worked at the electron-ics shop on the corner two blocks down. She'd kissed them both, had slept with the cop. And she had won-dered whether she was missing something, or if sex, like baseball, was one of those things the media had hyped into something far more interesting than it actually was.

Apparently not. Or rather, yes, she had been missing something, but it hadn't been the sex. It had been Dez. It always had been.

But as much as she had thought she knew that, she hadn't known it would be like this. She arched against him as he kissed her lips, her throat, his mouth as rough and demanding as his touch. She slid her hands beneath his leather, into the layer of heat that was trapped between the jacket's slick satin lining and the soft fabric of his tee, which she bunched up and dragged out of his waistband to touch him. He groaned and leaned into her, deepening a kiss that had already been impossibly deep.

Cool air touched her skin as he unzipped her sweater the rest of the way, pulled it off her arms and chucked it, then shucked out of his coat and tee. He still had her braced up against the wall, their bodies fitted together through the frustrating barrier of their jeans as they kissed and twined together, bare-skinned above, save for her lacy bra.

She was wet and ready, greedy for their jeans to be gone and him to be inside her. His bedroom, hers, the couch, the floor, up against the wall—she didn't care about the where; she cared only about the what, who, and when. Sex. With Dez. Right now. But when he swept her up in his arms and carried her to his bedroom, kissing her as they went, her heart shuddered in her chest. His bedroom. God.

In the small, sparsely furnished room, wan illumination came from a set of working emergency lights on the building across the way, limning his body in a sodium yellow that traced his muscle-ridged abdomen, then gleamed on the width of his shoulders as he lowered her to his bed and followed her down. She raked her fingernails down his spine, then down along his ribs until he shuddered against her.

He pressed his hot cheek to hers, so he was breathing warmly in her ear when he whispered, "Gods, Reese. Tell me I'm not dreaming this."

Her answer died on her lips. *Gods?* "What do you—"

He cut her off with a kiss that quickly became a clash of lips, tongue, and teeth, held more passion than finesse, and brought the salty tang of blood.

Without warning, he jolted against her and gave a strange, strangled cry that was more surprise than passion. Then a slash of electric awareness raced through her, sweeping her up and carrying her with a crazy-hot wave of passion and connectivity. For a second, she felt like she was *inside* him, feeling his heartbeat, his arousal, his confusion as the air around them took on a hint of red-gold sparks. She heard a strange buzzing noise and felt a hot, rushing sensation that was partly sexual, partly something else. Then the connection snapped as he tore himself away from her.

She blinked up at him in shock as the lights flickered and the power came back on, turning the darkness back into the reality of the two of them together in his normally off-limits bedroom. He was kneeling on the mattress beside her—shirtless and buff as hell, with his jeans unsnapped to show the sharply defined interplay of muscle and bone at his hips. If she had taken a picture just then, it would've read as sex personified. But this wasn't a picture, and the look in his eyes didn't read as passion. It was more along the lines of "oh, shit," and the sight turned the heat of moments before into a sharp stab of pain.

Heart thudding, she started to reach for him, then pulled back and curled her fingers into a fist. "Dez," she began, but then stalled on a slashing wave of disappointment, because what was left for her to say? She had made her play, and it hadn't been enough. He was already pulling away.

"I'm going out," he grated, avoiding her eyes.

"*What?*"

He stood, grabbed a shirt from the lopsided bookcase that served as his dresser, and pulled on the tee with jerky motions. He stalled at the bedroom door, though, made like he was going to put his fist through the wall, but slapped it flat-handed instead. Pressing his forehead to his knuckles, he grated, "This isn't about you. I'm . . . Hell, I don't know what I am these days, but it's not good. And I can't put that on you."

She glared at him, letting him see the hurt and the gathering tears. "Yes, you can, damn it. We're a team."

But he shook his head as he pushed away from the doorframe. "Not this time." Moments later, the door banged shut, and he was gone.

The weather was even shittier than it had looked from inside the apartment, but Dez stalked out into the teeth of the storm, hoping it would kick the crap out of him

like he deserved. Damn it, he'd let things get way out
of hand. And he'd made Reese cry.

*Shit.* He rubbed his chest, where throbbing pain
had replaced his heartbeat. But as the cold rain killed
the last of the electric sizzle that had come from lightning hitting right outside the window, he was damned
grateful for the searing jolt, because it had slammed
him back to a reality that said he couldn't take what
he wanted.

She had been dead-on in everything she'd said:
The apartment was just a place, safety a state of mind,
and they were damn good together. And, hell, yeah,
he loved her. He had for far longer than she probably
guessed, but had sworn he would wait until she was old
enough to make a real choice. By then, though, he'd had
another problem, one that might've lost traction when
she started kissing him, but was bigger than all the others put together: He was losing his fucking mind.

It had started with a deep, searching restlessness
that had driven him out onto the streets after something he couldn't name, couldn't find. Then had come
the dreams—sometimes dark, bloody scenes of wars
past and present; other times native-dressed men and
women bowing to him before slitting their own throats
and bleeding out. The nightmares had gotten worse
over time, as had his usual drive to do the most, be the
best, get the hell ahead, until those urges had eclipsed
everything else. He was pushing too hard and knew
it, but he couldn't make himself slow down, couldn't
bring himself to talk to Reese about it. Instead, he
stalked along the parallel rows of warehouses late at

night, looking for something that wasn't there and un-raveling more each day.

He headed there now, past the pitch-black tene-ments to the empty warehouse husks, which echoed hollowly in the rain.

He had tried to tell himself that the restlessness and nightmares came from subconscious fears about the idea of him and Reese taking the next step. It wasn't like he'd grown up with a good role model when it came to relationships, and while she might be a street kid now, she had come from wealth and comfort. She should be Ivy League–ing it right now, with a varsity boyfriend, a blinged-out cell phone, and a sports car out in the lot. He couldn't give her any of that.

And like that wasn't enough to give a guy mental heartburn, there was Hood, the *cobra de rey*, king of the Cobras. The sick bastard was coming up for parole soon, and rumor had it that he was even more fixated on Reese than before. Dez figured he was due a few nightmares on that one . . . but that didn't explain why, three times over the past month, he had awakened kneeling on the floor beside his bed holding a knife—twice a kitchen knife and once a switchblade he'd snagged from a street punk who'd been hassling the old guy who ran the convenience store on the corner. That third time, he had been bleeding from his palms: two shallow slices right along the old scar lines. Then last week he had woken up halfway to Reese's room, carrying a six-inch blade he didn't recognize. That had scared the shit out of him, point blank.

After that, he had added a second lock on the inside of his bedroom door, hidden the key, and booby-trapped the hiding spot to make hell and all of a racket if he went for it. He hadn't yet, but that didn't make him feel any better, especially as the restlessness had gotten even worse over the past few days. He could feel it now as he stalked past Warehouse Thirteen, his eyes slitted against the shit that was pelting out of the sky and cutting straight through his clothes, chilling him to the bone.

*I'm here.*

He stopped dead at the whisper, which hadn't carried over the sound of the storm. It was inside his godsdamned skull.

"What the fuck?" He could barely hear himself over the pounding rain. His head was spinning, his body numb, but his shock was blunted by a second surprise as he realized loud and clear that something inside him recognized the whisper. Or maybe he really *was* crazy. Gods knew he had been raised by a madman. Maybe it had been only a matter of time.

*Come and get me.*

Holy shit. What was going on here? His feet started moving before his brain could catch up, and he stumbled and nearly went down. Cursing, he forced himself upright and stood braced on locked legs, caught between wanting to prove he could walk away and needing to know what the hell was going on. And—just maybe—what he could do to make the craziness go away so he and Reese could have a chance.

*I'm here.*

"I heard you," he growled. "Keep your damn panties

on." Because the whisper—the insanity—was feminine. And it was pulling him toward Warehouse Seventeen.

That was where he'd first seen Reese, where he'd broken his own "don't fuck with the Cobras and they won't fuck with you" rule by grabbing her before Hood could make her one of his "girlfriends." At the time, he'd told himself it had been a spur of the moment thing, a decision he'd made because something in her eyes had reminded him of his sister, Joy. Later, he'd admitted that an outside force had pulled him to Seventeen that day, and he'd toyed with the idea of destiny. Now, he didn't know what the fuck to think. Hell, he barely *could* think, though he held it together enough to pull out his .44.

It was the only weapon he was packing. He didn't trust himself with a knife anymore.

The warehouse was a black box of a building fronted with broken windows, dangling fire escapes, and a big "17" painted over the seized-up garage doors that hadn't worked in years. Like most of the others, Seventeen had been abandoned by its owners, condemned by the city, and then ignored because nobody really gave a damn about what went on in the shit zone as long as it didn't amoeba its way toward more important real estate. Over the years Seventeen had gone back and forth between being a central Cobra hangout and being abandoned to the street rats, who tunneled from one warehouse to the next, always making sure they had a way out. Lately, even the street kids had left it alone, though nobody knew quite why.

*Come.*

Dez followed the whisper into the dark shadows near where a couple of steel panels had been turned into a hidden entrance. He ducked through, leading with his gun but not seeing anything worth shooting. The few emergency lights that still worked inside Seventeen illuminated a jumble of racks, catwalks, and other random discards . . . including a small bundle that lay in a patch of scuffed-up dust beneath one of the working emergency lights. The wadded-up cloth didn't look much different from the other garbage lying around, but he knew it was more. He *knew*.

His head pounded and spun; his senses fogged. A warning buzzer went off deep inside him, but he ignored it because this was what he'd been searching for. He was sure of it. Letting his gun hand sag, he crouched down and reached for the bundle.

A slight, wiry body slammed into him from behind, driving him to his knees.

*Shit. Ambush!* Adrenaline blasted through him, clearing his head in an instant. Reacting even as he cursed himself for walking dumb-assed into the trap, he jammed his shoulder into his attacker's gut and heaved. The move should've sent the guy flying into next week, but the runt countered, got an arm across his throat, and cranked down with a ferocity that grayed his vision and brought a stab near his collarbone. Tingling pain lashed down Dez's arm and the .44 skidded away.

Pissed at himself as much as at the other man, he lunged to his feet with a roar and then went over backward, using the little shit to break his fall. Something snapped—maybe bone—and the choke hold slackened.

He rolled away from his assailant and surged to his feet. "How'd that feel, mother . . . *fucker*." In an instant, the world telescoped down to the sight of familiar pale eyes in a sharp, tautly drawn face slashed through with six gnarled scar lines that ran across the other man's cheek and throat. "*Keban.*"

Dez hadn't seen his godfather in almost five years. And the last time, he'd nearly killed the bastard.

"Hid yourself well, didn't you, boy?" Louis Keban pulled himself to his feet, his sneer showing the jagged edge of a broken tooth. "But I found you. Always will." His mad, bright eyes went to the cloth-wrapped bundle. "You felt her, didn't you? That's because it's time—the war's coming, boy. The end of the world's coming. It's time for you to step up and do what you were born to do."

"You're out of your fucking mind," Dez grated, but suddenly he wasn't so sure about that. He had felt the pull, heard the voice in his head. And the air had sparked red-gold when he kissed Reese.

*They were just stories*, he'd been telling himself for years. *There's no magic, no doomsday countdown.* It had all been part of Keban's elaborate insanity.

Unless it hadn't been, he thought as the world started to swim around him. What if . . . "*Fuck,*" he spat when his vision fuzzed and he realized it wasn't just shock; the little bitch had drugged him. Swaying on his feet, he pawed his collarbone and cursed when his fingers hit the end of a snapped-off needle.

"Just a little something to help you get your magic." Keban turned, scooped up the bundle, and unrolled it to reveal a small carving. "This should take care of the rest. Courtesy of Montezuma." Made of shiny black stone and approximately the length of Dez's thumb, it was a woman with wide hips and a big head, more grotesque than pretty.

Dez hissed out a breath as a hard, hot force suddenly surged up inside him. *Mine*, it said. *That's mine.* He wanted to snatch the carved fragment away from Keban, wanted to hide it, to protect it, to have it as his own. He would kill to possess it, kill to protect it. *Kill.*

He was moving before he was aware of having made a decision, surging forward and reaching for the statuette. *Mine.* But when he was halfway there his knees folded and the world went gray, fog closing in on him until the only thing he could see was the flare of triumph in the other man's eyes. Then he was down and vulnerable, cursing in dread silence as Keban handcuffed his wrists in front of his body, positioning him so he was kneeling like a damned penitent. Then the bastard pulled a knife and cut Dez's palms along the old scar lines.

They had played this game before.

The pain sparked a searing rage that burned through the drugs. As his vision cleared, he saw that the other man was using the same stone blade he had used throughout the years—black obsidian with etched serpent glyphs that matched the one on the bastard's forearm: The mark of the serpent bloodline. *Son of a bitch*, Dez thought, reeling from both shock and drugs. *What if—*

Then Keban pressed the black statuette into his hand, and the world went haywire.

The stone flashed from cool to hot in an instant, searing his palms, and a strange, crackling buzz sizzled through him, reaching deep and sparking anger and greed, the lust for power, approval, recognition, respect. He bared his teeth and strained against his bonds as energy stabbed through his chest and behind his eyeballs. *The head and heart are the sources of a mage's power*, came Keban's voice in his mind, drilling the lessons into him along with the strategies of a thousand battles, the workings of a hundred political systems . . . and the future as it existed inside the older man's warped brain. *Your sister died so you could live. You owe me, owe her, owe the gods. Try harder. Be better, be more, or it was all a waste.*

The memories hammered through Dez as Keban got in his face and rasped, "Say the words, damn it. Jack in."

*Pasaj och.* The phrase whispered in his mind, but the spell wouldn't work, hadn't ever worked. It had just been an excuse for Keban to whale on him once a quarter, when he failed to tap into his so-called magic on the night of every solstice and—

Oh, shit. Tonight was the equinox.

And this was really happening.

A cold fist wrapped itself around Dez's heart and squeezed, cutting through the drugged fog and the power of the statuette. "Make your own fucking magic," he grated. "I don't follow orders."

The cool press of a gun muzzle touched his temple as Keban got in close and grated, "Jack the fuck in."

"Suck. My. Dick."

Face flushing an ugly brick red slashed with the six

parallel white scars, Keban hammered Dez across the jaw with his own .44, and then took a couple of steps back to aim it two-handed. "Say it." When Dez just glared, the other man's eyes went frenzied. "Say it!" he screamed with spittle-flecked violence. "Say the fucking spell!"

Dez saw his godfather's trigger finger tighten, saw murder in his eyes, and felt a flash of pure grief. *I'm sorry, babe. I didn't mean for it to end this way. I wanted—*

Two shots cracked, oddly syncopated. Dez felt something sting his shoulder, but it was Keban who jerked back and grabbed his upper arm.

Dez spun toward the second shooter, instinctively knowing who it was. Even so, his heart damn near stopped at the sight of her.

Reese was wearing the same snug black jeans and zip-down sweater she'd had on earlier. Now, though, she was dripping wet despite the raincoat that hung plastered to her body, and she was packing most of their weapons stash. Her short black hair was slicked to her skull, her strange whiskey-amber eyes were hot with anger, and she looked ready to kick some serious ass.

"You okay?" she asked without taking her eyes—or her .38—off Keban, who had collapsed near the wall, unmoving.

"I'm fine. But keep your guard up," Dez warned. "He's—"

"I know who he is. Jocko called to say that a guy with a scarred-up face was asking about you. I put it together."

And she had come for him even after the way he'd walked out on her. Love surged through him, further pushing back the fog of drugs and compulsion. He loosened his grip on the small statuette, making the handcuffs rattle. "He'll have the keys—"

Keban uncurled snake-quick and fired the .44 at her, point blank.

"NO!" Dez surged upright and then crashed back down when he hit the ends of his bonds. The cuffs cut into his wrists, the statue's hard edges dug into his slashed palm, and the whole world just fucking stopped for a heartbeat as the woman he loved went down in a motionless heap. "*Reese!*"

The storm, which had lulled briefly, flung itself at the warehouse with renewed fury. Lightning flared, strobing the cavernous space as wind-driven rain lashed through the broken windows. Electricity crackled around Dez, inside him, somehow expanding his senses so he saw more, heard more, *felt* more than he ever had before. And with it came a deeper, darker layer of hatred that was directed entirely at Keban as he raised his weapon and sighted again on Reese, his eyes carrying the same feral glee they used to get while he was lashing Dez with his belt. "Sorry about your girlfr—"

Surging against the cuffs and ropes, Dez shouted, "*Pasaj och!*"

Thunder cracked and a fat bolt of lightning dead-eyed the warehouse, sparking the old wires and haloing the steel girders with foxfire. Then the sizzle was *inside* him, radiating from the carving to his head and heart and back again. He was dimly aware of the bonds melting off his ankles and the metal handcuffs arcing with blue-white flame. Then pain lashed, flesh burned, and the shackles sprang open. They hit the floor with a metallic clatter. And he was free!

He lunged to his feet, roaring Reese's name.

Keban spun, eyes widening.

"Wait," said the *winikin*—because that was what he was, a *winikin*. It was all true, Dez suddenly realized as the lightning—the fucking *magic*—raced in his blood. Every last godsdamned story was true. He was a Nightkeeper. The last in an ancient line of magic users.

Keban had finally made him into a mage . . . And he'd used Reese to do it. *Blood sacrifice.* Nearby, she lay far too still, her body a dark blur in the shadows.

"No!" Pain and rage lashed through Dez, calling to something inside him, something that fed on the greed and hatred and then suddenly ignited. Power soared inside him, pressed on him, begged to be set free.

Going on instinct, he pointed at the *winikin*, stiff fingered. The power surged, a vicious crackle split the air, and a bolt of blue-white lightning shot from his outstretched fingers. It nailed Keban in the chest, blasting him back.

The *winikin* screamed and landed writhing, wreathed in sparks of blue-white electricity. His body arched; his hands and feet beat at the warehouse floor, and came away bloody.

Magic flowed through Dez. He gloried in it, heart racing. He was a mage, like Keban had always said. He could do anything, be anything, become—

Then, like someone had thrown a switch, the energy cut out, the crackle went silent, and his body shifted from fever hot to deathly cold in an instant. He sagged as fatigue hit him hard and he became, once again, just himself.

*What. The. Fuck?*

Weeping raggedly, Keban dragged himself to his feet and staggered for the door without a backward look, cackling a high, lunatic laugh.

"Son of a *bitch*!" Yanking himself out of the last dregs of magic, Dez jammed the statuette into his pocket, lunged for the fallen .44, and came up to his knees firing. The shots pinged off steel, the noise disappearing beneath a crack of thunder as Keban vanished into the storm. On one level, Dez knew he should chase the bastard, finish him off. But on another, more visceral level, he had a different priority.

"Reese!" He scrambled to his feet, bolted across the warehouse and dropped to his knees beside her. Ignoring everything he'd ever learned about first aid, he dragged her up off the floor and into his arms, cursing when her guns dug into him, feeling somehow more substantial than she did. Her body was limp and heavy. Deadweight that smelled of blood. "Godsdamn it, *Reese*!"

She stirred, then squinted at him through pain-blurred eyes. "Jesus, don't yell. My head's killing me."

He shuddered, groaning her name and holding on to her for a long moment while his heart hammered in his ears. Then he tried to pull himself together, easing away far enough to check for injuries with shaking hands. He was bleeding from his shoulder and his wrists howled where the cuffs had burned him, but she was hurt worse. She had a raised knot on her head that matched her blown pupils, and a through-and-through in her upper arm, the wound wide and angry and weeping blood.

She'd live. But they had gotten lucky.

"He's gone. I've got you. You're okay. We're okay." He said it over and over, not really sure he believed it until he stuck his hand in his pocket and touched the statuette. And for a second he felt a trickle of the power—the magic—he'd tapped into before. He sure as hell hadn't imagined the way his cuffs had come off, or the way he'd blown Keban off his feet. A guy who could do stuff like that could do anything.

Pressing his cheek to her temple, careful of the sore spots, he tightened his fingers around the statuette, as he said, "I'm sorry about what I said before. I didn't mean it—I love you. I need you. We'll make it work."

But suddenly he wasn't so sure about that, either. Because if the magic was real, then the other stuff was real, too . . . and what the hell was he going to do about that?

# CHAPTER TWO

Present day
*Cancún, Mexico*
December 5; one year and sixteen days to the zero
date

Reese had long thought that themed wedding hotels were tacky as hell, but she was pretty sure this one took the freaking multitiered, pink-frosted cake.

In case the velvet sombreros and striped serapes plastered on every available surface of the hotel lobby were too subtle, the decorators—and she used the term lightly—had lined the halls with a series of cringe-inducing tropical signs directing her to the wedding chapel. And when she got there, she found the entry-way decorated with what she suspected was meant to look like an ancient Mayan temple, but came across as papier-mâché gone horribly wrong.

Inside the chapel, a faux stone archway took the place of the usual flower-and-lattice bower, the aisle was lined with fake palm fronds, the rank-and-file chairs were wearing parrot-hued slipcovers, and the roll-away screen behind the main stage was painted with an art student's version of Chichén Itzá in its heyday, with the city intact, the ruins unruined, and cartoonish pre-Columbian natives thronging in the foreground, staring at the papier-mâché archway with creepy, goggle-eyed intensity.

Thank Christ the room was empty. It was bad enough she was semi-crashing. Be worse if she walked in and started laughing her ass off during the I-dos.

This so wasn't what she had been expecting. But then again, the expectations were her own fault: The moment she opened the FedEx to find a plane ticket to Mexico and a request for her to come talk about a job, her brain had gone straight to a tropical fantasyland, complete with umbrellaed drinks and bare-chested bartenders, far from Denver's drab gray winter.

Hell, it was probably just a run-of-the-mill deal for aging parents who had lost track of a kid and were feeling guilty in the middle of the sib's wedding prep. Typical locator gig.

But those cases still paid better—and were way safer—than her old job.

Tracking a low drone of voices that said "the party's over here," she crunched across the fake palm fronds to where an open doorway led to the reception area. Looking for a little advance intel—run-of-the-mill job or not, it was pretty extreme to fly her across the border just for a meet-and-greet—she tucked herself into the shadows and peered through to where a couple of dozen bodies thronged an open-air dining area.

Then she exhaled in surprise and eased back further into the shadows. Because whatever these guys were, it wasn't run-of-the-mill.

The twenty or so people, an even mix of men and women, were knotted together on one side of the room, the men in decent suits, the women in an eclectic mix of high-end, with no rent-a-tux'd groom or Barbie-doll bride in evidence. They were all wearing long sleeves, which was weird; it might be shitty with early December back home, but it was still pretty damn tropical down in the Yucatan.

Going into the figure-it-out-fast survival mode that used to be her only option, she scanned the room. Six of the wedding guests—three men, three women—were small and compact, their gestures quick, their eyes always on the move. Four of the six were in their sixties or so and hung together like family or old friends, while the remaining two were younger and new-coupleish: a military type in his early forties holding hands with a thirtyish cutie who had dark hair and laughing eyes. Overall, aside from a strange air of uniformity, those guys weren't too far off ordinary.

The rest of them, though . . . Whoa. Way not ordinary. Most in their late twenties, early thirties, they were uniformly huge—in height and muscle, with zero flab—gorgeous, and somehow *glossy*, like the overhead lights bounced off them differently from the others. More, they all held themselves at the ready, their body language saying they knew how to fight and would do it at a split second's notice.

There were a few exceptions: Two of the women,

one blond, one dark, were closer to average size, while a third—coppery dark hair, maybe a few years older than the others—sat at a table, staring vacantly, with a funny half smile on her lips. Beside her sat one of the men; he was huge and muscled like the others, but had his left leg strapped into a high-tech brace and propped on a chair. A pair of crutches leaned on the wall behind him.

None of those details changed the overall impression of deadly competence, though. Not one iota.

Reese's instincts checked in, making sure she was aware that she might, in fact, be an idiot. Suddenly, accepting the anonymous invite south of the border seemed less like a welcome getaway and more like a dumb idea.

Her new, more cautious self said she should do a vanishing act. But at the same time, another part of her—a trusted part—said that she should stay put. Because what if these guys were trying to locate someone worth saving? She'd seen it before. Hell, she'd *been* it before.

*You can't help everyone*, she reminded herself. But instead of doing a Casper and ghosting it, she hitched her small black carryall a little higher on her shoulder and checked out the setup.

The reception area was an open-air stone patio surrounded by a high, vine-covered fence. An overhead latticework hung with a gazillion fairy lights failed to disguise the fact that the hotel was smack in the middle of a bunch of other high-rises. There was only one door, which didn't compute, and not just because she was big on backup exits. In her experience, groups like this didn't let themselves get boxed in. Which meant they had another way out . . . Unless she'd misread them? She didn't think so. Even while doing the civilized wedding-brunch thing, they practically screamed "paramilitary." Or maybe something official, with an acronym most people wouldn't recognize.

She should walk away. Call Fallon. Let the pros handle things.

That common sense sounded awfully thin inside her, though, because the pattern didn't make any sense. When that happened, she got real curious—and, according to some people, stupidly brave. But *some people* weren't there right then, and they didn't run her life; she did.

So, glad she had stopped at a pawnshop to buy a decent .38 a mile or so past the airport, she stepped out of the shadows and into the doorway, pasted a pleasant expression on her face, and said, "Excuse me?"

Within seconds, every one of them had marked her, eyes flicking to her and then to each other, and there was a subtle shift in the room as some jackets got twitched aside, other bodies got out of the line of fire. The smaller six faded into the background with the exception of the soldier-type, who stepped in front of his girlfriend with an expression of "you want a piece of her, you're coming through me." A couple of the others looked over at the table, then away when the guy with the bad leg got big and capable-looking all of a sudden, and a dark-haired woman coasted over to join him.

Nobody drew down, though. They just waited, staring at Reese with an intensity that gave her a funny little skin-quiver, as though she had walked too close to a transformer.

Pulse upshifting, she held out her empty hands. "I'm not looking for trouble. I was invited." *Sort of.*

A pretty blue-eyed blonde off on one side glanced at the brown-haired man beside her. "We didn't invite you."

Okay. Bride and groom weren't the prospective clients. Didn't look like newlyweds, either; the rings weren't new, and they came across like a solid team. Were they renewing their vows, maybe? Or was this whole thing a setup? Reese didn't know, but she wasn't moving away from the door until she did.

"I invited her," said a big guy on the other side of the room, breaking the silence.

At that, the others gave way a little, telling her that he was the boss of this outfit. Wearing a charcoal suit with the slight awkwardness of someone who did better in jeans, maybe six six, two thirty, he was built like a bouncer and had killer blue eyes, dark, shoulder-length hair, and a jawline beard that made her think of a Renaissance fair. And he was vaguely familiar, but not from her present life.

*Oh, shit.* Again, her new self said to run. Again, she stayed put. "Do I know you?"

He gave her a once-over with those brilliant blues. "Where's all the black leather?"

She was wearing low boots, trim pants, and a subtly studded blazer, all in muted earth tones. Professional, grown-up clothes. "Dog's show turned it into a cliché."

Tipping her head, still not placing him, she said, "I could dig up the boots if you're interested."

"He's not." The smaller blue-eyed blonde moved up beside him and shot her a narrow-eyed glare.

Reese knew that look. Fallon hit her with it often enough. "You're a cop."

That intel eased her nerves a degree. Granted, there were cops who crossed the line, but fewer than the TV made it seem. More, she wasn't getting the "bad guy" vibe off this crew, and her instincts might not be infallible, but they had a damn good track record. So who were these guys? A task force working the wrong side of the border? If that was the case, why did they need her? And why not go through channels?

Unless they had, and Fallon had told them to fuck off. That, she could believe.

The cop nodded. "And you're the bounty hunter."

Most of the others relaxed a smidge at that one. The bride's mouth went round in surprise and, Reese thought, recognition.

Filing that, she stayed focused on the boss. "I used to be a bounty hunter. Now I'm strictly private." She paused. "Where do I know you from?"

"Three years ago. A burned-out warehouse in Chicago."

"Three—" She broke off as her stomach knotted. Keeping the poker face that had saved her life more times than she wanted to count, she nodded and made herself breathe past the stab of pain. "Right. Strike. I remember."

Would've been better if she could have forgotten.

She still had nightmares where she was back in the burned-out shell of Seventeen, breathing stale smoke as she crept up on the two men, one far too familiar, one an unknown who had a gangsta name—Strike—but wore normal duds and had shown up in a rented minivan.

With the other hunters closing in faster than she had anticipated, she had nailed her target from behind with her souped-up Taser and had her two quasi body-guards drag his ass back to lockup. After that, she had chased the other guy—this guy—back to his rental, labeling him harmless. Then she had locked herself in her hotel room, binged on Ding Dongs, and cried herself empty. Which wasn't the point right now. The important part was where she had filed Strike under "harmless" back then, now her instincts said that the man facing her was deadly dangerous in his own right. Which meant that either he'd changed over the past three years, or he'd been playing her before.

What the hell was going on here? And why did it have to be *that* day? The coincidence sucked.

A chill skimmed along her skin as a dead man's voice whispered, *There's no such thing as coincidence. It's all just the will of the gods.* Mendez had been big on quoting his writs when they made his point, especially toward the end of their time together.

*Keep your head in the real world*, she told herself. That part of her life had ended long before his death. Shifting the small black carryall so she could get to the gun tucked at the small of her back, she said cautiously, "I don't do find-and-grabs anymore."

"All you need to do is locate him," Strike said without a shift of expression or inflection. "We'll take care of the rest."

She should turn him down. Hell, she shouldn't have come out here in the first place. She was just starting to hit her stride in Denver after moving back from LA just under a year ago. She had a string of solid—if boring—jobs lined up and ready to go. And this crew had "questionable" written all over them. But that same questionability was what had her sticking. She knew what it felt like to be lost. Now she tracked down the lost and reunited them with their friends and family . . . or, if they were better off lost, she helped them stay that way. *Saving the world one person at a time*, Fallon had called it. And he hadn't even been mocking her. Not much, anyway.

"Tell me about the target," she said. Routine question, nice and open ended.

Strike's expression didn't change. "It's the same guy you bagged out from under me that day in the warehouse. Snake Mendez."

He said something else, but she couldn't hear him over the roaring that suddenly filled her head.

*Mendez. Oh, Christ.*

She had to lock her knees to keep from sagging when it all tried to come rushing back—memories, pain, guilt, betrayal, grief. *Keep breathing*, she told herself, struggling with her poker face. She couldn't go there again. Not now, when she was just starting to put her shit back together. Not now, when losing him had nearly killed her before.

More, there were warning bells beneath the pain. What the hell was going on here? How much did this guy know? Who was he working for?

Her instincts chimed in with a *Time to go!*

Feeling far shakier than she wanted to let on, she retreated a step toward the doorway. "Mendez is dead." She forced herself to say it, though the words tasted foul. "He was killed last year in Denver. The Varrio Warlocks got him."

His parole officer swore that Mendez had been playing it straight, but as far as she could tell, he had died as he had lived: trying to run the world one city block at a time.

"Wait." Strike stretched out a hand. "Don't go."

"You don't need me to find a dead man." Another step back put her in the doorway.

"He's alive."

The words didn't compute at first, coming one at a time, disconnected, echoing in her ears like someone screaming inside an abandoned warehouse. *He's. Alive. He's. Alive. He's alive. He's alive . . . alive . . . alive. Not dead.*

"Bullshit." The word was little more than a whisper. "The VWs claimed the kill."

"They lied. Dez has been working with us in New Mex for the past year. He took off two days ago, and we need him back."

"He . . ." She trailed off as the numbness grew teeth and bit in.

*Dez.* The nickname had been reserved for the inner circle. And three years ago, Strike had called him "Mendez," just as she had used "Snake," trying to remind herself what he really was. Poisonous. A manipulator.

Hearing the nickname now meant . . . Jesus, she didn't know what it meant. But her instincts said Strike was telling her the truth.

*They lied.*

Her breath rasped in her lungs and the world took a big spin around her.

Dez was alive. Holy. Shit.

The blond cop said softly, "He was more than a paycheck to you, wasn't he?"

Strike glanced at her, surprised, then looked back at Reese more closely. "No shit. What were you? Friends? Lovers?"

"We were . . ." What? She didn't even know anymore, couldn't think, could barely even breathe. Shock loosened her tongue and she blurted, "We knew each other as kids, as runaways. We watched each other's backs. At least we did until that night in the storm. After that . . ." Getting dizzy now, she pressed the back of a hand against her mouth. "Could I . . . Shit. I need a minute." Heart hammering sickly in her ears, she gestured back the way she had come, toward the restrooms she had passed on the way in.

"Of course." The cop shifted on her feet, like she was going to offer to go with her.

Reese waved her off, swallowing hard. "I'll be right back."

As she headed for the ladies' room, struggling to hold it together, she felt twenty-some pairs of eyes follow her across the tacky-assed chapel and through the door to the hallway beyond, which took her out of their line of sight. Then, with tears blurring her vision, she bolted past the restrooms. And straight out of the hotel.

*Fresh air.* She gulped it, feeling like she was drowning while pedestrians skittered around her like rats, glaring and squeaking when she interrupted their flow. Then, blindly, she headed for the nearest alley.

She might not know Cancún that well, but she knew cities. She knew the taste and smell of them, knew their dark underbellies, and the creatures that ruled them. She also knew that if Strike and his crew went looking for her, they would start with the airports, buses, and hotels, all the normal places that normal people went. So, heart thudding in her chest, she headed for what her gut told her was the bad section of town, moving through a warren of narrow streets that rapidly dwindled to alleys, losing layers of respectability in the process, and coming to look like a thousand other alleys in any one of a hundred cities she'd worked in over the years.

Scrawny cats and lean, hard-eyed mutts of both the human and animal variety slunk in the shadows. And, as she worked her way deeper into the maze, moving fast but not too fast, she was aware of beady eyes watching her from shadows, and the way they shifted, sending a silent message flashing ahead: *Grab her, we'll share.*

A minute and three alleys farther in, a lean-hipped youth with shark-dead eyes and a four-inch blade dangling from one hand moved out from behind a Dumpster and gave her a spittle-flecked "Hey, baby, you looking for me?" in English rendered almost singsong by his thick accent.

She rattled back in varrio Spanish, "Get these cops off my ass and you can have whatever you want."

"Fuck that." He disappeared, and the shadows melted away. They wouldn't stay gone for long, but the threat of the cops had bought her a few minutes, a little space to think.

Not that she wanted to think. It hurt too damn much.

*Dez. God.* Throat so tight it hurt to swallow, she kept going until her gut told her she had gone far enough, and then picked out a narrow, open-ended alley that smelled pretty much like every other alley on the planet—a mélange of piss, body odor, and rot—with a spicy overtone that said she was far from home. Putting herself about halfway down the alley, she scoped out her exits, both horizontal and vertical, and leaned back against a padlocked doorway hard enough that her .38 dug into her lower back. Then she braced her hands on her knees, let her head hang for a second, and concentrated on not losing her shit.

Dez was alive. Which meant . . . "Nothing," she told herself, hating that her voice cracked on the word. This didn't change anything.

She couldn't *let* it change anything. He wasn't her cowboy or her white knight, wasn't her best friend, wasn't her partner, wasn't *anything*. She had saved his life by putting his ass in jail long enough for Fallon to get the guys who were gunning for him, and then cutting the deal that had gotten him out again. Word had it that he'd even straightened up—to a point—while he'd been inside. She doubted he had found God, but she had hoped he had found some perspective, and maybe even a few shreds of the guy he'd been at twenty.

That had evened them up. A life for a life. Which meant she didn't owe him anything.

Her stomach rumbled. Some people snacked when they were bored. She binged when things got out of control.

*This isn't your problem.* She didn't need to get involved—hell, she *shouldn't* get involved. She should pass along the info, and let the task force decide what—if anything—to do about it. And if the thought brought a twist of grief and regret, she made herself ignore them both as she dug into her carryall, going for the false bottom where she kept a second set of IDs and a credit card that ought to keep her off the radar unless Strike and his people had major clearance, or a big-assed back door into the system.

Given that they were looking for Dez, the latter seemed a far stronger possibility. He hadn't been—wasn't?—an acronym kind of guy.

Dez. God. Could he really be alive? Her throat closed and a sob rattled in her chest, but she made herself keep going, her fingers shaking as she popped the bottom of the carryall. But then a strange tickle shimmied down the back of her neck and her instincts kicked hard.

Her heart lunged into her throat as she spun in a full circle without seeing a damned thing out of place.

But then an electric crackle laced the atmosphere, displaced air *whoomped*, and Strike freaking *materialized* right in front of her.

As Reese stared in shock, he glanced around, locked on her, and looked profoundly relieved.

Relieved? What the hell?

She went for her .38 as her mind scrambled, but before the gun was clear of her waistband, his expression shifted to one of fucking-get-it-done determination. Moving fast, he grabbed her wrist, twisted and chucked her gun, and then said, "Sorry about this."

Sudden vertigo slammed into her, tunneling her vision.

"What . . . ?" She reeled, tried to run, and staggered drunkenly instead.

Her brain went fuzzy and she felt herself falling, felt strong arms catch her in an impersonal grip. And the world went dark.

# CHAPTER THREE

Some immeasurable time later—maybe a few minutes, maybe a few days—Reese struggled back to consciousness. But instead of making it all the way there, she found herself caught, vulnerable, in the woozy dream state between asleep and awake, where she knew she should be afraid but couldn't muster the energy for panic.

Even more disconcerting, she wasn't alone inside her own skull. There was a strange presence there with her, controlling her. An unfamiliar voice echoed in her head, saying: *Show us.*

She was dimly aware that she was lying on a couch in a room that smelled spicy, like scented candles or incense. Strike was there, along with a younger, sharp-faced man who stared down at her, his gray eyes so intense they seemed silver. He was the presence inside her, she knew, without knowing how she knew it. *Show us the night of the storm,* he whispered in her mind.

She didn't want to go back there, didn't want to remember. But without meaning to, she did.

The images unspooled: She saw Dez, his eyes hot

and wild as he kissed her and carried her to his bed, saw the lightning, heard the thunder, felt her body go cold as he headed for the door. Then things sped up in a scatter shot of images and sensations: She heard Jocko's warning; felt herself racing through the storm, only to arrive too late. She saw the mad glee in Keban's scarred face as he leaned over Dez, gloating; felt the pain as he turned and shot her. Then there was Dez's rage. Chaos. Lightning. Thunder. Screams. Things happening that couldn't be real.

The memories sped up, becoming a blur of the weeks that followed and the growing pain that came, not from her healing injuries, but from the way Dez had changed, how he kept trying to call magic that didn't exist, and how each failure had pushed him further over the line. His temper sharpened. He quit his job, then got pissed when she cornered him about it.

*Show me*, the inner voice said. And she did.

*"Don't you get it?" he snapped, boots thudding an angry staccato as he paced the apartment like a caged animal. "The 'work your way up' thing is a fucking pipe dream. The only way people like us can get what we deserve is by being creative."*

*In the past few weeks he had gained a good thirty pounds of pure muscle, shaved his head, and gotten tattoos to cover the handcuff scars: twin bands of strange symbols done in dark blue-green ink. He was turning into a stranger, and a scary one, but that didn't stop her from putting herself in his path, making him choose between stopping and mowing her down. He stopped very close to her. Glared at her.*

*She glared right back. "And by getting creative you mean*

*working 'security'"*—she scorned the word with finger quotes—*"for the highest bidder?"*

*"How did—"* He bit it off. *"Shit. You fucking patterned me."*

It was her uniquely odd skill, an almost savantlike ability to put together seemingly unrelated pieces of information into a pattern, and from there a prediction that Fallon's gang task force could use, like where and when a drug drop was likely to be, whether a particular drive-by was random or part of a larger whole, or—and this was something she was keeping far away from the cops—that Dez was hiring himself out as muscle for the Smaldone wannabes.

The two-bit mobster types were trying to step into the vacuum left by the demise of Denver's once-great crime family. They didn't seem to get that there wasn't any vacuum; the gangs had already filled the niche. But while the Smaldone Lites were figuring that out, they had a habit of getting messily dead. Thus the bodyguards.

She shook her head. *"Jesus, Dez. How could you work for those guys after everything we've done to clean things up around here?"*

His face settled into the impassive mask she had quickly come to hate, the one where shadows darkened his eyes to an unfathomable murk. *"The money's good."*

*"It's a shortcut,"* she snapped, drilling a finger into his chest. It was like poking a building. *"Your job—"*

*"Wouldn't have gotten me what I need in time,"* he interrupted.

It was the first she had heard of any deadline. Oh, shit. Now what had he gotten himself into? Or, she had to ask herself, was he trying to buy himself *out* of something?

"You're getting a place of your own." She made herself say it. She had known he didn't like the way she had gone from practically throwing herself at him to "let's wait until we're getting along better," but she hadn't thought he would bail.

He looked offended. "Hell, no."

The tightness in her chest went down by half. "Then what is it? Tell me what you need the money for. Did you lose a bet? Are you trying to do something? Buy something?"

Her mind, stupid optimist that it was, flashed on the ring he had caught her trying on the other day in the local pawnshop. Not girlie—far from it—it was a finely detailed snake that curled around her finger and knotted around a polished black stone. Obsidian, the guy behind the counter had called it. She hadn't cared that it had probably belonged to one of the Cobras—to her it wasn't a cobra, it was a snake, like his given name. She had cared, though, that the pawnbroker wanted close to four months' rent for it.

"I need firepower," Dez said flatly.

That was so far off the ring fantasy that she just stared at him for a few seconds. "We've got guns."

"I don't think they'll be enough." He hesitated, then reached for her. This time he made contact, tracing a finger down her cheek.

But instead of heat, the move brought a shiver of dread. "Tell me what's wrong. Please."

He stared down at her. Then he said, reluctantly, "Hood gets out the day after tomorrow. And the word on the street is that you're going to be his first stop."

"He . . ." She trailed off as her stomach knotted and adrenaline kicked through her bloodstream as she flashed on sharpened teeth, scary-dead eyes, and a nose piercing that flared out to wicked points. Rumor had it that the incarcerated *cobra de rey* was more superstitious than ever these days, and had decided that making her his bitch would give him the power to add the VW's turf to his own.

They had known he'd be getting out soon. They just hadn't known when.

Or at least *she* hadn't.

"Why didn't I hear about this?" She was the one with the informants, the one with her ear to the streets.

"I paid Jocko to squelch it."

"You . . ." She stared at him, not understanding. "Why?" She could have been finding patterns, making plans. She could have been . . . oh, shit. Cold sluiced through her as she got it. She freaking got it. He hadn't told her because he was planning on killing Hood and he didn't want her trying to stop him. Or if things went bad, he didn't want her charged as an accomplice. Sick dread washed through her, bringing a new film of tears. "You're not a killer."

It was what separated them from the gang. She and Dez wore guns and walked tough, but the weapons were strictly for defense, and they shot to scare, to wound. Not to kill. Never to kill.

He cupped her face in his scarred palms and looked down at her, staring like he was trying to memorize the moment. And in his eyes, she saw more darkness today than yesterday. "I couldn't save my family," he said softly. "I can save you."

"You—" She broke off, knowing there was no point in arguing that one. It was why Dez had come to her rescue that *first night, when Hood had cornered her, coveted her. And it was why he was willing to sacrifice himself now.*

*That, and because he was a stubborn ass who didn't fucking listen.*

*She reached up and gripped his wrists, right over the new tattoos. "This isn't the only way. We can deal with him legitimately. We did it before—we can do it again."*

*His eyes burned into hers. "I'm not going to let him touch you."*

*"I'm not arguing with you there. But there are other options." She took a deep breath. "Let's leave. Fallon said the offer is still open. The department will stake us to a move, help us get started somewhere else."*

*For the past couple of years, Dez had wanted to bail and start over, but she had refused to be chased out of yet another home. Which she supposed made them a pair of stubborn asses, but if she had to give up on the neighborhood to save him from himself, she would do it.*

*He shook his head, expression bleak. "The Cobras aren't just a street gang anymore, Reese. They've got a long reach. Moving to a new city won't solve anything."*

*She wanted to argue that they could change their names, build new lives—she had done it before, could do it again— but she had a feeling that was just an excuse. As far as Dez was concerned, he had let Keban beat him that night in the storm, so he wasn't going to let Hood beat him now. Or, rather, he was going to be the one to do the beating.*

*Feeling suddenly sad, small, and desperate, she turned her face and pressed a kiss to his scarred palm. "Promise me you won't kill him."*

*For a second she thought he leaned into her touch, that his fingers tightened. But when he pulled away from her, his eyes were cool. "I can't."*

Tears stung Reese's eyes even in sleep, blurring the memories, which spun past faster now, mercifully showing as single images: Hood's eyes, open and staring; a ruby pendant; a ring box sitting in a pool of blood.

"That's enough," Strike said, his voice breaking through the memories and bringing her back to drowsy reality.

"You want me to block it out?" That came from the silver-eyed man who held her hand, his words resonating in her head as well as her ears. Through their strange mental link she learned his name—Rabbit— and caught a trace of wood smoke, sharp and acrid, along with a sense of worry.

"Not yet," Strike rumbled. "Let's wait and see what she . . ." The words faded.

*No!* Reese grabbed for consciousness as it started to slip away again. *Come back!* She fought against the grayness that crept in from the edges of her dream state, but couldn't stay awake. As she faded, another memory broke through unbidden, one that came from years earlier than the others.

*"Hurry!" Fingers biting into her wrist, the stranger dragged her along the outside wall of Seventeen while rain lashed down around them. As they ran, he muttered to himself, "Mendez, what the fuck are you doing?"*

*Behind them, shouts sounded as the Cobras pounded in*

*pursuit. They were cursing vilely that she had gotten away and threatening the guy who had helped her escape.*

*He dragged her over two buildings, to a pile of junk lumped haphazardly behind Fifteen. Then he let go of her so he could shove aside a metal sheet. Behind it, a corrugated pipe led into pitch blackness. "Get in," he ordered roughly. "They don't know about all of the tunnels."*

*In the light of one of the few unbroken outside floods, she saw that the guy who had risked his own ass to get her away from Hood was a couple of years older than she—maybe eighteen, nineteen? He was tall but whip-thin, his fierce eyes rendered colorless by the sodium lights, his dark hair plastered to his skull as the rain poured down. He wore the ragged, mismatched clothes of a castoff, but he wasn't anything like the other street kids she had met in the month or so that she'd been on her own. He had a presence the others lacked, an aura of capability and strength. There was a layer of menace, too, one that warned that he wasn't someone she wanted to fuck with.*

*She hesitated, shaking. He had gotten her away from Hood, but that didn't necessarily make him any better than the* cobra de rey. *He might just have wanted the fresh meat for himself.*

*When he moved, she flinched back, expecting him to make a grab. But he put his hand over his heart instead. "I'm one of the good guys, okay? And I swear on my sister's soul that I won't hurt you." Then he held out his hand to her, in an invitation that showed where a wide, slashing scar crossed his palm.*

*The sight should have scared her. Instead, it made her feel a strange kinship. Nodding, she darted past him and ducked into the tunnel as the gang members' footsteps got closer and she heard Hood shouting: "You're mine, bitch. You hear me? Mine."*

*"Not on my watch," Mendez grated as he pulled the metal sheet back into place, cutting out the light. Then he guided her fingers to the tail of his ragged denim coat. "Be as quiet as you can, and hang on to me. I'll take care of you, I promise."*

*Then, with him leading the way, they crept into the darkness together, leaving their enemies behind.*

The next time Reese aimed for consciousness, she made it all the way back, waking up to find herself lying on a couch. A thick blanket was tucked around her, its suffocating, too-warm weight threatening to trigger claustrophobia.

She didn't let the fear take over, though. Instead, she forced herself to lie still and feign sleep as she tried to get a sense of her surroundings. Given the weirdness that had already gone down, she needed all the intel she could get.

All she came up with, though, was that the air was clean and processed, the couch and blanket smelled fresh, and her surroundings were silent except for the background hum of appliances. She didn't hear anyone nearby, but that didn't mean they weren't there, waiting for her to come around and . . . and what? The fragments that came back to her didn't make any sense, didn't tell her where she was, or what Strike and the others wanted from her. Panic sparked. She hated not knowing things. Knowledge was power. Control. Safety.

*Shit. Breathe. In and out.*

Logic said they had drugged her—the impossible memory of Strike appearing out of thin air had to be some sort of retrograde hallucination. Then, after they had knocked her out, they had kidnapped her and interrogated her under some sort of hallucinogenic. But why? And how long had she been out? Had anyone realized she was missing yet?

The answer to that last one was "no," she knew. Not after she had made such a big deal about being independent and not needing to clock in or out.

*Breathe*, she told herself. *Pretend you're asleep.* She was pretty sure she was alone, though.

A minute passed, then two, and the panic leveled off. She took a deep breath, then another. Then she opened her eyes.

And froze, heart hammering anew.

It wasn't the sight of a generically furnished three-room apartment that caught her by the throat and ramped the panic back up . . . it was the view outside the window nearest her: a few buildings, a few trees . . . and a red-rock canyonscape that didn't look anything like the Cancún hotel district.

Where the hell *was* she?

Letting out a low moan of terror, she wrenched off the blanket and bolted for the door. It was locked from the outside, the intercom keypad beside it nonresponsive. *Damn, damn, damn.* Survival instincts clawed at her as she tried the windows, found them locked too.

Breath sobbing between her teeth, she grabbed a desk chair and swung it as hard as she could at the glass.

The chair bounced off with a reverb that sang up her arms and made her hands go numb. But she was only peripherally aware of the pain as she let the chair drop and stared, horrified, through the window, to where a pair of Jeeps and a dune buggy were parked near the steel building.

Holy shit. Oh, holy, holy shit. They were all wearing New Mexico plates.

And she was in serious trouble.

She hadn't told anyone where she was going or who she was meeting, had left only a breezy "Got a new case; call you when I get a chance" voice mail and turned off her phone. Now, her latest move in the "don't stifle me" argument had come back to bite her in the ass, because nobody would know where to start looking for her. They would have to track the GPS in her phone, and— *Her phone!*

She gave herself a hasty pat-down. She was still wearing all her clothes—wrinkled now and damp with fear. The .38 was gone, and her carryall was . . . no, her bag was sitting on a low coffee table beside a blue binder with some papers on top.

Ignoring the paperwork—though the pile sent a clear "read me" message—she grabbed the carryall and pawed through it. She wasn't really expecting to find her phone, but adrenaline jolted when her fingers glanced off its familiar shape. She yanked it out, flipped it open, started to dial, and then stopped.

There wasn't any signal. Not even a fraction of a bar.

"Shit." She started to flip the phone shut, but then froze, eyes locked on the upper corner of the display, where the little digital clock was trying to tell her that less than an hour had passed since she had walked into that tacky-assed Cancún hotel. Which didn't make any sense. There was no way they could have gotten her from the Yucatan to New Mexico in less than an hour. It just wasn't possible.

Yet there she was.

It had to be a trick. Someone had changed the time on her phone to mess with her head. She looked around, searching for a clock, for something that would verify that she wasn't crazy, that it was her phone that was wrong, not her perceptions.

Next to the sitting area, a breakfast bar separated out a small kitchen nook, with a bathroom beside it. On the other side, open doors led to bedrooms—one was furnished, the other looked empty. The decor was relentlessly neutral, all muted beiges and bare walls, the only stab at playfulness a small entertainment center on the wall opposite the couch.

The digital display showed the same time as her phone.

"Bullshit," she whispered.

Was she still drugged? She didn't feel woozy, but hallucinations were a better explanation than believing she had somehow been whisked from a Cancún alley to the New Mexican desert in the blink of an eye, like Strike had—*oh, shit*.

Her stomach knotted as the pieces started coming together in a pattern that was impossible. Abso-freaking-lutely impossible.

"No," she whispered, stomach knotting. But the denial didn't prevent her from remembering that New Mexico was where Dez's family had supposedly lived—and died—in a big-assed training compound hidden in a box canyon. Kind of like the one outside the window.

What. The. Fuck?

Once the idea took root, more pieces fell into place, in the sort of mental cascade that was usually a relief but in this case just freaked her out worse.

Strike and the larger members of his crew were all gorgeous, bigger and better than human norm. Much like Dez. *Shit*, she thought, pulse hammering thickly in her ears as she inwardly acknowledged that Dez could almost be related to the others. Or, if she wanted to go all the way into a bunch of bedtime stories that couldn't possibly be true, they could all be members of an ancient race capable of channeling psi energy with their minds. A race whose members had lived alongside humanity for millennia, together yet apart, waiting for the day they would need to defend the earth plane from the rise of the underworld.

"Bullshit," she whispered. But the pieces fit.

The smaller wedding guests, most of them a generation older, could have been the *winikin*, the hereditary protectors and tutors of the magi. And they had all been wearing long sleeves—possibly to cover the forearm glyph marks that denoted their bloodlines and abilities . . . like the ones Dez had been wearing when she had dragged him back to jail.

At the time, she had thought they were more tattoos, more signs that he was buying into his own hype. But what if they had been real? What if his magic had finally started working, after all?

Her blood ran simultaneously cold and hot as the pattern gelled into a theory that should have seemed impossible, but somehow didn't.

Strike and the others—and Dez—could be Nightkeepers.

*Holy. Crap.*

She had been so sure that the stories he had told her to pass the time had been elaborate fairy tales, creative lies Keban had used to brainwash Dez for the first sixteen years of his life. Then, later, she had talked herself into believing that the things she thought she had seen during the storm had been a concussion-induced hallucination. Because there was no such thing as magic.

Except that Strike had materialized practically on top of her, and then freaking *teleported* her thousands of miles. Then some guy named Rabbit had interrogated her. Or, rather, he'd *read her goddamned mind*.

Teleporter. Mind-bender. Oh, holy shit.

This wasn't part of a story, and it wasn't a hallucination.

More pieces fell into place, forming connections that left her reeling as she reached the logical—or illogical?—conclusion. Because if the magic and the Nightkeepers were real, then there was a good chance that the other parts of the stories were true, too. Like how the magi were blood-bound to defend the barrier in the years leading up to the end date, when terrible demons would break through and fight to conscript mankind into a hellish army that would make war on the gods.

She was keenly aware that the end date was a little more than a year away, not just because of the connection to Dez, but because it had been impossible to avoid the movies and documentaries, and the news stories about the tinfoil-hat brigades digging into their bunkers and acting like they knew something the rest of the world didn't. She had laughed all that off. Now she stared out the window at the back-ass end of a box canyon and wondered whether she'd been dead wrong.

Her knees went wobbly, and she dropped back down to the couch, mouth drying to dust like the desert outside. This wasn't happening. She was still drugged, still hallucinating.

Right?

Closing her eyes, she pinched herself hard on the arm. "Okay, Reese. It's time to wake up." But when she opened her eyes the only difference was the presence of reddened fingernail marks on her arm, which stung.

She glanced at the "read me" pile on the coffee table. *Don't do it.*

But how could she not? Knowledge was power.

On the bottom was a blue binder, half full of pages, with its spine marked "Open log, reunion onward" and fluorescent green Post-its flagging a couple of spots. Sitting on top of the binder was a short stack of papers that were clipped together at one corner. She flinched when she saw her name on the first sheet. But she couldn't *not* read the note.

*Dear Ms. Montana,*

> *Rabbit said that you'd rather have this in writing to digest at your own speed, so here it is. When you're ready to talk, dial 1313 on the intercom, and someone will come for you. At that point, it will be up to you whether to stay or go. If you choose to leave, you'll wake up in the hotel remembering only that you turned down the job, and you'll never hear from us again. But we hope you'll decide to stay, because we badly need someone like you on our side right now . . . and Rabbit says you've always wanted to save the world. Stick with us and you'll get your chance, gods willing.*

"Oh, shit." Reese sat back, crossing her arms over her churning stomach.

That was a seriously low blow, especially when it was those damned stories that had started her crusading in the first place. Back then, she had needed to believe that there were heroes out there, that someone was working behind the scenes to save her. She had been obsessed with Dez's stories of the Nightkeepers, had pictured herself fighting at the side of a brave and powerful warrior who wore a familiar face. And when Fallon—then an ambitious young detective—had offered her a choice between relocating or helping the cops go after Hood, it was because of the stories that she had chosen to stay. That, and because it had given

her a chance to fight, in her own way, at her warrior's
side. But that was then and this was now, and . . .

Screw it. She kept reading.

> *You may have already guessed, but if not, here it is:*
> *We are the last of the Nightkeepers, and the doomsday*
> *war is here. The blue binder contains a rundown of*
> *our more recent history, including the massacre that*
> *left us scattered as orphans, being raised in secret by*
> *our winikin; the events that led to our reunion three*
> *years ago; and the things we've seen and done since*
> *then. You're in there. You impressed the hell out of me*
> *in that warehouse—even more so now that I know that*
> *you were trying to save Dez's ass, and why. And you*
> *did a job for another of us, Patience White-Eagle, a*
> *while back. You found her sons and their winikin in*
> *hiding, and that should have been impossible.*

"The bride," Reese murmured, putting it together
with the funny look the blonde had shot her back at
the hotel.

She remembered the case clearly, not because she
had met any of the players—it had all been done by
remote control, highly hush-hush—but because it
had been a rare challenge. Given that the client had
provided her a last-known address, it should have
been easy to find a sixty-something couple living
with twin kindergarten-age boys. In actuality, she
had sweated the job, eventually dumping everything
else to focus on that one case, day and night, until she
had cracked it.

The guardians had been *winikin*, she realized now, hiding a pair of Nightkeeper children. No wonder she'd broken a sweat.

The note continued:

> *Your skills are part of why we need you. We're currently fighting a rearguard action against a Xibalban mage named Iago and the creatures he controls, and to do that we need all hands on deck, including Dez. Also, you'll find that there's a matchmaker inside most of us, because a Nightkeeper who has bonded with his or her rightful mate is so much stronger than before. I realize that you and Dez had problems, but—*

"Oh, no. You're so not going there." Crumpling the three-page note, Reese shot to her feet and strode to the window. But the sight of all that wide-open space made her long to be back in the city. Any city.

She glanced at the door, then at the intercom. She could hit the magic number and make it all go away.

Instead, she looked down at the letter. The words "rightful mate" jumped out at her.

"Better brace yourself to be disappointed on that score," she muttered. Until she shot her mouth off back at the hotel, Strike and the others hadn't had a clue that she and Dez had a history. It shouldn't have bothered her that he hadn't mentioned . . . *Shit*. She kept reading.

> *—realize that you and Dez had problems, but I think I can explain some, if not all of them. You know*

*how Dez changed after the fight with Keban? That
wasn't him, it was the effects of magic . . . or, rather,
a curse.*

Her blood iced and her palms started to sweat, but
she didn't stop reading. Couldn't have even if she had
wanted to.

> *That night, Keban gave Dez a small obsidian carv-
> ing of a star demon, a creature of darkness. We don't
> know where he got the carving or how he knew what
> it would do to Dez, but you experienced the fallout.
> Here's what we've been able to piece together: The star
> demon amplifies the darker aspects of a mage's person-
> ality until it overrides the good stuff. In Dez's case, it
> also allowed him to form a connection with the bar-
> rier, even before the magic reawakened. Although he
> couldn't use his powers afterward—he was only able
> to call the lightning that night because it was the equi-
> nox and, I'm guessing, because you were in danger—
> the effects of the star demon's power twisted him into
> the man who drove you away. But the thing is, he's not
> that guy anymore.*
>
> *A year ago, prophecy said that we had to offer our-
> selves to the gods and ask them to pick three of us to
> receive the powers and knowledge of our strongest
> ancestors. Enacting the Triad spell risked madness,
> death, possession . . . but forfeiting prophecy carries
> a heavy price, so we cast the spell. The gods reached
> out beyond us, all the way to Denver, and picked Dez.
> But instead of giving him the powers of his ancestors,*

*they gave him a spirit guide—a long-ago ancestor of his named Anntah—who entered his mind, undid the damage the star demon and Keban had done, and taught Dez what he needed to know. He awoke a new man: centered, powerful . . . and jonesing to make up for the things he had done. Or maybe "new man" is the wrong term—really, he went back to his pre-star-demon personality, his baseline self.*

Reese's breath rushed out in a hiss. "Bullshit. That's just bullshit."

The details fit the pattern; there was no question about that. But she didn't for a second believe that Dez had let some piece of rock control him. And if he was acting differently now, it was sure as hell because it suited his purposes, not because of some spell.

She gritted her teeth, flipped the page, and read on.

*We didn't believe his transformation at first, but Rabbit confirmed his turnaround, and over the past year Dez has worked his ass off to prove himself. Then, two days ago he disappeared without a word. Our usual private investigator found that he had received a letter via the old* winikin *drop system, but Carter couldn't track him beyond that. He suggested we hire a specialist, and I immediately thought of you. At the time, I assumed that was simple logic. Now, I'm reminded that what the humans call coincidence we call the will of the gods.*

*Don't believe me? Look on the next page. That's a printout from some security-cam footage that Dez*

*downloaded the night before he took off. At first, we
thought it was just some guy stealing a Puebloan artifact from a small museum outside of Santa Fe. After
Dez disappeared, we guessed who it might be. Now
that Rabbit has seen things through your eyes, we
know for sure.*

A cold chill sliced through her, and she was almost
braced for it when she flipped the page and found
Louis Keban staring back at her. The photo was blurry
and badly lit, and his scars were obscured by shadows,
but she knew his eyes and the slightly off-balance way
he held himself. Up until a year or so ago, she had still
seen him in her nightmares. Now, she had a feeling
those bad dreams would be back with a vengeance.

Last she had heard, he had been safely ensconced in
a locked mental ward. Apparently not anymore.

Below the photo, the letter finished:

*We're not sure why Dez didn't tell us what was go-
ing on or ask for backup. Pride, maybe, or something
in the letter. But we do know one thing for certain: We
need him back. The winter solstice marks the one-year
threshold, and the magi must be at their strongest.
More, we need to figure out what Keban is up to. He
clearly knows things we don't—and his history and
mental state make him dangerous.*

*So that's what we want from you, Ms. Montana.
Find Dez, find Keban, and figure out what the hell is
going on there, in the order of your choice. After that,
if you're willing to stay, we'll sic you on Iago. The*

*patterns of his recent attacks are . . . baffling. Maybe you'll see something we're missing.*

*I hope you'll take the job, both for Dez's sake and because it's the right thing to do. But if that isn't incentive enough, then how about this: It'll give you a chance to get back at the man who destroyed the life you could have had with Dez back in Denver.*

*Think about it. And when you've decided, dial 1313. We'll be waiting.*

*—Strike*

Reese lowered the letter and numbly stared out the window, at scenery that warned her that she was badly out of her element.

"Damn it," she whispered, glancing once more at the picture of Keban.

This was seriously and completely nuts, and it would be insane to even consider taking the job. But she *was* considering it, for all the reasons Strike had listed.

Damn the mind-bender for getting inside her head and figuring out which buttons to push. And damn her for being unable to resist the thrill of the hunt or be content with a safe, predictable life. More, she couldn't ignore the pressure that fisted beneath her heart as Strike's words circled in her head . . . *He's not that guy anymore . . . It was a curse . . . back to his old self . . .*

In the weeks after Dez's death—supposed death?—she had been buried in memories of the young man she had loved. The old Dez had driven her crazy with his stubbornness, but despite his protectiveness he'd never tried to box her in. The gang task force had been her thing, but he'd always had her back. He had nagged her into her GED, and had brought her chocolate and information, knowing they were neck-and-neck in her universe. And when the nights got cold and too dark, he had told her stories about magical warriors who could move things with their minds and hear each other's thoughts, and who drew their greatest powers from love.

*Back to his old self . . . a Triad mage . . . incredibly powerful.*

"Bullshit." She lurched to her feet, stomach knotting. The ache wasn't quite hunger, but it was safer to call it that, so she headed for the kitchen, figuring the apartment looked lived-in enough that it ought to have some staples, even if it was just a guest suite . . . or a prison cell with better-than-average amenities. That thought brought a shudder, but the moment she got the fridge open, both the queasiness and her appetite disappeared—*boom*, gone.

Oh. Shit.

She stood there for a long moment in the cold wash of air, shivering as she stared at the items that were clustered together on the top shelf, as if tossed back in after a snack: horseradish mustard, olive loaf, grape jelly, and pumpernickel bread. Four cans of Mountain Dew were racked in the door.

A low moan broke from her as her heart took up a heavy *thud-thud* beat in her ears. Nobody could come up with that combination accidentally, and there was only one person on the planet who would do it on purpose.

*Dez.*

Her hand trembled on the refrigerator door. There was no way in hell that this was his suite. It was too bland, too impersonal. There were no high-tech toys, no expensive clothes, no glitter and gloss, no leather or other indulgences. But there was pumpernickel, olive loaf, and the grossest condiment pairing known to mankind.

*He's not that guy anymore.*

Throat closing on a burn of tears, she whispered, "Damn it."

She thought about Denver, about the new life she was building there, and her determination to be a better person, one who didn't take the same sort of risks the old Reese had, who lived with less danger, less pain. Then she thought about the young man she had known, the one she had mourned even though their relationship had died years before his actual—or faked—death. She thought of the comfort of his spine pressed into hers, crowding her against the wall so she would be warm while he kept watch. And she thought about the puniness of saving the world one person at a time when she could potentially help save the whole damn thing.

*Don't do it*, her smarter self said. *Don't do it, don't do it, don't—*

"Shit." She crossed the room in a few strides, went for the intercom pad, and hit 1313 so hard her fingertip stung.

Strike came on the line immediately, voice sounding resigned and tired as he said, "Give me good news, Ms. Montana. I could really use it right now."

"I'm going to need whatever you've got on the museum break-in—provenance on the artifact that Keban stole, any cross-refs on similar cases, the works. Dez knows how to hide his tracks, so I'm guessing it'll be easier to find the damned *winikin*." She paused, toughening her voice to hide how small and vulnerable she suddenly felt, how deeply out of her element. "And for future reference? The next one of you who puts a spell on me without permission is going to be choking on his or her own spleen."

There was a pause. Then the king of the Nightkeepers said simply, "Welcome to the team."

# CHAPTER FOUR

*Aztec Ruins National Park*
*New Mexico*
December 10; total lunar eclipse;
one year and eleven days until the zero date

Well into hour three of his stakeout, Dez barely even twitched at the sound of a kid-sized stampede approaching from the visitors' center, followed by the nasal chirp of a teacher's voice doing the facts-and-figures thing.

He was well hidden, and knew that the human herd would stay on the marked path that crossed the huge circular footprint of an ancient kiva. From there, they would wind through a few of the hundreds of rooms belonging to the thousand-year-old stone-and-mortar structure, loop up to a smaller, heavily restored building called the Hubbard Site, then back around to the gift shop and picnic area. The tour groups didn't stray off the beaten path. Not like he had. And not like the man he hunted would do.

*Come on, you bastard. Where the hell are you?*

Ever since Dez had awakened from his Triad-induced coma and his ancestor's this-is-your-life-and-hey-you-suck reprogramming, he'd been working on curbing his impatience and maintaining control. But sitting and waiting still wasn't his strong suit.

He had been chasing Keban's dust for the past week, always two steps behind the bastard until—thank fuck—yesterday, when he'd finally crossed a fresh trail and recognized the sour scent and faintly off vibration that he'd caught a whiff of at the Santa Fe museum Keban had robbed. He'd followed it to a library downtown, got his hands on the same book the bastard had touched, found the map he had lingered on, along with a reference to shadowscript and the lunar eclipse, and knew he'd finally gotten the break he needed.

The *winikin* would be there at dusk. Not long now.

Dez had picked a spot just inside one of the dozens of low passageways that ran through what was left of the huge ruin. He was fifty or so feet and several chambers away from the self-guided path, but the alignment of the rectangular doorways and thick, rubble-filled masonry walls carried the teacher's words.

"Despite the name, these buildings weren't originally built by the Aztecs. The mistake was made in the mid–eighteen hundreds by scholars who believed the Aztecs had originated here and migrated south to Mexico. But this was most likely a trading center for the Puebloan tribes, and may have had ties to the Chacoans in the canyon country south of here."

"Try definitely had ties to the Chacoans," Dez said under his breath, shifting to get at his water bottle and take a swig. "This was one of ours." Even a thousand years later, the place vibrated with echoes of Night-keeper magic, warming him slightly as the sun started its downward slide and the shadows grew.

"Although early scholars thought the huge North Ruin might be an archaic apartment building, we now think there were maybe only a couple of hundred permanent residents, with thousands of other people gathering here during ceremonial days . . ." The kid-herder's voice faded as the group moved along the path.

". . . sooo bored," a straggler said, her ennui reaching Dez on an echo.

"I know, right?" said another. "This blows." Her voice dropped to a carrying whisper. "You wanna sneak back around to the gift shop? I've got my mom's AmEx."

"I—"

"No," interrupted an older, equally bored voice, though this one coming from an adult. Auxiliary kid-herder, no doubt. "Come on, let's go catch up with the others."

There were grumbles as the three moved off, with the first of the girls complaining in a put-upon voice, "Why do we have to know this crap anyway? It's so *old*. Why can't we learn about stuff that *matters*?"

Dez snorted to himself. "Consider yourself lucky somebody gives a shit whether you learn it or not. And the old stuff—especially *this* old stuff—matters more than you'll ever know." At least, she would never know if the Nightkeepers had anything to say about it.

The shadows lengthened further. The air chilled. The park cleared.

Dez tugged his fleece-lined cap down over his smoothly bald scalp and turned up the collar of the heavy desert-camo jacket he'd bought from an army surplus store, along with night-vision goggles and a KA-BAR knife. He should've gone with the lined pants too. He might still be in New Mex, but he was practically on top of the Colorado border, and the sharp wind smelled of snow. Not to mention that serpents didn't do too well in the cold, and the main effect of the Triad magic—aside from saddling him with a now-decamped spirit guide and some nasty dreams—had been to skew many of his senses closer to those of his bloodline totem.

The Triad magic had affected each of the chosen magi differently: It had given detail-oriented Brandt a mental filing system that contained all of his ancestors' spells and talents, yet the same spell had nearly killed Strike's sister, Anna. It wasn't clear whether that was because she lacked the warrior's mark, because she had forsaken the Nightkeepers to live out in the human world, or what, but she had suffered a hell of a cranial bleed. She was up and moving now, and the doctors said her scans were within normal limits, but still she ghosted from day to day, silent and foggy-eyed.

Seeing her around Skywatch had hammered home to Dez that he was seriously fucking lucky. The Triad magic hadn't just picked him; it had saved him, given him a second chance. And in the process, it had sleeked him down and enhanced his existing magic. Like a serpent, he used all of his senses, analyzing scent signatures by both smell and taste, and detecting minute changes in body heat. Not to mention that his warrior's talent gave him the sharpened reflexes and strategic thinking of a killing machine, and the lightning magic gave him some serious shock-and-awe. The three together made him a formidable weapon, and he was determined to be the best damned soldier he could be. He couldn't undo the past, but since waking up from the Triad transition, he had thrown himself into the Nightkeepers' war, taking his own ego out of the equation and doing whatever he was damn well told.

That is, until last week when he got Keban's strangely formal note—his fucking marching orders: *Prepare yourself—and the rest of the magi—to meet me at noon on the day of the solstice. Bring the black artifact. I'll gather the others that have been found, and on the proper days I will find the two that remain hidden. I will contact you with instructions when the time comes. Be ready.*

Bull-fucking-shit to that. Anntah had made it clear during Dez's mental Roto-Rootering that Keban had some of his rhetoric right, but he didn't speak for the serpent bloodline. He was sick and damaged. More, he knew far more than a *winikin* should about the magic, which made him dangerous. So Dez was prepared, all right . . . prepared to kill Keban and destroy the artifacts. And if there was some grim satisfaction in the chore, he figured he could live with that. He'd never claimed to be a frigging saint.

A trickle of dislodged rocks interrupted his train of thought and brought his head up. The sound was followed by the faint tread of footsteps coming not from the path, but from the back country on the other side of the park.

Heat flared as his warrior's talent came on line, sharpening his reflexes and bringing his fighting magic close to the surface. He bared his teeth when he caught the faintly sour smell he had been trailing for days. His enemy had arrived, and for once he was a step ahead of the bastard rather than chasing behind.

Easing from the cold passageway into the warmer air outside, he let his magic ramp up, the fine electrical currents making him acutely aware of each neuron and synapse. The sun was gone, the sky a clear, darkening blue going scalloped pink at the edges as he slipped from one shadow-shrouded doorway to the next, working his way through the interconnected chambers of the labyrinthine ruin. The small, furtive noises he was tracking headed for the northernmost point of the ruin, where eight-foot-high stone walls outlined a huge circular chamber.

Dez wedged himself into the shadowy juncture where an intersecting wall ran into the curve of the room's outer edge and a small window gave him a decent view of the inner courtyard. Moments later, Keban came into view. And even though Dez had braced himself to see the *winikin* again—and to kill him—the sight of the hunched-over body and scarred face shot his pulse into the stratosphere. In an instant, he flashed back on that night in the storm, and the look on the bastard's face as he had pressed the star demon into Dez's bleeding palms.

His final slide had started at that moment. The bad shit that followed had come from inside him, it was true, but Keban had set it free.

*Wait it out*, Dez told himself. *Let him get the artifact first.* He watched through slitted eyes as the *winikin* skimmed a hand over a section of the wall where the masons had worked a snakelike stripe of green stone into the red-rock background, then paused, lips moving as he read the shadowscript. After a moment, he turned and paced the diameter of the kiva three separate times, scuffing his feet when he hit the center. Then he stood in the place where his scuff marks intersected and started walking north, perpendicular to the plane of the setting sun. When he reached the wall, he dropped to his knees, pulled a folding shovel from his knapsack, screwed the pieces together, and started digging.

*Almost*, Dez thought, shifting restlessly in his hiding spot. A second later he realized that the twitchiness was more than his usual impatience—there was a new current humming in the air, an itchy heat that was familiar yet not. *Magic*, he thought, gut knotting on the realization. *Shit.* The buzz was coming from Keban, growing stronger the farther down he dug. It was from the artifact, a soft, insistent call that reached inside Dez, seeming to echo in his very DNA.

*Block it out*, he told himself, steeling himself against the siren song. He could handle it this time. He would *have* to handle it.

He started to sweat.

The *winikin* suddenly made a satisfied noise, ducked down and shoved his hands into the hollow he had carved alongside the wall. He came up with a bundle, started unwrapping a layer of rotting fabric, then paused and turned away to paw through his knapsack for something.

Digging his fingernails into his palms hard enough to draw blood, both as a crude sacrifice and to keep himself from doing something stupid, Dez called the magic for a shield spell, intending to turn it into a damned cage. Power raced in his veins as he spread his fingers and imagined the shield falling into place, but he didn't trigger the spell. *Wait for it*, he told himself. *Wait . . . for . . . it.*

Keban straightened, holding a flashlight.

*Now!* Dez unleashed his shield spell at the same instant that Keban turned on the flashlight. There was a spark of electricity, a flare of magic.

And the world went nuts.

A fat spark shot from Keban to Dez and back. The *winikin* cried out and dropped the flashlight, but a flare of blue-white power suddenly engulfed Dez, lighting his surroundings and totally fucking the element of surprise. Keban spun, took one look at him, and bolted.

*Damn it!* Dez slammed his crackling shield around the other man. Not invisible like most of the warrior's defensive spells, or concealing like the chameleon shields Michael or Alexis could call, Dez's shield was like most of his magic: loud, unsubtle, and supercharged. It arced with blue-white electricity, forming a weblike cage that stopped bullets and buzz-swords, and could make like a Taser if he wanted it to. And hell, yeah, he wanted it to right now. He wanted the bastard to burn.

Keban skidded to a stop in the center of the magic, and turned back as Dez approached the cage. The blue-white light showed a face that sagged like wax around the scars, eyes that were sly and calculating, but didn't track normally.

Nate's illegal hack into the *winikin*'s psych ward records had revealed that Keban had suffered an acute psychotic break a few days after that night in the storm. He'd stayed put for a decade, then vanished the day of the Triad spell, which couldn't have been a coincidence. He'd been rational enough to work out an escape, rational enough to send that letter and track down the artifacts he wanted. Now, though, he stared past Dez's shoulder, twisting his fingers in the filthy cloth wrappings, and mumbling to himself, looking more pitiful than rational.

Dez's rage didn't quite die, but it sure as hell faltered.

Up close, the man inside the glowing cage was a deflated, deranged version of the beast he had seen in his nightmares, year after year, until new demons took his place. He didn't look like the ruthless bastard who had dragged Dez to dozens of crumbling ruins as a kid and turned him loose with a knife and orders to find the temple's sacred chamber, make his sacrifice, and "for fuck's sake, get it right." And he didn't look like the man who had whipped him bloody each time he failed.

Instead, he looked old, sad, and defeated. And nothing like the man Dez had primed himself to kill.

"Shit." He scowled through the bars at his captive. "Now what?" His prior self would have stuck stubbornly to the original plan. The better man he was trying to be thought it might be safe to bring him back to Skywatch, after all. If he was this far gone, not even Rabbit would be able to get at the truth that needed to stay hidden.

Still looking off to the side, as if unable to meet his eyes, Keban held out the wrapped bundle and mumbled unintelligibly.

Dez hesitated. Then, dampening the shield spell so it wouldn't fry either of them, he moved in closer. "You want me to take it?"

The *winikin* jerked his chin in what might have been a nod, and went to work on the rotting cloth. Within moments, he had unwrapped a fist-sized chunk of white crystal carved into a head. The face was Mayan, the accoutrements those of a god with matching "T" shapes inscribed on both cheeks.

Dez didn't recognize the god or the glyph, but something inside him gave a liquid tug of longing. It wasn't the same as the way the black idol made him feel—this was softer and more grounded, almost sexual—but the two sensations were definitely in the same ballpark. This was another piece of the puzzle, no question about it.

He held out a hand, careful to stay on his side of the shield spell. "Give it to me."

Keban offered the bust, hands shaking and then sagging as he lost strength. Dez reached for the carving, stepping forward automatically to catch it before it fell.

The moment he made contact, power flashed through him, paralyzing him momentarily.

And in that terrible, vulnerable second, Keban's eyes focused and his fingers clamped on Dez's wrist to yank him closer. The *winikin*'s eyes flashed cruelly, and he was utterly focused and in control as he held up his free hand and blew a puff of white powder through the latticework of the lightning shield.

Dez yanked away as the fine particles peppered his face. "Son of a—" Pain lashed through him, starting at his nose and mouth and then racing through his body. His muscles seized up, his senses overloaded, and he doubled over in agony.

*Gods!* He fought for control, but crashed to the ground instead. The white god's head rolled away from his spasming fingers and electricity arced through him as his powers raged, veering and colliding. The shield spell shorted out, freeing Keban, who looked straight and strong, and nothing like the broken old man he had pretended to be.

He moved to stand over Dez. Pulling a wide-barreled gun from the small of his back, he shook his head, expression terrifyingly blank. "You couldn't just meet me during the fucking solstice, could you? You had to try and be the noble motherfucking Triad mage. Well, this'll slow you down a little." He took aim at Dez's kneecap.

*Fuck!* Dez rolled as automatic gunfire split the air. Through the haze of pain and the spinning disorienta-

tion that had come from the drugged powder, it took
him a second to realize that the barrage hadn't come
from the *winikin*'s gun. It had been one of the MAC-10s
the magi used for jade-tip combat.

Backup! Dez hadn't wanted it, didn't know how they
had found him . . . but he was damn glad for the help
as the autopistol chattered again.

Cursing, Keban grabbed the god's head and dove
through a doorway as bullets chewed into the thousand-
year-old masonry.

Lurching to his feet, Dez shouted, "Don't let him get
away!" He stumbled after the *winikin*, trying to summon his warrior's magic as he ran, but got sparks instead of a shield or lightning. He couldn't sense Keban's
heat signature, but he could feel the tug of the white
statue's magic, headed toward the Hubble Site at the
edge of the Aztec Ruin. Pulling a small flashlight from
his heavy jacket, he flicked it on. "This way!" Ducking,
he veered into a tunnel he had scouted earlier.

A single set of bootfalls pounded behind him, closing the gap as he burst out of the tunnel into the open
space separating the North Ruin and the Hubble Site.
But Keban wasn't headed for the second ruin. He'd
made it to his vehicle.

Dez skidded to a stop, swearing over the roar of an
engine as rear lights bounced hard and disappeared in
a cloud of dust.

"Son of a bitch." He spun toward his backup, aiming the flashlight. "We have to—" He broke off, the air
jamming his lungs when he saw, not a Nightkeeper,
but a stranger. A woman.

And a hell of a woman, at that.

The dark-haired beauty was fully decked out for a Nightkeeper op in black Kevlar-impregnated combat pants cut trim across her waist and hips; a tight black thermal shirt under body armor that didn't entirely camouflage her curves; a weapons belt loaded with guns, jade-tipped ammo, and a good-sized combat knife; and a gleaming black-and-chrome communications band around her upper arm that was part tech-ware, part magic.

The look packed a hell of punch, as did the shock of suddenly acquiring a new teammate, but then she took another step and her face caught the light.

And time. Fucking. Stopped.

Familiar amber-whiskey eyes framed in long, dark lashes turned a face he had labeled simply "beautiful" into something else entirely. Suddenly he saw the high cheekbones he had once ascribed to suburban royalty, the pert nose and dented chin that he'd called pixie-ish when he wanted to tease, and the elegantly curved mouth he had no right to dream about.

"Reese," he whispered, heart stuttering. Logic said that he was either hallucinating or flat on his ass un-conscious, because there was no way in hell Reese Montana would be wearing Nightkeeper gear and looking to back his ass up. She hated him, had cut him off, and with damn good reason.

Yet there she was. Which meant this had to be a dream. But in his dreams her hair was its natural blue-black, not a warm copper-streaked brunette. And in his dreams, she was looking at him the way she used to, before the storm and the star demon, and his mad slide into darkness. Not glaring at him like he was something she'd found stuck on the bottom of one of her silver-toed boots.

"Reese?" Shock seemed to have reduced him to that one syllable as it started connecting that this might not be a hallucination, after all.

"Guess they were right. You're not dead." She shoved her spare autopistol against his chest and stalked past him, headed for the second ruin. Over her shoulder, she shot, "I'm going after the *winikin*. And I'm not waiting for you."

Keban. The god's head. Oh, shit.

His warrior's talent took over, getting his feet moving while his brain tried to catch up. Being a Nightkeeper was all about priorities, and the *winikin* was getting away with the statue, so he did his damnedest to focus as he followed her to a thin stand of trees beyond the ruins, where she had stashed her vehicle. But he stuttered to a halt at the edge of the clearing at the sight of her ride.

She was driving an unassuming Jeep Compass with a generic silver exterior that gave zero indication of the rabid, snorting horses under the hood, and the other mods that had been retrofitted. He knew about them because he'd done some of the work himself.

Jesus, gods. She was wearing combat clothes and driving the newest and fastest of the Nightkeepers' cars. If he could've crafted a wet dream, that would be it, except for the part where she despised him. Because for all that he had remade himself, he was still the guy who had broken her heart, and worse.

"Get in," she snapped, slinging herself into the driver's side.

The engine roared like a racecar as he took shotgun and strapped himself in. He stared across at her. "Holy shit . . . Reese?"

"Not now." She hit the gas and aimed for the road.

But as the acceleration punched him back in his seat, he pointed northwest. "He's headed that way." When she narrowed her eyes, he added, "I can sense the carving."

She nodded tightly, spun the wheel, and sent them overland.

The next few minutes passed in a shuddering blur as they chased the *winikin* along a series of fire access roads that eventually joined the main road, where Reese muscled the heavy vehicle onto the tarmac and accelerated, two-handing the steering wheel as the odometer edged past ninety.

Dez stared at her badass pixie profile, the hard line of her jaw. And wished to hell he could have a do-over. "You came after me."

That was all he could think, that she had somehow figured out that he was alive, gone searching for him, and been recruited by the Nightkeepers. But why had she been looking? He would have thought she'd be glad to let him stay dead.

"I was hired to find you," she corrected coolly, staring straight ahead and handling the dark curves with grim proficiency.

"Oh." Which put a different spin on things. Due to the Triad magic, Strike wouldn't have been able to find him with magic, so the king must've gone old-school and hired the only bounty hunter he'd ever met in person. Then, once he figured out that she and Dez had a history and she knew most of the Nightkeepers' legends, he'd brought her into things all the damn way. "Jesus Christ," he muttered under his breath.

"Wrong religion, Mendez. Or so I'm told."

"Reese—" he began, but she cut him off.

"Are we gaining on him?"

*Focus. Prioritize.* "Yeah. Look for a right up ahead. He's off the main road." He didn't know how he knew that.

She accelerated around the next turn. "Good. This baby will out off-road the crap out of his POS rental in a— *shit!*"

He barely had time to curse at the sight of the empty rental car parked *across* the fucking road right in front of them. Then they were on top of it, going too fast to stop. Reese locked the brakes as they flew toward the dust-covered sedan. But it wouldn't be enough.

"Grab something!" he snapped, shooting a hand across the cab and pulling her seat belt extra tight as he called on his drug-depleted magic for a half-assed shield spell that crackled to misfiring electric life.

They hit with a slewing jolt of impact, a roar of destruction, and the muted gunshots of the airbags that *thwumped* into them from the front and sides. Dez's head snapped on his neck and he tasted blood. Keban's abandoned vehicle flew off the road and into a shallow ditch on one side, but the Compass caromed the other way and headed straight for the guardrail that marked off a steep embankment. Beyond was only darkness.

Reese's eyes locked on his for a second; he saw a flash of grief and heard her voice crack when she said, "It wasn't supposed to go like this."

"Story of our lives. Hang on." Spitting blood in sacrifice, he shouted, "*Pasaj och!*" A deeper barrier connection slammed through him, lighting him up and pouring out of him in a surge. He did his damnedest to fill the vehicle's interior with shield magic as the Compass hit the guardrail, peeled through it, went airborne for a few seconds . . .

And fell.

# CHAPTER FIVE

The SUV plummeted and hit with a bone-jarring impact, but instead of pain and the crash of breaking glass, Reese found herself surrounded by a sizzling noise and a whirl of lightning arcs. The blue-white strobes of Dez's shield magic—which wasn't like anything else she had seen in her five-day crash course at Skywatch—showed a rocky embankment that fell away from them on a steep slant, with jagged rocks at the bottom, trees beyond that. *Not good.*

Then the Compass bounced and all she could do was hang on white knuckled as the vehicle slewed sideways and rolled—*wham, wham, wham*—three dizzying revolutions that spun her head over ass and left her fighting for breath. They landed upright—thank Christ— and skidded down the incline, finally thudding into a pine tree that splintered and rained needles on them, but held.

It fucking held. And in doing so, it saved their lives.

In an instant that seemed to take forever, the crash chaos faded and the world went still.

And Dez's magic skimmed across her skin like a caress.

She closed her eyes, trying not feel it, to feel *him* sitting way too close beside her. By the time she left Skywatch, she had almost convinced herself that this was just a job, that she was doing what anyone like her would do given the chance to be part of the whole save-the-world thing.

But that was bullshit: This was about Dez, pure and simple. That was where anything "simple" ended, though, because she didn't have a clue if she'd come after him to get some sort of final closure, because she still felt like she owed him, because Strike said the Nightkeepers needed him, or because some weak, perpetually nineteen-year-old part of her wanted to believe he had gone back to being the boy she had loved.

It almost hadn't mattered, either, because she'd nearly killed both of them doing the high-speed-chase thing. She was supposed to have outgrown this shit. All of it.

"Reese!" He dragged off his belt, took his knife to the airbags, slapped on the overhead light and loomed over her, his eyes worried and so damn familiar they peeled back the years in an instant. "Gods. Are you okay?"

She swallowed hard and whispered, "Yeah. I'm fine." But she was suddenly having trouble breathing, and it wasn't because of the crash.

Intellectually, she had accepted that he was alive, that he had come into his full powers, not just as a warrior but as a Triad mage. And the five days she had spent at Skywatch had helped her get over her awe—or most of it, anyway—when it came to the Nightkeepers she had grown up dreaming about. The magi were big and glossy, yes, and they had powers she didn't. But on another level, they were normal people. Sasha shared her sweet tooth, Alexis had a thing for shoes, and Nate had kicked her ass twice on *Grand Theft Auto* before admitting that he'd been a game developer in his previous life. Strike was more distant, and seemed troubled, but she had gotten him talking baseball one evening and he'd seemed grateful for the diversion. Over the past week the magi had become acquaintances, some even friends, and she had thought, *Okay, I can do this. I can deal with seeing Dez.*

But she couldn't, she realized now. Because thinking about seeing him again wasn't the same as actually *seeing* him again.

She hadn't been prepared for the way the Triad spell had rendered him hairless, like his bloodline totem. His scalp was sleek instead of trimmed to stubble, his jaw unshadowed, his brows smooth. Where the sleeve of his jacket rode up as he leaned over her, his muscular forearm gleamed in the dashboard lights, which caught the edge of his bloodline mark: a gapemouthed, plumed serpent. And she hadn't been braced for that. She hadn't been expecting him to be wearing army surplus that looked far more like the secondhands they had scrounged as kids than the slick designers he had worn in later years. And she sure as hell hadn't been prepared for the way the years—or maybe the magic?—had honed his wide cheekbones, ridged nose, and sardonic mouth. How, when he lifted a hand to touch her cheek as if needing to prove to himself that she was really there, the fine tremor in his hand would make her heart shudder.

"Damn it, Dez," she said. She wasn't sure whether she would have invited him closer or warned him away, because her throat locked.

The moment spun out between them.

Then a car roared by up on the road, snapping her back to reality. The engine noise didn't change and there was no flash of brakes—the driver had either managed to miss the signs of a crash, or was pretending to—but the next one might not. "We can't stay here," she said softly.

He started to say something, then thought better of it and nodded instead. A shadow shifted across his expression, distancing him; it was his warrior's talent coming on line, she thought, blunting his emotions and shifting his priorities. Or maybe she just wanted to think that.

"I'll see how bad the damage is." He shouldered open his door and hauled himself up and out. Winter air rushed in to fill the void as he headed around to the back of the Compass, where the darkness swallowed him up.

She knew she should go with him, but instead sagged back against the seat, head spinning with the realization that she was in big trouble. She had told herself she was taking the job partly to prove how far she had come. Instead it was clear that she hadn't changed at all, not deep down inside: She was still the same adrenaline junkie who had damn near self-destructed.

Shaking her head in an effort to rattle some sense back into her brain succeeded only in waking a dull throb of a headache and making her neck twinge in protest. The pain got her up and moving, though.

The Compass was an accordioned mess of spider-webbed glass and skewed wheels, lit by a glowing fox-fire spell that followed Dez like a ghost, floating near his shoulder as he tried a crumpled door, muttering under his breath.

She touched the high-tech armband that connected her to Skywatch. "I'll call in, get us a 'port back to the compound," she said, sticking with the practicalities. They had lost Keban and killed the car. It was time to fall back and regroup.

"Don't," Dez said sharply, turning to face her. The foxfire trailed behind his shoulder, throwing his face into shadow.

The word carried the punch of a command, but she lifted her chin and met the darkness that hid his eyes. "Newsflash: I don't work for you."

His face went unreadable. "Don't turn me in this time. Please."

The jab lumped a hard pressure in her chest, as did him ducking her question. "I've got a job to do."

"Keban is my responsibility." He paused, the shadows deepening. "Go home, Reese. This isn't your fight."

She shouldn't have been disappointed . . . but, damn it, she was. She had told herself not to make excuses for why he had let her believe he was dead, not to think that the Triad spell was what had stopped him from reaching out to her because she wasn't a mage like him. Strike and the others believed that her long-ago brush with the magic had marked her, putting her under the gods' notice and making her part of the fight. More, they thought that she and Dez might have been destined mates, and that the gods were trying to make things right now by sparking the coincidences that had brought them together once more.

She had told herself not to buy into it, not to expect anything. But the prickle of tears and a sudden jones for tiramisu said she hadn't done as good of a job with that one as she had thought.

*Suck it up*, she told herself. *You don't need his permission to drag his ass back to Skywatch.* She didn't have her Taser anymore, but Strike was waiting for her signal, and the magi could take care of the rest. *You're just a locator these days, remember?*

But there was an edge of desperation in his eyes. A silent plea. And her instincts were suddenly telling her not to make the call, that this was one of those targets who might be better off staying lost, at least for a while.

When it came to Dez, though, history suggested that her instincts sucked. And the Nightkeepers' writs said it best: *What has happened before will happen again.*

She met his eyes. "You don't get to decide whether or not this is my fight, especially not when your king, my contract, an unlimited expense account, and the end of the freaking world all say it is."

"I could drop you with a sleep spell, call them to

pick you up, and be gone before they got here." He suddenly seemed bigger and more menacing than before, though he hadn't moved. The foxfire drifted ahead of him, illuminating his face but revealing nothing.

"I'd just hunt you down again," she countered. "And the next time you wouldn't even know I was there—I'd just dart you like a rabid dog." He didn't say anything, but for a second she saw something in his eyes. In another man, it would have been desperation. She softened her voice. "Come back to Skywatch. They need you."

"They're fine without me," he said flatly.

Which was a total crock. The Nightkeepers were bracing for massive attacks as the end-time countdown passed the one-year threshold. The prophecies hinted at disasters but were frustratingly low on details, leaving the magi scrambling for answers and needing all hands on deck . . . but Dez knew that. Yet here he was, out here on his own, tracking Keban. And he didn't want the others involved. Either his transformation wasn't nearly as complete as the others thought . . . or there was something else going on.

"What are you hiding?" The slight narrowing of those pale eyes said it was a direct hit. Taking a deep breath to settle the sudden churn in her stomach, the one that reminded her of other arguments, other secrets, she pressed, "What don't you want them to know?"

For a moment she thought he was going to ignore the question, or outright lie. But then he met her eyes. "I don't have any right to ask you to trust me."

The churn got worse. "Damn right you don't."

"I'm asking anyway. Let me go. I have to find Keban and the artifacts on my own. It's important."

For a second, she saw a flash of the boy who had saved her, the young man she had loved. Problem was, she wasn't sure if that was real or calculated. "You want me to tell Strike I couldn't find you?"

"I want you to go back to your life." His expression darkened almost imperceptibly. "And I want you to live this next year like it's your last, just in case it is."

Somehow, that hit her harder than any of the strategy sessions she'd sat in on at Skywatch. During those meetings, the magi and *winikin* had talked about the barrier and their enemies—both earthly and demonic—and the first real stirrings of war, but now she realized that part of her had held itself apart, treating the threats as another set of stories. Fiction. Maybe a big, flashy movie.

Dez's words, though, made her picture Denver a year from now, full of harried shoppers ramping up to do the holiday thing while bitching about the cold, and then—

Gone.

A shudder crawled down her spine at the thought, another as she tried to put herself into the picture. The offer was still open for Rabbit to tweak things so she could go back to that life, blissfully unaware that the tinfoil hatters had it right when it came to the countdown. Or she could return with her memories intact and, like Dez said, live the next year like it was her last. But those pictures refused to form. How could they, now that she knew about the Nightkeepers, knew what they were trying to do?

"I'm not playing you," Dez said when she was silent too long. "And I'm not going to hurt the Nightkeepers. I swear it on my sister's soul."

It was the same oath he had used to convince her to go with him on that very first night in the warehouse tunnels. Back then she had sensed his honor and loyalty, had believed he would keep her safe. Now, when she looked at the older, tougher version standing opposite her with magic burning bright in the air around him, she saw an achingly familiar stranger. He had an earnest intensity that made her want to believe. But history repeated itself, and theirs wasn't good. She shouldn't—couldn't—trust him. Yet her instincts said that she should let him go, that it wasn't time yet for him to be found. More, they said he needed help.

"Time to choose." Dez looked past her, up toward the road. "The cavalry is here." Sure enough, sirens throbbed just at the level of her hearing, then grew louder. He glanced back at her. "You going to let me go this time?"

She blew out a breath and went with her gut. "Not exactly. I'm coming with you."

His face blanked for a second, then clouded. "No fucking way," he said flatly. "That is *not* an option."

"Newsflash number two: You're not calling the shots here." Which was new, she realized. "So it's time for *you* to choose: You want to stay out in the field chasing your *winikin*, we do it together. Otherwise, I'm bringing you in." When he stayed stubbornly silent, she tipped up her chin. "Unless your Spidey senses are seriously long-range, you're going to need help finding Keban."

The first responders had arrived: The *aah-woo, aah-woo* of a police car was followed closely by the *bwip-bwip* of an ambulance, and colored lights strobed Keban's crumpled car.

"Damn it . . ." Dez glanced up at the road, then back at her, and his voice dropped. "This is some serious shit, Reese. I don't want you to get hurt."

*Losing you hurt. Every. Single. Time.* She didn't say that, though, because this wasn't about them. And if that meant she was thinking a little like a Nightkeeper, she was okay with that. So all she said was: "Pick a door, Mendez."

"Shit. Fine. We'll go after him together." He spun and stalked to the back of the Compass, where the rest of her weapons were stashed in a hidden lockbox. "Get your stuff," he ordered tersely, not looking at her. "We'll hike back to my truck. Overland, it shouldn't take all that long."

Reese ignored his tone and pulled her laptop and knapsack out of the wrecked vehicle. But although she had won the argument, she didn't feel any sense of victory. Instead, as she followed him into the darkness, her stomach was knotted into a hard ball of nerves and a panicked question was rocketing around inside her head: *What the hell are you doing?*

She didn't have a clue. But history was sure as shit repeating itself.

\* \* \*

*Skywatch*

When the landline started ringing in the main room, Sven ignored it to slouch deeper into the rec room sofa, his eyes glued to the screen. "Can someone get that?"

"Get it your damn self," JT snapped as he passed the door and glanced in, his arms loaded with storeroom boxes. "Playing *Viking Warrior* version whatever-the-fuck does *not* count as being too busy to get the phone. And I'm not your godsdamn servant."

Which would've been more cringe-inducing if the *winikin* didn't say it at least five times a day.

"I'm watching *Dog Whisperer*, not playing games," Sven muttered, but he headed out to the main room to grab the phone before JT came steamrolling back and made his point with his fists. A former army ranger who had spent the past seven years exterminating bat demons with a ceremonial knife and a bad attitude, he could more than hold his own.

So Sven got the phone his damn self.

"Skywatch," he said into the handset, keeping it simple because he'd gotten a month of kitchen duty a year or so ago when Carlos caught him answering with "Screamin' Demon Central. What is your emergency?"

"It's Mendez."

The low growl, coming with car noises in the background, brought relief. "Good to hear your voice." Sven checked the caller ID, saw that it was the cell that had been assigned to Reese. "Guess the bounty hunter earned her rep. You guys headed back?"

"No, we're staying on the *winikin*'s trail from out

here. She said she promised to check in twice a day with Strike, so consider us checked in. And I want you to get some info to the brain trust."

"Wait." Sven looked around for something to write on other than his palm. "Shit. Give me a second." He scored a pen and scratch pad. "Go ahead."

He copied down Mendez's message. "Statue. White god's head. 'T' glyphs on its cheeks. Got it."

"They can call us when they have something. We'll be on this phone."

"Good hunting."

Sven decided to walk the message out to the brain trust—aka Lucius, Jade, and the Nightkeepers' ancestral library, which had magicked its way into a cave at the back of the box canyon. It was a nice day, and he should probably work out some of the kinks. He had taken a pretty good hit the other day during a short, ugly fight with a dozen of Iago's *makol* near a ceremonial cave system down in Belize. Even though Sasha had hooked him up with some healing juju the other day, he still didn't feel right. So he jogged a little, trying to loosen up as he headed down the short flight of stairs beyond the pool area and hit the worn path that led past the picnic area.

With most of the others off on assignment—despite his protests, Strike had kept him back for a couple of days on injured reserve—he wasn't expecting to see anyone on the way to the library. He sure as hell wasn't expecting to find a standoff out behind the training hall. And certainly not one involving JT and Carlos.

Okay, JT wasn't much of a surprise, really. If there

was a fight, he was probably in the middle of it. But Sven knew firsthand how much it took to get Carlos all the way pissed off—been there, done that. His *winikin* was usually dead level no matter what crisis got thrown at him . . . except right now Carlos's face was flushed a dull red and his fists were clenched and even raised a little, like he wanted to haul off and slug the younger man.

"You know it's true," JT said. "Just give them some assurances."

Carlos bared his teeth. "That's not going to happen."

"Do you seriously not see how wrong this is?" JT's wave encompassed the whole of Skywatch.

Sven hesitated, not sure if he should come out from behind the training hall and mediate, or go back around the other way and let them work it out. Although the *winikin* acted as the Nightkeepers' support staff, and were technically lower than the magi in the hierarchy of Skywatch, by tradition they mostly governed themselves. Problem was, tradition hadn't been hacking it in the nearly a year since their former leader, Jox, had taken off.

The royal *winikin* had left the compound to help raise Patience and Brandt's twins in hiding, with no connection to the magic, no part in the war. Which had left a power vacuum. The rest of the *winikin* had done their best to adapt, continuing on in their usual roles and informally voting on group decisions, but they had lost serious momentum. Then the two unbound *winikin*, JT and his girlfriend, Natalie, had shown up. Natalie didn't have much baggage; she had been an infant when her parents smuggled her out of Skywatch just prior to the Solstice Massacre. JT, on the other hand, had been twelve or so. He had escaped ahead of the attack but his parents, key members of the resistance, had been caught and press-ganged into the fight. So it wasn't surprising that he hated the Nightkeepers' caste system with a virulence that bordered on pathological, and that he was calling for some major changes in *winikin*-land.

So far, Strike had been doing the "hands off, let them work it out for themselves" thing, but it wasn't getting better as far as Sven could tell. And frankly, he thought JT had a point.

Not that the older *winikin*—including Carlos— wanted to hear his opinion on that.

Making his move before he could talk himself out of it, Sven continued along the path, then hesitated, feigning surprise. "Oh, sorry. Didn't mean to interrupt."

Carlos frowned. "How much—" He broke off. "Did you need something?"

"I was just passing through, but I heard a little." To JT, he said, "You were talking about other *winikin*, weren't you? Other unbounds who got out ahead of the attack. Members of the resistance." Ever since his arrival, JT had said that he didn't know of any other survivors, that he didn't have a clue how to contact them if they were out there. Now, it seemed like he'd been saying one thing to the magi, but something else to the other *winikin*. Sven pressed, "You know how to find them, don't you?"

Carlos got in his face. "Don't repeat that. Don't even

breathe it. You owe me that much." His eyes were cold and hard, making him look like a stranger, and the sudden and unexpected shift sent Sven back a step.

For all that the two of them had had their problems, most of them stemming from Sven's relationship—*friendship*—with Carlos's half-human daughter, Cara Liu, Sven had always thought he knew where they stood. Back when he'd lived a treasure hunter's vagabond life, he had known that Carlos was pissed at him but would be there immediately if there was trouble. Even once they had come to Skywatch and Sven had made the decision to send Cara away, he and Carlos had managed to maintain a functional, if stiff, working relationship. Or so he'd thought. Now, though, he wondered if the two of them had drifted farther than he'd realized.

"I'm on your side," he said softly to the only father he had ever known.

"Maybe. But that doesn't make this any of your business."

"It is if it's starting to spill over onto the magi."

"Which it's not."

Sven could've listed off a half dozen recent incidents, but he wasn't sure if they were legit complaints or part of the natural equilibration that had been going on at Skywatch ever since Strike first brought his human mate, Leah, into the compound and she started in with "the *winikin* aren't your servants—do your own damn dishes." Which somehow sounded far less insulting when she said it, compared to JT. Besides, listing grievances would just embarrass Carlos and piss off JT. So instead, he said, "What about Jox's letter?"

In it, the royal *winikin* had named the person who should succeed him if the common-consensus experiment didn't work. It could only be opened if the *winikin* voted on it . . . or if Strike decided their lack of leadership was screwing up the war efforts.

JT bared his teeth. "Fuck that. The new system isn't perfect, but it's a damn sight better than using blood or magic as a reason to put one person in charge of another."

Sven shook his head. "The old ways have been evolving for the past twenty-six fucking millennia, all aiming to put us in the best possible position to defend the barrier on the zero date. Maybe you could just, I don't know, *go* with it for another year?"

"Spoken like a member of the ruling elite," JT snapped, looking seriously pissed now. He waved Sven off. "Why don't you go do . . . whatever you were going to do?" He paused, eyes narrowing. "And while you're at it, you might want to make sure that what you're doing is something your own ruling elite would like."

Sven bristled. "What's that supposed to mean?"

It was Carlos who said quietly, "You're not eating, you look like hell, and you're sneaking out nearly every night."

"I . . . huh?"

JT sneered. "Nice. Playing dumb."

"Seriously. No clue what you're talking about."

Carlos just looked at him. "Sven—"

"Never mind." Suddenly, he didn't want to be there, didn't want to be having this conversation. He needed to walk, run, burn off some steam. "Like I said, I was just passing through." He headed down the path that was the long way around to the library. And when Carlos called his name, he didn't look back.

Strike knocked on the door to Rabbit's cottage and waited for the "'S open" before he pushed through into the kitchen. The two of them were way beyond knocking formalities, but with Myrinne living there, he'd rather knock than catch an eyeful.

"You alone?" he asked when he found Rabbit spread out at the kitchen table with his laptop and a shitload of maps.

"Yep. Myr's out at the firing range with Jade. Michael's giving them some pointers."

"Good. That's good." Strike hadn't been entirely convinced Rabbit's human girlfriend—and quasi wiccan—belonged on the team, but she had worked her ass off for the chance, and had continued busting hump to make herself an asset rather than a liability. And there was no arguing that she had been good for Rabbit. Hell, he hadn't burned down anything unauthorized in nearly two years. "You find anything new?"

Rabbit sighed and pushed away from the table, rubbing his eyes. "Nothing concrete. Cheech says there are rumors of a third village being hit, but I'm having trouble getting a fix on the actual location from up here. He and his brothers are trying to get me some details."

Over the past few weeks, the populations of two

villages in the Mayan highlands had vanished, seemingly overnight. The media hadn't really picked up on it; the only reason Rabbit knew was because he had made some contacts down there as part of trying to learn as much as he could about his mother, who had lived in the highlands—maybe—and been Xibalban—definitely. Even though the Xibalbans were an offshoot of the original Nightkeepers and had given rise to Iago's bloodthirsty sect, the secrecy surrounding the groups meant that the Nightkeepers' archives were pretty useless in that department, forcing him to search farther afield. He hadn't made much progress finding out about his mother, but his contacts were proving invaluable now, as the Nightkeepers tried to figure out what the hell was going on in the highlands.

He flicked at a couple of printouts. "The probes Myrinne and I planted aren't picking up the sort of power flux that would indicate there's a *Banol Kax* in the area. I keep wondering if there's a human explanation for the disappearances, maybe a new guerrilla army or something."

"Fighting who or what?"

"Dunno. There were rumors of one of the big hotel chains trying to force a couple of villages higher into the mountains so they could clear cut. Or it could be a survivalist thing. According to Cheech, most of the highlanders are either ignoring the doomsday hype or treating the end date as nothing more than the start of a new calendrical cycle. But I'd bet you there are plenty of people up there who are stockpiling supplies, maybe getting together some extra weapons, just in case."

"Makes sense." Strike snagged two Cokes from the fridge, dumped one in front of Rabbit and popped the top on his own as he dragged out a chair and sat. "See any evidence of a guerilla compound where there didn't used to be one?"

"That's the thing. Granted, the forests make aerial detection tricky, but I'd expect to see *something*." Rabbit lifted a shoulder. "That was why I got to thinking about survivalist stuff."

"Underground bunkers? Maybe. But I don't think we can rule out Iago." Their opposite. Their nemesis. A Xibalban mage who had bound his soul to that of the Aztec god-king, Moctezuma, to become a nearly indestructible force bent on completing Moctezuma's planned conquest of the known world . . . which had gotten considerably bigger since the fifteen hundreds.

Rabbit grimaced. "Trust me. I'm not. But the thing is, even using Moctezuma's powers, Iago shouldn't be able to make *makol* out of innocents—as far as we know the demons can only possess the evil minded. And I just can't see him warehousing that many people who aren't *makol*. So where are the rest of the villagers?"

Neither of them said the obvious: *blood sacrifice*. But it hung between them, an almost tangible reminder of how serious things were getting, how much worse they were likely to get over the next year.

After a moment, Strike said, "I need a favor."

Rabbit raised an eyebrow.

"I need you to mind-bend me."

Both eyebrows slammed down. "Why?"

"There's something—" An alarm shrilled, interrupting.

The noise came from both of their armbands plus the intercom panel on the wall: three beats and a pause, three and a pause, which was the signal for a perimeter breach.

Normally, that would've sent them both running. Given the number of false alarms lately, though, they both stayed put. Sure enough, the alarms cut out after a few seconds. A moment later, Tomas's voice came over the system, sounding disgusted. "False alarm. Sorry, gang. It's nothing."

Strike pressed a button to activate his 'band. "You sure about that?"

"There isn't a damned thing on any of the monitors, visual, thermal, or magic. That's the best I can tell you. And you know how twitchy the new setup is."

"Yeah. Okay, thanks." Strike cut the transmission, grimacing.

Although the magic sensors that Jade and Lucius had created using her spell caster's talents were a huge help identifying magical fluxes, the gizmos were pretty hair-trigger. More, because of the increased traffic flowing into and out of Skywatch—deliveries mostly—Jade had tweaked a section of the blood-ward so the *winikin* could open and close the main gate without needing a magic-user. She was still in the process of fine-tuning the spells, though, and the alarms were crying wolf with annoying regularity.

Trying not to let it get to him, Strike drained his

Coke. Maybe the sugar and caffeine would give him the needed kick in the ass. Nothing else had, lately. He was off-kilter, and couldn't figure out how to get back on.

Aware that Rabbit was waiting for him to continue, he stared at the ceiling and said, "There's something wrong with me."

There. He had said it, and the world hadn't ended. *Not yet, anyway*, he thought with grim humor. *Give it a year.* Whether he liked it or not, he was the backbone of the fighting force; the fealty oath connected the magi and *winikin* to their king, making them susceptible to his will. So when the king went south, so did the Nightkeepers—case in point being the part where his father had gone a little crazy and a lot megalomaniacal, precipitating the Solstice Massacre. Which was a hell of a legacy.

Rabbit didn't say anything for a moment, just sat there, staring at Strike with an "oh, shit" look on his face. Finally, he said, "Has Sasha checked you out?"

"I came to you first." Strike tapped his temple. "I think it's in here. I want you to see if you can fix it."

He had wrestled with the decision, lying awake long into the night while Leah breathed softly beside him, and kneeling long hours in the royal shrine, praying for guidance from gods that couldn't talk to their earthly warriors anymore.

"What does Leah think?"

"She knows." Which was what Rabbit had really been asking. "She's the only one besides you. If Jox . . ." Strike trailed off. No point in going there. Jox was where he needed to be, with his Hannah and the Nightkeeper twins they were sworn to protect. "We're trusting your discretion on this."

Rabbit slowly closed the laptop, pushed it away, his silver-gray eyes troubled. "What am I looking for?"

"Something that would fuck some with my concentration and really screw with my 'port magic. I . . ." He flexed his fingers, denting the empty can. "I'm having trouble targeting. When I try to fix on a person or place, my mind starts racing and the travel thread gets . . . slippery, I guess you could call it." He looked back at Rabbit, found the blank shock he was expecting. "One of the few things we've got going for us right now is that I can put a team on the ground anywhere in the world within the time it takes to get geared up. If we lose that ability, we're screwed."

"But if you're not targeting properly—" Rabbit broke off.

"It's not that bad yet. I swear I wouldn't be jumping if it were. And sure as shit not with anyone else linked up." If he lost the thread midjump, he—and anybody else he was transporting—wouldn't just be screwed. They would be dead. "So . . . will you help?"

"I'll do my best. But . . ."

"I know. No guarantees." But as Strike cut his palm and held out his hand for the blood-link, he was hoping for a damned miracle.

# CHAPTER SIX

*Happy Daze Econo Lodge*
*Outside of Farmington, New Mexico*

"The star demon and the white god's head are made from different stones and don't really look like they belong together, stylistically," Dez said into the Webcam's pickup, "but my magic had the same sort of reaction to them, and Keban's letter made it sound like they were part of a set, along with the Santa Fe piece. Question is: a set of what?"

On the laptop he'd snagged from Reese, a video conferencing split screen showed Lucius's face on one side with the stone walls of the library in the background. The other side held overlapping pictures of the star demon, a grainy image of the Santa Fe artifact that Lucius had captured off the museum's security-cam footage, and Dez's own crude sketch of the white statue.

He hadn't wanted to involve the others for a number of reasons, but Reese's arrival—and her insistence on teaming up with him, if only because she didn't trust him as far as she could throw him—had changed that. Hell, it had changed a lot of things. He had thought he was over her—well, over the infatuation, if not the guilt. But one look at her and a few seconds of having her fighting alongside him once more, and he was halfway back in that crazy, wanting place, even knowing that their destinies weren't headed in the same direction. Maybe they had been, once, but not anymore. He wasn't a street rat now, or even a normal guy. And he wasn't free to make his own choices.

Damn it all, anyway.

"I think," Lucius began, but then his eyes shifted offscreen as Jade's soft voice said something in the background. "Hang on," Lucius said. "Be right back." Then he grabbed a crutch off the floor, lurched upright, and hobbled out of view.

As far as Dez was concerned, that was pretty impressive considering that a *makol* had sliced his damn leg off with a buzz saw less than a month earlier. Lucius's low-grade library magic and Sasha's *chu'ulel* healing skills had been enough to put him back together and give his recovery a running start, but without the accelerated recovery time of a Nightkeeper, he was stuck waiting it out. Humans just didn't heal as quickly as the magi.

Which was *not* a comforting thought under the circumstances.

Shifting back in his rickety desk chair, Dez took a look through the open connecting door that joined his and Reese's rooms. He knew he should've fought harder to convince her that he needed to deal with

Keban alone. Hell, he would have if it hadn't been for the go-to-hell glint in her eyes that told him she would have just doubled back and continued searching on her own. And, yeah, she was damned good at what she did.

"Louis Keban. No, it's 'b' as in 'bus stop,'" she was saying. She sat on the edge of her bed, facing away from him with her cell on speaker and a notebook in her lap.

She had showered, and her dark hair was sleek and slick, combed back along her skull and trailing down to dampen the collar of her T-shirt. If he could see her face, he suspected it would be bare of the makeup she had been wearing before, a professional gloss that added an edge and aged her a few years past her twenty-eight. He bet that was a deliberate move, because the Reese he had known never did stuff like that accidentally.

Then again, she wasn't the same girl, was she? For five years, they had known each other as well as two people could . . . but a whole hell of a lot had happened in the intervening decade. And a big chunk of that—if not all of it—was on him.

They hadn't talked about the past on the long walk from the crash site back up to his truck, or on the ride into the city. They hadn't talked about anything, really, but the past had sat between them like a hairy-assed mammoth. He'd let it stay, though, figuring it would be better for both of them if she remembered the bad stuff more than the good. Because as much as part of him—the part that still remembered every touch and sigh from the stormy night they had almost made love—wanted to make things right with her, even beg for a second chance, the man he was making himself into knew that couldn't happen. He was a Nightkeeper. More, he was a serpent, and what had happened before would happen again.

"Okay, I'm back," Lucius said, crutching into view. "Sorry about that."

Dez dragged his attention back to the monitor. "Jade have something for us?"

"For me, yes. For you? Not so much." Lucius tried for a leer that fell flat, as did his voice when he said, "Strike is sending her, Sven, Nate, and Alexis out to check another blip down in Belize."

So far most of the spikes reported by their magic-flow sensors had either been false alarms or teams of Iago's *makol* trying to take control of power sinks using small war parties that felt more like they were testing the Nightkeepers. But given the countdown, it was only a matter of time before hell broke loose.

"She's on a good team," Dez said. Nate's strategic thinking and Alexis's aggressiveness would counterbalance Sven's outside-the-box tendencies and Jade's lack of experience. "She'll be fine." Which was bull, because there were no guarantees.

"Yeah." Lucius brushed his fingers across the *jun tan* glyph on his inner wrist that marked him as a mated man, then cleared his throat. "Back to the carvings. If we assume that they're Nightkeeper in origin and go with ancient Mayan symbology, the 'T' glyph represents the wind. Which gives us a black star demon and a white wind god."

"Any idea what the Santa Fe piece might be?"

Lucius tapped a couple of keys and another picture appeared, showing a carving of a strangely proportioned, squat little man who stretched his short arms over his head, like he was holding something aloft. "I think it was this guy. He was one of the four skybearers who suspended the sky at the corners of the earth."

Dez frowned. "I thought the four *balaam* jaguars held up the sky."

"Depends on who you asked."

"Have you confirmed this with the museum?"

"The police report just calls it a 'human figure carved of reddish stone' and the curator won't tell me shit. He probably thinks it was smuggled up from Mexico after the ban on cross-border antiquities trading, and thinks I'm looking to come down on him."

"I thought it came from a Puebloan ruin."

"Supposedly, it came from the Puye Cliff Dwellings, which are north of Los Alamos on the Santa Clara reservation. But the Puebloans weren't really known for carved stone, and the artifacts found at Puye have been mostly red-glazed pottery with a . . ." Lucius trailed off, eyes sharpening on Dez. "Actually, they were big into serpent motifs. They believed that spirit snakes guarded their crops and protected them. That could be something, given that it's your *winikin* who seems to know all the tricks here."

Dez lifted a shoulder, playing it casual. "There are a ton of serpent myths out there, and they don't all track back to my bloodline."

Lucius nodded. "Fair enough. Hell, if they actually

did, I'd be tempted to think you guys were in charge, not the jaguar royals."

"Anyway. So we've got a black star demon, a white wind god, and a red skybearer. What does that give us?"

"A bad joke about walking into a bar?"

"Shit."

"Sorry. On the upside, they're all connected to the sky." Lucius stared at the pictures. "You said there was at least one more, right? That plays for me—these feel like they should be paired off. Black versus white. Red versus . . . Well, that's what we need to figure out, isn't it? We need to know what and where it is, and what Keban is planning."

"He mentioned waiting for 'the proper days' to collect the two artifacts that hadn't already been unearthed. If we figure one was tonight, the lunar eclipse, then what's the next day of barrier activity between now and the solstice?"

Lucius tapped a few keys. "The Gemenid meteor shower on the fourteenth."

"Which gives us three days to either grab Keban or find the fourth artifact and ambush him when he goes for it." The *winikin* wanted to meet on the twenty-first, but Dez didn't dare let it go that long. "Piece of cake," he said drily, glancing into the other room, and then going on alert when he realized Reese's voice had gone sharp. "Or not."

She was up and pacing, with the phone pressed to her ear. He couldn't see her face, but her shoulders were tight, her body language radiating annoyance.

She caught his eye, then looked away. But she didn't shut the door.

He straightened, letting his bare feet hit the floor in the narrow space between bed and desk. "You'll call when you find something?"

Lucius nodded. "It's not like I'm going to be sleeping tonight. Might as well use the time for research. I'll check into the powder Keban hit you with, maybe do a little more looking into the locations where these things have been found. I'll ping you in the morning with an update, sooner if I find something."

"Catch you later." Dez ended the vid-con and closed the laptop, aware that the room next door had suddenly gone very quiet. He told himself to leave it alone, keep his damn distance. Close the door.

"You done with the computer?" she called.

"All set." He folded it up and carried it through.

She was tipped back in her desk chair, eyes closed, one hand raised to pinch the bridge of her nose. Her hair had partway dried and was beginning to fluff out, and he had been right about the makeup—she looked younger without it, reminding him so strongly of the past that it made his chest ache. But her brows were furrowed and her face was etched with strain. And they were in this together . . . for the moment, at least.

He gave the laptop a gentle toss onto the bed, where it landed in the center of the sagging mattress. "You getting anywhere?"

"I've got a couple more threads to pull on the rental, but I have a feeling it's going to come down to grunt work. Then again, that's what I'm good at." She sighed, then pushed herself upright and swung her feet to the floor, wincing as they hit.

"You're hurting." It came out like an accusation, though he hadn't meant it to.

She shrugged. "It's nothing."

"Doesn't look like nothing to me." He jammed his hands in his pockets to keep from reaching for her. "And we did just roll the shit out of the Jeep—you've earned a few bruises." He paused. "The vending machine probably has Tylenol."

"I've already taken all the drugs I can if I want to be functional tomorrow. I . . ." She trailed off, pressed her lips together for a moment, and then said resignedly, "I was a little banged up to start with. A few years ago I got sloppy, and it caught up with me."

Knowing he had given up the right to have an opinion on what she did, or how, he pokered up. "Go on."

She sent him a measured look, but continued, "I was after a high-dollar bounty nobody else would touch, a real sleaze named MoJo, chasing his ass through this skanky apartment building, when I whipped around a corner and found him waiting for me. With an UZI." She paused, smiling with zero humor. "I kept going, right out a second-story window. Seemed like the better option at the time."

A chill washed through him. "Christ, Reese."

She held up a hand. "Neither of us wants to do the whole 'So what have you been up to for the past decade?' thing, so let's just leave the past where it belongs. But I figure you should know that I don't bounce back as fast as I used to. I was in the hospital and rehab for a while, then turned private locator when I was back on my feet, partly because I had lost the taste for bounty hunting, and partly because these days I do better with the finding than the grabbing." She rubbed the back of her neck. "I'm fine on a day-to-day basis, and Sasha worked some healing magic on me while I was at Skywatch, but all the rattling and rolling we did today threw something out of whack again."

"Why the hell didn't you say something before I dragged you hiking in the dark? If I had known, I would've—" He broke off because there wasn't much he could've done different. They had needed to get moving before the cops arrived, and calling for a 'port pickup wasn't an option. He had to stay the hell away from Skywatch until he'd dealt with Keban, or things could get seriously ugly.

"I didn't tell you partly because my instincts are telling me that you're right—we're better off staying out and here following our noses. Or, rather, your nose." That was the plan—if none of her inquiries yielded better options, they would return to the crash site in the morning to see if he could track the bastard's scent trail.

"If that was 'partly' it, what was the rest?"

"Because I'm perfectly capable of taking care of myself," she snapped, eyes suddenly flaring. "I don't need a man to tell me how to run my life."

"Whoa." He held up both hands. "Rewind. I wasn't—"

"I'm not talking about you." She glared at the phone she had tossed on the desk.

She hadn't been arguing with a contact, he realized suddenly. It had been a man. *Leave now*, he told himself. *Close the door.* Instead, he bared his teeth. "Boyfriend back in LA giving you grief about being gone?"

She shot him an unreadable look. "He's just a friend. And I'm in Denver now."

"You moved back?" That shouldn't have bothered him, just as it shouldn't have bothered him that she had a "friend." She had her own life, her own existence. And he didn't have any fucking right to comment on either.

And if he kept telling himself that, maybe it would sink in.

"I flew back when I heard the VWs had gunned you down. Then, after . . ." She hesitated. "I stayed. Denver was home." Or it had been once he was gone, he realized. And he couldn't blame her for that. She continued: "It wasn't hard to move the locator business. It's mostly Internet searches and phone calls, with the occasional plane ride and face-to-face for variety."

"When did you get hurt?" What she had described wasn't sloppy, it was suicidal. And if he focused on that, it would keep him from going where he *way* didn't belong.

"No." She crossed her arms, shaking her head. "No more 'remember when' crap. I only told you about my getting hurt so you would know I'm not the ass kicker I used to be. Not to get sympathy points, or what-the-hell-ever. So just leave it alone."

"You said a few years, which puts it right around the last time we saw each other." He had been pissed off about getting convicted for a bunch of small shit that he knew had come from her, deep in withdrawal from the black artifact having been locked away with the rest of his effects, and about bursting with rage and self-pity. And he had been fucking ugly to her. Hateful. Worse, even, than Keban at his nastiest.

He should know. It was one of the two scenes Anntah had shown him, over and over again, using the guilt, shame, and pain to break him down to nothing, so he could be rebuilt tougher and stronger, and ready to be a good Nightkeeper.

Reese didn't say anything, but although his instincts weren't as uncannily accurate as hers, they were good enough, and right now they were telling him he had nailed it. After that last visit, when he'd pretty much blamed her for everything that had gone wrong in his life, she had headed home. And she had freaking decompressed.

*Son of a bitch.* "If I made you—" he began, but broke off when she practically exploded out of the chair.

She got right in his face, and poked him hard in the chest, eyes blazing. "You can cut the big brother shit right now, Mendez. It won't play anymore. I'm responsible for my own choices, my own mistakes. Nobody *makes* me do anything."

She drilled him again, and he had to stop himself from catching her hand, holding it, holding her. His blood heated, and in the back of his brain something dark and greedy whispered: *Mine.* Except she wasn't his, hadn't ever been. Couldn't ever be, given the threat of the serpent bloodline.

And fuck it all, he should've knocked her out, called for a pickup, and left her with a note that if Rabbit didn't wipe her memory and Strike didn't 'port her home and leave her alone, there would be hell to pay.

He took a step back, which put him in his own room, and raised his hands. "Reese, calm down. If you—"

"*Don't* tell me what to do." She shot him a look of pure venom. Then she slammed the door that connected their rooms. And locked it on her side.

The next morning not long after dawn, Reese opened her side of the connector and tapped on the other panel. Expecting the click of the lock, she jolted when the door swung open immediately to reveal Dez, wearing desert-camo pants and a tight, dark brown Under Armour shirt that zipped up to his throat and showed every ridge and bulge. His sleeves were pushed up on his forearms, baring not just the dark blue-green tattoo bands that hid his scars, but also the three stark black glyphs on his right forearm: the swirling ovals of the warrior's mark; the plumed serpent's head; and the stacked, intricately decorated circles that identified him as a lightning wielder. She had first seen the marks the day she had grabbed him out from underneath Strike's nose. At the time, she had thought they were just affectations. Now, though, she knew they were real, understood what they meant.

*He's a new man*, Strike had written of Dez. But if that was true, why had he gone off on his own? What wasn't he telling the others? *That's what I'm trying to figure out,* she told herself, ignoring the twist of unease that warned her motives weren't so simple.

"Morning," she said to him, holding out a Dunkin' Donuts bag containing three egg sandwiches and a twenty-ounce Mountain Dew. "Here."

He took the bag with a raised eyebrow. "Making sure I've got enough calories on board to do the bloodhound thing?"

Her face heated. "More like an apology for losing it last night. I'd like to blame the pain meds, but the truth is that I probably would have melted down regardless. Yesterday was . . ." She trailed off.

"Yeah." He nodded. "Yesterday definitely was." He paused. "Feeling better?"

"Fine, thanks." And she was, physically. Emotionally . . . well, she would deal.

"You ready to get on the road?"

She exhaled, then nodded. "Yeah." The sooner they found Keban, the sooner she could get back to reality and away from a man who was simultaneously the boy she had loved, the guy who had broken her heart, and a stranger she didn't trust in the slightest.

They drove up a winding pathway, to the top of a forty-some-foot cliff overlooking the S curve where Keban had abandoned his car the night before. Reese's gut and basic logic said that the *winikin* had made his getaway in a second vehicle that he had stashed somewhere, and that the plateau would've made a good hiding spot. But Dez spent only a few minutes pacing back and forth along the flattened parking area before he shook his head. "I'm not sensing anything up here. You see anything down below?"

Lowering the binoculars she'd been using to scan the crash site, she said, "Nothing is jumping out at me." With the wreckers apparently having come and gone the night before, there wasn't much left of the crash beyond a crumpled section of guardrail, some skid marks, and scattered debris. "I keep thinking there should be more," she said, remembering the jolt of impact and the wrench of going over the edge . . . and then his magic feathering over her skin, making her feel like she was inside a giant Fourth of July sparkler.

He came up beside her, standing close enough that his sleeve brushed against hers. "There probably *is* more. If not right here, then somewhere along the trail."

"Booby traps, you mean."

Nodding grimly, he said, "He needs to slow me down enough that meeting him on the twenty-first is my only option. He'll want to call the shots and set the scene."

"Do you know what kind of a spell he's planning on casting?"

"He can't do magic. That's why he needs me." It was an answer of sorts, but she was keenly aware that he was avoiding her eyes.

*Damn it.* More disappointed than she should have been, she turned back to surveying the site. "If there's a trap down there, I can't see it."

"I'll keep my senses wide open." He shrugged out of his desert-camo jacket and hooked it over her shoulders. His eyes were unreadable behind dark, frameless sunglasses. "Stay up here and watch my back."

Until she was surrounded by his secondhand body heat, she hadn't really realized she was cold—her jacket was fine for A-to-B-ing it in the city but not much else, which meant that the weight of his coat was a major improvement.

Not wanting to examine her sudden flush of warmth any further, she nodded. "Will do."

As he headed down the narrow trail that led to the road, she folded back the sleeves and tried not to think that once upon a time, his simple gesture would have made her weak. Now it just made her hope they found Keban quickly, and that Dez's secrets would turn out to be no big deal.

A few minutes later, her armband gave a faint crackle on the short-range channel. "You reading me?" He was well back in the trees down at the base of the overlook.

"I'm here."

"I'm not sensing anyone else, and I'm not seeing or smelling anything that screams 'booby trap.' How's the traffic looking?" They had agreed it would be best for them to stay out of sight. Two totaled cars with no bodies or identifiable owners would have made local law enforcement curious, if not downright twitchy.

She scanned the road. "There are two cars coming toward you from the south and a smallish box truck coming the other way. Once they've gone past, you'll have a gap."

"Ten-four." He waited out the traffic, his shadow-dappled body so motionless that he practically disappeared into the tree line, even though she knew exactly where to look.

When the box truck had lumbered past with a gear-jamming belch and rattle, he slipped out of concealment and ghosted over to where shattered glass glittered blue-white in the sun. From there, he walked careful parallel tracks back and forth, searching.

She kept up a constant scan, watching not just the road, but also the forest and the sky, because Keban wasn't their only potential problem. The Nightkeepers were also fighting rearguard actions against Iago and his *makol*, and the missing villagers raised the gruesome possibility that a *Banol Kax* could already have slipped through the barrier. The sum total of it all made her feel very small.

Catching movement on the horizon, she straightened. "You've got company coming," she told him. "Three pickup trucks, matching paint jobs, orange bubbles. DPW, maybe? They're not cops, but it'd be a good idea for you to make yourself scarce."

"Ten-four." He headed for the trees, but stopped halfway there and crouched down near a small trio of stones at the edge of the parking area. "Wait. I'm getting something. I think he— *Fuck*. Reese, *run!*"

Vapor puffed up, and he went down hard.

# CHAPTER SEVEN

*"Dez!"* Reese screamed. Fear and adrenaline hammered through her in a terrifying fusillade as she raced down the trail, scrambling, stumbling, moving as fast as she could and deathly afraid of what she would find at the bottom.

When she hit level ground, she clapped an arm across her mouth and breathed through the heavy jacket sleeve, hoping to filter out whatever had taken him down. He lay in a heap, motionless. Heart pounding, she dropped to her knees beside him; sharp gravel dug into her shins, but she barely felt the pain as she clamped her free hand around his wrist, right along the tattoo-covered scar.

His pulse throbbed beneath her thumb. *Thank Christ.* But then a strange, spicy musk filtered through her makeshift face mask, coating her throat and putting a foul taste on her tongue.

She went light-headed, and fear kicked, hard and hot—but she didn't collapse, didn't convulse. And after a moment, the symptoms passed, though the smell remained. Either the gas was dissipating or it was Nightkeeper-specific. Risking it, she dropped her arm and took a shallow breath. Nothing happened. But it was one thing for her to breathe the tainted air, another for him. She had to get him out of there, but how?

"Dez?" She shook him, but didn't get a response, pulled off his sunglasses and cracked an eyelid, but didn't see anything but rolled-back white.

The ground beneath her picked up a faint vibration, followed seconds later by an engine hum. Shit. Even if nobody connected her and Dez to last night's accident and the untraceable Jeep, a trip to the ER would raise way too many questions. But if he'd been gassed, the ER might be the best place for him. Her throat tightened as she thought of Anna wandering the halls of Skywatch with her eyes unfocused, her mind far away.

She shook him harder, fingers digging into the heavy muscles of his upper arms. "*Come on!* Wake up. We've got to move." The trucks were getting closer.

He stirred. Groaned.

Relief slashed through her. "Dez!"

White gleamed through cracked eyelids; his mouth worked. "Son of a . . . *fuck.*"

"That about covers it," she said as the trucks rounded the corner and the first one did a wheel waggle of surprise and slowed down. There were forest service markings on the doors of all three, tools in the back of the first two and a big generator-compressor combo in the third.

"I told you to run," Dez slurred, cracking an eye to glare at her.

"I did. Just not in the direction you meant." She grinned at him. Logic said she should have been terrified, which she was. But suddenly, on another level she felt more alive than she had in a long, long time. Maybe she was reacting to the gas after all. Except that instead of being foggy, she suddenly felt functional.

The techno-magic armbands picked up some static of radio traffic, reminding her to strip them off. She snagged his gun, too, just as truck numero uno turned off and rolled in their direction. The other two rumbled past and accelerated away. Working quickly, she safetied her .38 and dumped it in one of the big inner pockets of Dez's jacket, which was too warm now, making her sweat. The heavy weight of the weapon pulled the coat askew until she balanced it off with his .44 on the other side.

"Come on." She crouched, grabbed him under one arm and around the back of his neck and helped him sit up. His body was heavy, his skin smooth and warm. "I need you to play pukingly hungover for me. Got it?"

"No problem," he slurred. "Son of a bitch left a trip wire, and . . ." His eyes rolled again and his head lolled to rest between her breasts.

New fear spurted through her as she realized that whatever the *winikin* had used this time, it was hitting harder, lasting longer. *Keban doesn't want him dead*, she reminded herself, *just slowed down for a few days*. Then again, the *winikin* had also spent nearly a decade in a mental hospital.

"Are you okay?" The guy who got out of the truck was in his late twenties, sandy haired and fine boned.

Wearing a gray-buff uniform with black stripes at the shoulders and pockets, and with a quick, jerky way of moving, he looked like a sandpiper picking its way across a beach.

Thinking fast, she dropped into fluttery female mode and gave him a wide-eyed, you're-my-hero look. "Oh, thank you so much for stopping!"

He puffed up. "I've got a first aid kit in the truck, or I could call for an—"

"He's not hurt, just hungover," she cut in before he called in more sirens and flashing lights. "He swore he'd be fine for a hike, but . . ." She trailed off, sending him a 'please-won't-you-save-me' moue. "Could you help me get him to the car?"

"I tole you I'm fiiine," Dez slurred. "You want to hike, lesss get going."

"Right," she said to him while shooting a conspiratorial eye roll at the sandpiper. "We're going. Straight back to the hotel."

"Oh." Rescue fantasies deflating, the spindly ranger nodded, his Adam's apple bobbing like a counterweight. But then his expression went dubious as he scanned the empty shoulder, then looked up to the plateau. "Your car isn't all the way up there, is it? He looks kind of, uh, big."

Not to mention that the ranger probably only hit one fifty after a heavy meal, her neck was already sore, and Dez was leaning heavily against her like he was settling in to stay. "How about you wait here with him, and I'll go get the car?"

The sandpiper's face brightened. "I've got water."

"Perfect." Together, they got Dez the dozen or so feet to the shade of the truck and propped him up against a rear tire that smelled faintly of dog piss. As she headed up the trail, she got a parting image of big, badass Snake Mendez being force-fed bottled water.

Not willing to bet that Keban was long gone, she kept a sharp watch on her surroundings as she retrieved the car, helped load Dez into it, thanked the sandpiper profusely, and got them on the road. Once they were rolling, she reholstered her .38 and headed back toward Farmington in case it turned out that they needed that ER, after all.

Then the shakes hit.

"Oh, shit." She gripped the steering wheel two-handed as her stomach rolled sickly and her muscles knotted in a series of whole-body shudders that left her feeling disconnected from the vehicle, from everything, really.

What the hell was she doing? This was way out of her league, way beyond the adventure she had been looking for when she boarded the plane for Cancún. She was sneaking away from the cops—or at least away from a government official—for the second time in two days, and that so wasn't her. This whole deal wasn't her. Where the Nightkeepers operated outside the system, she worked right smack in the middle of it. She had a Social Security number; she paid her taxes; she voted. She had a year-long lease on a third-floor apartment she rarely used, fifteen payments left on a spunky little Mazda, and an off-and-on lover who wanted to be much more. That was her world. This wasn't.

Beside her, Dez's breath rattled oddly in his chest.

Her hand shook as she reached for her armband.

"Don't." His eyes were still closed, his skin still gray, his voice a hard, painful-sounding rasp, but his words weren't as slurred as before. "I'll be fine in a few minutes. And if you call in the cavalry, this'll turn into a clusterfuck."

She told herself to ignore him and hit the panic button. Instead, she snapped, "You *won't* be fine in a few minutes. This wasn't the same as the powder."

"It's close enough, though stronger. Actually, it feels like a hell of a postmagic crash." He cracked an eyelid; the whites had gone pink. "Just find me protein, carbs, and someplace to sleep it off. I'll be fine once I recharge."

"For all you know, your brain could be leaking inside that thick skull of yours."

He reached across and touched her hand, brushing his fingertips across the inside of her wrist. "This isn't like what happened to Anna."

She could have held out against stubbornness. She had no defense against understanding. "Hands off," she snapped.

He withdrew, lay back against the far door, and closed his eyes with a tired sigh. But his color was better, his voice stronger when he said, "Just find me some food and a bed. While I'm sawing logs, you can do your thing."

*Dump him on his people and go home*, said her better

sense. But beneath the fear was a thread of adrenaline, a stir of heat . . . and the knowledge that he needed her.

"You just don't learn, do you, Montana?" she muttered. And she pulled into a Wendy's drive-through and ordered one of everything.

With Dez snoring softly beside her, she got back on the road, called Lucius, got his voice mail, and left him a rundown on the latest. Then she picked a chain hotel and used her alternate ID to rent two rooms. When the clerk asked if she wanted to pay the extra for early check-in, she was startled to realize that it was just shy of eleven a.m.

She hadn't even been around Dez a full day yet.

Returning to the car, she woke him up far enough to get him to his room. He leaned heavily on the wall as she swiped his key card and held it out to him, keeping a copy for herself in case she needed to get into his room. Like if he went catatonic. When the door opened, he grabbed the two big bags of Wendy's that she held out to him, and lurched through, saying over his shoulder, "Give me six hours before you even think of knocking." The door *thunked* solidly in her face.

Not letting herself be offended, and hoping to hell that she had made the right call, she left him and got to work.

Normally when she was off on a job, she liked to work in the hotel lobby or a café or something, surrounded by people and activity. But since she needed to be able to talk magic, she hit the vending machine for a Diet Coke and locked herself in her room to set up her computer and get down to business. She shot off a text to Lucius: *Wheels down. Hit me up as bulletins warrant.*

He bounced back a return almost immediately: *Consider yourself hit. Meet me on Webcam. Got something for you.*

"Finally, some good news." She hoped.

When the Webcam went live, it showed the stone walls of the library and the first few rows of racked artifacts. Moments later, Lucius crutched his way into the picture, looking as tired and strung out as she felt. He sat for a second, then shook his head as if orienting. "Okay. Okay, I'm here."

*Uh-oh.* She was afraid to ask, but she had to know. "Is the team back?"

He focused on her, his expression going rueful. "They're okay. Sorry. Didn't mean to scare you. In fact, it was over before they got there—they walked into an empty village. Rabbit's friend, Cheech, had lived there with three of his brothers, but now . . . there's no sign of any of them. *Poof.* Sixty, seventy people. Men, women, kids . . . just gone." He paused. "The team found Cheech's cell at the edge of the village, in a pile with a bunch of other personal shit. There was a little girl there, dead. Eight, maybe nine years old."

"Oh." Reese pushed aside her soda as her stomach knotted on the image. "Poor Rabbit." She hadn't gotten to know the youngest of the magi all that well—he had been in and out during her stay at Skywatch and had a territorial girlfriend—but she had the impression of a fiery but hardworking guy who was well endowed with both magic and opinions. She'd liked him instantly, and hurt for him now.

"He and Myrinne stayed down there."

"How is Jade taking it?"

"She's . . ." He exhaled. "Pretty broken up. But she'll deal. She's a fighter."

Which was different from being a warrior, she knew. Jade wore a tough outer shell, but was highly empathetic and lacked the emotional shields that came with the warrior's talent. But she had Lucius, who supported her in a thousand quiet ways, tried to send her off as strong as she could possibly be, and then waited behind, cursing his too-human healing rate and hoping—praying—she would come back safe. He didn't put that on her, though, just as he didn't try to coddle her, overprotect her, or guilt her into staying home. He was a good man. A good mate.

Reese had found herself studying the two of them together, not because theirs was one of the two human-mage pairings at Skywatch, but because it was so different from her own experiences with the opposite sex. "She's lucky to have you," she said softly.

"We're lucky to have each other." He cleared his throat. "Anyway, I've got something for you. Several somethings, in fact. I spent last night tracking down info on the injection and the powder Keban had used on Dez previously. Once I had an idea of what was going on there, it wasn't too hard to figure out the gas he was using today."

Reese closed her eyes on a surge of relief. "Tell me Dez is going to be okay."

Lucius nodded. "He'll sleep it off on his own, but I found an antidote that will speed up the process and immunize him against future attacks."

"Okay." She breathed through a too-strong punch of relief. "Okay. That's good."

"I'll shoot you the recipe in a minute—Natalie is transcribing it now. While we're waiting on that, I'd like to tell you what I've found so far on these potions, see if you pick up on something I've missed."

She gave him a "go ahead" finger wiggle. "Bring it on." It wasn't the first time one of the Nightkeepers had asked her to run through a pattern with them— they appreciated her special skills, especially given how much of their ancestral knowledge had been lost over the centuries.

"Well, the library came up dry, so I figured we must be dealing with bloodline-specific knowledge that Keban should've passed down to Dez, but didn't. I read up on the serpents, trying to figure out if they had a hidden guardianship, like the way the star bloodline was responsible for protecting the library." He shook his head. "If they did, they buried it well. But I found a reference that talked about how, around the turn of the first millennium, the members of the serpent bloodline left the Mayan Empire to establish a Nightkeeper presence among the native tribes to the north."

Reese narrowed her eyes. "How far north?"

"This far." Lucius tapped the stone table to indicate Skywatch. "They built the ruins later ascribed to the mysterious Chacoans and integrated into life up here. When the Conquistadors forced the other Nightkeep-

ers out of the southern territories, the serpent bloodline helped them get resettled among their tribal allies.
Hopi, mostly, though there were others."

"Thus, all the serpent myths in this area." It fit,
Reese thought. It played. So why was she getting a
low-grade itch that said there was more to the story?

Lucius nodded. "The Nightkeepers shared their tech-
nology with their allies, which would have made enemy tribes seriously jealous. That could account for the
inconsistency of snake myths among the tribes of the
Southwest, where they're either messengers for the
gods or deceitful spirits that bring death and disease."

Reese nodded. "Okay. So how does that tie in with
what Keban's been doing?"

"The native tribes didn't practice magic in the same
sense that the Nightkeepers did, but they discovered
certain plants and other materials could impact the
magic, especially that of the serpents, who relied so
heavily on the senses of smell and taste. The first formula Keban used, the liquid he injected into Dez the
night of the storm, somehow kick-started his powers.
So far I'm drawing a blank there, which may mean it's
something the magi and *winikin* of the serpent bloodline kept to themselves."

"If it was part of the serpents' initiation into the
magic, we don't need it." Dez already had more than
his share.

He nodded. "For the other two potions, I looked for
tribes that had 'bad snake' myths, and came up with a
dozen or so candidates. I think the powder was a general antimagic charm, probably something that Keban

kept on hand in case he ran up against a Nightkeeper, regardless of bloodline. Then, once he realized Dez was trying to stop him from getting the artifacts, he cooked up something specific to members of the serpent bloodline. Assuming I've called it right, the formula is similar to the powder but has a few additional ingredients . . . one of which is the New Mexico ridge-nosed rattlesnake."

His eyes gained a glint that upped her pulse. "I take it that's a regulated species?"

"It's endangered at the state level, threatened at the federal level, and tough to find at any level. I've already got Carter looking into possible sources. He'll e-mail you a list as soon as he's pulled it together." A low murmur off camera had Lucius looking up and away, then grinning. "Thanks, Nat." To Reese, he said, "Okay, the recipe for the antidote is headed for your in-box. It's part of the Hopi snake dance ritual, minus the two weeks of preparation and the actual snake-handling part."

Reese wrinkled her nose. "Glad to hear it."

There was motion at the corner of the screen, and Natalie—who was one of the two recent additions to the *winikin* and a former hotshot archaeologist in the outside world—came into view. She was bubbly, driven, and in many ways the opposite of her mate, JT. They made it work, though, with her softening his hard edges, him pushing her out of her comfort zone.

And Reese really needed to stop analyzing relationships.

"I had Sasha confirm the instructions," Natalie said into the Webcam, "but call if you get stuck."

Reese suffered a spasm of mild horror. "I have to cook?"

Natalie grinned. "If you can make tea, you can probably handle this one. The ingredients are pretty common. The black cohosh—aka black snakeroot—is native to the eastern part of the U.S. and probably would've been a high-value trade item back in the day, but you should be okay. If the health-food stores don't have it, try a homeopath."

Reese pulled up the e-mail on her phone, saw that she'd received the promised file, and nodded. "Okay. Guess I'm going shopping."

But as she said her good-byes and shut down her laptop, she was very aware of a low-grade churn in her stomach and the feeling that she hadn't asked Lucius exactly the right questions. She was missing something. And that was never a good sign.

The cashier at the natural food store sent Reese a funny look as she rang up her purchases: snakeroot, sage, maize, dried beans, measuring cups and spoons, and an industrial-strength coffee grinder. At first Reese thought the girl might have recognized the ingredients for the snake ritual . . . but when she got the same sort of look at the convenience store where she loaded up on Ho Hos and Diet Coke, she started to suspect they were looking at the tired rag that had formerly been her jacket. She had brought a couple of clean shirts and underwear on what she had anticipated would be a short trip to locate Dez, and her tough combat pants looked okay despite what they had been through in the past twenty-four hours. Her coat, though, was torn and tired, and looked like what it was: city gear that had been dragged through the mud.

"You're rationalizing," she said to herself, earning another leery look from the convenience store clerk. "Admit it. You want the leather."

She had parked near an upscale store that seemed to cater to either biker bitches that had money, or high rollers who wanted to look like biker bitches. Maybe both. Regardless, the mannequin in the window was wearing a hell of a jacket. Cropped in the front and dipping longer in the back, it was sleek and deceptively simple, with a square collar, off-center zip, and subtle studs on the sleeves—the good kind that wouldn't scratch the shit out of furniture or flesh.

Reese didn't covet often or easily, but she was feeling it now. A piece of it was probably leftover adrenaline, another piece of nostalgia. But she was also cold, and would rather have her own coat than borrow Dez's again. That had been far too . . . intimate. So, telling herself she would make it fast, she dumped her purchases in the car, stripped out of her bedraggled city coat and headed into the store.

"Can I help you find anything, ma'am?" The sales clerk had dark hair, decent body art, and a serious case of muffin top.

Reese pointed. "I want that."

She got an up-and-down, and a cautious, "It's handmade and one of a kind."

"And?"

The clerk named a price that wasn't nearly as bad as

Reese had been expecting based on what it would've gone for in LA or Denver. Besides, Strike *had* said "unlimited expenses," she thought with a grin, though it was doubtful she would turn in this particular receipt.

"Do you want to get it, or do you want me to?" she asked Muffin Top.

Five minutes later—and very conscious of the time, despite Lucius's assurances that Dez would sleep it off even without the antidote—she slipped into what felt like a second skin. The lining was cool and slick, the cut somehow ruthlessly fitted without restricting her motion, and the longer tail at the back would cover her .38. Even better, it had hidden vents and a thin, high-tech insulation that—at least according to Muffin Top—would keep her comfortable in temperatures anywhere between frosted margarita and lightly toasted. Whatever that meant.

Reese handed over her backup plastic. "I won't need a bag."

As she drove back to the hotel with the windows cranked down so she wouldn't sneeze her head off from the sage and other stuff, she couldn't shake the slightly queasy feeling that she always got when she spent more than a couple of hundred dollars on something that wasn't for work, wasn't essential. It had been a long time since she'd been a street kid, but those neural pathways were set for life.

*I thought you had outgrown the leather phase?* asked an inner voice that wasn't her own.

"The other one isn't warm enough, and it looks like

crap," she retorted, then stopped when she realized she was arguing with herself. "Shit."

She was an independent operator. She would wear what she damn well pleased, and come and go on her own schedule, and she wouldn't let anyone make her feel guilty about it. But although that logic sounded good, she was still going around in her head when she got back to the hotel, making it a relief to shove those problems to the back of her mind and ignore them while she focused on the job at hand. And if a whisper at the back of her brain said that things with the Nightkeepers—and Dez—had stopped being a job and become something more, she ignored that, too.

When she opened the door to his room, overheated hotel air wafted out, prickling her pores. A trail of clothing started just past the bathroom: coat, then tank, then cargo pants, socks, and boots. Faint snores came from the bed, where a huge mound of spare blankets and comforters moved rhythmically, more a mountain of bedclothes than any recognizable human being. Despite Lucius's reassurances, worry nagged as she hauled her purchases up from the car, using a side door so the desk clerk wouldn't give her any "no cooking in the rooms" static.

Then she stripped off her new leather, plugged in the in-room coffeemaker, and got cooking. By late afternoon, she had a feeling that poor Mr. Coffee had brewed his last pot—the upper chamber was gunked up and there was some gnarly sludge burned to the bottom of the pot—but she had about a cup of mossy-smelling syrup that, when she tried it, actually didn't taste all that bad. More, it made her head spin and sparked warm liquid shimmers low in her belly.

"Whoa. Potent stuff." Weaving a little, she left her room and headed down the hall. She hesitated for a second at Dez's door. Then she crossed her fingers, sent a small, wordless prayer to whatever higher power might be listening, and let herself into his room.

# CHAPTER EIGHT

On one level, Dez knew he was dreaming, that his mind was rebooting as his body healed and his magic rebounded. On another level, though, he was twenty-one again, and more jittery than he'd expected to be as he pushed through the door to the pawnshop a couple of blocks down from his and Reese's apartment.

*He relaxed—some, anyway—when he saw he had timed it right: Thin-faced, cadaverous Zeke was leaning on the glass display counter and there was no sign of Afternoon Bob, who couldn't keep a secret for shit.*

*"Hey." Zeke grinned, showing a glinting gold incisor that narrowed to a point, tagging him as a former Cobra, one of the lucky few who had gotten out and been badass enough—and useful enough—to not wind up dead in the process. "Got something good for me?"*

*He had been on the receiving end of a couple of Dez's recent jobs, which was pretty much glorified messengering of merchandise from point A to B, cash from B to A. Reese called it laundering—she had been getting tighter and tighter about that stuff alongside worrying about Hood's getting out of jail. But the way Dez saw it, he had a plan for Hood, and the transfers weren't hurting anybody—they were bringing high-value stuff into the neighborhood, and the jobs were low-risk for top-notch pay.*

He shook his head, playing it casual. "I'm not selling today. I was thinking about buying something."

"Ah." Zeke got his "I smell a profit" look. "Something like this?" He tapped the case under his scrawny elbows, where the higher-end jewelry lived. His finger landed right over the snake ring Reese had been drooling over the other week.

Dez had taken a good look at it, thinking he would find something similar—or, better yet, have it made—when the time came. But that had been before the storm. That was how he had started thinking of his life, as before or after the storm, because things had sure as shit changed for him that night. He hadn't just kicked Keban's ass, he had gotten a taste of the magic. Afterward, the dreams and restlessness had quit and he had started gaining the bulk of a Nightkeeper male, along with a warrior's confidence and ambition. It was all part of the maturation process, he knew . . . but Reese didn't want to believe it. She kept trying to reel him in and make him back into the guy he'd been before. Which so wasn't happening.

He dipped into his pocket to touch the smooth, warm bit of carved stone he'd won from Keban, the one the winikin had said would help him reach his full magical potential. He hadn't been able to work any of the spells yet, but he would do whatever it took to gain control of the lightning . . . and his first real taste of that power had come to him while he was kissing Reese.

*Thus, the ring.*

*Zeke modeled it on his spindly index finger. "This is the one, right?"*

*"Yeah," Dez said. "That's the one." He pulled out a fat wad of cash and handed it over. "This do it?" It wasn't that far short of the ask. No point in negotiating when Zeke had seen the way she looked at it.*

*The pawnbroker boxed the ring up nice and handed it over, and Dez slipped it into his pocket, where it banged up against the statuette. "Keep your lips zipped on this one, okay?" He wasn't sure how he was going to give it to her, or when. Or even what he really wanted it to mean, besides "I want to get laid."*

*Zeke pantomimed a zipping motion, somehow managing to make it obscene. Dez just rolled his eyes and headed for the street.*

The dream partway dissolved, leaving Dez swimming in the memory of the calculating bastard he had become under the star demon's influence. He braced himself, knowing there was more—there always was when Anntah sent the dreams.

Sure enough, images started forming around him once more. Only this nightmare wasn't anything like the others.

*He was his present self, wearing army surplus and carrying an autopistol on one side, knife on the other, but as he stepped out onto the street, the neighborhood was the way it had been back then: grimy streets lined with jacked-up cars, dated stores, and minimal foot traffic, like now-Dez had been plugged into then-Dez's world. He looked around, gut clenching.* What the hell am I supposed to do now? *he asked inwardly, but didn't get jack from his spirit guide. So he started walking, heading toward the apartment he and Reese had shared, thinking that maybe he was supposed to find his younger self and kick some sense into—*

*He was caught flat-footed when luminous green flashed from the shadows of a nearby alley, and gunfire erupted.*

*Makol!*

*There were screams and scurries as the other street rats made themselves scarce. Dez, though, bared his teeth, pivoted and dove, putting himself behind a parked car as he pulled his pistol and snapped off a burst of return fire. Adrenaline surged through him; his warrior's talent came on line, sharpening his focus and blunting everything but the fight.*

*The* makol *fanned out and took cover, still shooting— four big guys with filed-sharp teeth, wearing street clothes and a gang swagger, their eyes glowing eerie green. Then four more of the bastards came out of a second alley behind Dez's position, getting the damned drop on him.*

*"Shit!" Throwing himself flat as they opened fire, he rolled, got to the back of the car and came up blasting.*

*He knocked down two of the green-eyed bastards, but didn't dare break cover to finish them off. Bullets slammed into the car, bursting the windows and ricocheting. He nailed two more, but there were too damn many of them. Panic stirred at the realization that he wasn't wearing an armband, couldn't call for backup. Worse, the* makol *were spreading out, circling like nasty sharks.*

*When the air changed behind him, he spun, leading*

*with his pistol. And froze, his heart thudding at the sight of amber-whiskey eyes and sleek, dark hair. "Reese."*

*She nudged his gun away. "Didn't mean to startle you. What, did you forget the plan? Sorry I'm late. Those guys took longer than I expected." She jerked a thumb over her shoulder where dark, greasy ash piles marked where she had already reduced four* makol *to dust.*

*As the remaining* makol *opened with a renewed barrage, she dropped back down beside him, pressing close, so they were touching from shoulder to hip. She was wearing full combat gear and packing extra clips, two of which she tucked in his belt as naturally as breathing. Like him, she was now-Reese in then-Reese's milieu—her face honed here, softened there, her hair copper-streaked and sassy. But there were no shadows of hidden hurt in her eyes, none of the wariness that said she was just waiting for him to revert. More, when she bumped up against him, his body recognized hers with a soul-deep sense of rightness, a shimmer of connection that made him feel for a split second like they were sharing head-space, that he could see through her eyes and she through his.*

*Then she shifted away from him, lips thinning as she scanned the situation. "You ready to finish this?"*

*For a second he just stared as the realization hammered home: In the dream, they were the couple they could have been. He could dimly sense their history—how they had worked their way up and out, she as a cop, he as a real estate rainmaker. And how, when the call had come to reunite at Skywatch, there hadn't been a question of her staying be-hind. She was his mate, and they were a team. He hadn't spent a decade lost and alone, spiraling down into a black hell of his own creation. And he was free to love her, be with her, fight alongside her. Which was how he knew it was a dream.*

*The image wavered, but he reached for it, clung to it as his dream-self said, "Hell, yeah. Let's do this," and they came up firing as one.*

Reese hesitated at Dez's bedside, feeling hotter than the heated air in the room. Her head might be fuzzy with the effects of having tasted the syrup, but she was with-it enough to know that she was going to have to excavate him from the mountain of bedclothes in order to get the medicine into him.

And, yes, that was his underwear over there on the floor.

"You can do this," she told herself. "It's no big deal." But the heavy throb of her pulse said otherwise.

As she pulled off a couple of layers of bedclothes, she wasn't sure how much of the burn that suddenly fired in her blood was her inner teenager looking for closure and how much was a flat-out hormonal reaction to the man he had become—sleek, predatory, and dangerous. Then there was the magic—she had told herself it wouldn't be a big deal, but it was. Her skin still tingled from the shield spell he'd used to save her life the day before, warning her that she hadn't outgrown her rescue fantasies, after all.

"You know you can't trust him," she reminded herself.

He was lying on his side facing the door, angled diagonally across the bed, and he didn't even twitch when she pulled back the sheet, baring his upper body.

She didn't let herself gasp—at least she didn't think she did. The only thing she knew for sure was that she was staring at an acre or two of smooth golden skin stretched over a relief map of muscle and bone.

He. Was. Magnificent.

His face was fierce even in sleep, lines drawn between his brows as though he glared through closed eyelids. His mouth was a flat line, his jaw an aggressive jut below the long, hooked nose, wide-set eyes, and high cheekbones. Before, his lashes had been thick and full; now his eyelids were bare, turning him into something strange and primal. Back in the day, she had assumed he had started shaving his head to look tougher, and it had worked. Now, she wondered whether it had been a sign of his magic waking up, an impulse he hadn't fully understood at the time.

She touched his shoulder, intending to shake him, but then just let her fingers rest there. His skin was warm satin, his muscles living stone that poured across his wide shoulders and rippled down his abdomen to disappear beneath the sheet, temping her to picture the rest of him, muscle-etched, golden, and entirely smooth to the touch.

Reese, who waxed herself ruthlessly bare, felt a little envious . . . and a whole lot turned on, her insides gone molten, her skin dampening from more than the room's near-tropical heat, and—*And you're stoned*, she thought on a slow-moving churn of logic. *Or high, or something.* The antidote had put her in a major state. Her heart thudded and desire raced through her veins, making the past and future seem so much less important than that precise moment in time, and the way her skin looked against his as she touched him, stroking his shoulder, his arm, then trailing down to—

*Bad idea.* She pulled back, inhaling a shuddering breath that did nothing to calm the churn of heat and nerves. She should leave the syrup and go, get out while she could, clear her head. He could drink the damn stuff when he finally woke up. Except that Lucius didn't know how long that would take; Keban was out there on the loose; another village had disappeared; the meteor shower was two days away, the solstice ten . . . and the Nightkeepers needed her help to get their Triad mage back and make sure he didn't have a hidden agenda.

The heat amped a notch at the realization that she might be in over her head, out of her league, but she was *doing* something, damn it. She wasn't just making phone calls and tracking down last knowns. The realization, like the leather jacket back in her room, made her feel more alive than she had since she stopped nabbing bail jumpers. Back then, she had been saving her own piece of the world; now she had a chance to help save the whole damn thing. The blood beat beneath her skin with a mix of nerves and euphoria, a cocktail she had once needed like a drug.

Warning signals went off in her brain, but they were drowned out by the knowledge that she was doing the right thing here. And that for a change—maybe for the first time ever—she had the ability to fix what ailed big, badass Snake Mendez.

"Okay, slick." She stopped stroking him, shook him instead. "Time to wake up."

No response. He was out cold.

After a couple of more tries, she hitched a hip onto the bed. Ignoring the way the room spun around her just as much as she was ignoring the little voice inside her that said this was a really bad idea, she leaned over him, touched a fingertip to the thick syrup, and stroked it onto his tongue. Then she rubbed his throat, which rippled beneath her touch—smoothly, sinuously—as he licked his lips.

She stared at his mouth, transfixed. His heat surrounded her, making her skin prickle, and she suddenly felt like a voyeur in her own body, watching her hands and his mouth as she repeated the process a second time. And a third. The fourth time, he swallowed on his own, and she thought he might have been breathing a little faster than before. She definitely was. The room wasn't spinning anymore; it was throbbing. And she was in serious trouble. In some corner of her mind, two words whispered: *sex magic*.

She had read up on it back at Skywatch, had felt the way the air shifted around the mated couples when they shared a look, a touch. And now she felt it in the way the air vibrated, the fine tingles that ran along her skin, and how suddenly nothing mattered more than touching him. She wanted to run her hands over him, wanted him inside her with a ferociousness that couldn't be anything but a magic-driven compulsion.

She told herself to leave.

She leaned closer instead.

"Dez." When her voice cracked, she swallowed and tried again. "Dez, can you hear me?"

He groaned and shifted, rolling partway onto his back, closer to the center of the wide mattress. His thick erection was the center pole of an impressive tent; it drew her eyes, made her want to touch, taste. There was no thought process anymore, no real logic, only the magnetism that drew her onward, made her keep going. She got onto the mattress and knelt beside him, dipped two fingers into the syrup, and touched his lips. When he opened for her, the breath went thin in her lungs, and when he suckled, a hot wash of pleasure suffused her, leaving her tingling and wanting more.

Dimly, she was aware that she was doing exactly what she had sworn not to do, but she didn't care. She was a freelancer, an independent who didn't answer to anybody.

"Dez?" This time his name was little more than a whisper.

Finally, he opened his eyes, which were pale and luminous. "Reese." The word was a low rumble that seemed to come from the depths of the sensual storm raging inside her. "You're really here."

Relief had her smile going crooked. "Yeah. I'm here."

He searched her face. "Is it now or then?"

Not sure how to answer that, she eased over him, pressed the cup to his lower lip. "Drink this. It'll help bring you back the rest of the way."

He drank and she stared, transfixed by the rhythmic working of his jaw and throat, the bunch and flow of the muscles in his arm when he steadied the cup, the striking contrast of the black glyphs and dark blue-green cuffs against his smooth, golden skin. Then the cup was gone, thudding on the rug as he let it fall so he could wrap his hand around her neck and draw her closer.

His eyes were locked on hers, his expression open and heartbreakingly vulnerable. But instead of speaking, he closed the last breath of distance between them. And kissed her.

Oh, God. He kissed her.

He tasted of the syrup, rich and intoxicating. His lips were firm, sleek, and devastating as they moved over hers, his tongue a fascinating slide of heat and texture. His body felt like sin incarnate, all hard muscles and that smooth, warm skin sliding against her as he curled an arm around her and caught her up against his body. His very naked, very aroused body. The kiss was deep and carnal, a full-on press of lips and tongue, heat and madness. The sensations blanked out everything but the taste and feel of him, the rippling shocks unleashed by the press of his lips and the slide of his tongue.

She didn't trust his motives, didn't trust *him*. But she wanted him more than she wanted her next breath.

*Run!* said the practical, straitlaced, *boring* Reese Montana who had spent the past year wearing matchy-matchy suits and finding people for clients who probably could have managed the job with twenty bucks and a couple of Google searches. But the other side of her, the side that had just spent a month's rent on black leather, knew damn well they were both drunk and didn't give a shit, so she stayed put.

And kissed him back.

Dez was entirely aware that he wasn't dreaming anymore. He was really holding now-Reese, really kissing her and sliding a hand beneath her shirt to find the warm curve of a breast, the peak of a nipple. All that was happening in the here and now, in a hotel room somewhere in northern New Mex. But the dream stayed with him, sending sex magic to race through his body and charge the air around them.

The dream and the magic bore the touch of the gods; the woman in his arms felt like an angel and tasted like a prayer. She filled the emptiness inside him, the hollow ache of having been alone for so long. She wasn't the woman he'd dreamed of, the one he'd never hurt or betrayed. Yet somehow she *was* that woman—she had come after him and fought at his side, and now was right there in his bed, trying to heal him, to fix him.

Tightening his arms around her, he deepened the kiss, trying to tell her what that meant to him when he wasn't really sure himself. Logic said that if he truly cared for her he would turn her loose. Because if he couldn't take out Keban and the artifacts before the solstice, he would have to deal with the prophecy he'd spent half a lifetime running away from. Desire, though, didn't give a shit about logic when lightning raced in his veins and a woman—*the* woman, the only one there had ever been for him—arched in his arms, pressing against him and kissing him back with wild abandon. A decade ago, he had been able to make himself stay away from her until the time was right, only it never had been. Now, he didn't give a shit about the timing or whether it was right or wrong. He wanted her, here and now.

His honor was gone, his self-control out the window. She filled up the emptiness, sharpened the world around him, made him crazy. He wanted her, wanted to fill her, possess her, make her his own. Take her. *Take* her.

His blood thudded heavily in his veins as he kissed up alongside her jaw to her ear, then took her mouth again. She moaned, bit his chin, his jaw, then found his mouth again as she curled her calf around the back of his knee and moved her hips in a long, sinuous roll that left him bucking and shuddering against her.

The power of her response filled him, consumed him, had him rearing up and over her, and covering her body with his. Lightning arced as they met openmouthed in a hot clash of lips, tongue, and teeth that flashed heat to need, and from there to an absolute requirement: He had to have her like he had to have his next breath, the next beat of his heart.

And deep in his soul, a soft voice whispered: *Mine.*

Reese was out of her mind, out of control, and she didn't care. It felt so good to let go. Her better sense was long gone, her body turning to flames as she willingly lost herself. Dez was a furnace, an inferno; heat pumped off him in waves while she kissed him open-mouthed and touched him along the lines of his sides, the dips at his hips and flanks. Groaning, he pressed into her, tormenting her with his thick length and the barrier of her clothing, cupping her ass and pressing at the juncture, rubbing through the heavy cloth to make her moan and pant into his mouth.

Unable to stand the torture, she surged up and over, rolling them so he was on his back. He yanked off her shirt, then her bra, and she rolled away to deal with her too-heavy combat pants, boots, socks, all of it, so when she came back to him they were skin on skin, bare to bare, her legs wrapping around one of his, holding them both in place.

He cupped her breast, making the room spin as he kissed her. He surrounded her, took her under, drowning her in layers of sensation as he stroked her body, cupped her naked ass, slipped a finger beneath and groaned at the back of his throat. Sensations blasting through her, she skimmed a shaking hand across the hard bud of a masculine nipple, enjoying the indrawn hiss of his breath, the way his hands went still for a second. Then he shuddered as she caressed his taut belly, made a wide, teasing detour, and then trailed her fingers across the faint wrinkles surrounding his prodigious sac, which was drawn tightly up in excitement and seemed to come alive beneath her touch.

"Yes," he hissed against her mouth, gripping her hip, her shoulder, then digging his fingers into her hair to drag her mouth up to his for a fierce, wild kiss that tasted of sage and made her head spin. "Gods, yes."

He was hugely thick where she wrapped her hand around him, long from base to tip, where he was wide and blunt, and pressed eagerly into her hand. She curved her fingers around him, felt a thrill when she couldn't completely enclose him, another when he groaned and met her stroke with a jerky, desperate thrust.

There was slick wetness on her fingers, on her skin, between her legs where she gripped his thigh, rode it. She was feverish, her heart pounding with the desperation to take him inside her. There was no need for a condom; the magi used sterilization spells and didn't carry disease. And, despite the faint pinch beneath her heart, there was no need to wait, no reason to go slow.

At his urging she parted for him, arched into his touch as he cupped her, his hand gliding across where she, too, was sleekly bare. He pressed his forehead to her, his breath an excited rasp. "Fuck, that's sexy."

Then he slid a finger inside her, worked her with his thumb and sent her cartwheeling. Light flared behind her eyelids as a hard, hot orgasm barreled through her, paralyzing her for a moment with its raging intensity. She bowed up into him and rode out the pleasure that washed through her as he kissed her, held her, worked her, the whole time whispering dark, earthy curses that became love words in his rasping voice.

Every inch of her was sensitized to the fluid slide of skin on skin as she rose over him. She spread her legs wide to straddle him, the move changing the sensations and sending new urgency licking through her. Then she leaned in so they were nose to nose as she reached down to touch him, stroke him, center him at the entrance to her body. He let her have the moment, his hands gently kneading her hips, his eyes steady on hers, warm in the afternoon sunlight, then clouding as she eased him inside. The blunt head of his cock stretched and filled her, setting off chain reactions that began at her wet clasp and flared outward. The tightness eased as she moved down his shaft, then returned when he was fully seated within her.

They fit together tightly, with a seamlessness that brought a prickle of tears, a churn of emotion that she fought back. This was real. It was magic.

She closed her eyes and let her head fall back, then began to move her hips gently, experimentally. Heat flared through her, ramping higher as he slid his hands to her waist, up to her breasts. A long breath shuddered out of her and she rocked against him.

"*Fuuuck.*" As if unable to stay still any longer, he jackknifed up, wrapping his arms around her and kissing her hard and hot as he slid them, still intimately connected, to the edge of the mattress. He got one leg down, curled the other around behind her, and surged into her, his strong grip counterpointing the thrust. And again.

Heat detonated, wringing a moan from her. She floundered for a few seconds, awash in pleasure. They were face-to-face, belly-to-belly, locked in a kiss as he set a hard, fast pace that caught her up, swept her along, and left her no choice but to dig in and meet him stroke for stroke. She got a foot on the floor and used the leverage to buck against him, then cried out when he slid his hands down to cup her ass and exert a dark and dangerous pressure. Bucking against him, she whimpered against his mouth.

He rasped her name, his body shuddering, losing rhythm and then regaining it as he pounded into her, with her, taking them beyond the slap of flesh to a whiplash of pure energy that filled her mind and tightened her chest. Then he hit a sweet spot deep inside her, bringing a wave of searing pleasure, a gut-wrenching *oh, holy shit* of sensation. She dug her fingers into the heavy muscles of his shoulders and poured herself into a kiss as he found the spot a second time, then a third. And then she was coming in great, fluid waves of pleasure that crashed over her, rolled through her.

She cried his name on a long, guttural moan that should have belonged to another woman—someone who loved, and was loved. Then her orgasm coalesced and notched higher, wringing her boneless as he locked himself against her and came, shuddering against her, around her, inside her. "Reese," he said. "Jesus gods, Reese."

She turned her face into his, seeking his lips. They kissed for a long time, stayed locked together for even longer until, finally, his strung-tight body eased against hers and he pulled her down so they were wrapped together on the bed with her back to his front. He took an impossibly deep breath and let it out on a long, satisfied sigh. Then he wrapped his arms around her, and simply held her as the silence wrapped around them, bringing the smell of sage and black cohosh and the dragging fatigue of drugged sleep.

He was still holding her like that when she awoke the next morning, stone sober, with a single thought ringing in her too-clear head: *Oh, crap.*

# CHAPTER NINE

Moving quietly, heart thudding as she prayed he would stay asleep a few minutes longer, Reese slipped out of Dez's bed and did the clothes-grope thing in the muddy light of predawn.

She had her hand on the doorknob when he said, "Sneaking out?" His voice was clear and cool, fully awake.

She froze for a moment, then flattened her hand on the door. "I thought it would be easier to hash this out later, over coffee and some work."

"Probably would be."

She turned back to find him sitting up in the bed, cross-legged, with the sheet pooled in his lap. The morning cast him in light and shadow, picking out the heavy ridges of muscle across his chest and abdomen. The edges of his pale irises had gone shadowy, intensifying his gaze and bringing a quiver of nerves, along with the realization that her instincts were silent on this one. "So let it be easy," she said softly. "Let me go."

"That was the one thing I never could do." He hesitated, then said, "Yesterday, when you came in I was dreaming that we were fighting the *makol* together as a mated couple. When I woke up, there you were."

Her throat tightened, but she forced a smile. "Turns out the antidote was also an aphrodisiac. I think we should chalk it up as: It happened. It was fun. It won't happen again." *Please let's just leave it at that.*

His eyes darkened. "Is that all it was?"

"It was . . ." She swallowed hard as mental doors she'd long ago soldered shut threatened to reopen. "What else could it have been?"

He rose and started pulling on yesterday's clothes. Without looking at her, he said, "It was what I would have given anything for a decade ago."

A slow churn in her stomach said *yes.* "And now?"

Sending her a sidelong look, he said, "If I asked you to, would you go back to Denver and wait for me to call when it's safe?"

The heat—and even some of the vulnerability— faded as she realized she didn't know whether he wanted her back in Denver for her own good, or his own. Probably both.

"I'm not trying to stay safe," she said. "I want to make a difference." Which was the truth even outside of their reunion—the Nightkeepers and their war were too important for her to walk away.

Still, though, saying the words sent an ache through her. She didn't want to fight with him; she wanted . . . hell, she didn't know what she wanted anymore. To find herself dropped into another lifetime, maybe, where things had been different all along. Which was about as likely as her suddenly developing magical powers of her own—as in, not very.

"Reese . . ." Dressed now, and standing in the center of the room, he reached out to her, but didn't make contact. "The Triad magic broke Anna's mind, and a *makol* ripped Lucius's godsdamned leg off right in front of me—I was standing twenty, maybe thirty feet away, and I couldn't get my shield on him in time. Entire villages are disappearing. And now that Keban has seen you with me, he's going to be coming after you too."

The list sent a shudder through her, but she didn't back down. "You think I haven't thought about all that? Of course I have. But I'm not letting another bully run me out of town. Not Keban, not Iago, and not the *Banol Kax*." *And most of all, not you.* "Besides, I don't need you to protect me from myself. I'm tired of guys who think—" She bit off the rest. "Look, last night was . . ." *magical.* "I think it was something we needed to do in order to put the past behind us; sort of the night we never had together. It was . . . a moment, that's all. A memory." One that made her throat tighten and her body thrum, yes, but she didn't want to love a man she couldn't trust, and there was no way she could be involved with him and keep it casual.

"Damn it, Reese." Eyes flaring dangerously, he closed the distance between them, until he was crowding her, their thighs brushing as he angled to box her in. The warmth of his body—hell, the sheer physical punch of his presence—had liquid heat shimmying inside her even before he lifted a hand to touch her face, just a single finger stroke that left a trail of sparks.

"What if I don't want it to just be a memory?" His voice was low and intimate, and brought a hard throb of desire. "What if I want to repeat it?"

Her throat dried and her voice shook when she said, "I don't."

"Liar," he rasped. And brought his lips down on hers.

There were no niceties, no sweet seduction. His mouth crushed hers and his tongue plundered as his hands came up to grip her hips, fingers digging in.

Reese jerked back and he followed. She slapped her hands on his shoulders to push him away, but instead found her fingers spreading to span the wide breadth, then curving up and around the back of his neck. He kissed her deeply, bending her back until she felt helpless beneath his strength, trapped by his body and the wicked, clever things he was doing with his tongue.

Heat slammed through her. Greed. Without the safety of a drugged haze, she felt everything acutely, like each new sensation held the bright, sharp glitter of cut glass as they twined together and the air crackled with a static charge.

Then he made a harsh noise at the back of his throat and broke the kiss to press his forehead against hers, muttering an oath. He was breathing hard; they both were. And she was shaking with the desire that raced in her bloodstream, along with the hot flush of shame and anger that he had overwhelmed her so thoroughly, and with so little effort.

"Your body wants me," he rasped, taking a long stroke up from her hip to fist a hand in her hair, capturing her and holding her trapped. "But what does that brain of yours think? Can you be with someone you don't trust, aren't even sure you really like?" His voice was suddenly hard and intimidating, making her think of the other Dez, his shadow self.

Her hands balled into fists. But before she could decide between punching him or going with frosty politeness, the brain he had mentioned kicked back in—along with her suspicions. Instead of backing off, she leaned into him, pressing her lips near his ear to whisper, "You're trying to scare me into leaving, but it won't work. So why don't you just tell me . . . what are you hiding?"

He jerked away with a bitter oath and strode away a few steps, leaving her sprawled back on the bureau, body still imprinted with the memory of his. When he looked back at her, his expression was nearly blank. "I'm not hiding anything."

*"Don't lie to me."* The words cracked out of her far sharper than she had intended, riding a slash of anger and disappointment. "And don't forget that you're not a mind-bender . . . and Rabbit is. The way I see it, there are only two ways to keep me from diming you out, dragging you back to Skywatch, and hooking you up to your friendly local Nightkeeper lie detector: One, you tell me what's really going on here, and convince me to help you keep your secret . . . or two, you shut me up. Permanently."

He took a step toward her with a hard look that made her stomach lurch. But then he stopped and just stared at her, eyes dark and inscrutable. "Jesus, Reese."

She touched her armband. "Your choice."

Nothing.

Heart thudding, she activated it.

Still nothing.

She reached for the emergency pickup button.

"I know what Keban is up to." The words sounded as though they had been dragged out of his chest.

"Go on." Her hand hovered over the button.

He took a deep breath, hesitated, and then said slowly, "He used to talk about a Xibalban artifact that was so powerful, so destructive, that the Nightkeepers split it up and hid the pieces, on the very slim chance that its power was ever needed." He paused. "I think he's trying to rebuild it."

A chill skimmed through her at the sudden hollowness in his expression. She let her hand fall away from the transmitter. "What, exactly, does it do?"

"It's a damned WMD—it'll turn everything inside out, upside down, blow shit up." He shrugged. "All I know is that when I came out of the coma, I knew for damn certain that if more pieces of the artifact surfaced, it was up to me to destroy them. They're additive—each has its own power, with new levels being revealed as they're put together until they're all one whole. Which can't happen." He spread his hands. "That's why the gods made me a Triad mage: To keep the artifact out of play. Keban was convinced that rebuilding it was the only way to win the end-time war. But he's wrong. If it gets put back together, we're all fucked."

That read to her as the truth. But maybe not all of it. "Why not tell the others?"

"Because this says not to." He tapped a closed fist over his heart, tattoos and glyphs dark against his skin. "Something—my instincts, my magic, who knows?— keeps telling me that I need to do this on my own, that Keban is my problem, my responsibility." He paused. "I'm asking you to let it stay that way."

And damned if her gut didn't say she should go along with it, that bringing this back to Skywatch now would only slow them down at a time when every day counted. So she nodded. "Fine. I'll help you, and I'll keep it off Strike's radar. On one condition."

She couldn't read his expression when he said, "Let me guess. We won't be waking up together tomorrow morning."

That tugged—both the thought and the deadpan delivery—but she smiled coolly. "I'm capable of making that call on my own. No, I want you to promise me that you're going to destroy the weapon. Not . . . use it."

For a second she thought she saw something flash in his eyes, there and gone so quickly that she couldn't identify it. But after only the briefest hesitation, he nodded and said, "I promise I'll do everything in my power to protect the Nightkeepers." Then he crossed his wrists in front of his chest and double-tapped his thumbs to his chest, in a too-familiar oath sign.

Reese froze. Her mouth went dry. And something inside her said: *holy shit*. Not because of his promise, but because when he crossed his wrists, a new picture was formed by the narrow tattoos he'd gotten a few days after falling under the star demon's influence.

It was an "X" shape that she recognized as the world cross, representing north, south, east, and west. More, when he held his arms like that, in front of his chest, the four compass points became glyphs: the star demon, the wind god, the skybearer . . . and at the point representing "south," a two-faced mask that was half man and half screaming skull.

"Oh, shit," she breathed. "The answer's been in front of us the whole damn time."

Which damn sure ended the conversation about them sleeping together. And maybe—probably—that was for the best.

The next ten minutes were a blur of phone calls and photo uploads to Lucius, who agreed to track down a two-faced mask like the one hidden in Dez's tattoo. After that, and before she and Dez could get into any of the zillion unanswered questions that remained jumbled in her head, Reese made a flimsy excuse about packing, and escaped to her own room. Just inside it, she paused and leaned against the wall, closing her eyes as her heart pounded and the world threatened to spin around her.

Gods, she just needed a moment, a little breathing room. But she wasn't going to be doing much breathing in there, it turned out. Because the room reeked of boiled sage and looked like something out of a *Top Chef* challenge about cooking a six-course meal with a Mr. Coffee.

It was her space, though, and felt safe, even if that was an illusion.

After opening the window to air the place out, she

pulled on her new leather against the wintry chill, leaned back against the windowsill, and just freaking *breathed* for a minute while she tried to figure out if she was making a mondo mistake in agreeing to keep Dez's secret. She was all about going with her gut, but he was one of the few places where her instincts had failed her, repeatedly and badly. And how could there be logic in hiding the weapon's existence from the rest of the Nightkeepers? *Help*, she thought, but there was nobody to turn to. She was on her own.

Looking up at the sky, she said softly, "Is this what you want?"

The suburban universe she had grown up in had been largely Christian, but Dez's stories—the fairy tales that had driven back the darkness and the fear—had opened her to a world of many gods, each with a different area of expertise. Together with their earthly warriors, those gods were supposed to guard the barrier that closed off the underworld and protected mankind against evil. In theory, anyway. In reality, only a single god remained on the earthly plane right now: the sun god, Kinich Ahau. The others were locked up in the sky, unable to directly contact the Nightkeepers because Iago had destroyed the intersection beneath Chichén Itzá, the place where the earth, sky, and underworld had come close together. With the Nightkeepers unable to find another intersection or skyroad, they were cut off from their gods.

But, really, it didn't take a message from above to tell her what she needed to do next. And really, it wasn't about Dez or the end-time war, or even her job.

This was about her, about something she had put off for far too long.

She had kept hoping that growing up and slowing down would change her feelings. What did it say about her that a good man—a hero in his own right—had left her lukewarm and guilt-stung, where Dez set her on fire? *Hello, self-destructive tendencies.* Sighing, she pushed away from the window and headed for the bureau, where she had dumped her phone. And she hesitated when she got a look at herself in the mirror.

Wearing combat black and the new jacket, she looked nothing like the woman who had walked into that Cancún hotel a week ago. Yet as much as she liked what she saw, as much as this skin fit far more comfortably than the other, she wasn't sure how much of that was the core truth, and how much was her trying to go back in time and carve a different outcome for herself. Which was impossible.

"Shit." Grabbing the phone, she turned her back on the mirror and punched a familiar sequence.

The line clicked live on the second digital burble, and a familiar, resonant voice said, "Hello?"

She took a deep breath that didn't do a thing to ease the guilt-sting, and said, "Hey, it's me . . . we need to talk."

*Skywatch*

*The* boluntiku *rose above the king with a fingernails-on-blackboard scream. The lava-creature's vapor form exceeded the boundaries of the underground chamber, its scaly upper body rising up through the floor, its lower parts rooted in Xibalba. Many-fanged mouth gaping wide, it slashed at him with knifelike claws.*

*Pulse pounding, he fired off a burst of jade-tips and twisted out of the way. Then he spun, and grabbed the woman who was guarding his back. His wife. His queen. His heart.*

*"Go!" He pushed her toward a nearby door, the only way out of the circular stone room deep underground. "Get to the river!"*

*The boluntiku shrieked and followed as they raced along the narrow tunnel over dust gone muddy with blood.*

*When they reached the underground stream, he saw that the sacred water ran black, and was choked with the bodies of the fallen. His bodies. His fallen. None of them would have been there if it hadn't been for him.*

*There were others at the river, Nightkeepers and winikin formed up under the command of the royal advisers. "Fall back!" he shouted to them. "Get the hell out of here!"*

*The attack was a disaster. A massacre. All they could do now was retreat, blow the tunnel system, and hope to hell that was enough to cap off the intersection. The hellroad was wide open, the Banol Kax on the verge of breaking through. Gods help us.*

*An unearthly shriek rose behind him as the boluntiku began bubbling up from the floor, glowing orange and molten, and thoroughly pissed off. He turned, slapping home a fresh clip, feeling almost freed by the knowledge that it was time to make his stand, his sacrifice. His blood would amp the Nightkeepers' magic and slow down the demons' attack. Long enough, he hoped, for the others to get clear.*

*He risked a look at his queen, saw tears held back by guts and determination. "Go," he told her. "Get them out of here and blow the tunnel."*

*She closed her eyes for a second, whispered his name. But then she somehow found the strength to smile, and say, "I'll see you in my dreams."*

*He pressed his forehead to hers, felt a pulse of warmth at his wrist, where their* jun tan *marks linked them. His voice and heart broke as he whispered, "Go. Save yourself and the others, and get back to the compound as fast as you can." The children were safe behind the blood-ward, but . . .*

*She pulled away with a sob. A second later, her footsteps moved away behind him, the sound echoing off stone and bloodied water as he turned to face the creature of his enemies. And as he raised his weapon, his heart was heavy with the realization that he had been wrong all along. The king's greatest sacrifice wasn't his mate's life, after all.*

*Red-orange came at him, an eerie scream surrounded him, and a six-clawed attack slashed down with murderous intent.*

Strike flailed awake, heart hammering. Where the hell was his gun? He fumbled for it, couldn't find it, went for his enemy bare-handed. He grabbed the incoming blur, wrenched them both sideways and heard a cry of pain—human, female, familiar.

*Leah.*

Horror snapped the world around him into too sharp focus. The dream cave became a glassed-in bedroom; the darkness became dawn; his enemy became the woman he loved. He was kneeling on her, had his forearm across her throat.

"*Fuck!*" He jerked back and off her, hands spread and shaking, thoughts jumbling. "I'm sorry. Sorry. I didn't . . . *Shit.* Did I . . . are you okay?" His chest hurt; he couldn't catch his breath.

She pulled herself up to a sitting position, rubbing her throat. Her eyes were wide and worried, but she gutted out a wan smile. "I may never sing at Carnegie Hall . . . but then again, I never could sing for crap, so I can't blame that on you."

"*Don't* make this into a damned joke. I could've killed you." Blood raced through his veins, hammered in his ears. *Bodies in the river. Impossible choices.* Was that what he was going to face? Hell, was he facing it already? He was sworn to do whatever it took to get the Nightkeepers to the war in the best possible shape to win. But what if that required a greater sacrifice than he was ready to make?

She hesitated, then lifted a hand and showed him a compact Taser. "You had another five seconds before I booted you off and zapped you." Her cornflower blue eyes were shadowed with concern, her voice softening with regret when she admitted, "Given how bad the nightmares have been getting, I had a feeling something like this was coming."

"Jesus H. Christ." He dragged a hand through his sweat-tangled hair, trying to push back the dull ache that had been a constant throb ever since Rabbit had worked on his head. "You're sleeping with a stunner under your damned pillow." But in a way, this made things easier. It made the decision for him. "That's it. I'm moving back out to the pool house."

"Not without me, you're not."

"Leah, be reasonable."

"Walking away from you—or letting you walk away from me—when you're going through some traumatic-stress shit doesn't count as 'reasonable' in my book." She closed the distance he had put between them, cupped his jaw between her palms, and rubbed her thumbs along the line of his beard in a move that usually made him want to purr, but now just made his chest hurt. "I'm sticking with you," she said. "Deal with it."

"But . . ." He trailed off, seeing from her expression that it wasn't worth arguing—and not really sure he wanted to, as the dream-fever drained and his heart rate leveled off. His queen could take care of herself, and he needed her. Gods, how he needed her.

*Impossible choices.*

"Was it the same dream as before?"

"Yeah." Except that this time, he hadn't been entirely sure whether he'd been seeing the beginning of the Solstice Massacre through his father's eyes, or if he'd been himself in the middle of a battle that hadn't yet been fought.

"It's stress," she said firmly. "Not a vision. You're taking too much on yourself." She pressed her cheek to his. "As usual."

"I don't have any choice. I'm my father's son." Which meant he was the Nightkeepers' king, the last male descendant of the royal jaguars.

"Yes, you are. You're also your own man." She wrapped her arms around him, thawing some of the chill. "You won't make the same mistakes he did."

"No, I'll make new ones, with potentially the same consequences. What has happened before—"

"Hush," she interrupted. Her breath feathered across his earlobe as she reached to capture his hand, then draw it up to cup one of her breasts. "It was just a dream."

"Maybe," he said, pulling her down into a kiss that brought their bodies flush, freed their hands to touch, and turned the "maybe" into a growl of, "Oh, yeah."

But as he wrapped himself around her, sank into her, and lost himself to the *jun tan* magic and the power of loving his gods-destined mate, he was all too aware that the dream might be changing a little each time, evolving . . . but there was one thing that always stayed the same.

In the end, the king always sacrificed himself.

# CHAPTER TEN

December 13
*El Rey ruins*
*Cancún, Mexico*

When the theme from *Jaws* sounded from Sven's pocket, he winced but didn't answer. It was kind of hard to "can you hear me now" when he was fully up-linked, with Patience on one side of him and Jade on the other, their bloodied hands intertwined and magic flowing through them. Strike shot him a look but didn't say anything. They were too deep in the magic to be kibitzing about ringtones.

At the forefront of the arrowhead formed by the ten teammates, Rabbit focused on three man-sized stones that were inset into the ground. About the size and shape of coffins, the carved slabs cast a magical cloak, hiding the entrance to an ancient intersection beneath El Rey. If the Nightkeepers could get through the spell and get the doorway open, they would solve a whole shit-ton of their problems by getting the direct pipeline to the gods they should've had access to all along—aka, the skyroad. Problem was, the entrance was hidden by a dark-magic spell and Iago had broken Rabbit's hell-link, blocking him from the dark magic despite his half-Xibalban heritage. So far, nothing they had tried had even come close to reestablishing the connection, which left Rabbit scowling at the stones while Sven's phone rang on, the ominous music all too fitting.

A year ago, Sven would've laughed his ass off. Now, he just wished he'd remembered to mute the damn ringer. He was low on patience, felt like crap, and wanted to get this over with so he could get some space. Normally he loved the trips to El Rey—the ruin was right on the coast, giving him a rare chance to breathe salt and see endless blue-green ocean. Now, though, he had his back to the harbor and just wanted to go home. He wanted dust in his sinuses, dry heat on his skin, and packed earth beneath his feet.

"You okay?" Patience asked in an undertone.

"Yeah." Realizing he was bottlenecking the uplink, he refocused and channeled the magic as the phone went silent and dumped to voice mail. "Sorry."

She shot him a worried look. "Don't be sorry. If something's wrong, talk to me. Or if not me, talk to someone."

"I'm fine. Really." He lifted a shoulder in a casual shrug, covering the wince when the move pulled at the bandage he wore on one biceps, hidden beneath his pullover.

The damn wound was taking far too long to close up. He would've thought his healing skills were on the fritz, except that his other injuries were doing fine.

Which meant . . . shit, he didn't know. He couldn't even remember how he got the jagged slice. And he couldn't think about it now. Focusing on the uplink, he kept the magic zinging around the circle as Rabbit gripped the small carving he'd gotten from a dying Xibalban mystic the year before. Although the flattened stone didn't seem to have any real power, it had become his talisman. Now, he held it out in front of him as he leaned on the magic and cast a new spell that Jade and Lucius were hoping would work.

Magic flared around the uplink, moving smoothly and ramping up, making the air sparkle red-gold. More, the spell coalesced and took shape in an unusually visible form, a cloud of glossy glitter that was headed for Rabbit. It coalesced, sped up, took form and substance as it neared him, and then—

Without warning, it doubled back and accelerated straight into Sven.

*Holy shit*. He gaped as it *thwumped* into him feeling like a feather pillow doing forty. The impact sent him staggering back, breaking the uplink. Power flowed into him, arrowing to the injury high on his biceps, and from there dragging him straight into a vision that was more a series of impressions than anything: *He breathed dust, walked on hard-packed ground that burned his feet. He was searching, searching, missing something. But what? He heard a hawk's cry, a scurry of small feet, a death keen. Then wings flapping back up into the sky.*

"Sven?" Cool hands touched him, sending magic that brought him out of the vision. "Sven, can you hear me?"

For a few seconds, the words didn't make any sense; they were only sounds. Then they came clear, as did the sight of his teammates clustered around him as he lay flat out on the rocky ground. Sasha was bent over him, touching him, healing him.

"My arm—" he began, then broke off because she already had his sleeve up, the stained bandage off. But his skin was whole and unmarked, like he'd never been hurt.

*He was searching for something, needed something, didn't know where to find it. Hot sun. Burning feet. Thirsty.* The world tunneled down, blackening at the edges and withering inward until all he could see was Sasha's face, her eyes wide and worried, her lips shaping his name. Then dust washed across his vision and he coughed, fighting for breath, fighting the hands that tried to hold him, take him captive.

"The spell is linking to something, but I can't follow it," she said, her voice nearly lost beneath the howling noise of a sandstorm. "Rabbit, get in here and—"

*Blackness.*

*Somewhere off Virginia Beach*

Voices washed over Cara Liu, unintelligible at first and then slowly coming clear, followed by other sensations: a cool, wet deck beneath her, the gentle roll of waves, the smell of the ocean, the humid air that was at odds with her parched-dry mouth.

"Give her some room," said an older-sounding woman, the kind with the built-in cluck in her voice.

"Let the poor dear breathe!" The tone brought the image of a weathered sixty-something in a crazy pink sun hat as Cara's brain came back on line—sort of—and worked to match the voice with one of the forty-three passengers on the *Discovery III*.

Right. She was doing the naturalist thing. Or rather, doing the "ex-journalist pretending to be a naturalist" thing. Out at sea. Whale watching.

"What happened?" The voice belonged to a man, and sounded more excited than worried. Probably one of the three bored husbands who had congregated by the snack bar.

"She was talking about migration patterns and just fainted," clucked Crazy Hat Lady.

"We should sit her up." Another voice, young and piping, female. One of the dozen interchangeable bouncy teens who had taken the trip together. Gymnasts, maybe, or cheerleaders.

"Wait. No, don't move her. She might've hurt her spine. Someone should call the Coast Guard!" That was Bored Husband, far more interested in a possible medical emergency than humpbacks. Or maybe he just wanted to hitch a ride back to shore.

"She passed out," said Captain Jack, having apparently descended from the pilothouse to restore order to his little kingdom. "She didn't go overboard."

"But—"

"I'm fine," Cara croaked, cracking her lids and forcing herself to pull it together before Bored Hubby had her strapped to a backboard and being winched aboard a rescue chopper.

Flamingo pink straw eclipsed the sun. "Are you sure, dearie?"

"Positive. I just . . ." Cara trailed off, not sure what had happened or why. One second she had been talking about humpbacks traveling north from the Bay of Fundy, and the next, *click*. Lights out.

Captain Jack—fiftyish, grizzled, and straight out of central casting—eased Crazy Hat aside and held out a hand to help Cara up. "On your feet. No napping on the job, girlie." But his eyes were kind and concerned, telegraphing: *You okay?*

She had been on the *Disco* for only a month, but he had a daughter her age who was too busy to call, and Cara had daddy issues. They had bonded instantly.

"Sorry," she said aloud, giving him a nod. *I'm okay.* But she wasn't, really. She felt like unholy crap— woozy and tired, as though she'd been up for a week. Was last night's takeout coming back to bite her? *Ugh, hope it's not another flu.*

For the past few years she had gotten every sniffle and cough within a fifty-mile radius, to the point that some of her friends joked that she might as well teach kindergarten or work at a hospital. The doctors hadn't been able to find any real reason for it, had advised her to wear a mask. Since she couldn't bring herself to go out in public looking like something out of a disaster movie, she lived on Airborne, vitamin C, and echinacea, and took her sick days and then some. It had cost her several good jobs. Oh, her bosses hadn't said it directly, of course—it wasn't kosher to can people for health problems these days. But whatever the reasons that had gone into her files, her health had been the problem. She hadn't been able to put in the hours, and there had been a waiting list of junior reporters who could work ridiculous hours for pennies, and wouldn't call in.

That was one reason she loved working on the *Disco*: Not only had Jack still hired her even after she had warned him about being a sicko, but it had turned out that the sea air was good for her—she hadn't had to miss a single day so far. *Sigh.* Guess it was too much to hope that would last.

"You need to lie down?"

She shook her head at Jack's question. "God, no." Her sea legs were great when she was up and walking around or when the boat was moving, but she didn't do so well with sitting—never mind lying—down for long with the boat stationary and rolling beneath her in long, undulating waves. The sway was already getting to her: A low churn of nausea checked in to join the fatigue and deck spins. She needed to get up, breathe the salt spray, feel the wind in her face, and remember that she had come a long way from who she used to be.

Summoning a bright smile for the crowd that was still gathered around her, she said, "Thanks for your concern, everyone, but I'm good. I'm great. Let's get this show back on the road."

"Take it easy for a few minutes," Jack said. "I'll need to hunt up a new whale."

A glance over the railing showed that the gently swelling waves were cetacean-free. "Shoot. That was a good sighting." She sighed. "Sorry."

"No biggie. Won't be hard to come up with another." Meaning that there were plenty of big contacts on the fish finder or some chatter on the informal network of whale-watching boats and local fishing vessels that traded info in an effort to keep the cash flowing as the winter season got under way.

"Thanks." Taking Jack's hand, Cara boosted herself up and made it to the rail, where she breathed deeply, lungs aching when she tried to inhale all the way.

She let Crazy Hat press a lukewarm bottle of water on her and fuss about dehydration and sunstroke, even though it was only in the high fifties and she'd eaten and drunk the same thing she did every day. The clucking reminded Cara of better days, back before her mom died.

"*Cluck, cluck, cluck* . . . dehydrated. Unless, of course, you're pregnant."

Those last two words brought Cara's head whipping around so fast that a few white strands from her skunk stripe escaped from her ponytail and draped in her face. "*No.*" When the older woman recoiled, Cara exhaled. "Sorry. But no. No chance of that."

She might believe in magic, but she didn't believe in immaculate conception.

As Crazy Hat fussed, winding down, she chugged the rest of the water, which felt lumpy, like it was catching on something lodged in her throat. Beneath her, the *Disco*'s engines thrummed as they got back under way.

The others had dispersed, Bored Husband no doubt to the snack bar, most of the others to the railing, where they elbowed each other and scanned the horizon, competing to be the first to "thar she blows" it. Usually, Cara found the thrill of the hunt infectious; it was another of the reasons she had taken the job. That, and the surprising discovery that she, a born-and-raised Midwesterner, freaking loved being out at sea. Now, though, she couldn't summon any enthusiasm. What was more, she suddenly felt out of place, like she didn't belong there. Or, rather, like she needed to be somewhere else, *right now*.

Images flashed through her. Urges. She saw herself boarding a plane. Renting a car. Moving fast and traveling light, heading southwest, to where ancient pueblos overlooked wide-open canyons and the sea was a distant memory.

"Did you hurt your wrist, dearie?"

"No, I . . ." Cara trailed off as she glanced down and realized that she'd been rubbing her inner right forearm. *Oh, shit.* She should've caught on quicker, would have if she didn't feel so crappy. But although this wasn't the first time she had felt something echo through the severed blood-bond, it was by far the worst. Bad enough, even, to bring a stab of concern for a brother who wasn't hers by blood. "Excuse me. I need to make a call." She lurched away from Crazy Hat and headed for the stairs leading up to the wheelhouse, feeling like she was thirty fathoms down and walking against a stiff undertow, with everything happening in slow motion.

Jack met her at the door. "You're lying down. Now."

"I need to make a private call."

"Cara. Honey." He looked at her closely, and she

could practically see him adding twenty-something single female plus fainting plus nausea and coming to the same conclusion Crazy Hat had reached.

She didn't correct him, because it wasn't like she could tell him the truth. She just said, "Please, Jack. It's important."

He checked his course, made a couple of adjustments, and then got on the radio to connect to a landline. When it was ready to go, he waved her to his high swivel chair and motioned that he would leave her alone. "I'll need to get back in here in ten minutes or so. Charter says there's a couple of big males spyhopping up by them."

"This won't take long."

When he was gone, she took a deep breath. Or tried to, anyway. There wasn't room enough in her lungs for the oxygen she needed, strengthening the drum of fear until it overcame the dread. Almost.

"Number, please?" That was the operator, probably tired of listening to heavy breathing.

She gave it automatically, then listened to the call ringing on the other end. She tried not to picture the phone sitting on the marble-topped counter in the big open kitchen, tried not to guess who was on comm duty, who would be walking to the phone, picking it up, and—

"Hello?" a man's voice said.

She couldn't place it. Not her father, certainly. Had she been away so long that she had forgotten the others?

"This is Cara," she said. "I need to talk to my father."

There was a beat of silence. Then, "And who would that be?"

She wouldn't have thought she could feel any shittier and still be upright. *Wrong.* Breathing shallowly through a stab of pain, she said, "I'm Carlos's daughter." She should've stopped there, but couldn't help saying, "Out of sight, out of mind, huh?"

"Not really. I'm the new guy. Which is why I'm on comm and gate duty." He paused. "Well, that and because the others still aren't sure what to do with me." Before she could process that, he continued: "Carlos is out getting supplies. You want his cell number? Oh, duh. You probably have it."

No, she didn't. And she couldn't handle this, any of it. But it was clear that the *winikin*, at least the ones back at Skywatch, didn't know there was something very wrong. "You call him, please. Tell him he needs to find Sven, fast. There's something . . ." She trailed off, choked up. Whispered, "Just tell him for me, okay?"

She cut the call before he could say anything, ask anything, knowing that her father would do what needed to be done. Then she bolted for the head. And was miserably sick.

# CHAPTER ELEVEN

December 14
*Bandera Crater and Ice Cave*
*New Mexico*

The sign at the end of the access road identified the privately owned attraction as the LAND OF FIRE AND ICE. Which didn't half suck, Reese had decided.

The site offered two short hikes: one to ogle the blown-out cone of the Bandera volcano, the other to climb down inside a kiva-shaped cave where a combination of water seepage and convection airflow created a crazy microenvironment that never got above freezing. The underground pool at the bottom of the cave was perpetually frozen and glowed green in the sun, tinted by a strain of algae that was otherwise found only in the Arctic. Most of the long-ago tribes in the region—and those who traveled to it from afar— had called it Winter Lake and mined it for ice. But Lucius had turned up a reference in a British explorer's journal that described seeing thirteen warrior-priests wearing serpent-headed masks and making blood sacrifices to call the rain god.

Ancient sacred site, check. Pro-snake ritual, check. And it was located right at the southern point of the compass cross that could be drawn from the places where the other artifacts had been found. Granted, the pattern assumed that ten years earlier, when Keban had told Dez that the star demon was coming to him courtesy of Montezuma, he wasn't using an alternate spelling of the god-king Moctezuma's name, but rather talking about the Palace of Montezuma, which was a Pueblo ruin located just over the Arizona border. Given that the compass lines connecting north to south and east to west then crossed directly over Chaco Canyon, Reese was just fine with the assumption. More, one of the local black-market guys she had tracked down was holding an endangered rattlesnake for pickup by a guy with a scarred face, who had put in the order a week ago and paid cash.

This was the place. It had to be. And tonight was the night; the Gemenid meteor shower would be starting soon.

But as she and Dez, both lightly shielded by his magic, slipped past the locked entrance gate for the third night in a row and followed the cow pasture–flanked road to the trading post that marked the trailheads, it bothered her that they hadn't been able to pinpoint Keban. Hell, they hadn't even caught a whiff of him. Granted, the *winikin* had been trained to disappear, and he would have gone deeper under once he knew Dez was after him, but still. It didn't feel right.

"Come out, come out, wherever you are," she murmured as they passed the trading post and took the ice cave trail, the details gone green behind her night-vision goggles. She was very aware of Dez, sleek and solid beside her, his movements predator-smooth in the darkness. Despite her best intentions and the fact that they had been strictly hands off over the past three days, focusing on the job, his taste and the way he had felt inside her seemed burned into her neurons. "Can you sense him?" she asked, voice sharper than it needed to be.

He shook his head. "I'm not getting a damn thing." Which could mean that although Keban's potions couldn't knock him out anymore, they could still camouflage the *winikin*'s scent trail . . . or it could mean there was nothing to sense.

"He'll be here," she said as they moved off again. He had to show up. Not that they wanted to fight for the two-faced mask, but they needed to get their hands on the white god's head and the red skybearer, too. And they needed to do it before Iago got wind of the weapon's existence. The Nightkeepers had the black star demon safely locked up behind a heavy, magic-cloaking ward, but still.

*White, red, black, yellow*, she thought, because they were expecting the two-faced mask to be made of yellow stone. Once she had figured out the trick of what they had taken to calling the compass artifacts, Lucius had come up with another layer to the symbolism: In Nightkeeper lore, each direction was associated with a color and certain traits. Black-west was the power of shadows and dreams, as well as the ability to shake things up. Which was Dez in a nutshell, and explained why he had connected so strongly with the star demon, but hadn't felt the same pull to the white god's head, which represented truth, integrity, and the winds of change. Red-east represented inspiration, passion, and flashiness; no doubt he'd click with the skybearer statue when they got their hands on it. Not so much the two-faced mask, though, because yellow-south was connected with patience and balance, neither of which was his forte.

He was trying, though—or he seemed to be. In the days since their post-sex showdown he hadn't given her any new reason to distrust him. He was still stubborn and prone to shortcuts, but he listened to her, argued patterns with her, and had even won a few of those arguments, reminding her what it was like to debate someone who thought so far outside the box. But through it all she had been aware that a part of her was standing back and watching him, trying to figure out whether it was real or part of an act, even one he wasn't aware of putting on. He'd always had a knack for talking himself into doing what he wanted, after all.

"Look," he said, pausing to point through a spot where the dark tree branches gave way to the horizon. A streak of light crossed the night sky. Then another. The meteor shower had begun.

She suddenly was very aware of being alone with him in the darkness, attuned to his breathing and the soft click of his weapons as he shifted his weight and glanced over at her. But all she said was, "We should go."

"Yeah." But he looked at her for another long moment before he moved off toward the covered wooden staircase that led down to the cave. She followed him down, nearly piling into him when he stopped on the first landing and turned back to her. "Listen. If this turns into a firefight . . ."

"I'll stay close to you so you can shield me."

"But if you can't get to me, or if things get really bad, I want you to call in the cavalry."

She raised an eyebrow, trusting that he would see the move with his augmented vision. "What happened to 'I need to do this on my own. We can't involve the others'?"

"You happened," he said. And suddenly, the air between them held more than just the shield magic.

"Don't," she said, then couldn't get another word out, because he was lifting a hand to brush a strand of hair away from her face and tuck it behind her ear.

"It's one thing to risk my own life, another to risk yours. I couldn't . . . I don't want you hurt again because of me."

Her heart went *thudda-thump* and her breath thinned in her lungs, but she lifted her chin. "It's my choice to be here. I'm not your responsibility."

"Promise me you'll call for backup if things get hairy."

She nodded, because what was the point of arguing about something she was already planning to do? "I promise."

Without another word, he turned and moved ahead of her, pulling his .44 as he headed down the stairs toward the cave mouth, which was a huge, rounded opening the size of a highway underpass. Pulling her .38, Reese followed. And as she did, she told herself not to make the moment into something more than it really was. Which was nothing, really. Or at least nothing that could truly matter.

The air changed, the temperature decreasing with each step as they passed into the cave and descended the final short flight of stairs to where a wide observation platform overlooked the frozen lake. The night vision robbed her view of color, but it was still impressive. The frozen surface was roughly circular, edged with jumbles of rock and curving cavern walls that dripped with more ice, some of it in icicles, some as cascading waterfall formations.

That was all the same as it had been last night and the night before. Now, though, there was also a line of starscript glowing blue-white on the far wall, where the ice ended and the stone began.

Adrenaline kicked through her at the confirmation that they were in the right place at the right time. "Nice," she whispered under her breath, feeling a beat of optimism.

Dez swung over the railing. "Come on, let's take a closer look. Keep an eye on the door for me, though."

"Hell of a door." The cave mouth was a huge, gaping opening with multiple time-worn rock trails leading down. It would be far too easy for Keban to find a sheltered position up there and shoot down into the cave. *Which is why I'm sticking close to the guy with the magic*, Reese thought. She traded her .38 for the heavier firepower of the autopistol as they walk-slid across the frozen pool to the other side, then climbed over jumbled rocks to the starscript. Two outcroppings protruded slightly out into the pond; one was marked in blue-white starscript with half a man's face, the other with half a screaming skull. Behind them on the wall, running roughly between them, was a squiggling, serpentine line.

Dez kicked at the ice between the two marked stones. "Doesn't look any different than the rest of it."

"The cave adds ice every year. Depending on when the artifact was hidden, it could be pretty far down."

"Lucky for us, we've got—"

Without a buzz or hum of warning, the air cracked nearby and twenty men materialized in the center of the cave. Or not men, Reese saw even as she pivoted and brought up her autopistol, blood icing at the sight of glowing green eyes. "*Makol!*"

They wore long loincloths, quilted armor and feather-trimmed demon-faced masks, and they carried buzz-swords—wooden staves edged with spinning black blades that could detach like throwing stars. Her heart seized on a crazed thought of *Ohmigod they're real*, but then Dez shouted something and amped his shield to a blue-white latticework of energy, snapping her out of her shock.

She fired a panicked burst through the shield and a *makol* sprayed black blood and went down writhing. And for a second she froze, flashing back on another cavernous space, another gunned-down body lying twitching on the floor in a pool of blood.

"Reese!" Dez jerked her behind him and let rip with a blast of purple-white as their attackers spread out and rushed the shield, swords buzzing a high-pitched bee swarm of sound. The magic tore into the oncoming line, knocking back three of the *makol*, who went down twitching. "*Reese!* There's too many of them. Make the call."

She jerked from her paralysis and slapped her armband, but nothing happened. There was no little red light, no acknowledging beep. No reception, damn it. "We're too deep underground! We need to get closer to the door!"

"Wait. Close your eyes." Dez grabbed her, stripped off her goggles and got an arm around her, so her face was pressed into his chest and covered with the edge of his coat. Then electricity raced over her, through her, and the world went bright white as he unleashed a massive bolt of magic into the ice near their feet.

The blast was deafening. The ice heaved beneath them, cracking and tilting, and she clung to him without meaning to.

Then he let go of her, shoved the goggles into her hand, and snapped, "Get the mask and we'll make a run for it."

For a terrifying second, she was lost in a surreal world of pitch blackness lit only by luminous green eyes and his shield magic. Then she jammed the goggles into place and everything snapped back into focus: The *makol* had concentrated their efforts at one point on

Dez's shield and were trying to hack through with their swords. He stood opposite them, channeling lightning with one hand and firing an autopistol with the other, keeping them off balance and floundering. Bleeding.

"Move!" he bellowed.

Reese moved.

Spinning to where he had blasted away the ice and part of the rock near the starscript, she dove into the ragged chasm he had created. Her night vision was blurry at close range, but her fingers found a lumpy object wrapped in frozen cloth. She tried to pull it out, but the cloth tore and her fingers brushed a smooth, sleek, and intricately carved artifact. The mask! She fumbled, trying to get hold of it.

"Reese!" His voice cracked with the strain of holding the shield.

"Almost there." Her fingers found an edge and the disk popped free. "Got it!" She lunged to his side, held it out. "Here."

"Keep it." He jammed the autopistol into his belt and grabbed her free arm. A tingle ran through her at his touch, a sign that his magic was running hot. He grated, "Close your eyes on three. One. Two. *Now!*"

She slammed her eyes shut as he let rip with a huge bolt of magic that cracked and crashed, and made her hair spark with static.

"Come on!" He dragged her to a stumbling run over the torn-up ice, tightening the shield spell around them.

She caught disjointed glimpses of *makol* bodies, ripped limbs, black blood.

"Don't look," he ordered roughly, pulling her to his

side and trying to block the sight with his body. But she could still see the carnage, smell the blood.

When they reached the legs of the observation deck, he expanded his shield to include the wide platform, then offered her his cupped palms as a boost. "Come on." He gestured. "Up. I'll be right behind you."

Numbly, clutching the mask under one elbow, she scrambled up, away from the ruined ice pond. Her thoughts raced, but she kept wondering what the tourists would think in the morning. There was no way the magi could set the ancient cave to rights. *Pull it together*, she told herself, and called in the Mayday as Dez hiked himself up onto the other end of the platform.

"We're on our way," a crackling voice—she wasn't sure whose—acknowledged from the tiny transmitter.

She turned to Dez. "Did you—"

Without warning, a huge *crack* split the air *inside* his blue-white shield spell, and a man materialized on the platform between her and Dez.

Reese reeled back, heart lunging into her throat as her brain snapshotted the monstrous *makol*. He was as huge as any Nightkeeper and wore the same sort of black combat pants and boots, a weapons belt and long, carved knife. That was where the comparison stopped, though. He was bare-chested, wearing a ceremonial half robe of feather-worked crimson that was clasped at his throat and open everywhere else, revealing that his skin was ravaged, waxy, and runneled from shoulders to scalp. His features were lopsided and his eyes were the luminous green of the lesser *makol*, but with darker green pupils that burned with hatred.

*Iago.* Her mind supplied the name in the split second before Dez shouted, "Jump!"

She bit off a scream and flung herself backward off the platform as lightning magic cracked. But then unfamiliar shield magic whipped around her, burning her with greasy heat, catching her midair, and hoisting her back up. She kept hold of the mask but lost her autopistol, which went spinning over the edge. She heard it land with a crack as Iago's dark magic dumped her back on the platform. Dez roared her name and lightning flared, turning the world blue-white. But it didn't penetrate the dark shield that Iago had cast around him and Reese.

Mouth twisting, the Xibalban advanced on her, pulling a sickle-shaped stone knife as he came.

"No!" Rage and anguish roughened Dez's voice, which was muffled by the greasy brown of the dark-magic shield.

*She was trapped!* Panic lashed but she went into survival mode, ducking beneath Iago's knife swipe, and firing her .38 into his torso. The bullets chewed into him, dark ichor sprayed, and he fell back two steps, but the leathery flesh knit almost immediately and the wax-faced bastard laughed as he closed on her once more. Her pulse hammered, her mind screamed for her to *get out, get out!* But she couldn't get through the dark shield, couldn't— *Wait,* she thought, remembering how her other gun had fallen through the shield . . . and that the baseline shield spells were designed to keep bodies in but let projectiles out.

"Dez!" she screamed as Iago closed on her, starting

to draw the shield tighter so she wouldn't have any-where to run. "*Catch!*"

She hurled the wrapped bundle through the shield. It fell short, but Dez lunged for it as Iago roared in fury and slammed Reese aside. She hit the ground hard and slid, head ringing. Her vision blurred, but in the shield-lit darkness, she saw Iago dive for the artifact as Dez did the same. The men grappled as lightning and dark magic slashed around them in wild, furious bolts.

Breath sobbing in her lungs, she aimed her .38 just as Iago rose over Dez, his knife flashing in the moon-light. She screamed and fired, pounding two jade-tips into his knife hand. Blood splashed black in the moon-light and the knife went flying. Dez kicked his enemy up and off, then spun toward Reese and shouted once more: "Jump!"

But when she got to the edge of the platform, she saw luminous green eyes below. As one, the regener-ated *makol* warriors lashed out with their buzz-swords, letting rip with a salvo of deadly blades. Screaming, she threw herself back as the projectiles bounced around her. But when Dez started for her, she pointed. "Don't let him get the statue!" Iago was almost on top of the yellow idol.

"No!" Dez roared, lunging for his enemy.

Iago lashed out with a fat bolt that was part light-ning, part dark magic. Dez blocked with a shield, but went down hard, skidding heavily under the impact.

Reese's heart stuttered, her hands cramping where they wrapped around the empty .38. This was it. This was—

Brilliant silver light strobed the interior of the cave, painting the walls with *makol*-shadows that writhed and collapsed. When her vision cleared, she saw Michael silhouetted at the cave mouth, silver death magic flowing from his hands like mercury. In the same instant, Rabbit hurtled down the stairs, landed hard, and flung himself on Iago. Dark magic flared instantly.

"Rabbit, *no!*" Strike's voice bellowed from the other side of the cave, which was suddenly full of fireballs and ice as the Nightkeepers launched into battle.

Reese heard someone shout her name, but she was already falling back and twisting out of the way as a green-eyed *makol* appeared over the edge of the platform, its buzz-sword swinging down and—

Purple-white lightning hit it from one side, silver *muk* magic from the other, and the thing *exploded*, the chunks vaporizing to greasy ash before they hit. More silver flashed, more flames, and then there was a huge roar of magic, a mix of dark and light.

"*Rabbit!*" Myrinne's anguish split the air as his and Iago's images wavered and began to fade. Reese's heart stopped as Dez threw himself on the pair. Lightning detonated, burning her retinas with the afterimage.

When her vision cleared, he and Rabbit lay together on the platform.

Iago was gone.

Pulse hammering, she raced to the pair. On one level she was cognizant that the cave was lit blue-white now by a huge ball of fire that hung near the ceiling, illuminating the scene as the magi dispatched the last of the *makol*. But the rest of her was locked on Dez, who was pulling himself to his feet, ragged and battered, but alive. Alive! Her heart raced and a small sound escaped her, half laugh, half sob.

His head snapped around and their eyes met. And for a second it was as if the bad years hadn't happened, as if they had been on the same team all along, only the stakes were so much higher now. Then she was in his arms, crushed against his chest. It didn't matter that the moment came out of adrenaline and leftover fear. What mattered was that he was solid and real. And that he whispered her name and held on tight.

After a moment, he eased the embrace, but kept hold of her, tucking her against his side as he turned to face the others. "He got the mask."

Strike just looked at him, expression dark. "Are you ready to tell us what the hell is *really* going on here?"

When Dez hesitated, Reese tightened her grip on him. *It's time.* If Iago was involved, there was no way the two of them could handle the search alone. Finally, he nodded. "Yeah, I'll tell you. It's a long story, though."

"Then let's head home." Strike gestured to the others. "Link up."

Dez shifted his grip from Reese's shoulder to her hand, twining their fingers together to tug her into the forming uplink. She hadn't realized she had been holding her breath, but she must have been, because exhaling made her light-headed. Or maybe that was the realization that he was voluntarily turning himself in and asking for help.

It felt like they were coming in from the cold.

# CHAPTER TWELVE

December 15
Six days to the solstice
*Skywatch*

Dez sucked at meditation.

Despite a year's worth of practice, he still spent the first ten minutes or so sitting there cross-legged, staring at the small *chac-mool* altar he'd set up in the spare room of his suite, breathing incense . . . and going through a mental litany of "this is stupid," "how long do I have to sit here?" and "great, now I need to pee." Even after that, he usually had a hard time turning off the chatter on a good day. And today wasn't all that good.

He and Reese had briefed the team on the compass artifacts and the threat they represented. Strike and the others weren't thrilled with the way he had handled things, but the king had accepted his gut instinct as a reason for secrecy, because for better or worse, that was the way the magic seemed to work. And thanks to the fealty oath, where the king went, so went the magi. Which meant that Dez was back in the fold, save for some sidelong looks. And some of those were coming from Reese.

He sensed that she wanted him but didn't trust him, and he couldn't help her with that—her instincts had always been good. But as much as he told himself he should be doing his damnedest to drive her back to Denver where she'd be out of the line of fire, he couldn't make himself do it. In barely a week and a half, she had become intertwined with the Nightkeepers and the war efforts—almost as if the gods themselves had wanted her involved. Problem was, he didn't know how much of that was solid logic and how much was him finding reasons to do what he wanted to, deep down inside. He wanted her near him. Wanted to see if they could be the people in his dream. A couple. A mated pair.

*Shit*, he thought when warmth trickled through him. He was definitely talking himself into that one, ignoring the very real threat posed by his bloodline. But at the same time, he knew damn well that the war took precedence, and regardless of the other stuff, she was an asset to the team. He wouldn't have identified the third artifact or found the ice cave without her. She could find damn near anything ... and given what Rabbit had pulled from Iago's mind during their fight, the Nightkeepers badly needed her skills right now. Because there was bad news and more bad news: The Xibalban had captured Keban and the other artifacts. He controlled three pieces of the weapon, and the solstice was less than a week away.

On the upside, the Nightkeepers still had the star demon hidden away . . . and Rabbit had discovered that there were five artifacts, not four. There was one more out there, in play. But that was where the "more bad" came in. "I couldn't figure out what the fifth artifact looks like or where it's hidden," Rabbit had said, "because there's another problem. Iago isn't the dominant personality anymore; the demon soul of Moctezuma is in control now, and Iago's brain is *seriously* fucked up. I couldn't get anything other than what was floating at the top of his sicko soup." He had paused, a muscle at the corner of his jaw pulsing. "He's the one who has been taking the villagers. He's figured out how to turn them all *makol*, not just the evilest of them. He's got a fucking army brewing—hundreds, maybe thousands." Including men, women, children . . . and Rabbit's friends.

As for the rest, Rabbit had gotten hints about the solstice and a dark lord, but no specifics on who, what, or how to stop it.

Based on the new information, the Nightkeepers were scrambling to put together new recons, new strategies. Sasha was doing some healing work on Sven, who had turned quiet and strange since his inexplicable collapse and equally inexplicable reawakening the next day. Rabbit and Myrinne had gone back down south to keep looking for Iago's base camp. Reese had gone off with Jade, Natalie, and Lucius to try to figure out what the fifth artifact could be, where it might be hidden, and—

*Shit*, Dez thought, disgusted. *Meditate already.* He

would've skipped the routine, but he knew all too well how easy it was to start the downward slide. A missed prayer or a momentary grab for power weren't deadly in isolation, but for him they could be as dangerous as a dry drunk's first sip.

Staring at the wall, he drew a deep, incense-laden breath and blanked his mind. Then he relaxed his scalp, his face, his sinuses and jaw, working his way down, feeling the bumps and bruises, the psychic stink that came from having grappled with Iago.

Those reminders of the fight brought a thick stir of anger. The Xibalban had gotten the two-faced mask. More, he had almost killed Reese. *Damn it*, Dez thought, he should've tried harder to chase her off, should've found a way to send her back to Denver, even if the knowledge that she had a guy waiting for her made him want to put his fist through something. It would be better to have her safe in the arms of another man than risking herself with the Nightkeepers.

When a molar creaked, he made himself relax his jaw.

She wasn't as fast as he was, didn't heal like he did, didn't have shield magic or lightning. Worse, she was still stupid-brave. She might think she had grown up and slowed down, but she was wrong. She would still be the first one through any door if he didn't push her out of the way. Seeing her locked inside Iago's shield had just about killed him, as had watching the *makol* squadron advance on her.

*Blank wall. Blank mind. Drift. Breathe.*

This so wasn't working. He really, really sucked at this.

A knock at his apartment door had him lunging to his feet. "Thank Christ." It wasn't until he had his hand on the doorknob that he realized the thrum of his blood wasn't just coming from relief. The knock had been the syncopated four-tap that had been his and Reese's old signal for: *It's me. All clear.*

Except nothing was clear. He knew that for damn sure the moment he opened the door.

She was wearing dark jeans and a stretchy top that clung to her breasts and had desire hammering through him, racing on the afterburn of magic. He wanted to touch her, kiss her, back her up against the far wall and imprint his body on hers. Electric heat flared at the thought, saying *yes, this is right, this is what was meant to happen*, with a certainty as incontrovertible as the writs themselves. But back in the day, he'd thought the same about buying her that ring because he wanted to get laid, hadn't he?

Knowing that he couldn't trust his motives when it came to her, he made himself step out into the hall and let the door swing shut behind him. "Hey. Everything okay?"

She met his eyes, looking thoughtful and seeming oblivious to the ozone crackle that heated the air around them. "I was thinking . . . Skywatch is at the middle of the compass cross made by the other locations, right? So where better to hide the fifth artifact than inside the Nightkeepers' center of ops?"

That so wasn't where his brain had been that it took him a second to reorient, another to see that she might very well have nailed it. Because the pattern fit. The logic played. And he was damn grateful to have something else to focus on other than the heat that burned inside him.

Maybe keeping her close wasn't so self-indulgent after all.

He grinned fiercely. "I always said you were more than a pretty face." *Keep it light*, he told himself when his blood continued to hum in his veins and his body attuned itself to hers.

She stuck out her tongue at him, then lifted a flashlight. "Want to do some exploring?"

Caution said he shouldn't go off alone with her, not now when he was running so hot. But, damn it, this was their search and the compass artifacts were the responsibility of the serpent bloodline. And he might be tempted, but he was in control. He could handle himself. So, deciding caution could go fuck itself, he ducked back inside his apartment and grabbed his jacket. "Lead the way," he said.

But as they headed off, he couldn't help wondering where the slippery slide began. And how far he could let it go before there was too much momentum to stop.

Reese filled Dez in as he steered the Jeep along the looping trail that followed the perimeter of the box canyon. "The center of the compass is associated with the color green, and with—get this—lightning." When he shot her a look, she nodded. "I shit you not. The Hopi medicine wheel has a similar color arrangement, except that they connect the green center with their end-time prophecy, which says that the savior will return to save them. He's supposed to be a big, white-skinned god who wears a red cape and appears following a series of signs that include multiple earthquakes." Like the ones that had hit the previous year, courtesy of the earthquake demon, Cabrakan.

As they climbed out of the Jeep at the back of the canyon, he pointed out, "Only the royal bloodline wears red for ceremonies, which suggests that Strike is the guy they're looking for. Maybe it's his job to destroy the weapon." His tone was matter-of-fact, his expression anything but.

The intensity of his gaze, like the heat that had kindled in his eyes as they had stood together in the hallway, sent a shiver down the back of her neck and kicked her instincts into overdrive. Since their return to Skywatch, he had seemed . . . different somehow. He was darker and more closed off than he had been, yet at the same time she had caught him watching her possessively, with a feral, predatory gleam in his eyes. She wasn't afraid of him—she wouldn't have come out here alone with him if she had been. But the fragile trust that had started growing between them while they staked out the ice cave had disappeared, as had any easiness between them. Maybe encouraging him to return to Skywatch had been a mistake, after all. *Or maybe you're overanalyzing*, she thought sourly.

He looked up at the cliff face, to the triple row of

dark openings that led into a small Puebloan ruin. "Why are we starting here?"

"Since the other artifacts were all hidden at local native sites, I called down to Rabbit, who knows these ruins better than anyone. He was pretty sure that a few of the rooms have zigzag decorations suggesting serpent worship." She paused. "Granted, the compass points aren't exact, so the fifth artifact could be hidden in one of the main Chacoan ruins. Heck, given that Keban told you there were only two hidden artifacts left—the god's head and the two-faced mask—number five may be in a museum somewhere. And there's no guarantee you'll be able to sense it . . . But we've got to start somewhere."

An hour later, though, they were forced to admit defeat. The zigzags may or may not be snakes, but the surrounding stones were solid, with no evidence of anything being hidden there.

"It was worth a try," Dez said as he parked the Jeep back in its spot near the training hall, which was a short walk from the mansion. "Tomorrow we can start checking the Chacoan sites—Pueblo Bonito and whatnot."

The sun was setting, the sky going from salmon to bloodred as it filtered through the high canopy of the huge ceiba tree that had magically grown from the ashes of the *winikin* and children who had died in the Solstice Massacre. A grove of leafy cacao trees spread out beneath the bigger tree, forming a magical, out-of-place mini-rain-forest ecosystem that flourished between the training hall and the mansion.

Reese hopped out of the Jeep and walked partway

to the picnic area near the cacao, her mental wheels still turning. "How about planting some of those magic sensors around the Chacoan ruins? That way we'll know if Iago 'ports in to dig something up."

"We'll have to check if there are any left. Last I knew, Rabbit had set up most of them in the highlands."

It was a sobering reminder of the bigger picture. And the fact that they needed to find some answers, fast. "What about—" She broke off at a twig-snap. Her instincts flared. "Did you hear that?"

Still over by the Jeep, Dez looked over. "Hear what?"

She squinted through the half-light at the cacao grove, and raised her voice. "Is someone there?"

A shadow moved. Then luminous green flashed, followed by a high-pitched whine.

"*Makol!*" Reese spun and bolted, then screamed in pain when something slash-thudded into her shoulder. Another blow impacted low on her back, and then the creature was on top of her, tearing at her, growling vicious words in a language she didn't know. She heard Dez's furious bellow, saw a blast of lightning magic, felt the *makol* being ripped away and turned to ash. Then it was all pain and blackness. Then nothing at all.

"*No!*" Dez roared, dropping down beside her. "Reese!"

His shield sparked around them both as he dragged her up. He saw her blood, smelled it, felt it on his hands when he grabbed her and slung her over his shoulder, his heart pounding a sick litany of: *Not Reese. Please no. Not Reese.*

In the cacao grove, dark magic rattled and air *whoomped* with the sound of an outgoing 'port. Moments later, leaves parted and more *makol* poured through: men and women wearing the mix of loomed textiles and modern clothes favored by the highland Maya.

Pulse slamming, Dez reinforced the shit out of his shield and went for his armband, nailing the emergency alarms on every available channel. "We've got *makol* by the big training hall, repeat *by the fucking training hall*. Reese is hurt. I need Sasha here, *now*. And for fuck's sake put somebody on the star demon. I think Iago's here." The magic of the outgoing teleport had felt different, bigger.

Then he spun as a big *makol* with a nose ring and the robes of a village shaman-priest came out of the trees and lunged, slashing. The buzz-sword bit into and *through* Dez's shield. He felt the blow not just in his shield but in his body; pain roared in his shoulder and chest and he staggered back, went down. He landed hard and lost hold of Reese. And his godsdamned shield shorted out.

"Fuck!" He launched to his feet, putting himself in front of her as the big *makol* raised his buzz-sword for the killing blow. He tried to call his shield. Failed. Tried to call lightning. Failed. Went for his .44, but it was too late. The buzz-sword sliced the air and—

Foliage whipped suddenly as a furry grayish blur erupted from the cacao grove and leaped on the *makol*.

Dez froze for a split second, surprised as hell when the dog—wolf? coyote?—clamped its teeth on the shaman's sword arm and twisted. Inertia spun them around, and then the huge canine was on top of the *makol*, snarling horribly as it tore out the demon's throat and then bit down on its face with a terrible crunch.

More *makol* raced out of the grove and the big dog spun to face them with a chilling snarl, its jaws dripping blood and saliva. Then it leaped over the attackers, raced back into the cacao. And disappeared.

*Whump!* Air displaced as Strike and six more magi appeared in the middle of the fight. Immediately, they slammed shield magic into place and started blasting away. Rabbit and Michael were in front, wielding fire and *muk*. The deadly magical flows scythed through the bulk of the *makol* while the others napalmed with fireballs, then followed up with head-and-heart magic.

"Don't let them at your shields," Dez snapped. "One of them shorted mine out." He couldn't explain that. Couldn't explain the coyote. Couldn't explain how Iago had gotten inside the ward. Impossible, all of it.

Yet it had happened. And Reese had taken the brunt. *Fuck.*

He dropped down beside her, gathered her up, cursed when he felt the feverish heat pouring off her body and heard the way her breath sobbed in her lungs, strange and rattling. "Sasha!" he called harshly. "*Now.* She took a buzz-sword blade to the shoulder."

But Reese shook her head weakly and rasped, "The shoulder's just a cut. That's not . . ." She swallowed hard, then pushed up her sleeve and said faintly, "This is worse."

Her right wrist was swollen and angry, the flesh

dimpled in a semicircular bite that was blackened at the edges and wept clear fluid from the center. The sight sledgehammered Dez in the gut and chilled him down to his very soul. "Son of a *bitch*."

The magi had been lucky so far—none of them had been bitten—but they all knew what it said in the library about *makol* bites: They had to act immediately. And even then, the odds weren't good for a mage.

For a human, they were even worse.

# CHAPTER THIRTEEN

Strike zapped the entire fighting force straight to the sacred chamber in the center of the mansion, both because Reese would need all the help she could get, and because it was a defensible position.

Michael and Nate each took a door and cast heavy shield magic, because until further notice, no place was safe.

Dez carried Reese to the big *chac-mool* altar, which was set in cement made from the ashes of long-ago Nightkeepers. He slid down so they were sitting together on the floor, with him leaning back against the altar and her cradled in his lap, her back to his front, so he could brace her and hold her injured arm steady.

She moaned weakly, drifting back to consciousness to ask, "What are you doing?"

"We need to cut you and get the poison out right away," he whispered into her hair. It was the only way—it might be an old wives' tale for snakebites, but when it came to magic, the old remedies worked best. "We'll use a sleep spell. You won't—"

"No," she said. "No sleep spell." She shuddered. "Hate 'em." Her voice slurred, but her eyes were adamant.

He started to argue, but Sasha interrupted, saying, "I need her conscious. She has to say the spell." The worry was plain in her face though: As a human, Reese didn't have any magic. The spell might not have any power coming from her.

He met Sasha's eyes, saw her agonized sympathy. "Don't," he rasped. *Don't say you're sorry. Don't look at me like that.* "She can sense the magic," he said almost desperately. "Not loud and clear, but she knows when I'm jacked in." It was something he hadn't let himself think about too closely, because it only added to the self-serving logic urging him to take her as his mate.

"Then link up with her," Sasha ordered. "Gods know she's going to need all the help we can give her."

There was a commotion among the others, a flurry of phone and radio traffic. Dez caught the words "star demon" and "fucker got it" and his gut twisted with the knowledge that they were in deep, dark shit. Iago had at least four of the artifacts, might know where to find the fifth.

He cursed. They should have been safe inside the compound. What the hell had happened? How had the fuckers gotten in? He was furious—at Iago, at the whole fucking situation—but he shoved all that aside and bent over Reese. Her body was cooling from the spiked fever, but not in a good way. She was limp and clammy, her breathing labored. Her hand was swollen and hot, the blackness of the bite mark spreading along the webwork pattern of her veins. *Death follows quickly*, the codices warned about *makol* bites. And he could practically see her fading, see the darkness overtaking her. A tsunami of emotion hammered through him— rage, regret, guilt, loss, grief—all the things he hadn't fully felt when he lost her the first time. Back then, he'd been lost himself, and by the time he found his way out with the help of the Triad magic, it had been far too late for him to go after her. Now, though, he realized that he had kept her image inside him, and fought every skirmish with her locked in his heart, knowing she was out there in the world he was defending. He couldn't lose that, couldn't lose her.

He wanted to pray, but couldn't find the inner stillness he needed. So as Sasha used her belt to set a tourniquet above Reese's elbow, he pulled his knife and carved a jerky furrow in his palm, then hers. He clasped her hand, pressed his cheek to hers, and whispered, "*Pasaj och.*"

Magic flowed into him, but it weighed him down rather than lifting him up.

Sasha linked up on the other side, connecting her flow of life energy to Reese's. "Okay," the healer said, poising her knife over the bite mark. "On four. One, two . . ." She slashed on "three," bringing a gout of watery black fluid, followed by blood.

Reese stiffened and gave a harsh, strangled cry. Pain radiated into Dez through the blood-link—it was dull and unfocused compared to what he was used to sensing from uplinks with the other magi, but it was *there*, damn it. Something was getting through. So as Sasha slashed again, making an X, he drew as much pain as he could out of the link and sent his own energy back through it. *Come on, you bastard*, he thought, not sure if he was talking to himself or the poison inside her. *Come on!*

For a moment, nothing happened. Then a shadow rose from the wound, a formless miasma of dark magic. Reese moaned and strained away from it, pushing back into him. "I've got you," he said, over and over again, holding her tightly, the words becoming meaningless. "I've got you."

"Repeat after me, both of you," Sasha ordered. Her face was gray and drawn, and streaked with sweat.

Michael left the door to come up behind her and grip her shoulder, pouring his energy into her, the same as Dez was doing with Reese. Except it wasn't the same, was it? Michael and Sasha were both magi and fully mated, bound together by the *jun tan* bond. Dez could offer Reese only a fraction of what the other two shared. He hoped to hell it would be enough. *Damn it*, he thought, he would *make* it be enough. He bore down and took more of the pain, gave her more of his power. They said the spell, all four of them, with Sasha leading, the others repeating.

The mist coalesced malevolently around Reese's arm, flickering with arcs of luminous green. Dez gritted his teeth as pain came through the blood-link seemingly without end. He smelled blood and the foul, heavy stench of a *makol*'s evil, the two together overwhelming. *Come on, Reese*, he chanted inwardly, *fight!*

Then, unexpectedly, there was a wrenching jolt, and

for a second he was *inside* her, seeing what she saw, feeling what she felt. He felt his own solid grip enfolding her from behind, the stubborn determination that tethered her to consciousness, and the tendrils of sick, evil darkness that had made it beyond the tourniquet to root the poison within her body, holding it there.

More, he sensed her strength fading. And he sensed, for a second, a flicker of green that whispered to her, urging her to let go and rest, not to fight anymore. She was so tired, after all. Everything would be okay if she just relaxed and let things happen.

*Don't, Reese,* he projected urgently through the blood-link. *It's a lie!*

But his words didn't reach her. More, he felt the connection grow thinner as the *makol*'s darkness trickled through her bloodstream, an amorphous cancer of the soul that whispered over and over for her to relax, let go, let the darkness win. Panic kicked through him at the realization that she was losing ground. They both were.

"Take the tourniquet off," he said to Sasha, and heard his own voice through Reese's ears, creating a weird dissonance in his mind.

"But—"

"Take it off," he insisted, then said, "Trust me." Which was a hell of a thing to ask, because Sasha was one of the ones who still looked at him warily, not yet ready to believe he was reformed.

But she hesitated, traded a look with Michael, then nodded. "Okay."

"On three, and no tricks this time." They counted it down and she loosened the tourniquet.

Immediately, the dark mist raced back into Reese, flowing in through the gashes on her wrist. Going on instinct, Dez poured his energy into her, all of his reserves and more. *Fight*, he told her. *Fight, damn it! Don't you dare run away this time!* It wasn't until he said it that he recognized the truth of it, but the realization was quickly lost as his perceptions wrenched suddenly, and then he was back in his own head, his own body. He wasn't connected to her anymore, though he still held her hand in a bloody clasp, still felt the buzz of the uplink. "Reese," he shouted. "Godsdamn it, *Reese*!"

A long shudder ran through her body, and then she arched against him, trying to pull away from the blood-links. A deep, guttural moan tore from her throat and her eyes rolled back in her head.

"Gods!" Sasha gasped. The dark, wounded flesh rippled, runneling along her arm as though turbocharged worms were writhing beneath the skin, whipped into a frenzy by the poison. Michael's eyes went silver as he channeled more energy into Sasha's healing bond, but that didn't seem to help. Through the last little bit of the uplink, Dez could feel Reese slipping away. Dying.

Panic lashing through him, he shouted "Do something! We're losing her!"

"Call her," Sasha said. "Make her come back. If she's not conscious, she's not fighting it!"

But he had *been* calling her, and it wasn't working. He needed something better, something more. Something that would matter to her. He looked deep inside himself to the place where he normally kept the past locked away, but that had been breached the moment she lunged back into his life, wearing combat clothes and wielding an autopistol like she'd been born a warrior.

"Think about the dream," he whispered alongside her temple, feeling the words rip from his chest. "Think about Montana, all those mountains, and the streams, and the big open sky. I bet you never went there, did you? So fight, damn it. Get your ass back here. If you do . . ." He paused, feeling the churn and burn in his gut, but went for it. "Wake the hell up and we'll go there together." His throat closed on the ache of guilt, sadness, and regret that washed through him as he turned his lips to her temple. "Please, baby. Don't let it end like this." *Please gods*.

A long shudder wracked her body and she twisted against him, nearly bowing herself double.

"Shit," Sasha hissed. "Convulsion. Help me grab her and—"

Energy detonated soundlessly inside Dez, hollowing out his diaphragm and making him feel like his elevator had just hit bottom. At the same moment Sasha jolted, and Michael said, "What the fuck?"

Then Reese sagged, going utterly limp.

"*Reese!*" Dez surged out from behind her, rose over her with both hands wrapped in her shirt. "Reese, damn it!"

Sasha grabbed his shoulder. "*Look!*"

Dark mist was churning angrily from the weeping cuts, boiling out of Reese. It formed an angry, pulsing blob that went from black to green as it emerged.

Then *poof*. It disappeared.

He stared for a second, blinking at her arm. The X-marked cuts still bled and the bite was a dark, angry red. But the blackness was gone and the swelling was abating even as they watched. More, he could feel her breathing grow steady, her body temperature level off. And when he looked away from her wrist, he found her watching him with eyes that were blurry and unfocused, but held every ounce of now-Reese: a mix of the stupidly brave, crime-fighting girl he had known and the woman she had grown into, who dared him, challenged him, stood up to him.

She was back.

His throat closed on a hard, hot surge of emotion. "Hey." It was all he could manage.

Her eyes fluttered shut, but she whispered, "Montana, huh?" And she drifted off with a smile on her lips.

He let his forehead drop to his hands, which were still clutched in her shirt. Despite what he'd been through with the Triad spell, he still wasn't all that religious in the worshipping sense. Now, though, he sent a fervent thought-stream skyward: *Thank you, gods.* And he got, in return, a flare of heat that radiated through him, washing inward to his head and heart. He wasn't sure if it came from magic, the exhaustion he felt bearing down on him freight train fast, or some celestial source. But it made him feel a little less alone.

Groaning, he dragged himself to his feet, then reached down and gathered Reese to his chest. He felt the pull of muscles as he lifted her, the ache of fatigue as he held her tightly. But neither Nate nor Michael offered to take her. They were mated magi; they knew better.

He fixed Nate with a look. "Is the mansion safe?" Part of him wanted to hit the road again, find some anonymous hotel where nobody would think to look for them. He was never truly comfortable at Skywatch.

But Nate nodded. "We know how they got in."

"How?" Dez grated the word.

"A delivery van came through an hour ago and set off the ward. JT looked over the truck, didn't see anything, and figured it was another false alarm, so he waved them through, then reset the system."

"You're kidding. He fucking waved Iago and a truckload of *makol* through the front door?"

Michael's glower promised dire retribution. "Yeah. They crashed the system from the security hub to get out."

"Shit." Dez needed to get Reese someplace safe. But he also needed to crash. Another few minutes and he wasn't going to be worth shit. He glanced toward the garage. "I need to—"

"You need to get Reese settled and then get some food and rest yourself," Nate interrupted. He gripped Dez's shoulder. "We've got your back." Behind him, several of the others nodded, including Sasha, who for a change wasn't looking at him with trepidation.

It seemed that for all that he'd worked his ass off to earn their trust, it had taken him stepping up for Reese to win them over. And, oddly, he was okay with that. He nodded. "All right, I'm going. But first, what was with the coyote?" When he got blank stares, he briefly recounted the strange incident, which he would've been tempted to think he had imagined, only he hadn't. "It took off right as you guys got there. Big son of a bitch."

"We'll check it out," Nate promised.

"And remind Lucius there's still one more artifact out there. If we can—"

"Go." Sasha pushed him toward the door. "Turn it off for a few hours. We've got this, and you'll be useless until you recharge."

This was part of being a member of a team, he realized suddenly—not just having the others trust him, but trusting them in return. Which he hadn't done before. He nodded slowly, letting the others see that he got it. "Okay. Thanks."

Sasha followed him to the residential wing, ostensibly to make sure Reese's condition stayed stable but also, he suspected, to call for help if he went down flat on his face. He stayed on his feet, but just barely, hesitating at his own door and then continuing down the hall to the apartment Reese had claimed for herself.

Their suites had the same footprint, with a main room, small attached kitchen, two blocky bedrooms and one bath, but she had given hers more character in a handful of days than he had in more than a year. She would probably call the maps tacked to the wall "research" and the huge bulletin board and the smaller wipe board "practical necessities," but to him they were, quite simply, Reese. So, too, was the fat pottery jar in the kitchen, which he would lay money contained cookies. The air was lightly tinted with a spicy floral scent he suspected was her chosen shampoo—as opposed to the No-Tell Motel's finest they had been sporting the past few days—and a hint of coffee.

He carried Reese into the main bedroom. There was a pile of research books on the nightstand, a pair of silver-toed cowboy boots in the corner, and a trio of potted cactuses on the windowsill. One was blooming.

"Do you want me to get her cleaned up and changed?" Sasha asked from the doorway. But what she was really asking was: *Do you want to take care of her yourself? How close are the two of you?*

"Yeah," he said. "Thanks." Because he didn't dare put his hands on her while his defenses were shot.

So he set her down on the bed and retreated to the main room to raid a kitchen that was high on carbs, low on protein. She had Diet Mountain Dew, though, which surprised him because it had been his drink, not hers.

A few minutes later, Sasha appeared in the bedroom doorway. "All set. And her vitals are looking good." As she crossed the main room, headed for the hallway, she shot a look at the half-eaten cookie in his hand. "I'll have the *winikin* bring you some protein."

"I'd appreciate it. Carlos and Tomas know what I like."

She rolled her eyes. "I don't know how a guy with amplified senses can eat what you do."

"It's a guy thing?"

"It's a you thing." But her expression softened, just a hint. "Get some rest, Mendez. You did good back there with her."

"So did you. I owe you one." He could have left it at

that, but when she made an "I'll take off now" gesture, he said, "So, we're cool? You and me, I mean?"

He kept it vague so she could duck if she wanted. But she winced. "Shit. Sorry. I thought I was hiding it."

"I'm sensitive to vibes. And the one between you and me has always been off."

She hesitated, then nodded. "At first I told myself it was because you remind me of Michael when I first met him, back before he got control of the death magic. But that's not it, really. It's . . ." She shrugged apologetically. "To be honest, you make me a little nervous. Not in an 'I'm in danger' sense, but in a 'this guy is going to shake things up' kind of way." Crossing to him, she stretched up to squeeze his shoulder. It was probably the first spontaneous reach-out between them. "Seeing you with her . . . it helps."

*It shouldn't*, he thought but didn't say, because a cold, hard knot had formed in his gut at her words . . . because Sasha was Strike and Anna's little sister, and prescience ran in the royal jaguar bloodline. "Are you a seer?"

"Gods, no. My talent is tough enough to manage, I wouldn't want to be an *itza'at*. I'll leave that to . . ." She trailed off, then shook her head. "No. You just weirded me out, probably because all I knew about you beforehand was that you'd been in jail and your *winikin* disappeared right around the time you got out."

He relaxed a little. "My reputation precedes me." It wasn't a vision, then. Nothing he needed to worry about.

"I'm over it. And I'm sorry that I've been flinchy around you."

"Don't be. I'm a scary guy."

"Terrifying. So much so that I'm leaving you here with Reese, who I consider a friend." She patted his shoulder. "Eat. Rest. And don't stay uplinked for too long. There's too much shit going down for you to be drained hollow."

It was a given that he would be linking with Reese to feed her as much energy as he could. She was over the worst of the *makol* poisoning, and Sasha's healing had helped close the wounds on her shoulder and lower back, but she would need his help to recover. The magi could make do with IVs of saline and glucose; humans needed more. He shrugged. "She can have whatever she needs from me."

"Don't drain yourself," she repeated. "King's orders." But they both knew that Dez would make the call himself. Although the ancient writs placed the needs of the gods, the king, and the end-time war far above those of lovers and friends, the modern magi tended to put their mates and families first, starting with Strike's decision to break the thirteenth prophecy to save Leah. And although Reese wasn't Dez's mate, she was his lover. Or at least she had been, for one perfect night.

Chest tightening, he took Sasha's hand, gave it a squeeze. "Thanks for being there tonight. If you hadn't been . . . well. Thanks."

"You're welcome. Now get some rest."

Later, showered, changed, and fed, Dez lay down beside Reese in a darkness that was lit by outdoor floods,

warning that all was not well at Skywatch. He had his
.44 on the nightstand, an autopistol on the floor, and
felt the subsensory hum that said the others were sacrificing blood to strengthen the ward surrounding the
compound. He and Reese were safer in the mansion
than they would be outside, he told himself. And that
would have to be good enough.

When he took her hand and folded it into his, aligning his palm scar with the scabbed-over slash on hers
to form a touch-link that let his energy wash into her,
she shifted and turned toward him, murmuring, "That
helps. Don't let go."

"I won't." He tightened his grip. But as he let her
warmth seep into him and relax him one muscle group
at a time, he found himself thinking that he hadn't
planned to let go of her the last time, either. Yet he had.
As he went under, he heard himself whisper, as he had
done to bring her back, "Think about Montana . . ."

And he slipped into a dream, taking her warmth
with him.

*After nearly an hour zigzagging through the tunnels and
backtracking to make sure the Cobras weren't still after
them, Mendez led the girl to his current flop: a one-roomer
in a condemned apartment building that had been boarded
up a couple of years ago and scheduled for demolition, but
had then apparently been forgotten by the wrecking ball.*

*Squatting rights were held by a foul-mouthed weasel of a
man, nearly albino, who ran girls, drugs, and whatever-the-
fuck else out of the first floor, and "rented" the other rooms.
Dez wouldn't be able to make rent another week unless he*

*did something drastic—which didn't matter because the Cobras would be gunning for his ass now. But he was probably okay there for the night, at least. Or rather, they would be okay. Because suddenly it wasn't just him anymore.*

*In the light of the smoky lantern he had made out of an old soup can and fueled with leftover cooking grease that smelled like apples this week, the girl was thin and dirty, but he could see why she had caught Hood's eye. She couldn't be more than sixteen—maybe even less. Her chin was narrow and pointed, her wide-set eyes an interesting shade of rusty amber. And the dirt and ragged denim couldn't hide her long curves and the high bumps of her breasts. He didn't know what had drawn him toward Warehouse Seventeen that afternoon, or why he'd gone toward the sounds of a fight when he normally would've headed the other way, but he knew one thing for certain: She wouldn't last much longer on the streets without someone looking out for her.*

*"What's your name?" he asked.*

*She opened her mouth, hesitated, and then said, "Reese Montana."*

*He snorted. "No, it's not." For one, she had stalled. For another, it sounded made up. Then again, "Snake Mendez" wasn't exactly a winner in that department.*

*"It is now," she said.*

*That he got. Most of the street rats he knew had run away from more than just a location, and many of them changed their names to avoid being scooped back up.*

*Something mean and nasty worked its way through him at the suspicion of what she was running from. For a mid-upper-class suburban kid—he got that from the way she talked and the oldest layer of ragged clothing—without an obvious attitude or drug problem to be on the streets like this . . . yeah. A hundred bucks said there had been a family member with grabby hands. He was going with that over outright beat-you-'til-you-bleed because she didn't have that flinch-when-touched response. He should know.*

*It looked like she had taken—or at the very least ducked—a few punches recently though. She was squared off opposite him, ready to run or fight at a second's notice. Her body vibrated, strung tight as shit, and with good reason. He had gotten her away from Hood and his fanged freaks, but for all she knew, he was just looking for some privacy.*

*"You'll be safe here," he said for like the fifth time. "I'm not going to hurt you."*

*She didn't say anything. Just looked at him.*

*What the hell was he going to do with her? Teach her a few things and send her away? Keep her around? "You hungry?" he said when the silence got weird.*

*Her stomach grumbled in answer.*

*He grinned, then took a risk by turning his back on her to crouch and pull up the loose floorboard to reveal his food stash, which was heavy on the salt and protein his body craved, with some other randoms because a guy had to grab what he could get. "I've got pepperoni, mixed nuts, nachos, and this chipped-beef jerky crap. It tastes like cardboard and takes forever to chew, but it'll keep you going." When he looked up, though, he saw that she had crept toward him, her eyes locked on the edge of a bright orange wrapper. One of the randoms. He pulled it out, looked from it to her and back again. "Reese's, huh?"*

*She nodded slowly, then lifted her eyes to his. They packed even more of a punch up close, sucking him in and making him suddenly all too aware of his body, and hers.* She's just a kid, asshole. Hands off.

*A sad smile quirked the corners of her mouth.* "My dad used to get them for me." *Then she pressed her lips together, like she wished she hadn't said even that much.*

*He nodded, filing the info. The father hadn't been the problem then. Stepfather? Uncle?* Fucker. *Even after everything that he'd seen and done—or fought off—since he'd been on his own, it pissed his shit right off to imagine someone going after her like that.* I'll protect you, *he thought.* I won't let anybody else hurt you. *He would do it for the baby sister he hadn't been able to save. And he would do it for her, for this whiskey-eyed kid whose street luck had run out the moment Hood got his eyes on her and picked her to be the next in the rolling cast of disposable "girlfriends" he used up and tossed aside.*

*He needed to play it low key, though. Didn't want to scare her off.* "So why Montana?" *he asked over the open food stash.* "Is that where you're from?"

"No, it's . . . it's stupid."

*He wiggled the peanut butter cups, holding them just out of reach.* "Why Montana?"

*She scowled.* "That's blackmail."

"Technically, I think it's extortion." *But it had gotten her attention without scaring her.* "Why Montana?"

*Rolling her eyes, she said,* "Because when I was a little kid, before the—well, before things got bad—I had this poster of Montana in my room, on the wall over my bed." *She held out her hand.* "Pay up, Hannibal."

*Hannibal? Oh, quid pro quo.* "Not yet," *he said.* "What did you like about the poster?"

"It had these mountains in it, with a big blue sky, green trees, wide-open field, the works. There was a man and a woman riding double on a spotted horse, headed for the hills." She was flushed but her eyes were defiant. "At the bottom it said 'Escape to Montana.' And if you laugh, I'll break your nose."

"No laughing." He held up a hand. "Scout's honor."

Her eyes locked on the scar that ran along his lifeline. "You were a boy scout?"

"Nope."

"Mendez, right?"

It was what Keban had called him—that and "boy" or "pussy," depending—because he said he hadn't earned his bloodline name yet, probably never would. "Yeah, it's Mendez." But then he surprised himself by saying, "You can call me Dez."

"Dez," she said it slowly, trying it out, as if she somehow knew he'd never used the nickname before. Then she nodded. "Okay, Dez. What's the deal here?"

"Beats the hell out of me." He held out the candy. "Earlier today, something told me to go into that warehouse even though I usually stay the hell out of Cobra business. Now, that same something is telling me we should stick together, watch each other's backs, stay out of Hood's way. That sort of thing." Mentally, he added: get you your GED, a job, and up and out of this hellhole. *Because she sure as shit didn't belong down there in the stews.*

She took the chocolate, but shot him a long look under lowered brows. "That's it? Watch each other's backs? Nothing else?"

*His fingers tingled where they had brushed against hers, but he shook his head. "Not the way you're thinking."*

*Because although most of Keban's "lessons" might've been cracked crocks of shit, a few that made sense had stuck. And one that had gelled on a gut level said a man didn't take a mate until he had everything else under control.*

# CHAPTER FOURTEEN

December 17
Solstice minus four days

After being cooped up in emergency confabs all morning, Sven was feeling seriously squirrelly. The news was bad and more bad: two more villages had been taken, and Lucius and the others hadn't been able to pinpoint the fifth artifact, figure out what "dark lord" Iago planned to summon, or zone in on where the bastard was hiding or how he would attempt to set off the weapon now that he had at least four of the five pieces, maybe even the fifth. Reese was recovering, but slowly, and that had tied up Mendez, who refused to leave her for long. Strike was looking seriously ragged around the edges, and Nate and several of the others had been shooting Sven strange looks for the past couple of days, like they were afraid he was going to pass out again, or worse.

*I'm not your problem*, he had wanted to snarl at them, but kept that one to himself. He had been keeping lots of things to himself lately, including the headaches and the dragging fatigue. Sasha's *chu'ul* magic hadn't helped with the symptoms, so why bitch about them? For all he knew, they were in his head, just like the funky dreams he'd been having, where smells and sounds were amplified, his perceptions altered, and he awoke with a keen sense of loss, like he was missing something important.

Before, he would've taken one of the dune buggies out, or headed over to one of the nearby lakes and bummed a boat. Now, he prowled the halls of Skywatch, not sure what the hell he was looking for anymore. All he knew was that it wasn't in the mansion.

"For gods' sake, people, this isn't just about JT," Tomas's raised voice caught his attention as he passed the *winikin*'s wing. "Sure, he let the delivery truck through, but can we really say none of us would've done the same thing? We shouldn't be throwing blame around when the simple fact is that we're struggling. And that's unacceptable."

Sven paused as JT retorted, "Let me guess what you'd consider acceptable . . . opening Jox's letter and blindly accepting his choice."

"Yes, that is exactly what I think we should do. We're spending so much time trying to reach consensus that we're not getting our shit done. Period."

"Fine. So we vote in our own leader."

"That's not the way it works."

Sven kept going. It was no secret that things were coming to a head with the *winikin*—if they didn't make a change soon, Strike would make it for them.

More, Sven had given Carlos a choice between telling Strike there were other surviving *winikin* out there, and JT knew how to find them, or having Sven do it. He couldn't keep that from the king much longer; his fealty oath was already barking. Right now, though, the *winikin*'s problems weren't his priority. Searching was. His head pounded in time with his heart as he prowled out to the garage, grabbed a set of keys to one of the older Jeeps, and hit the button to open the big doors at the end of the hangar-sized building.

He had to puzzle over the stick shift for a second, which just showed how tired and strung out he was; he'd been driving standards since he was twelve, booting the ranch truck around to fix fences, and . . . What was he doing again?

Right. Driving.

But instead, his thoughts scattering, he left the vehicle idling and headed through the open door into the dry warmth of the great outdoors. *Yes*, he thought. *Yes*. There was sunlight on his face and hot hardpan beneath his feet as he struck out, drawn onward.

He looped around the back of the mansion, past the pool and out to the picnic area where the fight had taken place. Someone had raked away the scuff marks and greasy ash piles, but a picnic table was missing and several of the closest cacao trees bore gouged-up bark, scorch marks, taped-up branches, and other repairs. Moving past them, he pushed into the cacao grove. The air turned instantly warmer, moister, becoming that of a rain forest. He halfway expected to hear parrots and monkeys overhead, but didn't.

Instead, he heard a crackle of brush up ahead.

Adrenaline sizzled and he went on alert. Had Iago returned? He reached for his armband, but didn't hit the panic button. After a moment, his hand fell away as a simple, gut-deep urge swept through him: *Kill the enemy.* It was more impulse than words, an imperative that came with the thought of the green-eyed *ajaw-makol.* But on another level, something inside him said, *Search. Search and find. Complete. Up ahead.*

Lowering his head and baring his teeth, Sven stalked stiff-legged through the cacao grove. Something cracked behind him and he whipped around with a growl, but there was nothing there. Then a low whine came from the bushes nearby, and he froze in place, held motionless while something inside him crowed: *Found!*

As he stood, staring, a huge dog slunk out from between two trees.

Not a dog, he realized. A coyote. This was the big sucker Dez had seen, the one that had torn a *makol*'s face off, then disappeared. It pricked its ears, sat on its massive haunches, and looked at him, head cocked, as if it were waiting for him to do something. But what?

He moved in, doing his best *Dog Whisperer* impression, and—

"Now!" a voice shouted from behind him.

And all hell broke loose.

Sven howled as shield magic slammed into place surrounding him. A second spell pinned the coyote, which writhed and screamed, snapping at the invisible force. Adrenaline hammered, an atavistic surge that said: *fight, flee, survive!* Then he was suddenly seeing through the coyote's eyes. He smelled the magi, sensed their power, fought for freedom. He snarled and snapped, struggling to escape. *Escape!*

Terror lashed through him as big, hulking shadows drew close and unintelligible voices yammered orders. Then a noose dropped around his neck, and was cranked tight from the far end of a long pole. He gagged and clawed at it, trying to find words, magic, logic, anything. Something stung his thigh, bringing warm lassitude.

Then darkness.

For the next immeasurable period—maybe hours, maybe days—Sven faded in and out, aware of being strapped down, the sting of palm cuts, the shadows bending over him as he writhed and howled, his system hammering with the fear of being trapped. Then another sting would send him under. As he faded he heard them talking. Sometimes he understood the words. Other times he didn't.

". . . halfway bonded to his familiar. Carlos said he never showed any of the usual signs, that he didn't start to suspect it until just . . ."

". . . big son of a bitch. Must've been descended from the coyote bloodline's breeding stock. We thought they all died in the massacre, but I guess a few made it out. This one must've come looking for him, probably bit him to start the bonding . . ."

". . . a tricky one. Try it again, this time with . . ."

". . . much tranq can we keep on board without risking one or both of them? I don't want to . . ."

". . . think we have it this time. Everybody link up."

He felt hands take his, felt healing warmth spread through him like sunlight. Felt something shift inside him, realigning and forming new connections, blocking others. Something stung his forearm.

Then, finally, the clouds lifted from his brain. He blinked, surprised to find himself staring at the sky, which was reddish with dawn. *Skylight*, his brain supplied, the word feeling slightly foreign, like he was re-learning his native language.

Details came next: He was in the sacred chamber at the center of the mansion. And unless he was way off, he was strapped to the *chac-mool* like a damned sacrifice. Which was probably what he deserved, given what he'd been up to over the past few months. He hadn't even been aware of sneaking out at night, but that was what he had been doing—sleepwalking, trying to tame the big coyote's feral ass using tips from reality TV. What the hell had he been thinking?

He hadn't been, at least not the way he normally did. And now he knew why. *Familiar.* The word whispered through him, reminding him of the flashes, the snatches of conversation. Yeah, that played. The coyotes were one of the few bloodlines that could bond directly with their totem animals, the magic offered to a select few who were trained from birth to handle the blood-bound connection. He remembered Carlos trying to get him to help train a litter of ranch dogs, remembered the *winikin*'s quiet disappointment that Sven preferred dogfish over actual dogs. But now . . .

Now, everything was different.

He could tell simply by stretching his senses that the coyote lay nearby with its head in its paws, thinking that one of the humans had smelly feet, and food would be good soon. Sven could feel its light mental touch almost as an extension of his own mind, its thoughts shifted toward human patterns now, where before the connection had skewed his mental patterns toward canine: feral, untrusting, and reactive.

"He's awake," Jade said. Her face swam into view from beyond his right shoulder. "Hey there. How are you feeling?"

He woofed at her. Then he grinned through his stiff-feeling face at her look of absolute horror. "Sorry," he said, voice rough from disuse. "I couldn't help it."

"Ohh," she growled, flushing. "I could just . . . Urgh!" She stalked off.

"A little help with the straps, here? I promise I won't bite. And I've had my shots. At least I think I have."

"I'd say we should leave you here," Lucius said, hobbling into view on a single crutch, which he balanced on as he went to work on the straps that held Sven down on the altar. "But you'd just have your furry friend chew you out, right?" His expression said that he was asking about more than just a little jaw power.

"Yeah. I get what happened. I feel like an idiot for not seeing it sooner."

"You weren't yourself. You were sharing the coyote's perceptions and instincts, and those instincts said to stay the hell out of sight. Now that you're in control of the bond, it should work the other way around."

"You mean I won't wake up trying to lick my own balls anymore?" But where before the jokes had been a natural part of his hang-loose flow, now they felt forced.

"Here. Let's get you up."

Most of the other magi were in the sacred chamber, watching him as he sat up and let his legs dangle over the edge of the altar. Carlos wasn't there, though, which brought a thump of disappointment. Making himself ignore the feeling of being a damned zoo exhibit, he rubbed his chest where he had bruised himself struggling against his bonds, then his wrists, where the ties had chafed. He glanced at the red marks. Then he stopped and took a second, longer look. The warrior's mark and the translocator's talent glyph that meant he could move small things from point A to point B with his mind looked the same as before. But his bloodline mark was different now: it was enclosed in a circle with two domino-type dots in the upper right, indicating the number "two."

He was twice a coyote. Once for himself, once for the creature that was now inextricably linked to him.

He tuned in on the animal's low-grade thought stream, something about jackrabbits, smelly feet, and the coyote's contentment at having finally soldered the necessary connection with its Man. Beneath that was a solid, ineffable core of determination: the coyote would kill for its Man, die for him. It would be his weapon, his companion, his eyes and ears.

And this was going to take some serious getting used to.

Picking up on his sudden emotional surge, the coyote lifted its head and whined softly.

"Sorry, Mac," he said. "I didn't know what the hell was going on. I wish for both our sakes I had caught on quicker."

"Mac." Lucius nodded. "From *chaamac*. Coyote. Good name."

"Actually, I was going for the *CSI: New York* character. It's got Gary Sinese's eyes."

Michael snorted, but then did a double take. "You know what? You're right. Weird."

Sven pushed himself off the altar and stood, feeling far more balanced than he would have expected. "Mac isn't the only one I owe an apology to. I owe all of you one, and to the *winikin* and whoever I'm missing. I knew something wasn't right, but I didn't deal with it. I just . . . I don't know. Did an ostrich." He inhaled deeply, feeling the blood in his veins, the magic at his fingertips. "But that's over, starting right now. I feel clearer and stronger than I have in . . . hell. Months. Years."

Maybe ever. Had he been seeking his familiar all this time? He thought he might have been, because he felt suddenly centered and strong. He had a feeling he wouldn't have any more problems targeting his translocations, no more wet-firecracker fireballs, no more questioning whether he was really a warrior or not. Now, there wasn't a shred of doubt in his mind that he could—and would—kick some major ass. He could feel the latent power stirring in his blood, so much stronger than ever before.

Mac got up and heeled up against his side, Sinese eyes hard and businesslike. Sven dropped a hand to the top of his familiar's head, felt the stiff, bristly fur, and the click of connection that said: *finally*. And he looked at Strike. "Send me south, to the latest village that was hit. Maybe we'll be able to find something the rest of you missed."

It was time for him to stop fucking around and get to work.

# CHAPTER FIFTEEN

December 18
Solstice minus three days

By day three of Reese's magic-accelerated convalescence, she wanted to be free from the fuzzy bubble of lassitude that had lingered in the wake of the *makol* bite, out of her suite, and far away from Dez.

It shouldn't have been easy to live with him. They had spent five years together, more than ten apart, and they had become completely new people during that decade. But somehow none of that had mattered the first morning, when she had woken up beside him and felt his heartbeat as her own. And it hadn't mattered over the following three days, as he calmly but firmly refused to be fired as her nurse, remaining immovable as granite when she tried to get him to leave her alone to be her cranky bitch self—she didn't do sick well—in peace. Instead, he had stayed with her, hung out with her, and brought her revoltingly balanced meals, each time holding her dessert hostage until she had eaten what he considered an acceptable amount of the salad, stir fry, or whatever.

The food wasn't bad—quite the opposite, in fact—but the principle of it galled her. She was a grown-up. She would eat her damned dessert first if she wanted to. Yet even that pique had a hard time holding out against him as the first day turned into the second, then the third, and she was forced to admit, inwardly at least, that it wasn't so much about the past anymore, not really. She liked the man he was today. More, she was coming to trust him, because her gut said he was what she saw in front of her. He was solid and real. More, he was powerful, yet he was willing to be part of the team rather than its leader. A new man, just as Strike had called him.

During the day, he mostly acted as her data-crunching assistant, making library runs, phone calls, and whatever else she needed. There was still a hard edge in the "fuck the world, I'll do it my way" attitude he brought to every task, and the way his voice lowered an octave when her contacts gave him static. But then each night he lay beside her, holding her hand and channeling his warmth into her, healing her. Caring for her.

Something had changed between them since the *makol* attack, as if the blood-link he'd used to save her had connected them more permanently. She saw it in his eyes, felt it in the way the way the air sparked when they were near each other. Yet although they slept together each night, they hadn't even kissed . . . which had her alternating between frustration and relief. Part of it was her injuries, she knew. But as the days passed and she caught a heated glance with no follow-up, or found herself reaching out to him but pulling back before she made contact, she realized it was more than that. It was . . . everything.

Before that long-ago night in the storm, when she had been nineteen and love blind, she had resented the way he kept telling her to wait until they had a better place, better jobs, assured safety. Back then she had believed utterly that if he had wanted her—really wanted her—he would've taken her, no matter what. Now, though, she was starting to see his side. Because how could she and Dez devote time and energy to each other when they needed to be focusing on finding the fifth artifact and the location where the weapon was to be detonated? The Nightkeepers' mission was too important.

*You're rationalizing. He'd go for it if he really wanted to, and so would you. Which means you don't really trust him yet . . . and something's holding him back.*

"Shit," she muttered under her breath, and made herself get back to work, hammering away at her laptop. Dez was down south for a few hours, seeing if he could pick up a faint trail that Sven's coyote had found and then lost. "It might be something," he had said, "might be nothing." But Strike had figured it was worth checking out, because they were low on leads and running out of time. Meanwhile, she was working her ass off on locating the fifth artifact or, failing that, some clue to where Iago might have stashed Keban, the artifacts, and the *makol* army. "Come on," she urged under her breath as she scanned down the e-mail responses she'd gotten to her various queries. "Give me something here. We need a damned break."

Her heart gave a little shimmy when she saw a familiar e-mail address with the Denver PD's tag. She hesitated for a long moment before clicking it open and reading the message. Then she reread it, heart sinking because it was a break, all right, but not a good one: Iago had the fifth artifact.

"Damn, damn, damn." She hit up Dez's cell with a text: *Two-headed snake staff stolen from private collection three hours ago. All info is being suppressed in media, but the file is waiting for me in Denver.*

That was the small bright spot in what was otherwise shitty news: She had an excuse to get out of her suite and back into the field, because her PD contact had insisted that she pick up the file in person. She thought that the familiar sights and sounds of uptown would be a welcome change, for a few hours, at least. And it would give her a break from Dez, a chance to clear her head.

Or so she thought, until ten minutes after she sent the text when he strode into her suite. They were arguing by the eleven-minute mark, when he announced that he was going with her.

"What part of 'familiar face' and 'parole violation' are you not getting?" She glared at him, mentally calling him six kinds of stubborn. "You should stay the hell out of the city."

"And you should stay the hell in bed." He glared

back, standing too close, wearing desert-camo pants and a tight brown shirt. Among the magi, brown was the color of penitence. He had told her that he wore it as a reminder to stay humble, be a good soldier, follow orders. Apparently that didn't apply when she was the one giving the orders.

"I told you," she said through gritted teeth, "Lucchesi will only give me the file in person." *Let me go. I need the space.*

"And Lucchesi is . . . ?"

"Fifty-something and happily married. I've consulted on a few of his cases, made some suggestions." *No, he's not the guy. And what do you care, anyway?*

"You could get the report through other channels."

"Not this fast." *I know how to do my damn job.*

His eyes flared, warning that his temper was doing a not-very-slow burn. "Iago has to know who you are by now. You're not safe out there on your own."

"I'll take Michael. He scary enough for you?"

"We go together, or you don't go."

"You don't—" She bit off the snap. "Look. I get that you're worried about me. I even like it a little. But only a little." She indicated with her thumb and forefinger. "A *very* little."

He caught her hand, held it. "Reese, please. Be reasonable."

She damned the tingles, snatched her hand back. "I am. Eminently. But since you don't seem able to comprehend that having your parole-jumping ass with me in Denver would be a far bigger risk than me going with a death-wielder with a clean record, how about we get a royal ruling on it?" He was oath bound to follow Strike's orders, right?

Dez's teeth flashed. "Deal."

Three hours later, she was gritting her jaw as she waited in the great room for her traveling companion-slash-bodyguard. And she was cursing herself for having forgotten that the Nightkeepers were, at their hearts, incorrigible matchmakers. Hell, Strike had even warned her of it himself. "Shit," she muttered, disgusted.

But that wasn't what had her crossing to the main kitchen to filch one of Sasha's killer brownies for a much-needed chocolate hit. No, that would be the fact that she and Dez were headed back to Denver . . . and Luc wanted to meet in the burned-out shell of an old and familiar haunt.

*Warehouse Seventeen*
*Denver*

In some ways, Seventeen looked better than Reese remembered, in other ways worse. Structurally, it seemed pretty sound; the charred mess didn't seem ready to collapse on her and Dez as they loosened a couple of sheets of plywood and slipped inside, avoiding their old routes by unspoken consent. As far as the rest of it went, though . . . the place was an echoing ghost of its former self.

With the main gang focus shifting northward and some state money up for grabs, an investment group had started reclaiming the warehouses a few years ago. The debris had been cleared, along with the fire-damaged catwalks, lofts, and other inner structures; the roof and walls had been reinforced with thick steel columns and replacement panels; and a premature stab had been made at repainting. Then the economic crash had taken the investors and grant money down with it and the project had been abandoned, leaving Seventeen to sit empty and echoing, the hopeful paint job fading from whitewash to a dingy, graffiti-splashed yellow.

As Strike *whoomped* back to Skywatch and she and Dez headed across the echoing space, aiming for the eastern entrance where she had arranged to meet Luc, Dez looked around at the destruction. "Guess we can add this place to the long list of things I fucked up back then. Guess Rabbit and I have more in common than I'd like to think."

It took her a few seconds. Then her eyes widened. "You set the fire? Seriously?"

"Not on purpose." He slanted her a look. "It happened the day I jumped bail."

"The day . . ." She trailed off as the pattern started shifting into place. Before, she hadn't wanted to look too hard at that part of her life. Now, she let herself remember.

She had been living in LA, doing the bounty hunting thing she had fallen into after failing to make it in the cube farm corporate world, and then washing out of the police academy with high marks on everything, including insubordination. She had gotten word that the VWs were gunning for Dez back in Denver, but her old task force buddies had a plan. They had almost everything they needed to do a full-fledged crackdown on the old neighborhood . . . and they would trade Dez's safety for her getting them the last few pieces of the bigger puzzle.

She had done it, of course. He had saved her life, so she saved his, albeit in her own way. Unfortunately, a shark of a lawyer had wrangled Dez out on bail, laying him open once more to the VWs. Knowing that the only way to keep him alive would be to put him in a cage while the task force took out his enemies, she had flown back to hunt him down and drag his ass back to jail. At the time it had seemed sadly fitting that Seventeen had burned down the same night she got back into the city. Now, knowing what she did about the magi, she did the math. It had been the first day of summer. The solstice.

She stopped dead and stared at him. "That was the day the barrier reawakened. The day Strike figured out he was a teleporter and the end-time countdown was back on."

He nodded. "Yeah. I had been feeling progressively shittier and shittier all day, and holed up here like some wounded animal waiting to die. A couple of VWs found me, started working me over, and I snapped. Between that and the fact that I had the star demon in my pocket, like always, I jacked in automatically, got my bloodline and talent marks, and grabbed right back on to the lightning magic. I blasted the bastards off me, hit the wiring, and the rest is history."

So much of it was history, she thought. The past

suddenly crowded close, making her feel hemmed in. Yet at the same time, the warehouse that had once been their world was now alien and unfamiliar. More, *she* felt alien and unfamiliar in her black leather jacket, combat pants and boots, with a blue-green shirt that she had worn to put a splash of color into an image that had looked hollow-eyed and bleached in the mirror. Physically she was okay, not as weak as she would have expected given how sick the *makol* bite had made her. But she was far from being herself.

Then again, did she even know who that was anymore? She didn't want to go back to being the woman who had left Denver two weeks ago. She didn't want to be her dumb-assed nineteen-year-old self, either, or even the bounty hunter. She liked the work she was doing for the Nightkeepers—it was challenging, different, exciting, and, yes, she was helping save the world. Or trying to, anyway. The *makol* bite had been a sobering reminder of her mortality, but she'd never shied away from danger. Just the opposite, in fact. But although she wanted to be part of the Nightkeepers' war, she wasn't sure Skywatch was for her. Or, rather, she wasn't sure she could stay there with Dez if she wasn't really *with* him.

She didn't know quite who or what she wanted to be, or what she wanted to have happen next, leaving her feeling off balance as she and Dez crossed the echoing warehouse, automatically avoiding certain areas without speaking. She couldn't stop herself from glancing at the far end of the building, though, or the place where a set of catwalks had once led to a series of tunnels. And when she glanced back at Dez, he wouldn't meet her eyes.

Maybe the past wasn't so far gone, after all.

When they reached the eastern entrance, he checked out the short hallway that led from the outer door and past a trio of offices before opening into the main warehouse. "It's clear," he reported.

"You should hide in one of the offices. Luc transferred in a few years ago, but that doesn't mean he won't recognize you."

He grinned wryly. "And even if he doesn't, I'm not exactly the kind of guy who gives a cop warm, fuzzy feelings."

Although he wasn't fully geared out in autopistols and extra ammo, he looked deadly enough in camo and boots, with a double layer of thermal shirts and a thin black jacket zipped over the top, the collar turned up to his jaw. They had argued over weapons—she was meeting with a friend, after all, and he had his magic on the off chance that any *makol* showed up. Still, she'd bet money that he had his knife on him somewhere, probably his .44 as well.

He cocked his head in the direction of the outer door. "Showtime." Then he melted into the nearest office, becoming part of the shadows.

Moments later, she heard footsteps approaching.

She turned toward the door as it swung open, spilling pale winter light into the entryway and silhouetting her police contact. She started toward him, hand outstretched, "Luc, it's good to—"

She broke off as she realized two things simultaneously: One, it wasn't Luc. And two, she was in serious trouble.

*Oh. Shit.*

There had been no warning from her instincts, no gut quiver, no nothing, leaving her caught flat-footed as a tall, distinguished man with dark hair and a frost of silver at his temples stepped into the light, carrying a neat manila file folder. He wore a familiar herringbone wool coat over a cool gray suit that made his eyes look very blue. And the Tweety Bird tie clip she had bought him on a whim, trying to remind him to lighten up.

Her mouth went dust dry, her voice to a weak thread. "Fallon."

"Reese." His eyes searched her face. "Sorry for the bait-and-switch. I didn't think you would meet me."

"I . . ." She trailed off, because he was right. She wouldn't have met with him, at least not with Dez standing right there, unaware that the ambitious young detective who had recruited them once upon a time was now an established high-ranker, dabbling in politics. And that he had been, for the past few years, her sometimes lover.

Her pulse hammered; her brain raced. If she could have grabbed the file folder and fled, she would have. But Fallon deserved better. He always had.

"I needed to see you," he said, voice rough. "And to ask you to reconsider. You don't want to marry me, I get that. But that doesn't have to be the end of things."

Reese heard a sharp noise from the office and felt pain pierce in the vicinity of her heart. "Yes, it does," she said, making herself focus on the man in front of her rather than the one hiding in the shadows. "It's time. Me moving back here didn't change the fact that we're in two totally different places. You're ready to settle down . . ."

"And you're not," Fallon finished for her. "I know. I just thought . . . well, I don't know what I thought. Can't we forget about that and go back to the way we were?"

She doubted she would ever forget that night: fancy dinner out, candlelight, wine, violins, and a handsome cop with his sights set higher, asking her to be part of his life, part of making the city a better place. The proposal had been perfect, the ring a gorgeous diamond set in pale yellow gold. And she had felt like she was suffocating. "I should've ended things a long time ago," she said softly, "so you could've gone out and found someone who can give you what you want."

"*You're* what I want." He closed the distance between them, started to reach for her, then hesitated as if seeing her—really *seeing* her—for the first time: no makeup, a few pounds lighter, and back in black. Shaking his head as if telling himself to ignore the changes, he said, "I'll stop pushing. Whatever you want, just tell me. No more pressure. I promise."

"You'd be miserable."

He gave a sharp bark of laughter. "Like I'm not now?"

"We need a clean break, Fallon. It's time. We can't do this anymore."

He went very still, tensing like a predator, suddenly

all cop. "*We*," he repeated. "What happened to 'this is all for your sake, Fallon'?"

Guilt kicked. "Let it go. Please."

"This isn't really about a job in New Mexico, is it? All that stuff about watching the desert sunsets and searching your soul was all bullshit." He crowded her, face etched with raw pain and growing anger. "You met someone, didn't you? Someone who swept you off your damn feet the way I never could."

Her pulse thudded in her ears but she kept her voice even. "The job is real, and it's important to me."

"*I* was important to you." He grabbed her wrist. "Who—"

Pain exploded as his fingers put pressure right on the half-healed *makol* bite, obliterating the rest of his question and nearly driving her to her knees. She gasped and sagged, scrabbling against his grip. He let go the second he realized she was hurting, but it was already too late.

A dark shadow moved up behind him. A .44 appeared at his temple. And a pissed-off voice grated, "Back off. Right fucking now."

# CHAPTER SIXTEEN

Dez didn't look at Reese; he couldn't, not now when he couldn't get hold of his own thoughts. Fallon was one of the good guys, damn it. And even through the haze of anger clouding Dez's vision—at Fallon for going there, at Reese for not telling him—there was no question that the other man loved her. It was in his eyes, in his voice. He would protect her, care for her. And he had proposed. Probably even got down on one knee and did it right.

*She turned him down*, he thought. *Hell, she broke up with him.* But that didn't help, because he knew damn well the breakup had happened because of the night he and Reese had spent together. That was the way her brain worked.

"You don't want to do this," Fallon said. "I'm sure she told you I'm a cop."

He hadn't recognized Dez's voice. That gave him the option of backing off, disappearing again, not bringing it all out in the open, which was what Reese's eyes silently begged him to do. Hell, he could drop the cop with a sleep spell and they would be out of there with the folder before the guy woke up. No harm, no foul. If Dez were truly the better man he was trying to be, he would do exactly that, and maybe even find a way to point her back in Fallon's direction.

*Back off*, he told himself, just as he had told Fallon moments earlier. But he didn't. He couldn't. Not anymore.

The past week had reminded him how it had felt to be the stupid kid who hadn't fully realized what he'd gained the day he'd snatched her away from Hood. The guy he had been before the star demon's corruption. More, he had gotten to know the woman she had become, who wasn't the same as she would have been if they had stayed together. This Reese was quick-tongued and acerbic at times, but he liked that edge, just as he liked her self-sufficiency and the way she made him feel stronger just by *being* there. Before, he had waited too long and missed his chance. This time, he could very well lose her if the shit hit the fan and the artifacts came on line, unleashing the curse of the serpent bloodline. But if that happened, he wanted her to know what she was walking out on. He wanted both of them to know.

So instead of backing off and disappearing, he gave Fallon a briskly professional pat, relieved him of his piece, emptied it, and put it back. "That'll save you the paperwork of reporting it gone."

Then, still keeping his .44 trained on the other man's melon, Dez stepped around him, into the light, and put himself right beside Reese. To his surprise, his heart thudded in his chest, making the empty spots feel full. He saw in the widening of her eyes and the flush that touched her cheeks that she knew that he was staking his claim. And if that made him a selfish bastard, so be it. Maybe he wasn't as cured as he wanted to think.

They would hash that out later, though. Right now, they had a cop to deal with.

Fallon's face—more lined than before, but still bull-tough and square-jawed—went utterly blank for a two-count. Then it flooded with fury. *"Mendez."* Coming out of his mouth, it sounded like "motherfucker," but his eyes hollowed out like he was looking at a ghost. Which in a way, he was. Then his face set in deep lines as he added it up. His voice broke on aching disappointment when he said, "Oh, Reese."

She flinched but held her ground. Dez could only guess how much that cost her. She wouldn't have slept with Fallon if she didn't care for him, and she wouldn't enjoy hurting him now. Hell, Dez wasn't getting any satisfaction out of the agony in the other man's eyes. He could relate too damn well.

"I'm sorry," she began. "I didn't mean for any of this to happen. I tried to be what I thought you wanted—what *I* thought I wanted, but I just couldn't do it." She stroked a hand down the sleeve of her leather, over her injured wrist. "This is who I am."

Breathing hard, hands fisted at his sides, Fallon grated, "What about him? How long have you been—" He broke off, closing his eyes briefly in pain. "How long?"

"This isn't really about him."

"Fuck that."

"I never lied about my feelings, Fallon."

His ribs heaved. "I thought you would come around, that you would figure out that it's better to be with a good guy who loves you than an asshole who'll break your heart, probably get you killed." Transferring his glare to Dez, he grated, "Pretty brave with that gun, aren't you? How about you put it down and we'll see who's tougher?"

"I don't want to hurt you."

Fallon just sneered. "Don't want to go back in, you mean. Parole violation, weapons charges, I wonder what else you've been up to for the past year, and whether she knows all of it."

Guilt pinched. "She knows I'm not the same guy I used to be."

The detective snorted. "Found God in solitary, did you? Think He redeemed you?"

"Something like that."

"You'll have plenty of time to work on that once you're back inside."

Dez merely lifted the .44. "I'm the one with the gun here. And Reese is leaving with me." Then he just waited, knowing the other man would work the logic to its conclusion: If Fallon organized a manhunt, even an off-the-books, semi-quiet one, Reese would get caught up in the net for aiding and abetting. When he saw the knowledge hit, he felt a pang of sympathy at the hollow resignation in the other man's face. "Let her go, Fallon," he said softly. "She's made her choice."

Reese shot him a look at that one, but didn't argue

the point because she *had* made her choice—just not the one Fallon was assuming. She had chosen freedom over restraints, adventure over a sure thing.

Fallon's eyes cooled to ice as he looked from Reese to Dez and back. Then he gave a bad-tempered "fuck it" kind of a shrug, and grated, "Doesn't matter to me what a pair of ghosts does. I didn't see anything in here, didn't hear anything, just had a shitty lunch break in a crappy warehouse, waiting for a weasel who didn't show."

Then he spun on his heel, and headed out. He stiff-armed the door, paused, and chucked the file folder back at them with an angry swipe. The papers scattered and fluttered to the hallway floor, where they swirled in the current as the door slammed shut. They heard his footsteps, the bang of a car door, the rev of an engine, the chirp of tires . . . and then silence.

She inhaled a small sob, bowed her head and pressed her fingertips to her eyelids.

He lifted a hand. "Reese."

"Don't," she said. "Just . . . don't. Not right now. Just get us out of here, okay?"

*Skywatch*

The moment they were boots-down in the compound, Strike asked Reese and Dez to do a quick debrief-and-discuss.

Dez glanced at her. "Okay with you?"

"Yeah." She avoided his eyes, though. She could talk about the file Fallon had given them—thrown at her, really—but she wasn't ready to deal with the rest of it. Fallon had been a part of her life for a long time and she hated knowing that she had hurt him so deeply, hated knowing what he must think of her now. Part of her wished like poison that Dez had stayed the hell out of sight. But another part of her, one she wasn't at all proud of, had liked that he had broken cover for her, stood beside her. And that part of her wondered what it meant. It had felt like a signal, but of what? She didn't know, didn't dare guess, which meant that right now it was easier to focus on the job. It was also necessary, because as she looked around the room, it struck her that of the dozen people scattered around the great room, she and Dez were among the most thinly armed. Even Shandi, Jade's ultra-reserved *winikin*, was packing heat. Skywatch didn't feel inviolate anymore, Iago had all five of the artifacts, and they were three days away from the solstice.

"Okay, gang," Strike said, looking tired and drawn as he called the meeting to order. "Reese, you want to lead us off?"

Feeling strangely numb, like this was all happening to someone else, she went through the police report Fallon had brought her, which described a burglary that had turned into a double homicide when the homeowners had caught the thieves in the act. The victims had died from multiple stab wounds, there was no indication of how the killers had gotten in or out, and the only thing that appeared to be missing was a pale green jade staff that had strange indentations along its length and snake heads carved at either end.

*Serpents again*, she thought, glancing at the insurance photo, then passing it around.

Next, Lucius took over for a quick run-through of the sacred Aztec sites that were strong possibilities for either Iago's hiding spot or his next target. "Tomorrow, Strike is going to bounce a team—"

"Actually"—the king interrupted—"I'm going to have Rabbit, Myrinne, and Sven go check out the sites. They're already down south to." He glanced at Leah. "It'll work better that way."

A few knowing looks got traded, but nobody said a word. When Reese frowned in confusion, Jade leaned over and whispered, "Anna is . . . well, she's fading."

"Oh, no." The painful scene with Fallon receded slightly and she rubbed her chest, heart hurting for Strike and Sasha, who were losing their big sister, and for Lucius, who was losing his oldest friend and mentor. The others were losing a friend and teammate, the world its last living *itza'at* seer and the third Triad mage. And Anna . . . poor Anna. Reese had watched Lucius sit with her one day, going through her extensive collection of fake antiquities, talking about the ones they had found together at this market or that dealer's shop. That had cracked her heart. Seeing Strike just beyond the doorway with tears in his eyes had broken it.

*It's not fair*, Reese thought, though she knew firsthand that life wasn't fair. If it were, she would have been able to love Fallon, who had wanted to give her the stability she should have craved. Instead, like her chocolate obsession, the thing she wanted most wasn't good for her.

She had a feeling that the unfairness of Anna's condition went beyond "life ain't fair," though. The Nightkeepers—Strike, especially—couldn't catch a freaking break. They fought like hell for every gain, and too often things went the other way, seemingly in violation of the Doctrine of Balance that said everything would even out over the long run. It had taken some pushing and prodding, but she had finally gotten Lucius to admit that he suspected the bad luck was cosmic payback—whether from the gods or the Doctrine of Balance itself—for Strike having broken the thirteenth prophecy by refusing to sacrifice Leah. The magi supported him absolutely . . . but the shadow remained.

Suddenly exhausted, she only half listened as Lucius continued down the list of possible sites for the weapon's activation, focusing on serpent-related ruins down south, within the Mayan territories. And when the meeting broke up soon after, she was grateful to escape to her suite. She had been in there only a moment, though, when there was a quiet knock at her door.

It wasn't syncopated, wasn't the familiar "all's clear," but she knew it was him. She almost wimped out and pretended she wasn't there, but he would know. And she didn't want weakness to make her into a liar. So she opened the door.

He stood in the hallway with his shoulders hunched and his fists jammed in his pockets, looking like he'd been caught doing something wrong, and for a second reminding her so strongly of his teenaged self that her throat closed, trapping her breath in her lungs. Then he straightened, becoming once again the man he'd grown into, the sleek, sexy, powerful mage she didn't quite know how to handle. Which didn't make breathing any easier, but it did put her on her guard. Especially given that he was looking at her now like he had back in the warehouse.

"What do you want?" she asked, damning her voice for coming out breathy rather than tough.

He glanced away, then back at her. "Fallon's a better man than I am."

It took her a moment to process, another for anger to kindle. "Don't even think of trying to punt me back to Denver under his protection. I can make my own damn decisions about men, and I can take care of myself."

"I know you can. And that's not what I meant." He reached out, took her hand, and slid her sleeve up, over the bandage. The skin around it was almost back to its normal color. "Anna's dying."

And she had nearly died, too, his gesture said. Her heart gave a sharp *thudda-thudda* at his touch. "What does that have to do with Fallon?"

"Because death is guaranteed. Life isn't. And Fallon put himself out there, even knowing he was going to get shot down." He paused, then let go of her hand. Instead of moving away from her, though, he stepped closer, and lifted both hands to grab on to the lapels of her new leather. "I've never done that."

Feeling like she was on the cusp of the dream when she had least expected to find herself there, she nodded. "Not with me, anyway."

"Not with anyone. I don't know. Maybe part of me thought Keban was right when he said nobody would want me for anything other than my strength. Or maybe it was the other way around. Maybe I was so full of myself I thought I didn't need to work for it."

"I can see how you would think that—the second part, I mean," Reese said, not wanting to look too hard at the first part because she knew it would wipe out what little common sense and self-restraint she had left. She could picture all too well Dez-the-child hearing that, believing it.

His mouth quirked. "Because I was full of myself in general?"

"No. Because I would have done anything for you back then."

He went still. "And now?"

She hesitated. "I'm confused. Who are you, really? What do you want from me? And for gods' sake, what are you hiding? There's something. I can see it in your eyes, or maybe it's that I'm feeling it in whatever link we've got going."

He went very still. "You can sense the blood-bond?"

"That's not an answer."

"You're right, and this isn't going to be one, either. But I'm asking you to hear me out." His tone was serious, his eyes intense.

Her stomach fluttered. Or was that her instincts? She could never tell when it came to him. But she nodded shallowly. "Go ahead."

"When I left Keban I walked away from most of what he taught me. But a few things stuck, mostly about how the members of the serpent bloodline were typically ambitious as hell, borderline arrogant, and tough as nails. Even when I stopped believing in the Nightkeepers, I still knew that fit me. He also said that a serpent male, especially a powerful one, needed to make sure he had everything else straight in his life before he took a mate, because the serpents love obsessively, to the point that for the first while, nothing else exists for them. More, they need to pick a mate who can handle that, who can handle them, and keep them on an even keel."

Which wasn't anything she had expected to hear from him . . . but it explained a few things. She took a deep breath, then let it out on a sigh. "You weren't sure about me."

He rolled his eyes. "Don't be an idiot. I was worried about *me*, not you. Back then, I was having screwy dreams and weird impulses, probably because Keban had unearthed the star demon and was in the area, looking for me. And over the past year—and even the last couple of weeks—I've been trying to figure out how to make damn sure I can control what happens with Keban and the compass artifacts."

Her gut told her that was the absolute and final truth. She nodded slowly. "Okay, I get that. You need space to—"

"Not anymore." His knuckles brushed the sides of her neck. "That's what I've been figuring out over the past few days. It started when you got hurt, which made me wonder what the hell I've been waiting for. And then today, with Fallon . . . that sealed it. Because I'm not going to let myself get outdone by a cop."

He said the last with a faint sneer, which was so perfectly Dez that she felt her lips curve even as her heart beat an unsteady rhythm. "And?"

"You're mine, Reese." His eyes went luminous and his voice dropped to a whisper. "And I'm yours. I always have been, even when I got lost in the darkness."

She couldn't breathe. She couldn't think. All she could do was stare at him and wonder whether she was dreaming. But the throb of her body was very real, as was the tightness in her chest and the hot prickle of tears.

When she didn't answer right away, the fear that entered his eyes was almost tangible. More, it said that this mattered to him, that *she* mattered, more than he'd ever let on before. "Please tell me I haven't missed my shot, that you'll take your chances on a serpent mage whose life seems to be permanently out of control. Because I—"

She cut him off with a kiss. And if the move came partly from her not being ready to hear what she suspected he had been about to say, it quickly became more when Dez's lips slanted across hers. He shifted his grip from her jacket to the back of her neck, and shuddered against her, humming a low, almost awestruck noise at the back of his throat. That soft, needy sound, so very un-Dezlike, left her helpless to do anything but curl her fingers into his shirt and kiss him back with everything that was inside her.

She kissed him with the ache of having lost and found him again, the guilt of wanting him far more than she ever had wanted Fallon, and the fiery desire that came from not knowing what was going to happen tomorrow, next week, next year. Because he was right—they needed to take what they could now, because tomorrow wasn't guaranteed. Anna proved that. The attack inside Skywatch proved it.

Her entire world coalesced to the taste of him, the heat inside his mouth and the way his skin slid against hers. He vibrated with a raw power that fueled the longing that rocketed through her, the sense of *yes, there please, oh, finally*. They twined together, her arms around his neck, his hands at her waist, her shoulders, fisting in her hair as a groan vibrated at the back of his throat. But then she eased the kiss, slowly, softly, and drew away from him far enough that she could look up into his eyes, where she didn't see any secret shadows anymore. Heart shuddering, she reached up to stroke the strong, smooth line of his jaw. And winced when the move tugged at her bandage and the sting of pain echoed through her body to resonate with the other assorted aches and pains.

Catching her hand in his, he pressed his lips to her knuckles. "Weren't you supposed to spend the day in bed?"

Was it only that morning she'd been chafing at being stuck in her suite? That felt like forever ago. "Christ, I'm tired. Physically. Emotionally . . . God. I need some time to process." Slanting him a look, she said, "Your timing blows. You know that, right?"

His lips twitched. "Like I said, I'm through with waiting for the perfect moment." But he stepped away from her and pushed open her door. "Get some rest." He leaned in and gave her a lingering good-night kiss that was soft and sweet, and shifted something in her chest. "I'll see you in the morning. And do me a favor and keep a gun on you."

She pressed her cheek to his and closed her eyes at the grim reminder of the world beyond the two of them. "Count on it." But she appreciated that he was giving her the space she needed, and trusting her to be smart about her safety.

And she appreciated how, when she got out of the shower a half hour later, feeling warm, drowsy, and achy, she found a king-sized sleeve of peanut butter cups sitting just inside the door, like a sacrificial offering from an old friend who knew what she needed, and may finally be ready to give it to her.

It was nearly ten p.m. when Dez headed for the royal wing, but it had taken him some time to come down off the high of having finally made a real and honest move on Reese. She needed to think about things—he got that—but he thought they may finally—*finally*—be on the right track. But, given that, there was something he needed to do.

He tapped on the heavy double doors that led to the opulent royal suite. A moment later, Leah swung open the smaller, normal-sized panel inset into the carvings, but instead of inviting him in, she pointed farther down the hall. "He's sitting with Anna. Said for you to meet him there."

"Thanks."

The royal wing contained the king's huge suite,

along with apartments for the royal *winikin*—empty now that Jox was gone, though still kept exactly how he left it—and several sets of kids' rooms. The door to one of them stood open.

Dez tapped on the frame, got Strike's quiet, "Yep," and went on in.

Anna had taken the suite that she and Strike had shared as kids, though it had been redecorated in an eclectic mix of bright colors and choice pieces from her rogues' gallery of fakes. Strike was in the living room, sitting on a plush love seat with his feet on a circular wooden coffee table that was carved with the calendar round. Anna lay on a sofa nearby, curled on her side, eyes closed, breathing slowly. Her skin was very pale, her dark reddish hair a stark contrast. She could simply have been sleeping, but Dez knew it was much more than that. He had come out of his Triad coma within a couple of weeks. She had awakened the same day, but never came all the way back. And now she was drifting again, losing ground.

"You want to tell me why this is a priority all of a sudden?" Strike asked, setting aside the magazine he had been holding, and rising to his feet. "Or should I take a wild guess that it has something to do with our resident bounty hunter, who looks way more at home in guns and leather than she did in business casual?" A Nightkeeper couldn't take a mate without having sworn to his king.

"That'd be a decent guess." Reese wasn't the whole reason he wanted to take the oath, not even the primary one, but Strike would know the rest of it soon enough. He wanted to tell Reese first, then the others. Tomorrow. He would do it tomorrow.

"Want to take it outside?" Strike asked.

"Probably a good idea." Less messy than sacrificing onto the carpet.

They headed through a pair of sliders to a small patio that was enclosed by a sturdy metal railing. Two chairs and a small table sat off to one side near an unfolded awning. The night air was cool and dry, the stars washed out by the mansion lights, and as Dez faced Strike squarely, he caught a glimmer surrounding the other man—a halo of energy, maybe, or a hint of magic that didn't hit his other senses. He did a double take, but when he looked more closely, it was gone. Maybe hadn't ever been. Pulling his ceremonial blade, he nodded. "I'm ready when you are."

There was no fancy ceremony, no invocation. Strike simply looked him in the eye and said, "Who am I?"

Dez drew his knife blade sharply across his tongue. Pain slapped; blood bloomed salty in his mouth and ran down his chin to drip on the patio stones. Bending, he spat a mouthful of blood at Strike's feet, and said, "You are my king."

He felt the fealty oath take hold, felt the magic of the Manikin scepter—the barrier-bound symbol of the jaguar's rulership—forge a link with his soul, and knew the deed was done. He was bound to Strike, to his king. Gods help them both.

\*   \*   \*

Anna was nowhere. She was everywhere. She was nothing and everything. She hung in the fog of her own mind, lost.

Sometimes she remembered being a teacher, a wife, a normal woman living a normal life. Sometimes she was a visionary, a priestess, a warrior, a child, a mother. Sometimes she was a thousand women at once, living a thousand lifetimes strung together by a thin chain hung with a glowing yellow crystal carved into the shape of a skull. And other times, like now, she was almost herself. Those times, she could open her eyes and see the room around her, could comprehend it as "hers," knew she had been told that someone had repainted it for her, wanting her to feel at home.

But "home," like "hers," was nothing more than a vague concept in the fog, no more real to her than the memory fragments that shot past her mind's eye, glimpses of a thousand lives gone past—here, a baby; there, a lover. Never hers.

She felt a presence nearby, the one that she connected to the concept of "brother." Their shared blood formed a connection that echoed grief and worry into her. She had tried to reach through that connection, tried to latch on to something there that glittered in the fog, but it had slipped away from her time and again. So lately she had stopped trying and simply . . . drifted.

Now, though, she knew she couldn't drift. There was something she needed to do, something she had to say. She fought through the clinging fog, managed to find a body that felt dim and distant—her body. She made it turn to him and say: "He hides in the darkness, but must come into the light to act. Stop him and fulfill the prophecies, or Vucub will reign."

He said her name, reached for her, but she was already gone, slipping back into the fog with only that thin connection remaining. In her mind, though, she whispered: *Brother*.

# CHAPTER SEVENTEEN

December 19
Solstice minus two days

When Reese awoke she lay still for a moment and tracked the lightness in her chest, the sense of anticipation. When was the last time she had felt this way? Had she ever, or was it all sharper and more immediate because each minute, each hour, was more precious than it had been before?

She didn't know, but she knew who and what she wanted. He had said she was it for him, and the reverse applied. As long as they had that going for them, they could figure out the rest of it together, because he was right that there was no such thing as perfect timing, especially for them. She couldn't wait to see him, to talk to him, but her half-formed plan of sharing a quiet breakfast—and maybe more—went off the rails the moment she got out of the shower and found a "meeting in the great room" message waiting for her.

Dez had saved her a seat, but when she shot him a raised eyebrow, he shook his head. "I'm not sure what's going on." He paused and, after a quick glance showed that nobody was paying particular attention to them, lowered his voice. "How'd you sleep?"

"Just fine, thanks," she purred, and had the pleasure of watching his eyes go hot at her tone, and all that it implied.

She didn't get a chance to say more, because Strike came into the room then, looking strung out, and said without preamble: "Last night, Anna came around long enough to say: 'He hides in the darkness, but must come into the light to act. Stop him and fulfill the prophecies, or Vucub will reign.' Then she lapsed fully unconscious."

The warm fizz in Reese's blood flattened out as a murmur of surprise and dismay went around the room. "Oh," she said softly, heart aching.

"Hell," Dez bit out, voice sharp. When she glanced at him, he shook his head. "Poor Anna." But her instincts tugged, because that hadn't sounded like sympathy. Or was she overanalyzing again, looking for reasons not to commit?

She shook her head, trying to dismiss the Fallon-esque logic.

Lucius was talking now, referring to notes written in his crabbed scrawl, which was practically hieroglyphics in its own right. "Breaking down Anna's message, which we have to assume is legit, given her powers, I would say that 'he' refers to Iago. Then the mention of darkness could mean that he's hiding in the dark aspect of the barrier. That would explain why we can't find him on this plane—he's hiding between the planes, at the border of the underworld. He'll have to come out, though, to detonate the compass weapon during the solstice." He paused. "As for Vucub, who is also called Lord Vulture, he's supposed to preside over the twilight that follows the apocalypse, when day and night are no longer separated."

"Like a nuclear winter," Nate said. He glanced sharply at Dez. "The aftermath of the serpents' weapon, maybe?" Without waiting for an answer, he turned back to Lucius. "She mentioned prophecies, plural. Which ones are in play at the moment?"

"I'm working on it, but I—"

Sirens blared, cutting him off. Reese jolted to her feet along with the others, though Michael said, "It's probably just another false alarm."

Then the intercom crackled and Tomas's voice reported: "Long-range cameras show an old pickup truck headed our way. Single occupant, nothing on the magic sensors."

Up until a few days ago, the very rare random stranger who had showed up at the front gate had gotten one or two people responding—*no, we're not hiring; no, this isn't a celebrity retreat; yes, we can hook you up with directions and a couple of gallons of gas.* Now, all of the Nightkeepers, *winikin,* and humans headed out the front door, armed and dangerous. Dez and Reese hit the exit together near the front of the pack and moved out across the front of the mansion, staying off the main walkway, closer to the building where landscaping provided some cover. The other warriors, sorting into their mated pairs, did the same.

Through the wrought-iron gate, Reese saw the pickup—windshield cracked, paint color obscured by dust—roll to a stop. "It doesn't feel right," she murmured.

The truck door swung open and the driver got out of his vehicle—more like collapsed out of it—and went down on his face. He lay in the dirt, motionless.

"The monitors are picking up trace readings of magic," Tomas reported, voice coming from Reese's armband, and those around her. The information argued against this being a lost-in-the-desert thing.

"Everyone shield up," Strike said. "Nate, you man the ward—let us through, but close it after. Michael, once we're out, get a shield around the truck and the guy."

"Stay close," Dez said to Reese. Pulse thudding in her ears, she pulled her .38 and put herself right beside him, angled so his gun hand was free. He cast a crackling lightning shield around the two of them just as Nate dropped the ward magic.

"Go!" someone shouted, and they were hustling out to surround the truck and its driver as the air hummed with additional shield magic. For a second, everything seemed very surreal, like she'd been dropped into a movie—not the filming, but the movie itself, where she was living and breathing action scenes that didn't quite jibe with real life. Then things snapped back into focus as Strike crouched down beside the unconscious man, who was sprawled on his stomach, his hands outstretched toward Skywatch.

The king grabbed the guy by his dirty, torn shirt, and rolled him over. And Reese gaped, blood icing at the sight of a swollen and disfigured face, misaligned jaw . . . and a six-clawed scar slashing across his face.

It was Keban.

"Son of a *bitch*." Dez crossed to the *winikin*, dropped down beside him. There was no danger this time; the bastard was truly out cold. More, he'd had the shit kicked out of him. His wrists and ankles were raw and his forearms scored with deep, weeping burns. His face was gray, his breathing labored and shallow. But when Dez spoke, his eyelids flickered, then cracked, and his pale blue eyes fixed on Dez with dull recognition and more sanity than he had seen there in a long time. Maybe ever.

*Fuck me* was Dez's first thought, followed by *Why now?* Not just because they needed to assume that Iago had thrown the *winikin* at them, but because of how it was going to look if the whole truth came out now. *Our timing really does suck*, he thought, glancing at Reese to find her staring with worried eyes that asked if he was okay. He wasn't, but not for the reasons she thought. When he looked at Keban, he didn't feel his childhood fear, teenaged rage, or the bone-deep hatred of his adult self. He didn't feel pity or grief, either. He felt . . . numb. Because nothing good was going to come of this.

After shooting Reese what he hoped was a reassuring look, he leaned over Keban, aware that Strike and the others had stayed back to let him have first crack.

All except for Sasha, who was crouched down on the *winikin*'s other side, sending healing magic into him. From the looks of him, that was the only thing keeping him conscious.

Leaning in closer, Dez grated, "Did Iago send you?"

The *winikin*'s lower lip was split nearly to his chin. The scab cracked and bled as he said, "Not . . . sent. Escaped. Need to . . . warn you . . ." His head lolled, his muscles going limp as he lapsed closer and closer to unconsciousness.

"Can you bring him back?" he asked Sasha, but she shook her head.

"I'm doing my best, but he's in tough shape. Iago really did a number on him." Her eyes were shadowed and Michael had moved up behind her in support, reminding Dez that she, too, had been Iago's prisoner, and for far longer than the *winikin*.

Keban's lips moved, shaping words without sound. Dez leaned in. "Say that again."

The *winikin* coughed. "He and his army are in a mountain temple that hides in the dark barrier except on the cardinal days." Barely whispering now, he added, "You've got to stop him. He's going to use the serpent staff to make himself king."

Adrenaline hammered through Dez, not just because he'd just been outed, but because if Iago succeeded, they were beyond fucked. "He's not a serpent."

"He is. He's—" His eyes rolled suddenly back and his body shuddered . . . and went still.

"Keban." Dez grabbed him, shook him. "*Keban!*" But the *winikin* was gone, his face lax, the scars pale slashes against gray skin. In death, he looked small, battered, and used up.

"Dez?" Reese's quiet voice brought his head up, but he couldn't read her expression. Wasn't sure he dared. "What's going on? What was he talking about?"

Strike was on one side of her, Leah on the other, with the rest of the magi fanned out on either side, the *winikin* behind them. And suddenly it wasn't about him and Reese being a pair of outsiders who were loners otherwise, but knew they could rely on each other. Now she had some serious backup, and it wasn't coming from him.

Taking a deep breath, he dragged himself to his feet and stood opposite her. But he was talking to all of them when he said, "I want to make two things very clear first. Last night, I swore my fealty to Strike. He is my king, and not only would I never do anything to challenge that, I flipping *can't*." Once in place, the fealty magic wouldn't allow an oath-bound mage to harm the king.

Strike nodded. "That's true. In fact, it was right after he swore his oath that Anna woke up." His eyes narrowed. "I thought you swore the oath for Reese's sake."

"I did." He said it to her, urged her inwardly to believe it, but the wariness was back in her eyes. Risking it, he took her hands, holding them tight as he said, "That's the second thing I need to say—I promise you that everything I've done has been to stop history from repeating itself. I swear it on my soul and my bloodline."

Her lips trembled. "Okay. Now you're scaring me." She didn't pull away . . . but she didn't acknowledge his promise either.

Letting go of her, he jammed his hands in his pockets. When he realized he was unconsciously searching for the star demon, he put his hands behind his back and locked them there. Then, focusing on Strike, he said, "The artifacts, when activated properly, will transfer the Nightkeepers' fealty oaths to the wielder of the serpent staff . . . who must be a member of my bloodline."

"Son. Of. A. Bitch," Strike growled. "You want the fucking throne, Mendez?" Behind him, shock and bitter anger raced through the others.

"I took the oath," he repeated. But that didn't stop several of the faces around him from resetting in the familiar mistrustful lines. He had told himself to expect it, that it wouldn't matter as long as he knew he had done his best to make the right call. But it hurt. And the pain in Reese's eyes nearly did him in.

"You told me it was a weapon." Her face had drained of color and her knuckles were white where she was still gripping her .38.

"I told you that assembling the artifacts would blow things up. It will, just not the way I implied."

Her eyes burned into his. "That's not good enough."

"It gets worse." He took a deep breath. "According to Keban, Iago is—or believes he is—descended from the bloodline. If he manages to activate the staff during the solstice and our fealty oaths transfer to him . . ." The oath couldn't force the magi to act against their natures, but the contradictory impulses could paralyze them, leaving them vulnerable to the *makol*.

"Motherfucker," Strike grated. "If we had been on this from the beginning—"

"I know." But Dez held up a hand. "Let me finish. Then you can decide what to do with me." When the king sent him a clenched-jaw nod, he took a deep breath, locked eyes with Reese, and said, "For years I told myself that Keban was nuts, that he'd brought me up to lead an army that hadn't ever existed . . . but then, during the Triad magic, Anntah said it, too. There's a secret prophecy that's been handed down through certain serpent lineages . . . It says that in the end, the last serpent must kill his rival and take the throne." When the mutters died down, he finished: "Yeah . . . Keban raised me to kill Strike and take over."

"Over my dead body." That came from Leah, but the glares said the others were right there with her. The two royal advisers, Nate and Alexis, looked like they wanted to fly him up into thin-air territory and let him drop.

"I can't kill Strike," he reminded them all. "I took the oath."

"You're a Triad mage," Reese said. "The rules don't necessarily apply to you."

"That one does." He wished she hadn't been the one to bring that up, but at the same time, if she was arguing with him, she hadn't shut down completely. He hoped. "Think about it. I didn't make any move to track down the artifacts until I got Keban's note, and then only to destroy them."

"So you say."

He palmed his knife and held it out. "I'll swear it in blood if you want."

"You'd just tweak the wording." She pushed the stone blade aside and strode past him, headed for the main gate.

Dez started after her, then stopped and looked back, torn. His relationship with the Nightkeepers was crucial . . . but so was what was happening between him and Reese.

"Go on," said Strike. "We need to discuss this anyway." And by "we" he meant "everybody in the compound except you."

Every fiber of Dez's body told him to go after her. But he stood his ground and held his king's eyes. "For the record, the biggest reason I didn't come clean about the serpent staff and the prophecy is because you guys are doing something important here. And I wanted a chance to be part of something good for a change."

Strike's expression didn't change. "Well, I guess you fucked that up."

"Yeah. Guess I did." And, as he turned on his heel and headed after Reese, he hoped to hell he hadn't just destroyed that part of his life, too.

Reese's heart hammered thickly, jamming her throat. She couldn't breathe, couldn't think, didn't *want* to think, because if she did she would have to admit that she had bought into him again. Which hadn't been stupid-brave, it had just been *stupid*. She knew him, knew what he was capable of. And she'd fallen under his spell anyway.

"Reese, damn it!" He caught up with her on the covered pathway leading back into the mansion, grabbed her uninjured arm.

She spun on him, teeth bared, free hand going for her pistol. But then she stopped, refusing to give him the fight he wanted. In a low, measured voice, she said, "Let me go."

"I can't." The two words were stark. His eyes bore into hers. "I'm sorry, Reese. I'm so fucking sorry it happened like this. I was going to tell you this morning, I swear. Hell, I should have told you everything that morning in the hotel, but I knew what you would think, and I wanted us to get to know each other again first."

Her throat closed at the raw regret in his tone, which made her want to think that this, finally, was the truth. *He was going to tell you everything this morning*, her inner nineteen-year-old said, *but he didn't get a chance*. But her older, wiser self knew he'd had plenty of chances. "Let. Me. Go."

He tightened his grip. "No. Not until you've listened for a damn minute."

"That would've worked better last night. Or this morning. Or any other time *before* you got your ass caught out."

"Ever since I woke up from that coma and saw what was going on here at Skywatch, I've been hoping—praying—that it wasn't a real prophecy." He was talking fast now, as if trying to get it all in before she walked away. "The serpent bloodline is full of arrogance and ambition, but not seers. I thought the serpent prophecy might just have been wishful thinking that had morphed into something more than that over time. But once I got Keban's letter and saw the tape from the museum, I realized it might be for real. That's why I took off from Skywatch, and why I kept trying to chase you off."

"So I wouldn't catch on."

"No, damn it, so I would have the room to maneuver without worrying about flattening you in the process." He shook her slightly. "For gods' sake I don't want the damn throne. I've done everything I can think of to keep it from coming down to this. Don't you get it? This isn't what I want."

She twisted free of his grip. "You've made your choices. Now I get to make mine."

His expression tightened. "Before you do, consider this: Anna's prophecy, or vision, or whatever mentioned 'the prophecies,' plural. What do you want to bet that the serpent prophecy is one of the ones she mentioned?"

"So?"

"The team is going to need your help figuring that out, finding Iago's mountain, and a thousand other things between now and the end date."

Until that moment, she hadn't consciously thought about what she was going to do next . . . but she had been headed for the garage. Claustrophobia gnawed at her beneath the too-open desert sky. She wanted to move, keep moving, not let herself get tied down to something that was only going to get worse. She needed some distance, some perspective. *Let Strike and the others deal with this. I'm in way over my head.* She looked past him, unable to meet his eyes, and her gaze was caught by the brass plaque beside the main door. It had been Leah's way of christening Skywatch, which had simply been known as "the training compound" before her arrival. The sign was etched with the image of a world tree, with three words below it: *Fight. Protect. Forgive.* She could do the first two. She wasn't sure about the third.

After a long pause, she said, "What do you want from me, Dez?"

"I'm asking you not to run away again."

Fury flooded her. "You son of a bitch. I've never run away from a fight that was worth fighting." Which was true. By the time she ran away from home, away from him, she had already lost.

"So don't run away from this one. And don't run away from me." He moved in and, when she refused to flinch, touched her cheek. "I've learned my lesson, Reese. I'm not holding off anymore. The situation isn't perfect—in fact, it fucking sucks. But I haven't done anything wrong this time . . . and I'm not backing off."

Son of a bitch. Surprise roared through her at the realization that he actually thought he could play her, that he could—

Kiss her.

He covered her mouth with his before she could brace or defend. His lips were hard, quick and clever; his tongue didn't ask, it demanded. But if he was angry—with the situation, with her—then she was far angrier. Lust and fury mixed and amped, setting her aflame. She told herself to pull away, crack him in the jaw, knee him in the balls, make him pay for making her want to weep, rage, and scream. But the heat flared higher, bringing the crackle of magic. And instead of pulling away, she moved in.

She kissed him back, openmouthed and searching, got a handful of his shirt and pulled him closer. Their lips and tongues clashed, teeth nipped a sting of pain, a taste of blood, dark and inviting.

He broke the kiss, groaned her name, and pressed his forehead to hers. He was breathing hard, his eyes desperate. "Please, don't give up on me, Reese. Not now, when I'm trying to do the right thing." And he meant it, she knew. Problem was, he saw the world through serpent-colored lenses . . . and he could talk himself into almost anything.

She shook her head, pulled away. "I can't do this. I can't go through it all again." And, tears clouding her vision, she did what she had just claimed she never did. She ran.

Dez let her go. He didn't know what else to do, what else to say that would convince her he was telling the truth. *You can't*, a whisper said deep in his soul. *Either she believes in you or she doesn't.* He told himself not to blame her, that he'd given her a thousand reasons not to trust him, and only a few on the other side. He had hoped those few would be enough, though. Maybe not.

"Godsdamn it," he said hollowly as she headed around the corner of the garage. And was gone.

# CHAPTER EIGHTEEN

Reese ran until she couldn't anymore, then walked, pressing the heel of her hand into her cramped side. The winter sun shone down on her, making her light-headed. Or maybe the spins came from the endless expanse of sky above the canyon, which trapped her without walls or promises.

Sure, she could snag one of the Jeeps and start driving, but she would take way too much baggage with her—knowledge of Iago, Anna's warning, the serpent staff, the end-time war, all of it. How could she leave that behind, knowing that she could help? More, how could she abandon this odd group of strangers who had become her friends?

From the day she turned down the Denver cops' offer to relocate her and became an informant instead, refusing to let the Cobras win, she had been trying to make a difference. What was more, she had almost always been part of a team. She had drifted on the outskirts of those teams, it was true—as both a snitch and a bounty hunter—but there had been others around her, people who were also trying to make the world a better place. She had lost that when she went private, with her jobs becoming a one-man show and Fallon easing her out of cop work "for her own good." Stumbling onto the Nightkeepers' world had changed all that, though. She was part of a team here; she could make a difference.

She couldn't walk out on them, on what they were doing. That was a no-brainer. But she could work from anywhere, which meant that the decision to stay wasn't nearly so simple. Not when things had suddenly gotten far too complicated. Even if she stayed, even if she gave Dez the chance he had asked for, on some level she would always be watching him, waiting for him to make a move against Strike. How could she be with him like that? But she didn't think she could stay at Skywatch and not want to be with him, because when he had kissed her just now it had felt like she was his entire focus, like nothing else existed in that moment except the two of them. Finally.

*Damn it, Dez.* How freaking typical of him that when he finally got it, when he finally wanted her so much that he didn't give a crap about anything else, it was in a situation like *this*.

When the trail she'd been stomping along doubled back, she stopped, blinking up at the back wall of the box canyon. She hadn't meant to hike this far, at least not consciously. Now though, something tugged at her, drawing her onward.

Off to one side, the library door stood open, inviting her in. She could go in and begin searching for the mountain temple Keban had mentioned, getting a head start on Jade and Lucius. That was something real and tangible she could do, something that would put off the decisions she needed to make.

It wasn't the library she was being drawn to, though. The world spun gently around her as her feet—which suddenly seemed very far away from her head, as though the top and bottom of her had become disconnected somehow—carried her up the path to the pueblo. On one level, she was getting worried—was she dehydrated, feverish, suffering some new aftereffect of the *makol* bite? The larger part of her, though, was caught up in the sudden swirling conviction that she needed to do this, that it was important. *Come on*, the mud-daubed walls seemed to beckon. *This way.*

She found herself in one of the rooms where opposite walls were carved and painted with the squiggly petroglyph lines that might be water, might be wind, might be serpents. Dizzy and suddenly very tired, though she had really been up for only an hour or so, she put her back to the wall and slid down, so she was sitting with the serpent symbols right above her. The air was warm, the sun a honey-colored reflection from another room, making everything putty colored and soft, as her eyes . . . drifted . . . shut.

She awoke moments later, but she wasn't really awake. She was dreaming. She had to be, because there was a see-through warrior sitting opposite her, beneath the second set of petroglyphs.

He was timeworn, careworn, his face weathered, his skin tough, but even in his translucent state she could see that his hair was dark, with only a few threads gone gray. Wearing a brown robe worked with intricate patterns of beads and feathers, along with flat jade prosthetics designed to exaggerate his nose and sloping forehead, he struck a halfway point between Mayan and Hopi. His eyes were wholly black, with no whites at all, and his forearm was marked with the glyphs of the serpent and the warrior.

A tremor ran through her at the realization that either this was a really vivid dream . . . or she had been shanghaied by one of Dez's ancestors.

*You seek the serpent temple atop Coatepec Mountain.* His lips didn't move; the words sounded in her head.

"Is that its name?" Her voice echoed strangely; her body felt very far away.

*There, he must fulfill the prophecies, or the earth plane will suffer Vucub's twilight.*

Dread and excitement churned through her; an ancestor had come to her, was talking to her. But considering whose ancestor it was, she didn't dare take any of it at face value. Swallowing, she whispered, "Are you Anntah?"

The spirit guide nodded. "I called you here to bring him a message. Tell him that he must do as he was born to do, or the sacrifices that have led to this point are meaningless."

Hearing the familiar words from long ago, she narrowed her eyes as suspicions took root. "I've heard that rhetoric before. You got inside Keban's head, too, didn't you? You told him to sacrifice Joy and save Dez instead. It was you all along."

"Fool!" The word cracked in her brain, bringing a slash of pain. "Do not question me, and do not think that you are protected by destiny. You were never meant for him."

Her poker face failed her abruptly. "That's a lie."

The spirit's lips curved cruelly. "He was meant for the twins of the star bloodline. With them gone, he has no destined mate and must fulfill the prophecies alone. You must give him the message and leave, or you will answer to Lord Vulture when he arrives."

When his presence wavered, she reached for him. "Wait! What—"

His image fractured abruptly, turning into honey-colored shards that spun away from her and disappeared.

She blinked awake to find her body stiff, her heart racing, her stomach knotted with stress and heartache. The afternoon shadows said she'd lost half a day, and her pulse thudded in her ears as she tried to process the new information:

The mountain they were looking for was called Coatepec.

The threat from Lord Vulture was real.

Anntah was an arrogant, opinionated bastard.

And she and Dez weren't destined mates.

That last part shouldn't have bothered her the most, but it did, making her realize that on some level she had wanted to believe the gods were rooting for them to get together, maybe even helping. That would explain how she'd been brought back into his life, and why she sensed the magic, especially his, even though she was only human. But if she believed Anntah—and in this case she unfortunately did—then coincidences really did exist, and it was an accident that they were back in each other's orbits. If they weren't destined mates, then there was no grand plan for them, no cosmic interference, no hope of her ever wearing his *jun tan*. And, she realized with an embarrassed start, she had wanted that too. Somewhere deep down inside, she had let herself imagine them belonging to each other permanently, at long last.

How could she still want that, even knowing that he had hidden the truth from her, over and over again? How could—

"Enough," she said, closing her eyes and digging her fingers into her aching scalp. "You're not nineteen anymore, and the world doesn't begin and end with Mendez." Or, rather, their relationship wasn't central to the end of the world. Mendez himself could very well be, and the Nightkeepers needed to hear what Anntah had told her. Shoving the personal stuff behind a mental tape line that said "do not cross," she got herself up and headed down the trail to the library. Swinging open the door, she called, "I know what mountain we're . . ." She trailed off when she found the cavernous space deserted.

That put a shimmy in her stomach. Not that Jade, Lucius, and Natalie were chained to the place, but under the circumstances they should've been there working . . . Which suggested that something else had happened that took priority.

*Oh, God.* Suddenly aware that she'd been out of the

loop for hours, she reached for her armband, only to realize she wasn't wearing it. How had she forgotten it? *Stupid.* For a second she thought they might be off looking for her, then remembered that Strike could instantly lock on to her with his 'port talent. Or did the pueblo walls mess with that the same way rock and certain forms of magic did? Either way, she needed to get her ass back to the main mansion and see what was up.

She got lucky; there was a Jeep in the parking area, keys in the ignition. She dumped the vehicle near the mansion's front door, noting that Keban's body and pickup were gone. But she was far more concerned with what she was going to find when she pounded along the covered walkway and blew through the main door, her instincts shrilling a warning when she realized that the normal background energy of the place had dimmed. The magi were gone. "Hello?" she called. "Anyone?"

"In here."

She followed Lucius's voice, found him sitting alone at the breakfast bar, crutches leaning nearby. One look at him told Reese that her instincts had been right, as usual—he was waiting for news. "What happened?"

"The monitors caught a huge magic spike at a highland village called Xik. The team zapped down to pick up Rabbit, Myrinne, and Sven and then bounce to Xik, hoping to get there before the *makol* finish harvesting the village."

"Harvesting." Reese shivered at the hideous accuracy of the word. "Did Dez go with them?" she asked, but they both knew she was really asking where he stood with Strike and the others. *Please don't say he's locked in the basement.* She could see the logic, but didn't think she could stand to see him locked up again. The first time, it had been for the best. This time . . . hell, she didn't know what was right anymore.

"He took off right after you did. He said he was going to take care of Keban's body, drove off in the pickup." Lucius's tone was carefully neutral, but she heard the question in it.

"If that was what he said, then that's what he's doing. He's not a liar." Which was true. He omitted. He talked around issues and was occasionally guilty of some whoppers in the flawed-logic department. But he rarely lied outright.

"Without an armband, driving a vehicle that isn't hooked into the Skywatch system?"

"I didn't say he always plays by the rules. Just that he's not a liar." But her heart sank as she saw Lucius's mistrust. Softening her voice, she said, "Look, I'm not saying that his motives are always a hundred percent pure, but I believe him when he says he doesn't want the throne."

"Despite his history?"

"He's not the guy he used to be." It wasn't until she said it aloud that she realized she really believed it, deep down inside. She didn't know whether the change had come from maturity, breaking his bond with the star demon, the Triad magic, or a combination of all those things, but he was truly a different person now. A better man. "He took the fealty oath and swore on his honor." Which in his own way, he held sacred. "I think you should give him a chance."

"Is that what you're going to do?"

"Honestly? I don't know what I'm going to do. This is all so complicated." She paused. "And there's more. I had a vision, just now." His eyes fired as she described the spirit guide and repeated his warnings. Halfway through, Lucius grabbed a napkin and started taking notes; she could see the wheels turning in his brain. Although she was tempted to leave out the parts about her and Dez not being a destined pairing, she told him.

"I'm sorry," he said when she was finished. "That sucks."

She shrugged. "It doesn't change anything." But they both knew it did. "How about Coatepec Mountain? Do you know where it is?"

"Not offhand, but the name is sure as hell familiar." He pushed away from the breakfast bar and grabbed his crutches. "I'm going to collect Natalie and hit the books. You want to come with? We could use you."

"Later."

His eyes sharpened on hers. "You're going after Dez?"

She blew out a breath, then nodded. "He needs to know what Anntah said . . . and that I'm not running away this time. I don't know exactly what's between us at this point, but whatever it is, I'm going to fight for it."

But first, she stopped in her room for her armband and more firepower. As she headed back to the Jeep, her armband staticked and Jade's voice said, "We've got the others and are headed to Xik now. Wish us luck."

*Luck*, Reese thought. But so far, luck had been painfully short for the magi. And time was running out.

*The village of Xik*
*Mayan highlands*

As Strike triggered the 'port, Sven hung on tightly to Mac's ruff with one hand, the joined hands of Jade and Patience with the other, awkwardly touch-linking himself and the coyote into the circle. Mac whined, quivering. He knew what was coming, and wasn't a big fan: 'port magic freaked him out.

*Calm*, Sven sent to the big canine using the simple glyphlike command images that Carlos had been teaching him, and got a surge of deep suspicion in return. He was still getting used to communicating with his familiar, a process that hadn't exactly been easy, given that Mac was opinionated, quick-tempered, and a little on the flighty side. Their partnership was turning out to be less about Sven giving orders and more a constant state of negotiation, which was exhausting. Carlos had assured him that things would get better, but right now, it was all he could do not to lose track of his familiar. He'd learned his lesson, though—the last time Mac took off, it had taken Sven hours to track him down the rain forest based on oh-so-helpful thought-images like: *Leaves, leaves, leaves. Jaguar poop. More leaves.*

"Hang on," Strike said, and then triggered the 'port.

Sven braced himself against the familiar sideways lurch, the whip of gray-green barrier magic flying past, and then the universe reassembled itself around him.

Tightening his grip on Mac's ruff as the big coyote quivered and strained, sending a sudden flow of *Enemy! Run! Bite! Runbiterun!* Sven checked out the scene. And saw that they were too damn late. Again.

The magi had materialized in an open courtyard surrounded by twenty or so thatched-roof huts, several damaged, most untouched. Cooking fires still hissed and popped, one burning a pan of corn to shit, mute testimony that the place had very recently been inhabited. A radio played somewhere, Madonna crooning about being a virgin. And that was it. There was no other sound, no signs of life. The village was empty.

Rabbit cursed, yanked away from the circle, and strode away, boots ringing on the travel-packed ground. Myrinne followed him, but he waved her off with a sharp motion, then disappeared into the nearest hut. She stood for a moment, undecided, then unholstered her autopistol with a smoothly practiced move and headed into the next dwelling down. But she sent a long look back at the hut Rabbit had gone into, and it didn't take a mind-bender to sense her confusion.

Sven was staying out of it—being relationship-defective and all—but he had found himself way more aware of those nuances than he normally would be. Then again, he didn't used to wake up in a cold sweat, hard and aching, with his heart racing in the face of an overwhelming conviction that he was supposed to be looking for something, doing something, only he didn't know what. Carlos said that, too, would go away eventually. But he'd avoided Sven's eyes when he said it.

"Split up and search," Strike ordered, though there seemed little hope of survivors.

"I'll take the perimeter," Sven offered, and got a nod, which was a good thing. He needed to move, and he didn't know how much longer he was going to be able to hold the coyote back in the face of all the run-kill-bite-enemy stuff going through his furry head. "They're gone," he said in an undertone. "We're too late."

Mac growled deep in his chest.

"Yeah," Sven agreed as he headed out of the village, keeping a tight mental leash. "I feel the same way." The Nightkeepers couldn't continue chasing Iago's tail like this. Something needed to change . . . but it needed to be the right something. Strike had given him, Rabbit, and Myrinne a clipped report of what sounded—reading between the lines, anyway—like a major shitstorm of Mendez proportions going down at Skywatch. But as far as Sven was concerned, prophecy or no prophecy, he and the others could—and would— take Mendez if it went that far. Strike was their king. Period and no discussion.

He let Mac range a little farther once they got a distance from the village and started making a wide loop around it. Their passage flushed out countless bright, flashy birds and sent squadrons of butterflies into the air. Ignoring them, Sven kept his eyes on the ground, searching for tracks while staying attuned to the coyote's thought stream, which had gone from warnings about the enemy to a growing sense of edgy frustration.

Or was that coming from him? Gods knew he'd been hair-trigger lately. Carlos said the new restlessness and aggression—like the dreams and the hormone surges—came from his magic getting used to the impulses of his familiar, that he would level off soon and go back to being the guy he was. But Sven had a feeling it was the other way around, that he was finally coming into his true self and would stay that way. It felt like he had been sleepwalking for so long, and was just now waking up, just now—

Mac yowled and exploded, diving into a cluster of bushes nearby. *Enemy!*

Adrenaline hammered through Sven. Yanking his knife and calling up a shield, he hollered and plunged after the big canine. Branches whipped at him, deflecting off the shield as he burst out of the middle growth and into a small, sun-dappled clearing.

There, Mac stood over a villager. For a second, Sven's heart leaped at the thought that they had found a survivor, but then he got closer and saw otherwise. The man's body was twisted unnaturally, unmoving, but his face was animated and his eyes shone luminous green as he hissed at Sven, face alight with bloodlust.

"Nice job, Mac," Sven said, reaching for his knife and prepping himself for the head-and-heart spell. But he paused when something nagged at him. It took him a second, but then he got it: The *makol* wasn't regenerating. Something was wrong with it.

He started to crouch down for a closer look, but Mac

pivoted over the *makol* and stood with his legs braced, head lowered, and teeth bared. A bloodcurdling growl rumbled in the coyote's throat.

Sven froze. "Mac? What the hell?"

The coyote sent a stream of glyph images that spelled out *friend-enemy-friend*, which didn't make any more sense than him protecting the *makol*. But Carlos had impressed on Sven that he needed to trust his familiar, and experience had shown that Mac would get in a snit if ignored. And a hundred-pound coyote having a temper tantrum was not a pleasant experience. *So think it through,* Sven told himself. Analysis had never really been his thing before, but he'd been getting better at it lately. The coyote had saved Reese's life by attacking a *makol* back at Skywatch, but he wouldn't let Sven near this one, and was even acting protective of it. So what was different? Did it have something to do with how this one wasn't regenerating?

*Friend-enemy-friend* came again, this time along with a sharp, mossy smell.

Moving slowly, Sven crouched down again, sending peaceful, nonlethal thoughts. Mac's growls subsided and he gave way.

The *makol's* human host had been a young man, maybe early twenties. He was wearing jeans and a grayed-out wife beater, and had a small, new-looking leather pouch hanging around his neck. The mossy smell Mac had noted was coming from the pouch. With a mental flick that would have been ten times more difficult before his familiar had come into his life, Sven translocated the pouch into his outstretched palm. But the second it vanished from around the *makol*'s neck, the creature shuddered and arched, and a terrible, screaming keen ripped from the host's throat.

Luminous green flashed, blinding Sven, who dove back and yanked up his shield. When his vision cleared, though, there didn't seem to be any danger. Instead, the other man's eyes were those of a human once more, filled with pain and grief. He looked at Sven and his lips moved, but no words came out. A second later, his eyes dulled and a last breath leaked out of him.

For a moment, Sven just stood there, clutching the leather pouch that was still warm from the other man's body.

"Holy shit," Alexis said from behind him—softly, reverently. "Did you just cure a *makol*?" He hadn't heard the others approach, but they were there now, staring down at the corpse, which hadn't gone to greasy ash, hadn't required a head-and-heart spell.

"He died," Sven said hollowly. "That's not much of a cure."

"But he died human, and he was killed—or at least fatally wounded—in battle. He's destined for the sky now." Which was far better than staying a *makol* and being automatically consigned to the ninth layer of Xibalba.

"Yeah." Sven held up the pouch, let it dangle. "The demon flashed out when I took this off him."

"Shield it and bring it with you," Strike ordered. "We're getting out of here. There's nothing more for us to do here, and work to do back home if we're going to find Iago and neutralize the fucking serpent staff before the solstice." To Rabbit, he said, "You want to take care of the body?"

The younger man nodded tightly, and made short work of the ritual cremation. Moments later, he joined the loose circle where the others were linking up for the dispirited 'port home. Sven made sure he had a really good hold on Mac, who was squirming and whining even harder than usual as Strike took a deep breath, tapped into the uplink, and triggered the 'port. And the magic went haywire.

"No!" Heart hammering, Strike lashed out with his mind, trying to recover the fat yellow thread of magic that connected him to his destination during a 'port.

He couldn't believe he'd lost the fucking thread. One moment it was there, waiting for him to grab on with his mind and give a tug. The next it had slipped through his mental muscles, whipped past the mental blockades Rabbit had set up, and got sucked into a whirl of thoughts and feelings he didn't recognize. Instead of the usual order, his head was a whirlwind of half-understood images—men and women dancing in ritual robes; warriors locked in battle with dark terrible creatures that breathed fire and bled acid; a huge house in flames.

Forcing himself to focus through the maelstrom, he thought of the great room at Skywatch, pictured it, tried to connect with it . . . and failed. Adrenaline pounded through him as, instead of the familiar sideways lurch and grayish blur of teleportation, the world spun and dropped, doing some sort of crazy carnival shit while magic sparked and flared red, gold, and gray, and wind tornadoed around them.

"Don't let go!" he shouted to the others over the wind noise, and he clutched the hands linking him on either side—Rabbit on the left, Leah on the right, linked from there to the others. Jesus gods. He was going to kill them all and wipe out mankind's last and best hope. And Leah. *Oh, Leah. My love. I am sorry.*

In reply, love came pouring through their *jun tan* bond to fill him with warm understanding and support, along with an edge that was hers alone. A millisecond later, raw power came into him from the other side as Rabbit opened the floodgates, not trying to mind-bend him or anything, but just *being* there and offering himself up. *I love you*, whispered in his mind, coming from Leah, who hadn't believed in magic before she met him. *I trust you*, said Rabbit, who didn't trust anyone, not even himself.

Gathering his magic, focusing it when it wanted to scatter, Strike thought again of Skywatch, visualizing the great room where so much had happened over the past few years, good and bad. It was where the Nightkeepers had first met as a team, where they had bonded and mapped out their plans. And it was where they needed to be now.

The world spun, the wind tore at him. Then, finally, a thin thread appeared in his mind's eye. He reached for it, touched it, wrapped his mind around it. And pulled.

*Crack!* The great room took shape around them

as the magi materialized right where they belonged. Unharmed.

*Thank the freaking gods.* Strike went limp as relief poured through him and his power cut out, drained by whatever the hell just happened. He would have sagged if it hadn't been for Leah on one side, Rabbit on the other. They kept him up, made it look casual, steered him through the crowd.

Incredibly, none of the others seemed all that shaken up. He heard a few jokes about turbulence and barf bags, and Sven's coyote actually *was* barfing, but nobody seemed to realize how close they had just come to dying, or that their king had almost lived up to his father's legacy by finishing off the Nightkeepers. But once Leah and Rabbit got him to the royal suite and into bed, he stared through the glass ceiling of the solarium they used as the master and cursed himself bitterly because *he*, at least, knew how close it had been. And he knew something else: He couldn't keep going on like this. He had been gutting through the fogginess in his brain and rearranging things to minimize the number of 'ports he needed to do in a given day, but this . . . shit. What the hell was happening to him?

And it couldn't be a coincidence that the jaguar king was losing it just as a challenger was stepping up. Dez claimed he didn't want the throne, and Strike sure as shit didn't want to lose his kingship—never mind his life here on Earth, with Leah—but there were prophecies in play, just like Anna's message said. *What do you want from me?* he sent into the sky, envisioning Kulkulkan, the god that had been his and Leah's special guardian before the destruction of the skyroad. *What am I supposed to do?*

There was no answer. Just the slant of the afternoon sun that should have been pleasant but instead was a reminder that their time was running out.

# CHAPTER NINETEEN

*Pueblo Bonito*

It was sunset by the time Dez was finally finished with Keban. He had refused to cremate him on the sacred ground of Skywatch—and suspected that the others, particularly the *winikin*, would object if he had tried—but when it came down to it, he hadn't been able to just dump the bastard in a ditch, either. So he had come up to Bonito, the Chacoan castle built by their ancestors, and he had built a funeral pyre.

The humans considered the ruins a soaring mystery, the last remnants of an elusive tribe that had lived a thousand years earlier, leaving behind a grand stone-and-timber castle with many floors, dozens of kivas, hundreds of rooms, and tricky interplays of light and shadow that could be used to tell time or plot the stars. Some scholars thought it had been a trading center, others a home for the gods. In a way it had been both, though not even his serpent ancestors would have been ballsy enough to call themselves gods. He hoped.

Either way, this was the serpents' castle, and whatever else he had been and done, Keban had served the bloodline by saving its last male descendant. So Dez built a small pyre in a sheltered spot near a curving wall and lit it with a combination of diesel and magic. He watched the smoke curl, blocked out the smell, and listened to the hiss-pop of the fire, let himself drift . . .

It was the day of the Nightkeepers' planned attack on the intersection, and the training compound was a beehive of activity overlain with tension.

Dez's vantage was all feet and knees, his perceptions those of a three-year-old, but he felt the tension in the air as the huge, battle-armored warriors and their winikin gathered in the courtyard. Knots of men and women were being kept under guard as they prepared for battle—Dez had heard them called dissy-dents; he wasn't sure what that meant, but he could see they were mad, and most everyone else was mad at them.

Elsewhere, the younger winikin were herding all the kids into the Great Hall; the grown-ups were all pretending like it was a party—a movie first, dancing later, with pizza and cake. But their eyes were worried, and Dez's mother and father had hugged him too tightly just now. They had done the same to baby Joy, making her cry. She was still sniffling as Keban tucked her into her bouncy chair.

"Son."

Dez craned around, but it wasn't his dad, it was Keban's father, Keru. The two winikin hugged briefly, looking very alike, though one was old and the other young.

"We've got everything packed like you said." Keban kept

*his voice very low. "If things go wrong, Breese and I are out of here with the kids."*

Dez sat up straight. Breese was his winikin—*she was soft and nice, and smelled like strawberries. Were they all going somewhere? He wanted to ask Keban, but didn't dare. He was nice to Joy, not always so nice to everyone else.*

*"Be strong," Keru said. "And whatever you do, preserve the bloodline. Because gods help us if we have to go into the war without a serpent king."*

*The men hugged again, and Keru went off toward the warriors, where Dez's parents were helping each other with their gear. Keban turned, found Dez staring at him, and started to scowl. Then he seemed to catch himself, and sighed. "Come here, kid. Let's go find Breese. The four of us need to stick together, okay? No wandering off on your own tonight." Dez nodded, but the* winikin *looked unconvinced. He hunkered down and gestured for Dez to come closer. "Hold your sister's hand for a second."*

*Dez complied, sticking out a finger and letting Joy curl her chubby fist around it. She smiled at him, sniffles forgotten.*

*"Do you know what an oath is?" the* winikin *asked.*

*Surprised, because Keban didn't usually say much to him, Dez nodded.*

*"Okay, I want you to say, 'I swear I'll watch out for my sister tonight. I won't leave her, no matter what.'"*

*Dez stammered his way through the oath, feeling very grown up and protective all of a sudden. His father had told him Joy was his responsibility before, but nobody had ever made it his job to stay right with her. It all seemed very important, and a little scary, but it gave him the courage to ask, "What's going on?"*

"*Nothing you need to worry about as long as you stay right with your sister. Because if you don't, bad things are going to happen.*" *Keban looked up when someone called his name.* "*There's Breese. Come on.*" *He picked up Joy, bouncy chair and all, grabbed Dez's hand, and headed for the doors to the Great Hall. At the stairs, though, he stopped and looked back. It seemed like a lot of the* winikin *were doing that.*

*Dez looked back, too, his eyes zeroing in on his parents. His mother's laughing eyes were very serious, and his father's face was drawn, his serpent-bare scalp hidden beneath an armored helmet. He was saying something to Keru, who was his* winikin. *Dez's stomach gave a funny shimmy, and he called out,* "*Mom! Dad!*"

*They didn't hear him, and Keban tugged him to keep going, but just as they went through the doors, Keru looked straight at Dez, meeting his eyes. He touched his heart and then his wrist, letting his fingers linger where rows of serpent glyphs sat above the image of a hand cupping the face of a sleeping child.*

The vision dissolved, leaving Dez floundering for a moment as his perceptions shifted back to those of his adult self, the one who knew that the glyph was the *aj winikin*, and the gesture meant "I serve you, serpent." Keru had been swearing fealty—not just his own but that of all the serpent *winikin*, who had guessed that the attack would fail and had made clandestine plans to save Dez and Joy.

Staring into the fire, Dez tried not to think how different his life would have been if Breese had made it out, or if Keban had been able to save both him and

Joy. If it had gone down like that, the *winikin*'s mind wouldn't have gotten fucked over by the magical backlash of him having sacrificed his blood-bound charge. He would've been a normal *winikin* instead of what he had become, and Dez would've come out a better man, maybe even a man fit to be a king. Now, though . . . the gods might have done their best to patch him back together with Triad magic, but that didn't make him the man he should have been. Which made it damn lucky—or the will of the gods—that the Nightkeepers had Strike.

Shaking his head, he added more gas to the fire, and watched it burn. When it was over and the *winikin* was little more than a smudge of ash and some shitty memories, he scattered the embers and headed back to the parking area, strides purposeful. He had given Strike and the others enough time to hash things over without him, and now it was time to step up and defend himself, make whatever promises they wanted him to.

He didn't know if the vision had come from Anntah or his own head—but it had brought home that they were all on the same team. It wasn't the serpents against the other bloodlines, or him against the world; it was about the Nightkeepers against Iago and the *Banol Kax*. And the Nightkeepers needed all the help they could get, even if it came from a guy like him. Which meant there was no way in hell he was quitting the team; he was there to stay, and they were going to have to find a way to believe that he didn't want the throne, that the serpent prophecy—if it had ever been anything beyond a serpent-fueled dream—no longer applied. The same went for Reese—he wasn't letting her go without a fight. He just had to figure out a way to convince her of that, convince her to give him another chance to prove that they were meant to be together.

His steps faltered slightly when he came out from between two high stone walls and saw the remaining Jeep Compass parked next to Keban's pickup. Reese was sitting on the hood of the Compass, waiting for him, a silhouette in black leather highlighted by the oranges and reds of the setting sun. As he drew closer, he tried to read her expression, but failed. He wasn't sure if her poker face had gotten better, or if his perceptions had gotten worse, fouled up by how much this mattered. How much *she* mattered.

Swallowing past the fist-sized lump in his throat, he moved to stand in front of her, caging her in, yet leaving himself wide open, his defenses down in more ways than one. He took her hand and turned it over to trace the nearly healed cut. Without preamble, he said, "I was afraid you would leave if you knew about the serpent prophecy. Or that you would tell Strike and . . . well, things would blow up."

Her expression was lost in the shadows. "And now that it's happened?"

"They learned to trust me once. Hopefully I can convince them to give me another chance." He paused. "And, yeah, I should have told them everything right up front." If he had, they wouldn't be up Hell's creek without a scepter.

He expected her to tell him he'd been an idiot, which he couldn't argue. Instead, she turned her hand

and twined their fingers together, giving him a jolt. "They'll forgive you eventually, because they'll see what I see in you."

The heat that had flared at her touch was joined by something strange and unfamiliar. He thought it might be hope. "What's that?"

"They'll see a man who, even after everything Keban did wrong, still does the right thing for him in the end." Her gesture encompassed the ruin. "You did good here, Mendez." And coming from Reese, that was high praise.

He exhaled, letting it go. "In his own way, he was obeying the gods."

"Um. It wasn't the gods talking to him. It was Anntah."

"It was . . . What?"

"I saw him in a dream, talked to him." She briefly described her vision. "He told Keban what to do, though not how, which was his mistake. I don't think he realized how badly losing Joy had damaged him." She paused. "He gave me a message for you. He said to tell you that you need to fulfill the prophecy or Vucub will reign. Which isn't news, but it underscores what Anna said."

They were out in the open, but invisible walls seemed to press in on him from all directions, hemming him in. He tightened his grip on her hand. "The man the prophecy was talking about doesn't exist." But he knew that wasn't good enough; the messages suggested that what mattered was fulfilling the serpent prophecy, period. "I won't challenge the king and I sure as hell won't kill him."

Though back in Denver he had done exactly that, and history repeated. Could he really promise that he wouldn't backslide straight into being the bastard he'd once been?

Yes, he decided, he damn well could.

When Reese was silent on that point, his heart sank a little, but he said only, "Was that it for Anntah's message?"

"Not exactly." She turned away so the setting sun lit her face. "I'm supposed to tell you what he said and leave, because you're supposed to fulfill the prophecy alone. And"—her voice got a little smaller—"we're not destined mates. We never were."

"Bullshit," he said flatly.

She lifted a shoulder. "I'm just telling you what he said."

It wasn't until that moment that he realized he'd been taking it as a given that she was his gods-chosen mate. Why else had he locked on to her from that very first moment? Why else had he known he had to save her, keep her, be with her? Why else would she have come back into his life now? It had to be magic. Nothing else made sense.

When he didn't say anything, she put in, "According to him, you would have fallen for the star twins if they had lived. They were your true mates."

"Twins? Really? Damn."

She scowled. "Be serious."

He sobered, willing her to believe him when he said, "I *am* serious . . . about you. I always have been, even when I had my head up my ass." He moved in closer, putting a hand on the Compass's hood on either side of her and leaning over her, crowding her back on the vehicle's hood. "If you're planning on leaving because Anntah told you to, or because the gods, or destiny, or what the fuck ever didn't mean for us to be together, think again. Because *I* say we belong together. So what if it wasn't magic? We'll call it something else and move on. The only destiny I give a shit about is the one that's right in front of me, right here, right now."

He was braced for an argument, pumped for it, even. Instead, she looped her arms around his neck and touched her forehead to his, so they were leaning on each other. "Say that again."

"Which part?" But he knew. He lowered his voice and whispered, "We belong together, baby." And then he kissed her for real, because he was through waiting for the perfect moment.

Reese's heart raced, heating her blood and making her exquisitely conscious of the cooling night air when it brushed against her skin and rushed to cool the dampness as he kissed her cheeks, her throat. She caught his ear between her lips and savored his groan, tugged up his shirt to revel in the feel of muscles strung tight with need.

Driving up here, she had known it would end like this, or at least she had hoped so. It might not be what she had pictured when she woke up—God, had it been just this morning?—but that didn't make it wrong. The overanalytical part of her wanted to worry that she was making excuses, but the rest of her knew better. He wasn't the boy she had loved or the criminal she had hated, or even a mix of the two. He was a new, better man, a mage. And that was who she wanted.

Flashes of desire built quickly to greed as they kissed and touched, twining together. Then he pulled away and stared down at her, his eyes unreadable in the gathering darkness. He touched her cheek, traced her jaw, brushed his thumb across her lips. "Come home with me?"

Something shivered deep inside her at the way those four simple words suddenly took on greater meaning. Once, she had dreamed of making a home with him. Now, she was dreaming of tonight. Tomorrow. The day after. But no more than that. She didn't dare. Brushing aside a poignant sting at the thought, she kissed the thumb he held pressed to her lips, took the tip in her mouth for a longer, moister kiss, and had the satisfaction of hearing his breath catch. He urged her legs up around his hips and slid his hands to cup her ass, his thumbs working delicious pressure through her jeans as they kissed. The world spun around her and she cried out as a small orgasm caught her unawares, bowing her against him in a rush of unexpected pleasure.

He shuddered against her. "Gods, Reese. That was so fucking sweet."

The rasp of passion in his voice set off chain reactions inside her, turning the fluttering nerves to an imperative: She had to have him. Now. She slid off the Compass's hood, letting her body graze down his. Then, when he reached for her, she dodged and shoved him toward the driver's side. "You're driving."

She might be channeling some of her inner nineteen-year-old's long-ago crush, but now it came with a woman's experiences and fantasies. And this was one of them. Because if the world was on the brink of disaster, the future unclear, she was taking this for herself.

Once they were off the road and onto a relatively flat stretch of hardpan where they couldn't get into too much vehicular trouble, she checked her armband to make sure there weren't any messages or emergency transmits. Reassured that no new shit had hit the fan—or at least none that they had needed her for—she gave herself permission to take tonight, starting now. So she stretched her belt to the limit and slid over to him, enjoying his hiss of pleasure when she slipped an arm around his neck and caught his ear in her teeth. He stroked his free hand along her ribs to her hip, then lower to trail across her upper thigh and inward.

Her heart raced and her breath caught, but no more so than his did when she got his fly undone and freed his hard, thick length. When she ringed him with her hand, he surged up into her touch in a reflex arc that skewed his foot off the gas.

"Keep going," she whispered, "I'll make it worth the trouble."

He responded with a stream of curses in a low, reverent voice that shivered along her nerve endings and sent fire into her bloodstream. But he followed orders and accelerated, though going slower than before, breaking his shaky concentration to skim his hand down to her knee and back up, trailing fire to her center even through her jeans.

She closed her eyes and stilled her stroking hands for a second, absorbing the delicious sensation. He chuckled, low and masculine. "Like that?"

"I like all of it." She suckled his ear, his throat, then shifted without warning to tongue the flat plane of his abdomen where she had his clothing open.

"*Shit.*" He jammed the seat back farther, giving her room as she closed her mouth over him. He went utterly still or a moment, the engine revving and then slacking, creating harmony when he gave a raw, ragged groan.

She tasted the wide, flat head, explored the crinkle of rougher skin at the juncture, and the long, sleek length of him, where the rigid veins pulsed and throbbed, making him jump against her hands and mouth. After that first moment of shock, he fisted a hand in her hair, both guiding her and protecting her from the steering wheel as she slicked her tongue over him, under him, suckling and teasing as they surged over a series of low mogul-like dunes she knew put them in view of Skywatch.

She was dizzy with the motion of the car, with the rush of blood and desire as she took him deep and reveled in his harsh rasp of breath. His hard flesh jerked and his hips shifted restlessly, but he held it together, slewing them around the mansion to jam on the brakes at the back of the residential wing.

He slammed the transmission, killed the engine,

popped her belt, and dragged her face up to his for a wild, raucous kiss broken only by his whispers: her name, graphic descriptions of what he was going to do to her, dirty words made wondrous by the passion in his voice. Then he was dragging up her shirt and bra to feast on her breasts, bending her back against the steering wheel as she clutched his jacket for balance.

"Dez," she panted, "Christ. Inside. Get me inside. I want to feel all of you."

"Fuck, yeah." He kicked open the Compass, tried to lunge out with her in his arms, and got hung up on his seat belt. Then they were snickering and shushing each other as they wrestled out of the SUV and crossed the short distance to the mansion.

Reese headed for the door, but Dez scooped her up, slung her over his shoulder, and carried her to the side of the building.

"What are you . . . no, you're *not*."

She was laughing so hard that when he let her down she had to lean against the building for support as he balanced on a chunk of stone landscaping, popped the latch on his sitting room window, and slid it open. He gestured her through, eyes agleam. "What can I say? It bugs me to have everyone all up in my business."

"Why does that not surprise me?" she said, then boosted herself up and went through the window, making sure to give him a shimmy on the way by.

He was right behind her, up and through almost before she could turn around, crowding her up against the couch as he slapped the window shut and caught her against his body in almost the same movement. Outside, the hours were counting down to the solstice and the Nightkeepers' options were dwindling. But inside Dez's suite it was just the two of them. At least for tonight.

Laughter turned to heat, teasing to mad joy as he grabbed on to her and overbalanced them, taking them both over the back of the couch so they fell together with him on the bottom. The sturdy couch gave off an ominous splintering noise when they hit. It listed off to one side, sparking more giggles that quickly morphed to kisses, then to a full-bodied wrestling match as they hastily got naked. They wound up with the sofa shoved against the wall, her perched on the edge of the seat, him on his knees in front of her, gloriously naked, his eyes hot and wild as he kissed her, his tongue delving deep.

Her body was screaming for him, mad for him, and he was shaking against her, trying to keep some thin thread of control. Glorying in the crazy power they were making together—not magic, but raw passion—she touched herself and then him, slicking the head of his cock with her wetness in mute invitation.

Biting off an oath, he gripped her hips, pulled her lower down on the couch, and thrust into her in a long, strong surge. He entered her, invaded her, filled the space that had been waiting for him, only for him. She hissed with pleasure, dug her fingers into his waist, his ass, ground herself against him as he hit the sweet spots inside and out.

He kissed her openmouthed, lips and tongue working her to a frenzy of moans and threats as she twisted against him, trying to get him to move when he just held himself there, rooted in place and huge within her. She arched. "Please. Oh, please."

He chuckled low. "Made you beg."

She would have cursed him, would have fought her way free just to prove that she could make him beg in return, but she lost those brief impulses the second he began to move. There were no pretty preliminaries, no warm-up moves. He set a hard, fast rhythm immediately, shocking her system and ripping a cry from her throat. His pelvis pinned her, his arms held her against the force of his thrusts, his mouth commanded hers. He possessed her, dominated her, took her. And she loved every second of it. "More," she chanted into his mouth, "yes, there, more, harder."

He shoved her higher on the couch, then rose over her, his body bowing with the force of his pounding tempo as she urged him, ordered him, clutched at him, and then arched and screamed as pleasure exploded inside her, shattering her and then sweeping the pieces along on a pulsing wave. He thrust into her twice more, invading and prolonging the pleasure, and then on the third he locked himself to her, seated himself deep within her, and cut loose. His arms tightened around her, binding them together as long shudders ran through his body, flexing his hips in an atavistic echo of what they had just done. He groaned, pressing his jaw to her temple, his mouth in her hair, his breath hot and fast as the pleasure peaked, crested, and then faded to an echo itself.

"Reese," he whispered, the word full of awe.

She exhaled softly, trying not to let it matter too

much too soon. "Jesus, to think we could have been doing that all along. And that's Ms. Sex Goddess to you, buster."

He chuckled and eased back to frame her face in his hands and look intently into her eyes. His were warm and wondrous, sending new warmth through her system. She felt slippery inside and out, and even though he was still lodged inside her, softening and slipping free, she felt a twinge of greedy need, a stirring of new interest. "What does that make me?" he asked on a purr.

"The guy who's about to get his ass paid back for making me beg."

Dez held out for longer than he would have expected, but eventually he begged, and was damn glad to have done so.

Then, later, after they had raided his fridge and cabinets for a truly random collection of calories not unlike what they had scrounged as kids, he liberated the scented candles from his meditation area—given the nature of the magic, the gods would understand—and used them to give the bedroom a soft, incense-laden glow as he worshipped her, slowly and thoroughly with his hands and lips, until they were both shaking with the need to join their bodies. And even then it was slow and thorough, and when the end came, it was different than it had been, different from anything he had ever experienced before, to the point that he couldn't even give it a name. All he knew was that it was different. *He* was different.

Gods help them all.

Afterward she lay curled up against him, with her head on his chest, as he idly stroked her arm. His body was finally sated—for right then, at least—but his brain had unfortunately come back on line, insisting on churning over the events of the past day, the past week, the past year, his whole lifetime.

He told her about the vision he'd had by the pyre. "I wonder what things would have been like if Breese was the one who lived, not Keban."

"Don't think about it," she said softly, touching his mouth. "What's done is done. What matters now is what we do next." In other words: *Don't bring down the room. Not tonight.* So he kissed her palm and murmured something behind her muffling touch. She moved her hand. "What was that?"

He surged up, locked his lips to hers, and rolled her beneath him in one powerful move, surprised to find that he wasn't wrung out, after all. She squirmed and beat playfully on his shoulders for a few seconds, then stilled, her hands relaxing to splay across his back, travel down, grab his ass, and pull him closer as their kisses sparked and new heat built. Pulling away slightly, he grinned down at her. "I said, 'If what matters most is what I do next, then let's get busy. I'm pretty sure I've got this part right.'"

She arched a brow in an "oh, really?" look. "You're doing okay so far."

He fell into the tease, finding her single small ticklish spot and playing his fingers over it until she shrieked and writhed beneath him. "Is that a dare?" he demanded. "I think that was a dare." Then he pounced on her, laughing, and they wrestled like a couple of idiots, making way too much noise and not giving a crap because right then it was about the two of them, the heat they made together, and the way his name sounded in the back of her throat when she came.

Afterward, he finally slept.

In sleeping, he dreamed.

And in dreaming, he fell into the nightmare.

# CHAPTER TWENTY

*Dez walked the streets as rumors flew, whispered sight-ings of the king returning from captivity, bent on revenge.* Hood's coming back, *the shadows gibbered.* He's going to take his woman and kill the man who stole her.

*That Reese had never been—would never be—Hood's woman didn't matter. All that mattered was reality as the* cobra de rey *saw it. He had the streets that firmly under his spell even after all the work Reese had done to break the gang's hold, with Dez at her back, keeping her safe, protect-ing her. Despite what she seemed to think, that was all he was trying to do now—keep her safe. And after Hood was gone . . . Well, Dez's plans weren't set, but he was working up to a big score, something they could both be proud of and that would take the sad, worried shadows out of her eyes.*

*So he walked the streets, listening to the whispers and watching for his moment to finally take the bastard down, once and for all.*

*He hadn't been able to repeat the crazy electric magic he'd wielded that night in the storm, but he was armed with more than just the guns on his hips and the knife on his belt.*

*The small black statue tucked into an inner pocket reminded him of everything he had already survived, its solid presence giving him the confidence he had lacked. And the ring box concealed on the other side, right over his heart, reminded him what he was fighting for—his rightful place, his rightful mate.*

*As he skimmed past Warehouse Fifteen, he avoided the tunnels and stayed visible, out in the open, partly hunting, partly waiting to be found. "Come on, come on," he muttered as he turned down the alley beside Seventeen. His gut said that the bastard was very close by. "What are you waiting for, you sons of—"*

*Figures exploded around him, four guys closing fast.*

*Adrenaline spiking, Dez spun, ducked a swinging pipe and jammed a shoulder into a hard gut, sending the guy flying back on his ass with a bunch of "motherfuckers" spewing out of his mouth. A strange, humming sense of power flared in his bloodstream, making things sharper—smells, sights, and sounds were all amplified. He felt the weight of his clothes, the faint drag where the black statuette outweighed the ring box, pulling his leather slightly askew as he spun past a knife slash and kicked a second guy's leg out from underneath him, sending his knee sideways.*

*He recognized all four of the guys—they were part of Hood's top muscle, his enforcers—but their guns were tucked, their weapons seriously old-school, heavy on the crowbars and chains. That said Hood wanted to take Dez himself, but wanted him tenderized a little first.*

*Fine. He could have it his fucking way.*

*Dez ducked the third guy a little too slow, let the meathead tag him with a glancing blow on the back of his skull, and reeled like a drunk. They closed on him, kicking and punching, and getting in a couple of good whacks. He took the beating, held on to consciousness as they frisked him roughly, pulling the .44 and the carved stone knife he had paid an arm and a leg for, and was probably fake anyway. One guy pocketed the weapons, another took the statuette and the ring box. Dez forced himself to let them go— temporarily—memorizing which pocket they went into as the enforcers dragged him off the street and through a main door into Seventeen.*

*Hood was waiting for him in a pool of light that came down through a broken window high up on the wall, like he was trying to seem divine or some such shit. As far as Dez was concerned, he just looked like a thug, with prison tats on his knuckles and a fanged sneer creeping across his pasty-assed face as he watched his enforcers drag a woozy Dez over. Around the edges of the warehouse, shadows drifted and whispered, outer-ring gang members looking to get some attention, or maybe just a free show.*

*"Where's your girlfriend, Mendez?" Hood licked his lips. "She back at the apartment getting all pretty for me?"*

*Rage poured fire into Dez's veins, but he kept himself limp.*

*Hood scowled at his enforcers. "You weren't supposed to kill him. Just quiet him down a little."*

*"Got a soft head for such a big bastard," one said with a shrug. He held out the statue and the ring box. "Had these on him."*

*The fanged bastard's face lit like it was Christmas. "No way." He grabbed them, shoved the statue in his pocket and practically drooled over the ring, gloating before he even got* the box open, saying it over and over again: "No fucking way!"

On one level, Dez was snarling with rage. *Don't you fucking touch it.* But on another, he was cold and calculating, watching as a second enforcer crossed in front of him, reaching too eagerly into his coat and paying more attention to the thought of adding another present to Hood's stocking than he was to his positioning.

"He had this on him too." The guy pulled the carved stone knife, started to offer it to Hood.

Dez intercepted it. Moving faster than he ever had before, spurred by something he didn't understand, he grabbed the knife, buried it in the enforcer's throat, and yanked sideways hard and fast. Blood geysered, splattering him and getting in his mouth with a salty tang that just ramped the rage higher. He went down with the first guy, got his .44 back, and nailed two more of the enforcers while they were still gaping and going for their guns. Bullets killed far more neatly than the knife, he discovered at that moment, but there was no added buzz with so little blood. He skipped the fourth guy, ignored the shadows, and zeroed in on Hood.

Then he got the buzz, hard and hot, as he locked on his enemy. *Kill,* something whispered inside him as Hood spun and took off, his mouth splitting in a yell that Dez couldn't hear over the voice inside his head, the one that was saying, *Kill him and take what is rightfully yours.*

Roaring, he lunged after Hood, taking him down with a tackle that sent them both sprawling. He recovered first and got a knee into the small of Hood's back as the bastard scrambled and yelled, trying to get free, to get away, a schoolyard bully bolting when things weren't going his way. Dez dug *in the other man's pocket and got the black statue, felt the kick of power and righteousness.* Kill him now. *He grabbed Hood's forehead, bowed his head back with one hand and slashed his throat with the other. Then he held him there, the wound gaping, the arterial spurts jetting out and painting the warehouse floor as the bastard shuddered and went limp beneath him.*

*Dez smelled the blood, tasted it, felt it on his skin. It took him to another place, another time, and something whispered:* head and heart. *They were the seat of a mage's power, the ultimate sacrifice to the gods.*

*Breathing fast now, barely aware that the shadows had closed in and two guys were holding them off, he flipped Hood over. The bastard was glassy-eyed. Dead. Dez took the knife to his jacket, his shirt, baring a caved-in chest that seemed too narrow for all the things Hood had done. Metal gleamed at the dead man's throat, a thick chain that triggered a spurt of possessiveness, a sense of the inevitable.*

*But first . . . He knelt beside the body, lifted the knife, and—*

*"Dez!" The word was just a whisper, but it cracked through the warehouse like a bolt of lightning and nailed him right in the heart. He jerked away from the corpse and lurched to his feet. The room spun around him as he looked up.*

*Reese stood just inside the warehouse, haloed in the light that spilled in through the door she had left open at her back. She was holding her .38 at the ready, had more firepower slung across her back. She had come to back him up, but her eyes were wide, dark, and hurt as she took in the bodies, the enforcer, the gang shadows—fifty of them, a hundred, with hungry, calculating eyes—and him, covered with blood, holding a knife that dripped onto the floor.*

In the distance, a police siren started up. She must have called them when she heard the shots.

Damn it. He had wanted to keep this under wraps, under the radar. But now . . . shit. He didn't know what came next. This wasn't how he had pictured it looking, how he had imagined it feeling. Part of him was sick as shit, puking in a corner of his mind, terrified that what he'd done was inside him. He wanted to go to her, grab her, and run like hell. But another part of him saw a door opening, a new opportunity presenting itself. Another way to get them up and out, and make sure she was safe from men like Hood.

But safe or not, her face was etched with horror.

He stretched out a bloodstained hand to her. "Reese—"

"Mendez." A sinewy hand caught his arm in an iron grip. "Think about this."

"Let the fuck go of—Zeke?" He wasn't sure which was higher on the "does not compute" front, seeing the pawnbroker smack in the middle of Cobra business, or the fact that Zeke was packing a nine mil that was accented with pink mother of pearl. "What the hell are you doing here?"

"Watching your back." Zeke's eyes flicked to the shadows; a shift of his gun hand sent two of the hungrier street rats scurrying back. But not for long. "Maybe I'm not out of things as far as I make it look. And maybe I've been seeing the direction you've been heading, and want in on it."

"There's nothing to be in on," Dez said, aiming the words at Reese even as another part of him said, Yes. This is what was meant to be.

"You two want to fix up the neighborhood, right? This

*is your chance. You've got the balls and the connections. Take the chain, step up as the new* rey, *and you'll have the resources you need. We'll back you." He indicated three other guys, armed, holding back the shadows. One was Afternoon Bob from the pawnshop. Dez didn't know the other two.*

Take the chain. *The words whispered in his heart. His eyes dropped to the pendant hung around Hood's neck: a silver cobra curled around a ruby the size of his thumb, its color that of blood.*

*"Dez." Someone touched his arm. He flinched back and almost swung, but pulled the punch at the sound of Reese's voice. He hadn't sensed her approach, hadn't heard the others gathering nearby, but when he looked up he saw that they weren't shadows anymore. They were people—some street rats like him, others neighborhood kids. They stared avidly, some at him, some at Hood's body. A few at Reese.*

*"Don't you fucking look at her." He bristled, grabbed the pendant, and made a move toward the nearest, growling low in his throat. Then he turned back to Reese. "Come on. Let's get out of here before the cops . . ." He trailed off, hearing himself.*

*Eyes wide and wet, poker face shaky, Reese glanced from his face to the knife, down to the four bodies, and then to the blood-smeared pendant that hung from his fingers. "We need to stay and tell Fallon what happened," she said softly as the sirens got louder. "It'll be okay. It was self-defense." But the dull horror in her eyes said she had seen him attack Hood from behind, slaughter him like the animal he was.*

*Deep inside Dez, anger bloomed. "Of course it was self-defense. He was going to kill me, use you up, and then kill you."* He closed the distance between them, lowering his voice to rasp, *"Trust me. This was the only way."*

*"Okay."* She swallowed hard. *"Okay. We can deal with this. We'll tell them—"*

*"Nothing,"* he interrupted before he even realized he was going to. He looked at the pendant clutched in his hand, at the faces that said silently, Will you lead us? Will you make us better? *At least that was what ran through his head, humming through his veins like a song. That, and the sudden conviction that this was what he had been leading up to for so many years. Maybe even what Keban had been babbling about all along. His heart raced as the possibilities opened up in front of him.*

*"Don't,"* she whispered. *"I'm begging you—please don't do this."*

*Energy flared. Conviction.* *"It's all for you."* *Why didn't she get that?* *"As* cobra de rey, *I can keep you safe. I can give you everything that you need."*

*Her whiskey-amber eyes went stark in her face.* *"All I need is you to go back to the way you used to be."*

*"I like myself better this way."* *He looked around, saw the ring box, fished it out of a pool of blood.*

*Her eyes welled at the sight and she pressed the back of one hand to her mouth, and for a crazy second it was happening exactly as he used to dream it would when they finally got to this point: shock, tears, disbelief. But then instead of the blinding, blazing joy he had pictured, her face crumpled.* *"Jesus, Dez, what's happening to you?"*

*He bared his teeth, aware that the cops were closing in, that Zeke, Bob, and the others were getting restless.* *"This is who I am, Reese. I'm not your cowboy and I'm not your backup. It's my turn." He looped the chain over his neck, felt it settle against his skin, warm from a dead man's body.*

*"Dez, please." Tears swam in her eyes.*

*His head spun with power, with the mad perfection of it all, as he held out the ring box. "Come with me." He flipped the top, revealing the serpent. "I'll make you a queen." Then, seeing that he needed something more, he added, "I love you."*

*A year ago, when he had finally admitted to himself that he loved her as more than a sister, the concept had been huge and all consuming. Now it was just three words he used to get what he wanted.*

*She closed her eyes, tears spilling free. When she opened them again, he saw deep, tearing grief. "I love you, too. But I love the old you, not this one."*

*He went cold inside. "There's only one me. This is who I am."*

*"No." Her lips shaped the word without sound.*

*"Yes." He picked the ring out of its nest, held it out. "Come with me. You said you wanted me, that you'd do anything to get me. Well, prove it. Take the ring." The cops were almost there. Another minute at most, then some dicking around at the perimeter. Three minutes, tops. His heart picked up a beat and adrenaline stirred, making him feel powerful, invincible. But not powerful enough to make his woman do what he wanted. Because she was backing away, shaking her head and mouthing "no" over and over again. "Reese," he grated, and took a step toward her. Zeke shadowed him, as did several others, closing on her, cutting off her escape.*

*"No!" Eyes going wild, she broke. She spun and bolted,*

*her boots pounding on the floor, weapons slapping against her back as she raced up a short ladder to a platform, where a slider led into the tunnels, and from there to dozens of bolt-holes and back doors. There, she turned back and looked across the warehouse at him, tears streaming down her face. "Dez," she whispered, so softly that he wasn't even sure he heard it for real. He may just have imagined it.*

*"Mendez," Zeke said. "We need to go."*

*He glanced over and nodded. When he looked back, Reese had disappeared into the tunnels. Into safety. Anonymity.* I'm so fucking sick of being anonymous, *he thought, nursing the burn of anger when the rest of him went hollow.*

*The enforcer glanced at him. "You want her back?"*

*"No," he rasped, though that was a lie. "None of you touches her," he grated. "And you kill anyone who tries."*

*He would show her. He would make the Cobras into something good, something worthy. He grabbed the ring and stuck it on his pinkie, tossed the box. He would keep it for her, saving it for the day she saw that he was right, that this was the way it was meant to be. But as the cops burst in and the shadows melted away, and he went with them into the darkness, something deep inside him, something that sounded very different from the other voice, whispered brokenly:* Mine.

*Only she wasn't his anymore. She was gone. And he was alone in the crowd.*

Dez shuddered in the throes of the memory, living it on one level while knowing it was a dream vision on another. Then the nightmare sped up to a flicker-flash of images, impressions showing how very wrong he had been, how quickly he had grown into the skin of the *cobra de rey*, justifying each slip and slide down into darkness. *We need more cash to clean up our act, need more men, more power. We can't go legit right now or the VWs will level the neighborhood. Can't do it now when the Smaldone wannabes are making their big move.* Then, before he knew it, he had found himself at the head of his own syndicate, part gang, part mob. All his.

More, the nightmare threw his words back at him— *I'm doing this to keep Reese safe . . . to prove to her that I'm not what she thinks . . . for the neighborhood . . . for street rats like me.* But really it hadn't ever been about anyone but him. He had done exactly what Keban had taught him to do: take over, lead, control, command. And not give a shit what anybody else thought or said about it.

Another flicker. Another vision.

*He woke sharp and alert—always did, always had, no matter what he'd been into the night before. His mind cataloged the morning inputs: decent bed, too-flowery perfume over the funk of stale sex, a woman's arm over his waist. Nothing to trip his inner alarms. Opening his eyes gave him a look at a decent apartment, a woman's hand trailing across his stomach, wearing fake nails and bloodred polish. Cheap sheets, expensive manicure.*

*Naked, restless, and hungry, but not for her, he got out of the bed, not really caring whether he woke her or not. He headed for the bathroom, snagging his jeans on the way, his initial mood smoothing out some when he felt the weights in opposite pockets: his .44 and the little black statuette that brought him luck.*

"Hey, lover," a feminine purr said behind him. "Going somewhere?"

He barely glanced back at . . . Darla? Carla? Something like that. She had big tits, big hair, a bitchy sense of humor, and knew the score. Which was why he was surprised she had even asked. He came and went as he fucking pleased. "Things to do," he said, and hit the bathroom. When he tossed his jeans, something bright pinged off the vanity and plopped in the toilet.

"Shit." He peered in, caught a wink of silver, a gleam of obsidian, and flashed hard on dark hair that framed amber-whiskey eyes that were full of vibrant joy, a love of adventure, a thirst for justice . . . and adoration. "Reese," he whispered, his heart clutching as he remembered her as more than just a flail he used to drive himself. His mind raced on a moment of strange clarity, one where he felt like he was waking up from a terrible dream. In it, he had become a monster, a demon. A dark lord come to earth. Jesus. How had it all happened? And Reese. God, Reese. A hollow ache clutched at him. She was long gone, but she would hate what he had become. She would hate—

A static buzz whined in his ears, derailing his thoughts and making his vision go momentarily black. He shook his head to clear it, realized he was crouched over the john like he needed to puke, but didn't.

Whoa. Maybe he was feeling last night more than he thought. He took another look at the ring, debated fishing it out, decided not to bother. It didn't really fit him anyway.

Mind skipping ahead to the meeting he was having down at the pawnshop in a couple of hours, he pissed and flushed, and when the artificially blue water stilled, the ring was *gone. But when he dragged on his jeans, he had the important stuff. Gun, check. Good luck, check. With those two things in hand, he could get everything he needed, everything he wanted. Look out world, the* cobra de rey *was coming.*

The dream vision fragmented. And before he was really ready for it to be, it was the morning of the day before the solstice. One year and one day to the end time.

He woke sharp and alert, and his mind cataloged the morning inputs: familiar bed; the faint smell of smoke from the pyre; the stronger scent of good, earthy sex. His body was curved around a woman's, his arm over her waist, their hands interlocked beneath her cheek. There was no irritation, none of the faint self-disgust of that vision-memory. There was only a poignant ache at the wish that he could snapshot the moment, frame it, keep it inside him: Him and Reese together at long last.

"Bad dream?" She turned in his arms, looked up at him, eyes soft and filled with all the things that had flashed through him in the vision, plus something even more precious: trust.

He pressed his lips to her brow. "Just Anntah—or maybe my own subconscious—making sure I don't forget about my sins." He told himself to leave it at that, but her eyes were steady on his, her fingers twined between his, hanging on as if she didn't intend to let go. "I keep seeing myself kill Hood, keep reliving the way everything twisted itself around inside my head, so the wrong things seemed right." When her expression turned sad and serious, he lifted their joined hands, pressed a kiss to her knuckles. "I should've seen what was happening, should've fought harder, but I didn't. And I'm sorry."

She closed her eyes, took a breath. And when she opened them again, the poker face was gone, tears were welling. "I told myself I didn't need an apology, that it was enough that you got out from under the star demon's influence."

"*You* helped me get clean," he said. "If you hadn't gotten me into jail and away from the statuette, I don't think even the Triad magic could've brought me back."

"You saved my life; I saved yours," she whispered.

He owed her so much more than that. And he wanted to give it to her, wanted to be with her, watch her soar. "You may not need an apology, but you've got one anyway." He kissed a tear away, felt something shift in his chest. "I'm sorry." He kissed her other cheek. "I won't be that guy." He kissed her lips, tasted the salt of her tears, and felt warmth flicker in the cold place that spawned the nightmares. "Never again. I promise."

Magic sparked beneath his skin, sealing the oath as she opened to him, deepening the kiss and shifting against him, sleek and bare and already wet.

He hissed in a breath as all the blood left his head and went other, more interesting places. In the back of his mind, he knew they had to get up and out, that she had work to do and he needed to see what it was going to take to prove that he wasn't secretly plotting behind Strike's back. And . . . His thoughts scattered, lost to hot, openmouthed kisses. Hands sliding over soft skin. Reese rising over him, taking him inside her.

He arched up beneath her, going rigid with the hot, wet pleasure as she surrounded him, squeezed him, worked him. He touched her, kissed her, lost himself in her. Then, as she tightened around him and cried out, he reversed their positions and pinned her, surged into her, loved her. She was his, always should have been. Screw Anntah and his blithering about destined mates. She had been meant for him from the very beginning. He had just been too fucked up to see it.

"Reese," he breathed against her temple as she came apart in his arms, shuddering and calling his name. "Jesus, Reese."

He surged into her, planted himself deep, and cut loose. And as he came, he gladly lost a part of himself to her.

The orgasm went on, spun out, felt like magic . . . and left him just as ready to crash when it faded. His arms quivered where he was braced over her and his body was practically numb. From the look of her glazed-over eyes, she was in a similar state.

He rolled onto his back, taking her with him. "Gods, woman. I can't feel my toes."

She chuckled. "Was that a complaint?"

"Hell, no. It was—" He broke off at the sight of a light flashing on the nightstand. His armband. Someone had left a message in the past few minutes.

Reese followed his gaze, then looked over to where her transponder sat on the floor tangled with her discarded shirt. It, too, was blinking. "Guess they're looking for us." She glanced back at him. "You ready for this?"

He thought about it for a second, then nodded. "You know, I guess I am. Way more than I was yesterday afternoon, at any rate." He caught her hand, kissed her knuckles . . . and stalled on what to say next. He wanted to thank her for coming after him, believing in him, taking him as he was; he wanted to tell her she was beautiful, smart, sassy, honorable, and on some levels way out of his league; he wanted to let her know that he was going to go into the next couple of days stronger because she was behind him, and that he was damned grateful for the chain of events—whether destiny or coincidence—that had brought her back into his life. But all those things wound up jammed together in his chest, so in the end, all he said was, "Cross your fingers that they don't nail me with a Taser and pack my ass down in the basement."

She winced. "Not funny."

And not that far from possible, he thought ten minutes later as, showered and wearing fresh clothes, they headed to the main room together, holding hands.

The sunken great room was jammed with bodies, and everyone there looked up pretty much simultaneously when Dez and Reese came through the archway leading from the mage's wing. He got the glares he was expecting, with a few notable exceptions: Leah was pale and unusually shaky; Rabbit was glowering, but not at him; and Sasha was looking at him with a hint of pleading, which didn't make any sense. The decision wasn't in his hands. It was the king's call.

Strike was standing on the riser that ran the perimeter of the room and opened into the kitchen, leaning against the wall near the big-screen TV. When he saw them, he straightened and came over. He glanced at their joined hands, nodded fractionally, then tipped his head toward an empty love seat. "Have a seat and we'll get started."

Dez swallowed. "I have a few things I'd like to say." Strike hesitated, expression guarded, and Dez's gut knotted. "You already made your decision, didn't you?"

"It's not what you think." The king pointed to the two-seater. "Chill. Sit. Listen. Some things have happened that . . . well, let's just say the circumstances have changed."

Dez glanced at Reese, who looked just as confused as he was. So they followed orders and sat. But it was evident that whatever they had missed, it was big. And from the looks being shot back and forth among the others, he and Reese weren't the only ones in the dark on what was going to happen next.

# CHAPTER TWENTY-ONE

Reese's instincts were shrilling a major warning as Strike leaned a hip against the sofa where Leah was sitting, as though he wanted to be near her but couldn't sit still. He looked serious and strung out, and she couldn't quite squelch the thought that under the writs, the punishment for treason was execution. The Nightkeepers wouldn't go there, would they? What would she do if they did? Visions of her and Dez shooting their way out of the compound locked horns with the memory of Strike's sleep spell and Rabbit's mind-bending. Would she wake up back in Denver and wonder why Fallon wasn't speaking to her?

Dez reached for her hand, twined his fingers through hers, and held on tight.

After what felt like a long pause, Strike took a deep breath, and said, "There is something very wrong with me. I'm having brownouts, suffering from what I guess you could call psychic brain lesions . . . and yesterday, bringing everyone home from the highlands, I lost the teleport thread. If it hadn't been for Leah and Rabbit propping me up with their magic, none of us would've made it back."

That so wasn't what Reese had been expecting to hear, that it took her a moment to process what he'd just said. The same thing seemed to be happening to most of the others, because there was a moment of absolute, blank silence broken only by the muffled sounds of Leah's jeans and shirt against the sofa when she shifted to take Strike's hand and press it to her face. A single tear leaked down her cheek.

It was Alexis who finally broke the silence. "I take it Sasha has checked you out?" She was sending the healer a "what the hell?" look, but Sasha was staring at her white-knuckled hands as Michael, himself grim-faced, whispered something into her ear.

"Both Sasha and Rabbit have done everything they can," Strike said. "Lucius has scoured the library, and I've had all the relevant human-style scans we can think of. The scans came back clean; it was Rabbit who found the lesions. He's done his best to put me back together, but it's not holding."

"There's a shadow," Sasha said without looking up. "It's like a phantom blood-link or something. I can't get a handle on it. Nothing I do makes any difference." Strike started to say something, but she held up a hand. "I know, I know. It's not my fault, I'm doing the best I can, blah, blah." She looked up to glare, red-eyed, at him. "What I don't get is why the gods gave me this talent but won't let me heal my own big brother. My king." She shook her head. "Godsdamn it, I fucking

hate this." And for her to drop an f-bomb was as unexpected as Leah crying, making everything suddenly
very real.

A low murmur built as brains started to unfreeze.
Reese glanced over at Dez and found him staring at
Strike, eyes gone utterly hollow. And she got it: The
serpent prophecy said that Dez had to kill his adversary to take the throne, and the prophecy needed to
be fulfilled in order to keep Lord Vulture from arising.
And Strike was sick. The blood drained from her head,
leaving her dizzy as she flashed back: *the gleam of a stone
knife as it slashed an upturned throat, blood gouting . . . and
that other Dez, the one the star demon had turned him into,
watching with hot, satisfied eyes as the* cobra de rey *died
beneath him.*

She must've made some noise, because Dez looked
at her. His fingers tightened on hers and his throat
worked, but he didn't say anything. And for the first
time in the time she had known him, he looked terrified. But beneath the terror she thought she glimpsed
something else . . . or rather some*one* else. And that
made it even worse.

"It started with the dreams," Strike said, then went
on to describe being in his father's perceptions during
the Solstice Massacre. "The details changed over time,
until it seemed more like it was me in the dream. The
one thing that didn't change, though, was this moment
of realizing that I had it wrong, that when the thirteenth prophecy called for the last jaguar king to make
the 'ultimate sacrifice' before the four-year threshold,

it wasn't talking about the king sacrificing his mate. It meant that he was supposed to . . . that *I* was supposed to sacrifice myself."

Sasha made a low, broken noise and pressed her face into Michael's arm. He shifted to hold her, hanging on tight. Leah sat there, still and white-faced, staring at the floor with the look of a woman who had argued herself sick on a point, and was gearing up for another round. Reese's heart hurt for them, and for pale, pissed-off Rabbit, who would be truly orphaned without Strike. She hurt for Nate and Alexis, whose parents had been advisers to the prior king, and who had helped steer this one, to the extent he let himself be steered. And she hurt for all of the others, who were staring at Strike with expressions ranging from disbelief and anger to blank shock. She hadn't yet begun to hurt for herself. She knew it was coming, but didn't try to brace for it, because how could she buffer herself against something like this?

*What has happened before will happen again.* Fucking writs.

"There's no question that our luck has sucked since I broke the prophecy," Strike continued. "Given everything that's happened over the past couple of weeks, I think that the gods are giving me—giving us—a chance to make up for my having not fulfilled the thirteenth prophecy when I was supposed to." He paused, voice cracking with renewed regret. "I think maybe the sun god chose Anna as a Triad mage because the gods needed her to deliver the message, and wanted to be sure that I would pay attention."

He shifted his tired, hollow gaze to Dez. "Which is where you come in."

"No," he said hoarsely. "Don't."

But Strike kept going. "I want you to be my successor and—if it turns out to be the only way to keep Lord Vulture trapped in the underworld—my executioner."

"Hell, no!" Dez shot to his feet and faced Strike with his hands balled into fists. His shout was echoed by a bellow from Nate, cries from Jade and Alexis, and various other shocked noises. But it was Reese's softly indrawn breath that cut through him; she was trying very hard not to cry.

Strike stayed leaning hip-shot against the couch, waiting for the furor to die down. When it did, he said, "Setting aside the prophecies for a second, my sickness, whatever the hell it is, has driven home the need for me to name an heir, if you will."

"Not me," Dez said flatly. *Dear gods, please not me.* Not when he and Reese finally had something going right for them after all these years.

"Then who?"

"Nate," he said immediately, preferring this debate to the other one, because how was a guy supposed to argue an execution with his own potential victim? He continued: "Michael or Brandt would work. Hell, why stick with a patriarchy? Choose Leah or Alexis. Someone who knows the current system, who knows how you run things and how to keep things on an even keel for the next twelve months."

"I've been doing the even-keel thing, and it's not

working. We've become a reactionary force, moving in to fix shit after the fact—sometimes way too long after. We need someone who's going to go out and find the fight, kick ass, take names, shake things up."

"Shaking things up," Reese said softly, with a broken little hiccup in her voice. "The western compass quadrant, the one associated with the star demon, represented the ability to transform and shake things up."

"Reese, no." He caught her hand in his. "No." But she wouldn't look at him.

Leah said, "We read back through all the info we collected on you, back when we were trying to figure out whose side you were on." She paused. "From a former narc to a former gangbanger, I have to admit, you were a hell of a *rey*. Under your command, the Cobras expanded their territory and operations, even dabbling in some legit businesses. The local mob wannabes fizzled and died out, the crime and death rates went down slightly in the areas you controlled, and the per capita incomes went up."

"Great," Dez grated. "I was a better criminal than Hood. Give me a fucking cookie. Not the Nightkeepers."

But Reese cleared her throat and said, "She's right. You made the Cobras into something better than they were. Even Fallon admitted it."

"That doesn't mean I'd make the Nightkeepers better."

"I'm not asking you to," Strike countered. "I'm asking you to take the team that's already been built and use them to win the end-time war."

Leah's voice flattened, and some of her deeply hidden emotions broke through as she said, "Gangs are essentially urban armies."

Strike added, "You're ruthless, ambitious, arrogant, and don't give much of a shit about anybody's rules but your own, and even those are flexible when it comes down to doing what it takes to win. You're a warlord, and we're headed into war."

"Jesus." *I don't want to be that guy. I promised not to be.* "You're acting like naming a successor is the only issue here. What about the prophecies? What about Iago?"

Strike's tired eyes bore into his. "This is the serpents' solstice. All the signs point to this being your time."

"What fucking signs?"

It was Lucius who said, "Aside from you and Iago being the only two people left on the plane who have the potential to wield the serpent staff? Well, the Hopi believe that their snake dance will call a great white god wearing a crimson cape, who will turn back the apocalypse and allow the earth to enter a new age. And if you consider the whole 'what has happened before' doctrine, it seems significant that the last time a Triad was summoned, the peccary bloodline lost the throne to the jaguars. Add to that the fact that the sun god basically sacrificed one third of the Triad magic to send you a spirit guide and get you back on track . . ." He shook his head, dispirited. "Yeah. The signs suggest a power transfer."

Dez couldn't think. He couldn't fucking breathe. "Are you ordering me on my oath to do this?"

"Take a few hours and think about it," Strike said,

which wasn't really an answer. He included Reese in his look. "Both of you. We'll meet back here at noon, and go from there." And with that, they were dismissed whether they liked it or not. King's orders.

Strike watched Dez struggle inwardly for a second before the other man snapped off a nod, and tugged Reese away. She went with him, shell-shocked, yet gutting it out because she'd be damned if she'd lose it in public. Strike knew the type; he lived with a prime example.

If the parallel was as close as he thought, she would . . . yep, there it went: the pause in the hallway, the short, intense conversation. He even knew the script, such as it was: Dez would want to be on his own to process the shock, but he'd push her to come with him, not wanting her to be alone. He wouldn't do it right, though, or she would see the well-intentioned lie. There it was now—the small shove, the head shake, and then the two of them moving off in different directions to nurse their wounds so later they could present a united front in public.

*Or—hello—maybe you're projecting all of that, and they're going to meet back up in his suite in five for some raunchy, desperate, "We've got less than thirty-six hours before everything goes to hell so screw the other stuff and let's get it on" sex.*

"What are you thinking?" Leah said, rising from the sofa to sit beside him on its arm, close enough that he could answer in an undertone.

"That the fun is only half over," he said wryly, not

because any of this was a joke, but because if he didn't keep his head in a semi-normal place, he would explode. He was barely hanging on as it was, trying to deal with logistics, grief, anger, and despair—his, hers, and more to come—with a brain that felt like oatmeal. Exhaling, he turned toward the others. Their faces—some looking up at him in disbelief, others looking away, angry or tearful—pretty much encapsulated everything he was feeling. He'd been trying to deal with it all since he had awakened in the middle of the night, finally understanding what the dreams were trying to tell him about the thirteenth prophecy: that he was his own greatest sacrifice. And the prophecies needed to be fulfilled.

Alexis scowled. "This is a trick, right? You're testing his loyalties."

"I wish. No, this is for real."

Beside her, Nate shook his head, letting a rare flash of grief show through his normally controlled exterior. "I'm sorry, man. I wish . . ."

"Yeah." Strike had to push the word past the huge lump in his throat. "Ditto."

"Isn't there anything else we could try?" That came from Patience.

"If you've got a suggestion, I'm all ears. Doesn't matter how far-fetched, I'll try anything at this point, because the pisser of this thing is that we don't know *what's* going on. Hell, it could be a new talent trying to come through and doing damage in the process. It could be Kulkulkan trying to find a way to communicate without using a skyroad. It could be . . . Shit, I don't know. Lots of things other than fatal. But there are the prophecies to consider."

"Break 'em," Nate said promptly. "We've made it this far with the fates pissed at us. We can make it the rest of the way."

Several of the others nodded, all magi. The older *winikin*, though, didn't. They knew how bad things could get when a king went off the rails. More, they weren't just talking about Skywatch now; they were talking about the whole damn world, and he couldn't put himself ahead of that, no matter how badly he wanted to. He might buy himself a few more hours, days or even months, but at what cost?

"Lord Vulture symbolizes a nuclear winter," he said quietly. "I don't think we *can* break them."

"We might be able to reinterpret them," Lucius said. Strike had brought him in to things just past one that morning, and it showed in his haggard face. But his red-rimmed eyes gleamed. "Some of the prophecies have had tricks to them, loopholes. Like the way I avoided pieces of the library prophecy because it specified the magi, and I'm human."

"You find me a loophole and I'll owe you a beer." Hell, a lifetime supply.

"Deal."

Strike looked around the room. "I'm not giving up," he said, giving each word extra weight. "I'm going to fight this thing in my head every step of the way, and I'm sure as shit not going to roll over and play—" Bad word choice. "I'm not going to throw myself on anyone's knife voluntarily. But in the meantime, I can't ignore the other shit that's going down here. And neither can any of you."

Leah shifted beside him, tense. This was where she wanted the conversation to end, period. She wanted to pour every resource and every waking minute into figuring out what was going on with him and how to stop it. And, yeah, if the situations were reversed, he would want the same thing—hell, he would find a way to make it happen, even if it meant knocking her out and locking her in the basement for her own good. Been there, done that. But the thing was, as much as he considered her his equal in most things, his superior in some, she wasn't the jaguar king of the Nightkeepers. Saving her had created ripples . . . but if he went against the gods now, it would make waves. And putting everything they had into this fight would be self-indulgent, which had never really been an option for him.

For one, Jox would kick his ass. And, damn, he missed the old guy. He had lost his *winikin*, was watching Anna slip further away each day . . . and now this. Where was it going to end? Or was that the point? Was this it for the jaguars?

"Which brings us to Dez," Nate said, as if reading his mind.

"Exactly." Strike scrubbed a hand over his eyes to clear the grit, then stopped when he realized the problem wasn't with his eyes. The fog was back, creeping in around the edges of his vision. Swallowing, he said, "I'm sure some of you have issues with my naming him heir and putting him in charge of ops—trust me, I've been through all the what-ifs." He paused, sobering. "The thing is, the prophecies are there and the logic is sound. If you guys can poke holes in it, be my guest. But if not . . . then he needs to be the guy, and you're going to need to deal." Which would be easier for some than others.

There was a round of low murmurs and some curses, but nobody spoke up. In the relative silence, he was conscious of a faint hum coming from the strange, knotted pulse that had taken up residence at the back of his brain just that morning. He was very carefully *not* thinking about it, because when he did, the fog got worse and his mind started playing tricks on him, replaying one fragment of Anna's message over and over again: *The prophecies must be fulfilled or Vucub will reign.*

"Oh, come *on*!" JT jerked to his feet, eyes gone nearly molten silver with frustration. "This is bullshit." Beside him, Natalie winced a little, but stayed quiet. Which meant she agreed with the content, if not the delivery. JT continued, "Tell me you're not serious. The guy's unpredictable, and as far as trusting him, forget it. There's a big difference between a guy who comes out of prison having learned his lesson and one who comes out having learned to beat the system. He's not the first kind, I'll bet my right arm on that." He paused, looking around the room. "Yesterday morning, half of you wanted to kick him out of the compound for hiding the truth about the serpent staff. Now you're acting like it makes sense to not just put him in charge of tomorrow's op, but to make him *the frigging heir apparent*."

Strike moved to get in his line of sight, knowing JT wouldn't look at him unless he was forced to. The unbound *winikin* might have agreed to become part of the war effort but he was far from ready to forgive and forget. When the other man sent him a sidelong look, Strike said, "The situation has changed. We're talking about prophecies and nuclear freaking winter here, so you'll have to forgive me if I think we should hit things with the biggest hammer we've got. Right now, whether we like it or not, that's Mendez." He paused. "This isn't what I had planned for. It's not what I want . . . but it might be the only way for most of us to get through this solstice intact."

Leah made a soft noise, but didn't say anything.

Some of the tension went out of JT. "Look, I'm sorry about what you're going through. Seriously. If I could do something to help, I would. And if it comes down to it, I'll follow orders. But I've gotta ask . . . Are you sure this is coming from the right place?"

"Because a jaguar king acting on his dreams is your worst nightmare?"

"You said it, not me." The unbound *winikin* looked around the room at the others. "And you guys are all oath bound. You've got to go along with it."

Lucius grated, "What would you rather have us do, sit around and count votes for the next thirty-six hours? There's a structure here, a way of doing things that's evolved over thousands of years and exists for a reason.

Strike knows what he's doing . . . and so does Leah. I'd follow either of them into the heart of the nuclear storm. So, yeah, even without the prophecies, I'm on board . . . and I'm not bound by any oath." He rose and held out a hand to Jade. "Come on. Let's crack some books."

Natalie got to her feet, too, and when JT glared at her, she glared right back. "I shouldn't have to remind you that I came here to help the Nightkeepers protect the barrier, not to play politics." But she reached out and straightened his collar. "Don't be too big of an ass, okay?"

He stared after her as she followed Jade and Lucius out through the sliders that led to the pool deck, shoulders slumping a little as the fight drained out of him. "Shit," he said under his breath, following that up with, "Damn it all to hell."

With any of the others, Strike would've clapped him on the shoulder. Instead, he said, "You'd be an idiot not to be scared."

"I'm not . . ." He shook his head. "It didn't use to matter so much. Bosnia, the Middle East, the death-bat caves down south. I didn't care if I died, really. Now I do."

Strike glanced over and caught Leah's eye. "I know the feeling." But as much as he couldn't imagine leaving her behind, he couldn't do what she wanted either.

JT slid him a look. "I'll fight alongside you and the others. But I'm fighting *for* her."

"Better watch it or I'll start liking you."

The *winikin* snorted. "Give it five minutes, it'll fade." As he moved off, Strike saw that the meeting was breaking up slowly, awkwardly, with lots of looks in his direction that said each of them wanted some one-on-one with their king. But he was cold and tired, and the humming whine in his ears was pissing him off. He just wanted—Shit, this wasn't about what he wanted. They needed face time, and he would give it to them, even if it was going to feel too damn much like saying good-bye.

"Out!" Leah ordered suddenly, making shooing motions that sent Sven's coyote skittering with a low snarl. "There are fifteen doors in this room. Use them." She had the room cleared in minutes.

He exhaled slowly. "I seriously love you."

"Back atcha." She flowed into his arms, pressed her face into his throat, and clung, hard.

He felt a fine tremor run through her, and held her tighter. "Hey. It's okay, I'm not giving up, okay? I'm going to fight until . . . I'm going to fight. I promise."

But as she tipped her face up to his and their lips met and melded, he heard that damn humming, and a soft whisper of: *Fulfill the prophecies or suffer Vucub's wrath.*

# CHAPTER TWENTY-TWO

At the lower end of the firing range, the Nightkeepers had built a training ground peppered with fake ruins that mimicked the places where they did most of their fighting. The replica temples, stelae, and crumbling walls were mostly made of cinder blocks and plaster, and the big pyramid at one end was steel and cement.

Reese had always liked it there. It was the closest she could get to being back in a city. She sat atop the big pyramid, some three stories up, even though the sweeping view of the wide canyon, with its clustered buildings and out-of-place rain forest grove, made her ache for skyscrapers and gritty alleys, and the feeling that she was one among many, even when she was alone. Here, she was one of a chosen few; her actions, her choices, carried a different sort of weight.

She wasn't going to run. Dez had pissed her off when he accused her of having a history of bolting rather than seeing things all the way through to their bitter end, but there had been a kernel of truth to it. Over and over again, she had gotten to a certain point in a struggle when the walls closed in, trapping her—with her parents and stepfather, with Dez, with her work in LA . . . and with Fallon—and each time she had gotten to a point where she just snapped and took off. Every. Single. Time.

Her entire life, people had called her stupid-brave or a variation on the theme, so it was a hell of a thing to realize that she was a coward when it came to her own life. This was different, though—her comfort level didn't do much to tip the scales, given what was on the other side of the balance. So she would stay, and she would help the geek squad find the patterns they needed, help the warriors think more like street rats.

If the worst went down and Dez wound up fulfilling the serpent prophecy, she didn't think he would survive it, not as the man he was now. Killing Hood—a truly vile soul the world had been better off without—had put him fully under the star demon's spell. What would happen to him if he was put in a position where he was forced to—or worse, chose to—kill Strike and take possession of all five artifacts? She wrapped her arms around her body, though the sudden chill came from within. "That won't happen," she said aloud. At some point, the Doctrine of Balance would have to kick in and the Nightkeepers would catch a break.

But even as she tried to tell herself that Strike would pull through and the team would find some way to get the staff back from Iago and prevent Lord Vulture's nuclear winter—and that was a hell of a laundry list, dragging at her forced optimism—she ached inwardly at the knowledge that Dez would still be named heir. It was inevitable. And, like an alcoholic taking "just one sip," he would start the downward slide.

Unless he didn't.

Over the past few weeks, she had learned to believe in the man he had become—a powerful yet self-controlled mage, a good soldier, and the kind of guy who would sneak her peanut butter cups when she'd had a bad day. She liked this Dez, respected him. He fascinated her, frustrated her, challenged her, and pissed her off. And she felt more alive than she had in a damned decade. Love was too simple a word for it—or maybe her onetime perception of love was too simple. Back then, she hadn't had any doubts that they belonged to each other, and that they could make it work if they both tried hard enough. Now, her feelings for him were deep, dark, and unsettled. He may be addicted to power, but she was addicted to him—she wanted him, craved him, needed him. Or was that how love was supposed to feel? Maybe this crazy, insecure emotional roller coaster was normal. Maybe she needed to trust her feelings and the man he was today.

"Flip a coin," she said softly. "Heads I'm fooling myself and heading for self-destruction. Tails he's for real and history isn't going to repeat this time."

Moments later, a quarter pinged between her feet, took a crazy bounce, and went clinking down the pyramid steps to land somewhere on the packed dirt below.

There was a pause, then Dez said from behind her, "I pictured that going differently. And for the record, it was tails."

Her skin heated; she hadn't sensed his approach.

Stalling, she leaned over and pretended to look for the coin, which was long gone. "Kind of symbolic, really."

"Yeah. When it finally stopped, though, it was still tails."

She looked back at him, found him standing there looking unbearably sexy in fatigue pants and a brown pullover, with a .44 in his belt and shadows in his eyes. "You can see it?"

"No. But I'm for real, and history's not going to repeat itself this time." He hesitated, though, and said, "Strike got the others on board for a sort of compromise. They're not happy about it, but . . . if I agree to it, they'll transfer their fealty oaths to me."

*Oh*, she thought, breathing through a sharp stab of pain. "That's . . . logical." And it scared the piss out of her.

He sat down beside her. "I won't have the full powers of a king, but it'll increase our chances when we go up against Iago. Strike is afraid that whatever's going on with him is going to spill over into the bonds if he doesn't transfer the oaths."

She put her head on his shoulder, very aware of his arm against her, and the place where he would wear the *hunab ku* if he truly became king. "I want to beg you not to do it, to ask you to run away with me . . . But this is too important."

He took her hand, threaded their fingers together. "We're important."

"What I wouldn't have given to hear that at eighteen."

"But not now?"

"I like hearing it. But this is bigger than us." Way, way bigger.

They both knew he would agree to Strike's plan. He didn't have a choice—they needed to attack Iago the moment he stepped foot back on the earthly plane, the king wasn't fit to lead, and the prophecies said the task should fall to Dez. But the thought of him taking over the power of the fealty oaths put a nasty churn in her stomach.

"You thought about us running away together." He paused. "So stay with me, instead. Give me a chance to prove myself to you."

"It's not . . ." She trailed off, because in a way it *was* about him proving himself. He needed to prove—not just to her, but to himself and the rest of the Nightkeepers—that he could handle power and tell the difference between temptation and a strategic move. He had to show them that he wouldn't fall back under the star demon's spell when the artifacts were put in play. If it came down to worst-case-scenario time between him and Strike, he needed to make the most honorable choice he possibly could, without any taint of self-service. And after that . . . No, she didn't want to think about what would happen if he became king, or even if he just kept hold of the fealty oaths and became Strike's heir.

How long would it be before she trusted him not to revert to his old self? Or would she always be watching him, analyzing every move? God, that sounded exhausting. And dysfunctional. But how could she be sure that he wouldn't backslide?

"I know we said that life doesn't come with any guarantees," he said, "but I promise you this: I'm going to do my absolute best to be a good soldier and serve my king, and if shit goes south and I wind up wearing the *hunab ku*, I'll do my best to get that right, too. And no matter where I wind up in the hierarchy, you'll be right there with me. I don't want to lose you again, Reese, and I'll do whatever it takes to keep that from happening." His eyes were determined, his tone resolute, and the warmth that flared through her at his words carried a spark of lightning and a hum of magic that almost drowned out the tiny, irritating voice that warned it wouldn't last.

*Screw that*, she thought, and leaned in to kiss him, pausing to whisper, "I don't want to lose you again, either. So be warned: if I see you starting to go off the rails this time, I'm going to do my damnedest to beat some sense back into you."

His lips curved against hers. "Deal. Though I'll try not to make it necessary."

"You—" *Do that*, she meant to say, but lost the words when he closed the final fraction of an inch and kissed her.

It hadn't been all that long, really, since their lovemaking that morning, but so much had happened, so many emotions had wrung her out and filled her back up, that she felt like they hadn't kissed in a year. Warmth was a sweet ache that turned to heat as she touched the back of his neck, his shoulders, and he crowded closer with a rasping groan and deepened the kiss. After not nearly enough time, though, they drew apart. Her lips felt soft and swollen, her breasts were heavy, her skin tingled all over.

She would have given anything to take the afternoon off, with him, and pretend the rest of the world didn't exist. But it was the whole "world not existing" thing that had her climbing to her feet. "I think we need to hold that thought and head back."

"Rain check," he agreed, and she was struck by the strange normalcy of the exchange, like they had been lovers all along. But the heat between them was bright, fresh, and new as they headed down the pyramid.

At the bottom, he stopped and bent to pick up a small, shiny bit of metal.

"Heads or tails?" she asked, telling herself there was no reason for her mouth to go dry. The U.S. Mint didn't imbue their coins with prescient magic.

He just shook his head and put the coin in his pocket.

*Heads*, she thought, grateful that at least he hadn't lied. Besides, it didn't matter whether she was on the fast track toward self-destruction. She had made her choice. Taking his hand, she laced their fingers together, conscious of the way their shadows merged in the slanting afternoon light, stretching larger than their true selves. "Come on," she said, tugging him in the direction of the mansion. "Let's go tell the others that you're ready to take their fealty oaths. The looks on a few of their faces should be good for a laugh, at any rate." She would take whatever jollies she could get, because the next day and a half had the potential to get seriously grim.

\*    \*    \*

*Virginia Beach*

As the *Disco* churned up to its mooring, a thousand or so pint-sized whale watchers—okay, technically more like a hundred, but it had felt like there were a thousand of them—leaned over the railing, waving and hooting at nobody in particular while Cara and the school group's chaperones made sure that was all they were doing.

"I'm pretty sure we got all the Silly String, but I don't trust those guys when they start clumping up," Too-tight Facelift said as she buzzed past on her way to eagle-eye the group that Cara had mentally dubbed Juvies-in-training. Meanwhile, Stern Teacher was rooting the I'm-too-sexies out of the forward ladies' room and Nurse Nancy was keeping Pukers One through Three corralled on the lower deck, just in case. Because being barfed on from the observation platform just sucked. Been there, done that.

"Excuse me, Miss Cara?"

"Yes?" She turned to find one of the Actually-has-a-brain—this one had borderlined on Smarty Pants, but Cara had decided to give her the benefit of the doubt—standing there with two other girls behind her, all looking owlishly serious. Where most of the others had tweaked their navy sweaters, tan pants, or plaid skirts into fashion statements, this group just let their uniforms look like uniforms, as if saying "This is only temporary—why bother?"

"You can ship the sperm," the first girl announced.

"Excuse me?"

"For the right whales. You said the populations here and off California were dying from inbreeding, but there was no way to ship whales across the country to mix things up."

"I did," Cara said faintly. It was part of her "how the whaling practices of the seventeen and eighteen hundreds are still screwing us up today" spiel. This was the first time it had sparked a convo about sperm, though.

"My mom raises horses, and she just has the semen shipped." Smarty Pants—it was confirmed now—lowered her voice to a conspiratorial whisper. "Make sure you call FedEx and let them know it's coming, though. It's only good for a few days."

Choking back a snort, Cara nodded. "Thanks. I'll keep that in mind." No way she was going into the midocean-orgy factor of whale mating behavior or the unlikelihood of getting a diver in there to collect sperm, never mind what the heck they would do with it on the other end. Nope, not going there. But she was grinning as she stood by the gangplank and said her good-byes to Stern Teacher and the rest.

"You look happy," Cap'n Jack said from behind her as the last of the Juvies filtered through.

Cara tipped her head back and inhaled a deep lungful of air. "I am. I feel better. No. Not just better. Fabulous." It wasn't just that the not-flu was gone, either. Energy coursed through her, making her feel like she could take on the world.

Jack came up beside her, leaned on the gangplank railing. "Any particular reason you're happy-dancing today?"

"It was a good day. A good group, good sightings, good energy."

"If you say so. Seemed about average to me."

She made a face. "Don't poop on my party."

"Sorry." But he was grinning. "We still on for later?"

"Lasagna night? Wouldn't miss it. Tell Beth I'll be there at six, brownies in hand." It felt good to have that connection, too. Jack and Beth made her feel like family.

"You can bring a friend if you like. There's always plenty of food."

She laughed. "What friend? You're my friends."

But he nodded down at the dock. "Looks like there's a guy waiting on you. Thought he might have something to do with you feeling better these days."

"A guy? No way." She shook her head, glancing over. "There's no—" Her mouth dried at the sight of a swimmer's body inside painted-on denim and a tight techno-fabric jacket. Familiar blue eyes looked out from beneath familiar blond hair that was cut in an unfamiliar military brush. Her brain said *it's not him—where's the ponytail? where's the surfer gear and perma-tan?* But in her heart she knew exactly who it was. "Oh," she said. As in, *oh, shit.* As in, *oh, that's why I feel like the world has come back into focus.* Damn him. Damn all of them, and the accident of birth that had thrown her in with them. "Sven," she said, the word coming out more like a wistful breath than a name.

Jack chuckled. "Thought so. No problem if you're a lasagna no-show—Beth'll understand. Or like I said, feel free to bring him along. The dog can come, too. If it acts up, Pegleg will just hiss and go hide somewhere until the coast is clear."

"What— Oh." How had she missed the big, buff-and-gray creature that sat beside him? *That's no dog*, she thought half hysterically. *Shaving it down doesn't make it any less a coyote.* Which was another shock—Sven had a familiar. The realization sent a shimmy through her.

"Go on and talk to him." Jack's eyes narrowed on her as he caught the vibe. "Unless you don't want to?"

She really didn't. "It's okay," she said softly. "But don't expect him for dinner."

"Whatever works." He gave her shoulder a brief squeeze before he turned away. "If I don't see you tonight, I'll see you tomorrow."

"See you," she echoed, hoping it was the truth. Hoping Sven hadn't come to bring her back to the desert because . . . *gods*. Had something happened to her father? Sudden fear rocketed through her, sending her racing along the gangplank and down to the lower level, where man and coyote waited unmoving.

"Carlos is fine," he called the moment her feet hit the dock. "Don't freak."

She slowed, blowing out a breath and pressing a hand to her stomach as the quick panic drained. Okay. That was something, anyway. But even as the fear for her father subsided, new disquiet took its place. Because if Sven wasn't there because of her father, then he was there because of her.

As he watched her approach, his eyes—the muted blue of a sea under hazy skies—were cool and assessing, making her wonder what he saw. She couldn't tell from the way he was watching her, and that made her nervous. So, too, did the realization that the changes in his clothing and hair, and the addition of the coyote weren't the only things that were different about him. He was leaner than he had been, his face honed down to its basic Michelangelo perfection, his body big and broad, but spare. More, he stood perfectly still, not jiggling from foot to foot or looking around in search of the next adventure, the next diversion. That change, more than anything, made him seem like a stranger as she stopped, squared off opposite him.

She blew out a breath when her heartbeat picked up again. How had she forgotten the physical punch of a mage? Or had he become even more potent than before, his beauty amped by magic and the power of a familiar? She didn't know. All she knew was that a part of her wanted to bow, scrape, and worship. And she despised that part of herself. So she tipped her head and shot for casual when she said, "It's been a while."

"It has. You look good."

"Whatever you've got to say, say it fast. I've got a date." Which was true. Sort of.

The coyote gave a low whine in the back of its throat. She glanced over, but it was looking past her, to where gulls were squabbling over an unidentifiable something.

"Cancel it."

She bared her teeth. "Newsflash: I don't have to follow orders—not from my father and not from you."

He shook his head quickly, "That wasn't what I—"

He broke off when she shoved the sleeve of her Windbreaker, sweater, and shirt up over her forearm. His eyes widened when he took in the lack of any decoration save for the thin bracelet that curved inward and touched her seasickness pressure points.

"My marks faded. I don't work for you anymore."

The coyote stirred, but he dropped a hand to the top of its head and it quieted. "I've come to bring you back," he said simply. "Skywatch needs you."

She started to answer, but then hesitated, frowning because that really didn't compute. If anything, she had been a distraction within the training compound—a young half-human *winikin* who hadn't been raised in the program and didn't care for the hierarchy. "How does that work? I didn't fit in there. I didn't make any *sense* there."

"Things have changed. They need to keep changing." He dug into a pocket, held out a note. "From Jox. You've been promoted."

Heart racing, she took the note, careful not to let their fingers brush. She didn't open it right away, though. Instead, she hesitated, looking up at the bulk of the *Disco* as she rode solidly at the wharf.

He looked up, too, expression going wistful. "I never figured you for the sea."

"Me neither." And that was all he was getting.

She hesitated, then opened the letter and read it. Then she reread it. Twice. The words dipped and wheeled like gulls: . . . *too stuck in tradition, need to modernize . . . perfect for the job . . . end-time war needs you . . . calling you back to duty.* "Jox wants me to lead the *winikin*," she said dully. The surf roared in her ears, though the water beyond the marina was glassy.

"I know. And there's more, something that Jox didn't know about." As with the letter, his words ran together: *... more survivors ... unbound* winikin *... members of the resistance ... Mendez wants them brought in ... JT wants to meet you first ...*

For a moment, she flashed back on the pain and terror of her father calling the magic to mark her with the *aj winikin* and the coyote glyph, indenturing her to Sven. He hadn't raised her within the system that to him was the natural order of things—he had focused on Sven, leaving her to her mother, and then had the gall to be surprised when she hadn't been able to make it work at Skywatch. She had hated the place, the people, and the hierarchy that said she was little more than a glorified servant to the shallow, egotistical golden boy her father had raised.

"... and tomorrow's the solstice," Sven said in conclusion.

She lifted a shoulder. "First day of winter. Big whoop."

He looked out over the water as if just noticing there was an ocean there. Or maybe he was stalling. Maybe this was just as awkward for him as it was for her. She had outgrown her long-ago crush on him, had decided to file the rest of it under "things I did when I was young and stupid" and move on. But while that might have worked if he had looked like the guy who had finally sent her away from Skywatch before they killed each other, the man who looked back at her now was a stranger—tough and capable-looking. "Strike and Anna are sick," he said quietly. "Maybe dying. Red-Boar and Woody are already dead. Jox and Hannah are in hiding with the twins. And tomorrow . . . hell, unless the skies split open and drop a damned miracle on us, it could all be over tomorrow and this whole conversation is pointless. But if we make it to next week, we're going to need the unbound *winikin* to have any chance. And to get the survivors, we need you."

"This JT guy—"

"Isn't an option to lead the *winikin*. None of them are. You're Jox's choice." His voice dropped an octave. "We need you, Cara."

A warm, heavy body pressed against her leg. She looked down to find the coyote leaning against her, looking up with pleading eyes. "Nice try," she said, figuring Sven had told the animal to ham it up. But when she looked back at him, she found him staring at the coyote with a faint wrinkle between his eyes.

She told herself that it didn't matter, that *he* didn't matter, at least not any more than the others. But that was a lie. *You've told me what everyone else back there wants. What do you want?* But asking that would imply that he had the right to an opinion, which he didn't. She didn't wear his bloodline mark anymore, wouldn't ever have worn it in the first place if her father had given her a choice. She had a choice now, though. "I'm not doing it," she said finally, even though her stomach was churning, her bones aching. "I'm staying here. I like what I'm doing. I'm good at it."

"You'd be good at this, too."

She almost laughed. "You must be desperate."

"I want you to come back willingly."

"That's not going to happen." But a chill shivered through her at the implied threat. "And for the record, if any of you are thinking of knocking me out and dragging me back, be advised that Jox isn't the only one capable of leaving sealed letters with friends. If I disappear, you guys are going to get some unexpected—and official—visitors." The Nightkeepers weren't a strictly secret organization, but they definitely preferred to stay far off the government's radar.

His eyes narrowed. A low growl vibrated in the coyote's throat. "You're bluffing," Sven said quietly.

"Try me." She stared him down until he looked away. Satisfied, she nodded. "Sorry," she said, completely unapologetic. "I've got to go. Like I said, I've got a date."

Spinning on her heel, she marched to the staircase that led up to the parking area. She didn't need him, she reminded herself, refusing to look back. Right now all she needed was to drown herself in friendship and lasagna, though the thought of eating anything made her want to hurl. Then, when she got home, she would figure out how to stash a letter to Jack and Beth, telling them that if she disappeared without warning they should start the search in a small box canyon near Chaco, New Mex. She probably should have done that a while ago, but until she came to work on the *Disco*, there hadn't been anyone who would have noticed that she was gone.

Now, though, she had a life. And it didn't have

anything to do with a dozen magic users and their servant-slaves.

Mac chuffed anxiously as Cara hit the top of the staircase and strode out of sight without looking back, leaving Sven with the impression of her dark and mysterious eyes, exotic face, and the startling streak of white in her hair. Along with those images, though, came the sinking sensation of failure.

He had known it wouldn't be easy to see her again, even harder to convince her to come back with him. He didn't know what else he had expected—the awkwardness they had parted with, maybe, or even the air-clearing fight they probably should have had years ago. But whatever he'd expected, it hadn't been for her to be coolly indifferent and turn him down flat. He looked down at Mac. "Now what?"

The coyote whined a little, still staring after her, projecting: *friend-friend-friend.*

Apparently his familiar was already a fan. Poor sod. Sven shook his head. "I'm not so sure she would agree with that one." Problem was, he didn't have a choice in the matter, because Dez's order had been crystal: *Do whatever it takes to get her back here.* He had taken command a few hours ago, and while the transfer of the fealty oaths actually hadn't turned out to be that big a deal—Sven didn't feel a difference, at any rate—the new commander's first order had made some serious waves. Long overdue waves, maybe, but waves nonetheless, because he had told the *winikin* to "crack the fucking envelope and put Jox's replacement in charge already."

So, despite JT's blustering, the deed had been done, and a name had raced through the room: Cara Liu.

That had been a hell of a shock for most of them—Carlos had seemed like the obvious choice—but once Sven got past his initial "no fucking way" and a whole lot of other emotions he was ignoring, he had seen the logic. She wasn't part of the system, wasn't really outside it. She would have as good a chance as anyone—except maybe Rabbit—to convince JT to cough up the resistance's old contact protocol, bring in the rest of the unbound *winikin*, and find a way to integrate them into the hierarchy—or build a new one. More, she didn't want to do it. She hated Skywatch, despised the idea of being anybody's servant, resented her father, and wasn't overly fond of the Nightkeepers. Which, again, made Jox's choice a damned good one under the circumstances.

For maybe ten seconds, he debated following her and taking another crack at convincing her to come willingly with the added bonus of scaring off her date. But then he shook his head and tapped his armband instead, hitting up Strike for a ride home. Rabbit had shored up the king's 'port talent once more, and Strike swore he was fine to 'port himself and one or two others. Besides, it wasn't like they had another option—with thirty-some hours to go, there was no time to waste on traveling.

Once Strike was on his way, Sven stuck his hands in his pockets and looked out over the harbor, feeling only a small tug at the sight of the wide-open sea. He figured that he would give Cara a day or two to think it over and set up her fail-safe letters—or even disappear entirely, if that was what she wanted to do. Dez would be pissed, but he would deal with that if it happened, because as far as he was concerned, some things were better left in the past. And not everything that had happened before would—or should—happen again.

# CHAPTER TWENTY-THREE

December 21
Solstice day
*Skywatch*

In the hours after Dez took over the Nightkeepers' fealty oaths, things broke loose in a big way, to the point that he started getting sidelong looks that were more speculative than hostile. Reese didn't know whether the breakthroughs were a sign of the gods' approval or just a case of timing working in their favor for a change, but suddenly she had information to work with.

It started with the charm that Sven had taken off the dying villager, which they were assuming was how Iago was turning innocents into *makol*. The leather pouch had turned out to contain black cohosh, sage, and a couple of other ingredients shared with the antidote Reese had cooked up for Dez, along with a small, crudely carved stone that was slippery with dark magic. It all seemed to corroborate that Iago was descended from the serpent bloodline, which had gotten

Reese and the others talking, throwing ideas around the library's main stone table.

With Dez closeted in the royal quarters hashing over the plan for tomorrow, and no real private time in sight, she had geared up for an all-nighter. Lucius was dividing his time, brainstorming with Reese, working on whittling down the sites where Iago could be hiding and trying to find a cure for Strike. Jade and Natalie were in and out, helping when they weren't needed elsewhere. And by the time the sky was lightening with the first pink smudges of dawn, Reese had a working theory that she felt was spot on.

Lucius had made the connection that the serpents had left the Mayan territories and established their northern outposts right around the same time the Xibalban sect had split off from the Nightkeepers. It was Reese, though, who had figured it out. "The codex you found said the serpents were sent to settle the outposts because the jaguars considered them particularly loyal, but what if that was spin control? What if the jaguars were getting rid of them? And what if that was related to the Xibalban split?"

"You're thinking about a failed coup?" Lucius had said, surprised . . . but then nodded. "Yeah, I see it. A group of serpents lose sight of their balance and start getting in deep with the dark magic . . . and the next step, given their makeup, would be the throne. Maybe there was already a legend about a serpent king, maybe it started there, who knows? Either way, they got their asses kicked, the jaguars kept the throne, and the bad serpents became the Xibalbans."

"Which left the jaguars with the question of what to do with the rest of the serpents. So they sent them north as a 'reward'"—Reese finger-quoted the word—"for their loyalty." It fit. It played. And she wished it didn't, because she could seriously use a break from thinking about the serpents and their ambitions.

Over the next couple of hours, they used the new info to narrow down the list of possible sites for Iago's mountain temple. With Strike's ability to teleport severely limited, the magi would be able to check out only five or six of the most likely sites. But even selecting for mountains with Mayan or Aztec connections plus a snake legend left them with fifty-two possibles and nothing more to go on, really. Reese's temper sharpened as her rumbling stomach escalated from twinges to a bad-tempered mutter.

"There's bread in the bowl over there." Without looking up from the codex he was translating, which had a slim chance of being able to help Strike, Lucius made a vague gesture behind him. There, a carved stone jaguar fountained water from its mouth to gather in a bowl between its paws, while a second bowl held maize cakes. Both were always fresh and fully replenished.

"The magical bread-and-water deal is cool, but I was thinking more along the lines of a decent doughnut." She hadn't had a really great doughnut—plain, with just a little crunch around the edges—since arriving at Skywatch.

"Would Belgian waffles count?"

She jumped at the sound of Dez's voice, and her

edginess smoothed out some when she saw him standing in the doorway with a picnic cooler. "With whipped cream?"

"Freshly made, plus strawberries. Not to bring down the room, but apparently, Sasha cooks up a storm when she's upset."

Reese sobered. "I wish we had something that would help."

"That wasn't a complaint." He crossed to her and kissed her cheek.

She leaned into him, closing her eyes for a second, then realizing that was a bad idea when fatigue washed through her. He was warm and solid, and smelled like breakfast and the outdoor air. In another lifetime, they would have woken up together and made leisurely love, then made breakfast together, sneaking kisses and copping feels in the process. But it wasn't reality, she knew—she was pretty sure neither of them could cook. Not to mention that they had a world to save, and she was stuck. Sighing, she straightened away from him. "Let's eat."

They cleared a section of the stone table and laid out the feast he had brought—not just the waffles, but fluffy eggs, toast, and a thermos of coffee for Lucius and one of tea for her, along with a two-liter of Diet Mountain Dew and a plate of brownies that he left in the cooler with a mock-stern glare. "Those are for later. Or at least wait until I'm out the door before you dig in."

She flipped him a salute, and made do with a waffle piled with enough whipped cream and syrupy strawberries to make him wince.

Breakfast was a brief but lively meal, with Jade and Natalie joining in halfway through. Dez caught the researchers up on the battle preparations, including the welcome news that Rabbit had gotten in contact with an older brother of his *makol*-abducted friend, Cheech. The older brother, who worked in Mexico City and was far more mainstream than his relatives, had heard about the village and was frantic for his family. When Rabbit, posing as a member of a secret U.S. government agency, had "recruited" him as a local asset to help locate the guerilla group responsible for the village raids, he had jumped at the chance. With the help of several trusted friends, he was redistributing the magic sensors throughout Mexico City; built atop the Aztec's capital city, the backfilled lake region was where Iago typically hung out. "It won't give us much warning," Dez finished, "but that's better than none."

Reese squelched her instinctive bristle, well aware that her pissiness wasn't aimed at him. She hated that the patterns weren't coming this time, when it mattered so damn much. When they figured out the connection between the serpents and the Xibalbans, she had been so sure it would point them toward Iago's hideout. And maybe it would, but not fast enough . . . and they were running out of time.

Lucius outlined what they had so far, finishing with, "If Strike could 'port us—"

"He can't," Dez said flatly. "As it is, Rabbit's going to have to ride shotgun inside his head to get us down south when we figure out where we need to be." He said "when" but Reese heard "if."

"Then I should get back to work on this." Lucius tapped the codex he'd been translating. "We need our teleporter back in action."

"We need to find the mountain," Dez corrected.

"Exactly," Reese agreed, chasing a last forkful of waffle. "Which means that we need to get some magi down to the potential sites to sniff around."

But as Lucius moved to the other end of the table, where he'd been working, Dez said, "No, I mean that I need you to stop dividing your efforts and focus on the mountain. Not Lord Vulture, the serpents, or Strike's illness. Find. Me. That. Mountain."

Reese's stomach knotted and the breath backed up in her lungs. His eyes held regret . . . but she thought she saw something else there too, something hard and implacable, almost daring her to argue, as if he would welcome the fight, the excuse to push her away. She knew that look, though she hadn't seen it in a long time. *Don't overreact,* she told herself. *You're tired and frustrated.* What was more, like a cheater's wife imagining another woman's perfume or a junkie's mother searching her kid's room, she was primed to see problems where they may not exist. "We need Strike's help," she said carefully. "He's our best bet of narrowing down the search."

Dez shook his head. "Find another way." Impatience tightened his face. "There's a difference between exploring all the avenues and getting stuck in a dead end. And—" He broke off. "Shit. Sorry." He leaned back, exhaling. "This sucks. I hate having to make this call, but someone has to. We need that mountain, guys. We've got to get to Iago before he activates the serpent staff."

It was a good apology, good logic. But was it the whole story or only the tip of a lurking iceberg? *Stop it*, she told herself.

"You're right." Lucius sat heavily. "I know you're right. It's just . . . Shit." He scrubbed his eyes with the back of his hand. "No. You're right. I'll stop buzzing around. Damn it to hell." He hadn't said it, but Reese knew he was hoping that curing Strike might somehow help Anna, who still lay unconscious—not getting any worse, but not getting better, either.

Dez nodded. "Thanks. I hate having to make the call, but . . . thanks." He paused. "We okay?" He directed the question at both of them, but he was looking at Reese.

She hesitated, then nodded. "We're okay," she said softly, and told herself to believe it. But as he collected the trash and cooler—leaving the soda and brownies behind—and headed out, her stomach stayed uneasy, her instincts prickling.

Ten minutes after he left, though, they got the break they needed.

"*Got it*," Lucius hissed triumphantly, eyes gleaming. "I've fucking got it."

Reese's heart jolted. She had been running scenarios while waiting on hold for the past ten minutes—way longer than it should have taken her contact to check an order for the one rare ingredient found in the *makol* amulet: a certain type of snub-nosed snake. Now she hung up and crowded in beside him as relief spiraled through her. "Show me."

His laptop showed a photo of an ancient ruined city with a main street, offshoots, a shit ton of building footprints, a few more complete structures, and two huge rubble mounds that had been partly restored back to pyramids. A modern suburb sprawled in the near distance—was that a Wal-Mart behind the pyramid?—and mountains loomed in the background.

"That's Mexico City," he said. "And this"—he indicated the ruin—"is Teotihuacan. It's not Aztec or Maya, which is why it wasn't a primary focus of our search. It was a sort of spiritual tourist attraction for the Aztec, though, kind of the way we treat their ruins now. And you see these mountains?" He highlighted the distant peaks. "Moctezuma built temples on them. When you draw lines connecting the temples with the pyramids of Teotihuacan, it measures out the Long Count."

"Aztec temples that refer to the Mayan calendar predicting the end date." Reese nodded. "That fits with what we're looking for."

"So does this." Lucius did the *tap-tap* thing and brought up a line drawing of a temple made of upright pillars carved into gape-mouthed serpents. "Got this from a Spanish missionary's journal. These are the same three mountains back in the mid–fifteen hundreds." When he zoomed out, the temple was shown located atop the middle of three mountains, with other temples hinted at on the other two, a ruin roughed into the foreground. "This," he said, "is the one on the left in close to real time." He tapped and the line drawing was replaced by a bird's-eye photograph of sparse tree cover and a jumbled ruin. *Tap.* "The one on the right." Another greened-out photo, another temple footprint. *Tap.* "The middle." Green. But no ruin, not even a shadowy depression or some broken rock to mark where one might have been. "Lower down, sure, the forests can grow over anything in zero time flat. But up there? We should see something . . . unless it's been deliberately hidden. Like on another plane."

Reese nodded, pulse upping a notch. "Works for me. Let's—" Her phone rang with a digital bleat; it was the snake guy. She answered, "Montana here."

"Got the info here," he said in accented English. "The guy's name was M. Zuma, and they were shipped to a cantina in Pachuca." He rattled off the address. "That help?"

"It does. I'll put a thank-you in the mail tomorrow."

"I take PayPal."

"Of course you do." What self-respecting black marketer didn't these days? She wrote down the info, shaking her head, but as she hung up, she shot a hard-edged grin at Lucius. "M. Zuma bought three of those snubnosed snakes last week, and has bought a couple of dozen over the past few months, all for delivery to a bar in Pachuca. How close is that to your mountain?"

"Damn close."

"Okay, let's pull together all the info we can find on this thing, and I'll take it to Dez while you get back to work on that codex. And let's not tell Dez he was right, okay?" But she was grinning as she said it, because what mattered was that they had found Coatepec Mountain . . . and they might have a fighting chance after all.

By noon of the solstice day, when the full team assembled in the great room and the briefing got under way, Dez had the beginnings of a plan and a hell of a stress headache.

The migraine had hit him the second he accepted the first of the fealty oaths: Strike's. He suspected the shit hurt because the power that had come with the oaths—a strange and vibrant sort of feeling in the depths of his chest—wasn't balanced by the responsibilities that came with the true kingship. Sasha had taken the edge off the headache, bringing it down to a dull roar. She hadn't been able to do anything about the stress, though.

He wasn't sure if he'd been too young, too stupid, or too firmly under the star demon's control when he led the Cobras, but he didn't remember it being this complicated. Back then, when he gave an order somebody got it done. Simple. This, on the other hand, was anything but simple. He was trying to coordinate a dozen magi who were waiting for him to screw something up, along with a bunch of *winikin* who weren't sure they liked each other, never mind him. Strike was shaky and Anna was barely hanging on, which meant that the people closest to them were distracted. And Reese hadn't said anything, but he had seen her flinch when he cracked down on Lucius. She seemed okay now, but it had put him on edge.

He couldn't vet his orders through her, didn't intend to—he'd been put in place partly because he was a colder-blooded leader than Strike, and he needed to be that guy. But it worried him. *Hang on, baby*, he urged her as she briefed the others on the discovery of Coatepec Mountain. *We've just got to get through today, and things will settle down.* He hoped.

"We should have a new set of updated images in the next thirty minutes," she was saying, having taken over the briefing so Lucius could stay in the library. "One of my contacts thinks he can get us some penetrating radar shots as well, which could give us a better idea of the temple's footprint, maybe even a hint at the tunnels mentioned in the missionary's journal." She sent it back to Dez with a nod.

To Nate, who had the ability to shape-shift into a powerful man-sized hawk called the Volatile, he said, "Once we get in there, I want you up flying recon."

"Alexis and I are on that."

"Not Alexis. I want you to take Patience." Very aware of the low mutterings, he held up a hand. "I know that means splitting up two mated pairs. But think about it logically. The *makol* can sense Alexis's chameleon shield because it's a spell, but they can't detect Patience when she goes invisible, because that's an inborn talent. Which means she and Nate, invisible, can take recon footage without being seen or sensed, and potentially blasted out of the sky." He thought about asking if they were cool with that, but didn't, because this wasn't a democracy. Moving on, he said, "We'll 'port into this clearing here." He indicated a spot on the satellite image being projected on the big flat screen, and glanced at Strike. The king sat beside Leah, gray-faced but otherwise looking okay. "You're confident you can make the jump?" Not like they had another option. There wasn't enough time for them to get to the mountain any other way.

The king nodded. "Yeah. Rabbit's going to do the driving. We've done a few practice hops, and we're good to go."

"We'll use the clearing as a staging area," Dez said, because there was really no point in dwelling on the teleport. It would work because it had to work. "From there, we'll monitor the recon and figure whether we can 'port into the temple, whether we'll have to fight our way in, or if there's a third option, maybe using the tunnels." He continued, hitting the necessary points and then tagging the warriors with their areas of responsibility, keeping it vague because the whole damn plan was too damn foggy. He didn't like how much of it was going to come down to last-minute decisions and thinking on the fly. "That'll do it for now," he said, and dismissed them.

As the others filtered out, Reese came up beside him. "Nice job." At his sidelong look, she lifted a shoulder. "I'm not a big fan of breaking up the mated pairs, but I can see the logic. And the rest of it is as good as it's going to get, I think."

"All thanks to you and Lucius finding Coatepec."

"I wish we could've done better—a map of the tunnels, a cure for Strike, something more concrete than a vanishing temple."

"Well, a vanishing temple is all we have to go on

at the moment." And he was stalling. He took a deep breath, knowing what he had to do next . . . and that she wasn't going to like it one bit. He had even tried to talk himself out of it, but his warrior's instincts, which in the wake of the oath ceremony had become so powerful they were almost tangible, said: *This is the only way. The right way.*

Hopefully, she would understand.

# CHAPTER TWENTY-FOUR

As Dez fell silent, no doubt running through the plan yet again in his head, Reese turned to watch the *winikin*, who had started bringing in the heavy plastic crates that contained jade-tipped ammo, and the high- and low-tech communication devices that the Night-keepers would be taking with them. Catching sight of the box containing the computer stuff, she said, "I assume you'll want me on the satellite?" Computer work wasn't her favorite, but she was good at it.

"Actually, I'm going to have you stay here and run this end of the uplink."

She turned and rolled her eyes at him. "Like hell you are. Try again." But then she faltered, because he didn't look like he was teasing. In fact, he looked wary, as though he knew she wasn't going to like what he had to say. Which meant it was for real, and made her stomach give an unsteady churn.

Voice too serious, he said, "Having you back here will let Lucius keep working until the last possible second, and it'll give us two sets of very good eyes analyzing the recon footage with Skywatch's equipment."

Staring at him, she tried to see past the wariness to the truth below. She wasn't sure what she found, but it wasn't good. "This isn't about equipment or the recon," she said slowly. "What's really going on here?"

He hesitated, then glanced around to make sure nobody else was in earshot. Lowering his voice to a near whisper, but sounding far more like the Dez she knew, he said, "I don't feel good about this, Reese. There are too many damn unknowns, too many gaps in the plan." When she drew breath, he held up a hand. "I'm not trying to box you in or overprotect you, or if I am, it's for my own benefit."

She told herself not to overreact. "Because you'd be worried about me? That's thin, Mendez."

"It's more than that." He pinched the bridge of his nose, wincing. "My damn head isn't just killing me, it's stuffed full. I'm trying to juggle too many pieces of intel right now, and I'm afraid that if I get distracted, even for a second, I'm going to drop the wrong one at exactly the wrong moment, make the wrong decision, and get someone killed. Or, worse, get us all killed."

She saw the truth in his eyes, read it in the trickle of energy between them. "Then let me help."

"I would, I swear. But you've never been in one of these things before. Take the bloodiest gang skirmish you can imagine and triple it, and then imagine that everybody on the other side keeps getting back up and walking back into the line of fire. Take Iago as you saw him in the ice cave and make him ten times more powerful, because he'll be on his own turf and channeling the solstice. And then put the Nightkeepers in the middle of that. Yeah, we'll be amped up on the solstice, too, but we're going to be making it up as we go along, and we'll probably be fighting our asses off the whole way."

"You don't trust me to watch your back?" The stomach churn had escalated to a full-on roil, but she wasn't sure if that was because she was missing something, or because she could actually see his point and didn't want to.

He raised a hand and skimmed his knuckles along her jaw. "I trust you."

"But?"

"It's me I don't trust. I've only been doing the Nightkeeper thing for a year, and I've been in charge of this circus for, what, twenty-six hours? There's no way I can lead the team at the same time that I'm thinking about where you are, whether you're safe." He touched her lips, smiling slightly, though his eyes stayed serious. "I know you don't want that to be my responsibility, so let's call it my prerogative as your lover. Or are you going to tell me that you won't be worried about me?"

She closed her eyes briefly as his question brought the fears she'd been trying so hard to suppress. "Of course I'm going to be worried. But I'd be way less worried if I were right behind you with a gun."

"Well, I'd be *more* worried, because if you're watching out for me and I'm giving orders, then nobody's watching out for you."

And, damn it, she didn't have an answer for that.

He saw it in her eyes, but to his credit, he didn't gloat. "Gods willing we make it through today somehow, there'll be plenty more fighting to do, once I've got my feet under me and my head back on straight." He took her hand, lifted it to his heart, and held it there for a moment. She felt the steady beat beneath her scabbed-over palm, and the vibration of his voice as he said, "I know I promised no more waiting around for the perfect moment, but I'm asking you to give me this one. Stay with Lucius, please."

She hesitated, then nodded. She wanted to fight by his side, yes, but not if it would jeopardize the others. "Okay, you can have this one. But I get the next one."

"You can have anything you want." He leaned in and touched his lips to hers in a barely there kiss that seared through her, kicking shimmers through the thin thread of energy that connected them. She reached up, got him by the collar in a pose that had come to mean so much to them, and drew him down for a deeper, darker kiss. The energy amped and flowed, and for a second, she had that strange, disjointed sensation again, the one where she imagined she was inside him, feeling his heartbeat and desire as her own. It was only for a flash, though, and then she was back in her own perceptions as he ended the kiss and whispered against her lips, "Thank you."

"Don't worry. I'll get you back later." Moved, and all too aware that there may not be a "later" for them— for anyone—she turned away before he saw the glint of tears. "I'll go see how Lucius is doing."

"Yeah. I should go get suited up."

She turned back. "Oh, and—" Whatever else she may have said died instantly the moment she caught sight of his profile and saw his expression: pure relief, underlain with a look she hadn't seen in years, but had once been all too familiar. It was the one that said, "I played that one perfectly."

Her blood iced and her breath backed up in her lungs. "Son. Of. A. Bitch."

He whipped back around, expression blanking. "Reese? What's wrong?"

"You finished congratulating yourself for playing me?"

"I wasn't . . ." He checked himself—a brief hesitation that spoke volumes. "It's not what you think."

Emotions slammed through her in quick succession—shame on the heels of anger, followed by a massive dose of "oh, shit" as she got it. She freaking got it, like it was lit up in neon across his wide chest. "Leaving me behind isn't about safety or distractions, or some such bullshit, is it? You don't want me there because you're planning something and you're afraid I'll call you on it, warn the others."

His eyes cut left and right, making sure they were still alone. "Of course I'm planning something—it's called a battle, and as tough as you are, Reese, you're not tough enough for what we're going to be up against today."

"You're trying to divert me by pissing me off. Which means I'm right. What—" She broke off as the hated images flashed through her mind: *Hood lying dead; a serpent ring in a pool of blood.* Pain sliced through her when the pattern fit, repeated itself. Holy shit, he was going to take out the king regardless of what else happened. He would make it look like an accident, an enemy attack, a slip with the shield spell at the wrong moment. "Strike," she whispered aghast, then realized her mistake when Dez's eyes changed, hardening and going cold.

*Run!* her instincts screamed, suddenly far clearer than they had been in weeks. She ducked, spun, and bolted for the nearest door, knowing there was no way she could take him down without help. She had to get to the others, had to warn them!

A shield materialized in front of her, spitting static and making her hair stand on end. She slapped her palms against it and screamed, "Hel—" Fatigue slammed into her and her muscles gave out, dropping her to her knees, then the floor.

She landed on her side, unmoving, but fought the sleep spell with everything she had, forcing her eyes to stay open even as her vision blurred and the darkness crept in. A camouflage-clad blur moved in front of her, then crouched down. She couldn't see his face, but she could feel his anger. "Damn it, Reese, I didn't want to do that. But you had to be a stubborn—" He broke off as footsteps sounded in a nearby hallway. "Shit."

He gathered her up and lifted her easily, cradling her close to his chest. She could hear his heartbeat, quick and agitated at first, then slowing as he got her through the archway to the residential wing. *No!* she cried inwardly. *Someone, help!* Not because she was afraid that he was going to hurt her physically, but because she knew what he *was* going to do: Keep her out of sight and mind until it was too late.

Sure enough, he carried her, not to her room, but to his own—the one with the sealed-shut windows and the lock on the outside of the door. He set her on his bed, then leaned over her as though to kiss her. Instead, he braced himself on one hand and stared hotly down at her. "If you can't give me the benefit of the doubt for two damn seconds, how am I supposed to prove I can handle the power? And for the record, the only thing I was hiding back there—the thing I was congratulating myself on *not* having to tell you—was that I couldn't have you on the op because I can't filter every decision through whether or not you're going to approve—especially when my damn job is to push the team past their limits, which means doing things you're not going to like. And I can't have you putting doubts into the others' heads, like you were about to just now in the great room. Fealty oath or no, if they think I'm taking aim at the king, they'll be distracted, which is going to get them dead." He paused, shifting to pinch the bridge of his nose.

The vantage put his marked forearm right in front of her face, bringing the serpent, the warrior, and the lightning god into focus. More, she saw the images made by his wrist cuff: the star demon and the red sky-bearer. West and east. Transformation and rebirth. Her head spun.

Dropping his hand to the side of her face, he bent even closer, so his breath feathered along her jaw and made the side of her neck tingle as he said, "Either you trust me or you don't . . . and I guess we've got our answer there." He paused, voice going sad. "Maybe it's not that we've got bad timing. Maybe we just missed our chance."

Tears stung her eyes as he whispered a string of unfamiliar syllables into her ear, repeating the sleep spell. She felt a drop break free as her eyelids turned into lead and dragged shut. Then, as she spun toward unconsciousness, she felt his lips on hers in a chaste, achingly tender kiss, then his hands moving gently over her body, taking her armband and phone, her .38, and even the cute little .22 she wore on her ankle. The tendril of energy between them pulsed, filling her with warmth as red-gold sparks shimmered behind her eyelids.

Then there was darkness, punctuated only by the sound of a door easing shut and a lock clicking into place.

# CHAPTER TWENTY-FIVE

*Coatepec Mountain*

The 'port went off without a hitch, with Strike and Rabbit collaborating to land the team safely in the small clearing downhill from the mountain's crown, right on target. Once they were there, though, Strike doubled over and retched miserably.

"Jesus." Dez stared at the king as the sharp sounds broke through his dark roil of emotion: regret, remorse, anger, grief. Reese would hate him for knocking her out and locking her up, but what other choice had she left him? He'd been telling the truth, damn it. Maybe not all of it, but the part that he'd left out hadn't hurt anyone but her, and he hadn't dared risk having her destabilize an already fragile team. Especially not when parts of it were getting shakier by the second.

"Sorry." Strike straightened painfully, waving off Leah when she tried to help, though softening it with a quiet, "I'm good." That was an overstatement, though;

he was gray and peaked, and his combat gear hung on him even with extra holes punched.

Dez was painfully aware that a couple of the others were thinking the same thing he was: If it came to it, Strike could very well die today, by his hand. There had been no more messages, no miracle cure from Lucius. The prophecies stood, the danger clear and present: The king had to make the ultimate sacrifice and the last serpent needed to take out his adversary and become king.

As if sensing his thoughts, Strike limped over to him, Leah hovering at his elbow. The king's eyes were still the same vivid cobalt blue, his hair black and thick, tied back at his nape. But beneath the jawline beard, his face was gaunt and drawn. When he reached Dez, he held out a hand. "Whatever happens today is on the gods, Mendez. Not you."

Aware that the others were watching, Dez inclined his head in a shallow bow. "If we go down, we go down fighting . . . Sire." He'd never called Strike that before, probably never would again. But in that moment, it felt right. Then he took the king's hand, aligning palm to palm, and, going on instinct, opened himself wide, trying to pump energy into the other man, shoring him up as he had learned to do with Reese.

For a moment, he made the connection: The king's eyes widened and color stained his throat. "Don't drain yourself on my account."

"I'm good." In fact, he was better than good—the power flowed around him like blood, thick and warm. It coalesced, pulsed, surged. And then suddenly it was rushing away from him, flaring outward as if magnetized to a distant point, and "good" went to "oh, shit" in an instant. His magic was wild, crazed, jacked on the solstice rush. Damn it. He yanked away from Strike, trying desperately to rein in the power that poured through him, strange and sinuous.

The king pointed. "Look!"

A section of air near the mountain's peak shimmered and dark magic hissed as, with a *whoomp* that sent Sven's familiar scattering, the serpent temple appeared, its snake-carved pillars and open-roofed structure completely enclosed within a shield that had a strange, pearlescent sheen. The moment it was fully in place, the energy flow cut out and Dez sagged, suddenly drained. *Shit. Shitshitshit.* "What the fuck was that?"

"I'm guessing it was you summoning the serpent temple," Leah said drily. But her eyes telegraphed a silent thanks for the color in Strike's face, and the fact that he looked like he might be able to fire a weapon without the recoil flattening him.

"We're still ten minutes from the three-hour window," Michael reported. He tossed Dez a pair of binoculars. "And check it out. I don't think they were ready for the big reveal."

The scene jumped into focus: a robed shadow knelt within the shield while the green-eyed villagers scrambled to surround the temple, their weapons at rest position, deactivated. "Fuck the recon," Dez said, making the call. "We hit them now."

As the others sprang into action, digging into the

crates for guns and ammo rather than computers and tactical equipment, Strike said in an undertone, "You know this is either a brilliant tactical move, or suicide."

"Story of my life," Dez said, telling himself that bad timing was his and Reese's thing, not his alone. But as his team formed up around him, he heard something that chilled his blood and made him wonder whether his tactical move wasn't entirely self-serving. It was a soft, feminine whisper at the back of his brain that said: *I'm here.*

*Skywatch*

*Anna, for fuck's sake, get up!* The mental snarl cut through the fog, harsh and familiar, yet so out of place that it jolted her to a semblance of focus, bringing a flash of hard gray eyes and anger.

"You're dead," she whispered. She felt her face move, but didn't hear any sound.

*You'll be dead, too, if you don't get moving and open your godsdamned eyes.*

"There's nothing but the fog."

*Those aren't the eyes I'm talking about and you damn well know it.*

Her heart shuddered. "I can't."

*You have to. He needs you to wake the hell up and open your fucking eyes.*

She knew who "he" was. Brother. The one who sat beside her, sad and silent, looking like he had the weight of the world on his shoulders. Because he did. "I can't." This time the whisper came with a breathy sound. Her own voice. She heard the noise on the air, felt the vibrations in her throat. And part of her despaired, because the fog was safe and familiar. It didn't take anything from her or force anything on her. It didn't show her tunnels and flames, didn't make her die over and over again in her dreams, didn't—

*They need you.*

She didn't want to be needed, not that way. She wanted her little house in the suburbs, her office at the university, her students, her husband, a baby . . .

*Bullshit*, he snapped, plucking the thoughts from her mind. *You just don't want to face the truth.* A pause. *Why am I even bothering? You always were such a girl.*

"Screw you."

There was no answer, the voice was gone, lost again in the beckoning fog. Her anger, though, didn't go with it. The burn stayed inside her, refusing to let her slide back into the grayness of her own mind. And along with it came whispers, not in his voice, but in the thought-images and sensory memories of a thousand lifetimes, a hundred thousand visions. *Get up,* they said. *You have power—use it! Help him, or you both will die.*

She saw Brother's face, still and cold, caught a gleam of luminous green, and her heart shuddered. To her surprise, that progressed to a full-body shudder, then a prickling wash of sensation as long-unused neurons flared to life and she became cognizant of the space around her. She was in a room—*bedroom*, her brain supplied—with things arranged on shelves and hung on the walls. *Artifacts. Fakes. Cheap knockoffs.* Just like she was a cheap knockoff of a true *itza'at* seer, unable to control the talents she didn't want. But one of the fakes caught her attention. The stone knife was unwieldy and poorly balanced, its hilt carved with gibberish glyphs from wildly different periods—she knew that because she knew the knife, had used it to open the occasional letter. But now she locked on it, and the building urgency inside her said: *Yes.*

She lurched to her feet, was up before she was aware of the effort it took, made it across the room in a stutter-step parody of walking on long-unused legs, and grabbed the knife from its little display stand. Without thinking or pausing, she drew the knife sharply across her right wrist. And power flared through her, bringing images of death.

In the next wing over, Reese awoke and blinked up at the ceiling, then around at her surroundings, aware of a deep pit in her stomach. Dez's bed. Dez's bedroom. No Dez. Memory returned like a knife through the heart. He had left her here, locked her in so she wouldn't warn the others.

"Son of a—" She cut herself off and launched off the bed, adrenaline clearing the last of the sleep spell. She slapped for her armband, but it was gone. A vague memory stirred of him searching her, disarming her. *Bastard.* Moving too fast for all of the things he had said to her to catch up, too fast even for her gut instincts to find her, she flung herself into the suite's main room, cursing when she found the house phone gone, the intercom deactivated. No doubt he'd told Lucius and the *winikin* that she was working alone on a special project, and not to disturb her. That was what she would have done.

"Damn it!" She glared around at the austere apartment that lied as slickly as its occupant, making it look like he'd changed when, really, some of the glossy shine had been rubbed off but the rest was the same. At the thought, her eyes went to the coffee table. Or, rather, to the small rectangular rug that lay beneath it.

It was the only rug in the suite, save for a shaggy bath mat. And he was the same guy he'd always been.

Breathing a quick prayer to whatever entity might be listening, she shoved the table and rug aside. Disappointment churned when all she found was more of the same hardwood that was everywhere else in the suite. But when she got down close and brushed her fingertips along the surface, she found the faint line of a seam.

"Didn't totally trust them, did you?" Or maybe he was hardwired to hide things. The thought brought a pang, but she ignored it.

A quick search uncovered a hidden pressure pad. She hit it, expecting it to pop up and reveal a lock. Instead, the larger panel loosened with zero fanfare. Apparently, he hadn't been that worried about his teammates . . . or else he had assumed he was far away from anyone who would know where to look.

Heart tapping, she used her nails to pry up the panel and reveal a small arsenal—MAC-10, a couple of decent .44s, a snub-nosed .22, and ammo all around. But that wasn't all; he'd also stashed some nuts and jerky . . . along with a couple of packages of peanut butter cups. She stared at them for a three-count while her instincts and the things he had whispered before leaving caught up with her—things about her proving that she didn't trust him, and how he couldn't let her distract him or the team with her suspicions.

If she took her emotions out of the equation, she thought those things fit the pattern and sounded like the truth. Only they weren't, because she had long ago learned that she had to listen to what Dez did, not what he said. So she chambered a few bullets in one of the .44s, and stood to take a bead on the door. Then she yelled, "Fire in the hole!" and blasted two rounds through the lock.

Wood splintered and cracked, the panel shuddered. It would've been very satisfying to kick it open, but it opened in, so that would've been more work than necessary. Instead, she tried the knob, jiggled it, put her shoulder into it, and got the door open. Stepping out, she exhaled a quiet, "Yes!"

"Freeze!" a man's voice bellowed, and a big figure lurched into view two doors down, pointing a machine pistol at her.

"Shit!" Fight response flaring, she flattened and ducked back into the room, whipping up the .44, all too aware she had loaded only four rounds. Scenarios flared—the compound under siege with her unaware, *makol* in the hallways . . . but a *makol* wouldn't have yelled for her to freeze. And that was Lucius standing there, crutch under one arm, MAC-10 in the other.

His expression quickly ran from determination to surprise, and from there to confusion. He let his weapon sag. "Reese? What the hell's going on?"

"Long story." She lunged back to her feet. "Are they gone yet?"

"Maybe ten minutes ago." Confusion turned to alarm. "What's wrong?"

"I need to talk to Strike." She hesitated for a second, unnerved to find that a piece of her still didn't want to blow the whistle on Dez, still wanted to think he was telling the truth. But the outrage was too much—the story came out of her in a clipped précis, like one she would have given to the task force. She finished with, "So I need you to put me on a tight band transmission to Strike or Leah. Or failing that, anyone but Dez. They should still be doing recon. We've got time."

But Lucius sagged back against the wall, his face draining of color. "They skipped recon and attacked when Dez's magic pulled the temple out of the dark barrier ahead of schedule. Right after that, the satellite cut out. I've got no ears, no way to transmit."

"He cut the feed?" Even as the knots in her stomach tightened, a dumb-assed part of her kept saying, *Maybe he's not doing what you think.* "We need to get it back up."

"I thought it was barrier interference. The closer we get to the end date, the wonkier the atmosphere gets during the cardinal days. If he cut it, though, there are a couple of other things I could try."

"Let's go." Shoving the .44 into her waistband at the small of her back, where it pressed awkwardly into her spine, she headed down the hallway toward the great room. Her thoughts churned as a ragged pattern assembled itself in her head. "I bet he meant for me to stay asleep longer than I did, long enough so it wouldn't matter. Maybe the blood-link warned me that he was making his move, woke me up early." She was going full steam now, pieces falling into place slightly askew. "I bet he sensed that I was coming around and knew he had to move his timetable up. So he—"

"Wait." Lucius caught her arm and swung her around in the archway leading to the main mansion. "Stop. Back up. What blood-link?"

"We don't have time for this." She tugged at his arm.

He didn't budge. More, his normally easygoing demeanor had hardened and a glint had entered his eyes. "Yes we do. It's important. Start talking."

She didn't want to think about it, because the link, too, was a lie. But she trusted Lucius. "It started when I was bitten by the *makol*." She quickly described the thin trickle of energy that had fitfully connected them ever since their blood and energies had mingled. "And when we . . ." She faltered as a stab of grief ripped through her.

Lucius finished for her. "And when you make love, sometimes it seems that you can feel what he's feeling and see the world through his eyes."

Hating how the reminder brought a prickle of tears and made her yearn, she snapped, "Like I said, a blood-link."

But his eyes had taken on a strange glint. "A blood-link comes from shared DNA—siblings, parents and children, that sort of thing. What you're talking about is the early stages of the *jun tan* connection. The mated bond."

"Bullshit." The word burst out of her.

"Not bullshit. *Jun tan*." He tapped his wrist, where he wore the curving glyph. "And, especially when it's newly formed, the bond won't activate unless the two of you are open to each other, not holding anything back. Which means he was telling the truth about why he locked you up."

Shock took her breath and she sagged against the nearest wall. "You're kidding." Her heart leaped at the possibility, but twisted as she warned herself not to talk herself into believing what she wanted to. "The spirit guide said we weren't meant to be mates."

"Looks like you're falling in love with each other anyway."

Her mouth went dry. "No." The whisper wasn't a denial of her feelings, but of the hope that suddenly swept through her. "Oh, God." Could it be true? She pressed a hand to her suddenly jittery stomach as her mind skipped around, thoughts jumbling into a mishmash of yearning and regret. "He's a Triad mage," she said, heart beginning to pound with excitement even as her practical side poked at the gaps in the pattern. "He could've manipulated the magic."

"Not this kind of magic," Lucius said with quiet assurance. "The *jun tan* doesn't answer to anything but true emotion."

"But I . . ." She didn't know what she wanted to say, didn't know how she felt, but as the new information sank in and the pattern rearranged itself into something that fit perfectly, she heard his parting words whisper in her heart. *Maybe we missed our chance.*

She must have looked suddenly panicked, because Lucius's expression took on a tinge of empathy. "It's early yet. If this isn't what you want—"

"I need to talk to him," she interrupted, her heart suddenly beating hard and fast in her ears. "I need him to know . . . No. Wait." *No distractions. Let him keep his mind on the fight.* But what if he didn't make it through? What if he died with her angry words and his quiet despair the last thing between them? *He dies, we all die,* logic said, because without the serpent king to stop him, Lord Vulture would arise.

"Come on." Lucius steered her through the archway and onto the upper landing of the great room. "Let's get some brownies and try the satellite feed again, and when that doesn't work, I'll introduce you to the suck-fest called 'stuck at home, waiting for news.'"

Reese let out a shuddering breath as they turned for the kitchen. "Okay. Deal." She glanced over at him. "Fair warning. I'm not very good at waiting."

"There's a shock. I—" He broke off as his crutch slipped out from underneath him, then hissed as the move jarred his bad leg. Reese grabbed his arm, steadying him as she looked down, expecting to find spilled water, maybe a leak.

Except it wasn't water. It was blood.

She hissed as all of her quick fears about *makol* in the compound came racing back. Yanking the .44 and going into survival mode, she said in a low voice, "Check on the others. If they're okay, have them get armed and get out here."

"Oh, shit," he said, face going stark. "This isn't good." But as Reese moved away, she heard him activate his armband, heard a reassuringly calm answer from one of the *winikin*, elsewhere in the compound.

The blood started thinly—a few gravitational drops near the archway leading to the royal quarters, a couple of smears tracking to a nearby hallway. Then it got heavier as it turned down another hall and started weaving, then turned to bloody scuff marks as it turned through the doorway leading to the sacred chamber. Pulse hammering, she tucked herself beside the door, crouched, and took a look around the edge, staying low. Then she froze for a second, mind refusing to process the horror-movie scene.

Anna lay motionless near the altar, wearing blood-soaked pajamas. More of the red liquid was splashed on the altar, the floor, the curving walls, even the glass ceiling, creating reddish patches on the floor where the sun shone through. She was alone. There was no *makol*, and the ceremonial knife clutched in her hand, the vivid slashes on her wrists, said there never had been.

"Jesus." Reese was up and into the room in a flash, jamming the .44 in her belt as she dropped down beside the motionless woman. The cuts were fresh and running, showing a sluggish pulse. Reese's stomach grew queasy as the salty tang of blood invaded her lungs, her sinuses, but she grabbed the other woman's wrists, gripped tightly, and lifted her arms above the level of her heart. Her blood was warm and wet, sticky in spots.

She heard Lucius's uneven steps out in the hallway. "It's Anna," she called in scant warning, hurting for him. "She's—"

"Oh, gods." His voice was low and broken, as if he wasn't all that surprised. He stood for a half second in the doorway, then limped to let himself down on Anna's other side, his leg sticking out at an awkward angle as he wedged himself behind her, up against the altar, so he could support her upper body while Reese kept the pressure on.

"We found her quickly," she said, but almost couldn't hear herself over the thunder of her pulse. Then she realized the thundering noise was the sound of boots on tile. The others were coming. Natalie was the first one through the door; she gave a low cry and went pasty when she got a look at the scene. Several other *winikin* were right behind her; their faces mirrored her shock.

"Make a hole," a voice barked, and JT came through carrying a medic's duffel. He took one look, dumped the bag, and started yanking out IV materials. "What the hell happened? There wasn't a damned thing on the monitors. Nothing got in or out of here."

"She was holding the knife when I got here," Reese said.

"The solstice must've triggered something inside her," Lucius said raggedly. "But she should be healing. Why the hell isn't she healing?"

Without warning, Anna's eyes flew open and she

gasped—a long, sucked-in breath that arched her body, tipping her head back and raising her chest until she was supporting herself on her ass and the crown of her head.

"She's seizing!" JT went for the IV line with a loaded syringe.

Lucius grabbed his arm. "No, wait. Look!"

Anna's mouth worked and her head lolled wildly, but then her movements smoothed out as she scanned the room . . . and locked on to Reese. Suddenly, her hands twisted in Reese's, reversing their grip until she wasn't holding pressure on Anna's wrists anymore—the other woman was holding hers. Instinct told her to wrestle free, but she made herself stay put and meet Anna's eyes, which were clear now, with none of the fog that had clouded them for more than a year. But at the same time they were vacant and uncomprehending. Which made it doubly eerie when she said, voice cracking, "The serpent staff cannot be wielded without balance—without it, the temple will become a doorway without a door and the vulture will be set free. You must stop the serpent prince from tipping the balance!" Then, like a switch had been thrown, the fog snapped back. She shuddered and let go of Reese's hands.

"Move." JT shouldered her aside and got to work, issuing low orders to Lucius—*hold this; press here*—but to Reese those were peripheral inputs that barely dented the spinning whirl inside her, the shock and horror as the pieces once again rearranged themselves, this time forming a compass within a circle, with the black opposite red, yellow opposing white, and green lightning at the center.

They fit together. They balanced. And if any one piece was taken away, the outer shell fell apart, releasing the lightning in a terrible explosion of nuclear proportions . . . and bringing Lord Vulture's twilight.

Iago would have no compunction against activating all five of the artifacts. But if it came to it, Dez—the man he was now—may try to leave one of the pieces out of the puzzle, needing to prove to both of them that he was a better man than before. And then . . . *boom*. She looked at Lucius, heart racing. "I have to talk to Dez. I think he's going to kill us by trying to do the right thing."

# CHAPTER TWENTY-SIX

*Coatepec Mountain*

*I'm here. Come and get me . . . get me . . .* The whispers echoed in Dez's head, getting louder every foot the Nightkeepers fought toward the temple, hacking through the *makol* lines. It wasn't just the one voice now—there were three others, quieter whispers that pulled at him, seesawing him from honor and balance to upheaval and revolution.

Lightning crackled around him, deflecting buzz blades, bullets, and whatever the fuck else the *makol* were throwing at him. He killed when he had to, knocked down where he could, aware that the other Nightkeepers were doing the same, though it was a bloody, thankless task. Yanking off the amulets turned out to disable but not kill them, and when they went down, the others turned on their fallen comrades and ripped them to shreds. So the magi were knocking the villagers down, over and over again, hoping they would find an answer in the temple, where Iago was casting the spells to activate the staff. Dez could feel the pulsing, hissing magic that was both dark and light, and pure serpent. If he didn't get in there soon and stop Iago, they were fucked.

Overhead, Nate's hawk incarnation soared and wheeled alongside the sun god in its firebird form, the two of them acting as air support. Dez tapped his armband—the solstice had knocked out the long-range communication, but short-range still worked, sort of. Into the hissing static, he said, "Now!"

As one, the hawk and firebird wheeled and dove, accelerating to a blur and swooping across the battle-field, strafing a fiery path between the Nightkeepers and the scaly, pearl-colored shield that enclosed the temple. *Makol* went down in flames, screaming, and Dez plunged up the hill with several of the others at his heels. A few of the magi were already up there, working on the shield. As he ascended, the whispers got louder, more urgent. *We're here. Come and get us!*

Up close, the temple was actually a series of arch-ways leading from one to the next, undulating like a sea monster swimming through the earth. The floor was carved stone, the roof open to the sky. Iago stood inside, a dark, robed form kneeling before a curving, serpentine throne. On it, fitted into holders, rested the five puzzle pieces, the staff across the arms, the four compass artifacts set around the back piece of the throne, which fanned out like a green sunburst that ended in white, red, yellow, and black.

*Come and take us. Bring your knife and come and fight for us!*

The magi who had come up behind him turned back to cast a shield and defend the perimeter against the *makol*, buying him and the others already up there some space to work. Sven's blond hair was streaked with ichor and blood ran from a cut on his cheek. The coyote stood at his side; for a second, the two of them seemed to blend together in Dez's vision, until there was a single creature there. Then the moment passed. Beyond Sven, Rabbit had tears in his eyes, but he was holding the shield, napalming whichever of the villagers got too close. The others were all there, all accounted for, and they had a temple to breach. There was no sign of the tunnel entrances shown in the missionary's journal. They would have to go through the shield.

Magic sizzled around Dez, edging higher as he approached the huge, arching shield, which was formed of pearly scales that overlapped in sinuous patterns of dark and light. Michael was trying to punch through using a thin stream of his deadly magic, with Strike and Leah standing beside him keeping watch.

"We're not getting anywhere," Strike reported as Dez came up beside him. The king was deathly pale, but he had fought with the others, grim-faced and determined, and the blood on him wasn't his own.

He was running on magic and balls, Dez thought, and hoped it would be enough to see them all through the day intact. "Let me try," he said, waving Michael back. "This is serpent magic."

Leah said something, but her voice was drowned out by the coaxing whisper in Dez's mind: *Kill your*

*rival and take what is rightfully yours. Kill your rival . . .*
*your rival . . . your rival.* And he got it. He freaking got
it. Reese had been right when she said this solstice was
all about the serpents.

"Son of a bitch," he grated. "The prophecy wasn't
about a serpent killing a jaguar king . . . it was about
two serpents fighting each other, one-on-one, one
wielding light magic, one dark." But when Leah's eyes
sparked with hope, he shook his head in warning. "It
also says that the usurper who kills his rival will take
the throne."

Strike reached out and gripped his upper arm, right
where the *hunab ku* would go. "Kill him, Mendez. No
matter what happens after that, I want you involved,
not him." His eyes were bright cobalt chips in a pasty
face.

Dez nodded. "I'll kill him. But I'm not taking your
job."

"Let's blow that shit up when we get there."

"Deal." Acting on instinct and the way the whispers
kept focusing on his knife, Dez stripped off his armband, .44, autopistols, belt and clips, and tossed them
aside, then looked down the Nightkeeper line. His
team was holding back the *makol* with a combination of
shield magic, fireballs, and jade-tipped ammo, fighting
fiercely as warriors. As teammates and saviors. "Stay
alive," he ordered, then pointed to Strike. "And keep
*him* alive."

He didn't know how the thirteenth prophecy fit in,
but he knew the voices had gotten one thing right: This
was his fight. It always had been. Blood pumping, he

faced the glistening shield for a moment, then used his knife—his only remaining weapon—to slice his palms. The magic amped as he pressed his palms to the surface, which was glassy and smooth, and cool to the touch. *Ready or not, here I come, you bastard.*

On the other side of the shield, Iago knelt before the altar with his head bowed in prayer. He, too, was wearing only a knife. He didn't seem to be paying any attention to the world beyond the temple—either he was too deep in the magic to notice that the Nightkeepers had made it through the *makol* defenses or he wasn't concerned with them.

*That's what you get for sacrificing all your teammates,* Dez thought. *There's nobody left to watch your back.* But then he winced when the concept hit too close. He hadn't been letting thoughts of Reese distract him to this point, at least not that much. But as he summoned his magic now, her image formed in his mind—soft-eyed and drowsy as she had been the few precious mornings they had woken up in each other's arms. As she came clear in his mind, the magic of love flowed through him. Because he did love her—maybe always had, on some level. But she didn't trust him. He really had waited too long this time. He still needed to prove himself, though—to her, to himself, to the magi who had entrusted him with their oaths. So he focused, drawing on the magic of the Triad and the fealty oaths, and deep down inside to the core of his serpent self.

And then, holding her image fixed firmly in his mind, he let the magic flow out of him as he had done earlier with Strike, when he had inadvertently brought the temple out of hiding. Power crackled as it flowed into the shield, sending sparks arcing across its surface and warming it beneath his hands.

*Yes!* the whispers rejoiced, *come!* But nothing else happened.

He dug deeper, poured more magic into the shield.

Warmth. Electricity. The glimmer of an image. *Reese.* He focused on her, saw her, felt her in his heart. And as he did, the shield magic softened and gave, letting him through. Because light magic burned brightest when it came from love, he realized.

As he passed into the shield, his magic went dead, utterly nullified by the spell—he felt it cut out, and had the strange sensation of his skull echoing as the background hums of power cut out. Not for long, though, because the moment he was through, he felt the power of the statuette, heard her voice, so much louder than the others. *I've always been yours. I've never turned away from you, never left you, never let you down.* With the words, a terrible urgency slammed into him—the need to touch the statue once more, hold her, have her. Before, he hadn't been able to use her magic. Now, though—

*No!* He tried to sweep away the temptation, but he'd never been good at clearing his mind, and now was no exception. So instead, he filled it with an image of Reese, sporting black leather and a .38, and ready to kick some ass.

Iago roared and exploded to his feet, crimson robe flowing around him as he put himself between Dez and the artifacts, whipped out a wickedly curved stone knife, and dropped into a fighter's crouch. There was no hint of dark magic, save for the eerie green glow of his eyes. That was just fine with Dez, because he knew how to handle a knife.

Iago charged and Dez met the rush, dodged the knife swipe by dropping to his knees, and then surged up, leading with his skull and driving his head into his rival's solar plexus. It was like headbutting granite, but the *makol* flew backward to slam into a pillar and slide down it, leaving a streak of blood that was very red on the white limestone. The *makol* twisted, watched the wound regenerate, and hissed in satisfaction.

Which so wasn't fair. How come he got to keep some of his magic?

Cursing at the disadvantage, Dez reversed his grip and charged as Iago hurtled toward him. He ducked a chest-high stab and slashed upward. He felt the knife bite, heard Iago howl English curses mixed with ancient Aztec as fabric tore and the blade skidded across his abdomen. Dez yanked back, narrowly avoiding the bastard's backswing. Blood splattered from Iago's wound and he staggered. Seeing the opening, Dez lashed out a kick that connected with the Xibalban's knife hand, sending the weapon flying.

Iago screeched and spun, not toward the knife, but toward the throne. The whispers gained sudden volume in Dez's head—*Yesyesyes!*—as he lunged in pursuit, but Iago got there ahead of him, grabbed the serpent staff, and swung the three-foot-long snake-shaped stone artifact at his head like a fucking Louisville Slugger. Dez lunged forward, took the blow on his shoulder, and got inside Iago's guard for another stab. The collision drove them back against the throne, and the second he made contact, the whispers became shouts. He blocked them out, but the split-second hesitation cost him as Iago rammed an elbow into the side of his head, dazing him.

Fog. Urgency. The sight of Iago rearing back to jam the gape-jawed end of the serpent staff into his face. *Shit!* He skidded off the throne bare seconds before the blow landed with a crack of stone-on-stone. He hit hard, rolled . . . and came up holding the black star demon. He didn't remember grabbing the statuette, but the familiar shape was suddenly there. Confidence flared through him. Arrogance. The utter conviction that he was doing what he was meant to do, what he was born to do. The spinning in his head didn't matter; nothing mattered except the feel of the stone warming in his blood-streaked palm.

But those were lies, he knew, because he had nothing to be confident about. He was bleeding from cuts on his face and shoulder, and his fucking head hurt. He was holding his own for now, but there was no way he could win. He and Iago were evenly matched as fighters, and the bastard regenerated.

*Take me. Use me. I am yours, have always been yours.*

He blocked the whisper, thought of Reese. Saw her, eyes wide and worried for him. And that more than anything told him he was in deep shit.

Iago came at him hard and fast, swinging the staff. Dez feinted a second too slow, and the *makol* caught him in the head again. The world grayed and Dez went down, Iago following him with a roar, his green-on-green eyes glowing with murderous rage as he twisted Dez's knife out of his hand, reversed it, and reared back for a killing blow.

Despair hammered through Dez. Inevitability. "I'm so fucking sorry," he whispered to the Reese in his mind. But to save his teammates and the war, he had to damn himself. And so he let go of the tight reins of his control, opening himself to the black star demon's magic. Power hammered through him. Greed. Lust. Violence. He stopped being himself and became something else. And that thing he became bared its teeth and went for Iago with a single thought in its mind: *Kill!*

*Skywatch*

"The serpent is unbalanced. He seeks the darkness. He must take the others, must take them all, or the dark lord will come, the end will begin." Anna heard the words, knew she was saying the same thing over and over, but couldn't stop. She could see the world around her, but she couldn't control the words that were coming out of her mouth.

*Open your eyes*, the spirit—figment?—had said, but her eyes *were* open. She was channeling visions without seeing them, not sure she could reconnect with that part of herself when she'd spent so long trying to block it off. Or even if she really wanted to.

It would be easier to close her eyes and let go.

"Come on, Lucius!" snapped a dark-haired woman

with scared eyes. "You transported the whole damn team out of the underworld."

"But once I got the library to earth, the conduit magic stopped working," the man opposite her said. "I can't do it. Period, end of sentence." His familiar face was etched with pain and stress. *Lucius*, Anna thought, the name almost latching onto memories. She ached to talk to him. To *connect*.

"I've got to get to Dez." The woman's voice shook as she took Anna's hand, leaned close to her. "Please," she whispered. "I can't warn him about the balance if I can't get to him. I need you to tell me how."

The raw longing in her voice touched something deep inside Anna, making her consciousness quiver like a plucked guitar string, and bringing a single humming note.

*Magic.*

She almost didn't recognize it. Had the magic ever been this pure and sweet for her? She didn't think so, just as she didn't remember it being so strong and sure, flowing through her, suddenly flooding her with memories—like the good, solid feel of her brother's arms around her, holding her tightly and making her feel like everything was going to be okay. *Strike*, she thought, putting a name to him at last. But how could it feel as though he were right there, holding her, when he wasn't? How did she know that he was far away, that he was very sick, yet still using his magic to fight? She could almost picture him there, with Leah on one side of him, Rabbit on the other.

As she concentrated on the image, it grew clearer.

And, unexpectedly, the humming note inside her found an anchor inside him, and the strange, searching magic ratcheted higher. The power coalesced and the spirit whispers of her ancestors floated around her like the ghosts she had seen in her dreams since she was a little girl, the ones she had fought so hard to block out. Now, though, she reached for them, because after all these months she would take ghosts over the emptiness. She stroked her mind along one wisp and felt visions stir, touched another and felt the fierce focus of the warrior she had never been. And then she touched the third, and a golden thread shimmered to life in her mind, beginning with her and stretching into infinity.

It was a travel thread, she knew. In life, the ghost had been a teleporter. Or was it a ghost at all? Because suddenly it felt as though the Triad magic had captured a piece of Strike inside her, too. Which should have been impossible.

*Link with me*, the magic whispered.

"What?" Reese said, leaning in closer.

Had she actually said that aloud?

"Link. With. Me." That time she was sure of it, had actually made her mouth say the words she wanted. "Need. You. Both." And her senses sharpened, bringing the real world more into focus, connecting her to herself, to her power. And, dimly, she saw the glimmering outline of a vision: two cobras, hissing and striking at each other inside a glowing dome. *Get her there*, something whispered. *Now.*

"Link up," Lucius said. He pulled a combat knife and used the tip to score his palm along the scar line.

"She must need a boost, and we're the only ones here. She'll have to make do with human blood." He clasped Anna's hand, over the cut that she, too, had made over old scars.

Power surged and the golden thread solidified inside her.

"Hand it over." Reese took the knife, fumbling with the cut and then gripping Anna's other hand.

More power. More solidity. The golden thread glowed, thrumming with the magic and calling to her. *Take it. It will get you where you need to be if you want it enough.* Remembering how Strike had described teleport magic, she reached out with her mind and touched the yellow thread. Grabbed on to it. And pulled.

Magic lurched, sending all three of them sideways in a stomach-jolting roller coaster. Then the familiar gray-green nothingness was whipping past them, a blur of incalculable motion that went on. And on. *Too long*, she realized. Panicking, she clutched the thread, only to have it dissolve suddenly. She screamed as the whip of motion curved in on itself, arcing in a tightening spiral, a whirlpool drawing them down into the formless gray that wasn't quite the barrier, wasn't anywhere else.

"Help me!" she screamed as the maelstrom sucked her down, taking the other two with her into the nothingness.

*Coatepec Mountain*

Strike jerked at the sound of a female scream, audible even over the burr of shield magic and buzz-swords, the screams of the *makol* and the roar of the Nightkeepers' magic. He looked wildly around, didn't see the source, but then felt a sick surge in his magic followed by a stomach drop of epic proportions. Then he heard words: *Help me!*

It was Anna's voice.

"Anna!" he shouted, and bolted toward the sound.

"*No!* Rabbit, help me!" Leah grabbed his arm, slowing his mad charge.

"It's Anna! She needs me!" He tried to free himself, but then Rabbit got his other side and the two of them dragged him back against a stone pillar and pinned him there.

The screams died out; reality returned. And he realized that he had started to head out into the *makol*. Leah was plastered against his chest, looking up at him, her eyes asking in silent agony, *Is this it? Is this where it ends?*

His head was suddenly pounding. He couldn't get enough air, couldn't get control. He hated this, wanted it to fucking stop. And by all that was sacred, he didn't want to die. He wanted to stay with Leah, with the Nightkeepers. Gods, please not now.

Wrapping his arms around Leah, he held her close, leaned into her. "I'm sorry. I didn't mean . . . I'm fine." He wasn't fine; he was losing it. "It was just—"

It happened again without warning: a stomach drop, a surge, a skitter of his malfunctioning 'port magic. *Son of a bitch.* Bile soured the back of his throat. But there was something else now, he realized. Because for the first time, the heavy thud of his heart was echoed in a thrum of magic, a tingle in his bloodline mark.

Rabbit was moving in to help, but Strike held up a hand. "Wait. Hang on. There's something . . ." He trailed off as it connected.

He had been dreaming that he had lived the massacre through his father's eyes, had heard whispers that weren't his. Then there were the odd power surges, strange lesions in his mind, and the ghostly connection that he could almost feel but Sasha couldn't track . . . Because a healer couldn't track the blood-links of her own line. *Oh, holy shit.* It had been a blood-link all along. Anna's subconscious had reached out to him through their shared DNA, giving him part of her injury and taking part of his power in return. He hadn't known it, but he'd been helping her heal. And now she was in trouble.

"I've got to go after her!"

*"What?"* Leah tightened her grip. "What's going on? Talk to me, damn it!"

"It's the Triad magic." He gave her a quick, hard kiss as excitement burst inside him. "I love you. And I'll be right back, I promise." Then, trusting that she had his back, always and forever, even when she thought he was losing his everfrigging mind, he left his body behind and sent his consciousness into the magic, into the neverwhen of transport leading to the barrier. He went in without a destination, without forethought, diving after the tingle in his blood and leaping straight into the storm.

Gray-green lashed at him instantly, slamming him

in one direction and then another, flipping his consciousness end-over-end. But he wasn't alone—he glimpsed something yellow-gold trailing nearby, sent himself after it, suddenly feeling strong and sure, and completely in control of his power and himself.

The teleport line was tangled around someone. Several someones. He caught the end, reeled them in even as he was buffeted by the blurring force of uncontrolled 'port magic. Anna was clinging to the string, but so were Reese and Lucius, their terror palpable. Jesus gods, what was going on here? *Doesn't matter. Get them out of here.*

He could do that. He touched his magic—suddenly strong and pure and perfectly in control—and returned to his body, taking them with him.

As the gray-green whipped past, he fell into a waking vision.

*Footsteps moved away behind the king, the sound echoing off stone and bloodied water as he turned to face the lava monster. And as he raised his weapon, his heart was heavy with the realization that he had been wrong all along.*

*The king's greatest sacrifice wasn't his mate's life, after all. And it wasn't his own life, either.*

And suddenly, Strike knew what the ultimate sacrifice was meant to be.

Then air *whoomped* away and they materialized in the middle of the firefight, scaring the shit out of the others and sending Sven's coyote skittering between his legs, growling. Leah jumped back and went for her gun, then checked herself as it registered that Anna, Lucius, and Reese were tangled together at Strike's feet, gasping.

Jade gave a low cry and rushed to Lucius's side as he lurched up and then stumbled on his bad leg, his crutch nowhere to be seen. The other magi looked shocked as hell but stayed at their posts, holding the shield and keeping the *makol* in check.

"Where the fuck did they come from?" Michael demanded as Sasha dropped down beside Anna, partly to check her over, partly to just hug her.

"They were pretty close to being lost for good in the barrier," Strike answered, his voice breaking as his emotions threatened to overload from the weight of his father's final revelation. But then, knowing the time for that would come, he focused on the here and now. He reached for Leah, caught her against him, and whispered into her hair, "It was Anna's blood-link making me sick. We're both okay now."

She gave a glad cry and clung to him fiercely for a moment. "Thank the gods." Her voice was low and fervent, her eyes wet. "But why are they *here*?"

"Because it's a damn sight better than where they were." Delayed reaction set in at the thought of how close the three of them had come to simply disappearing. *Boom, gone.* He dropped down beside Anna, balancing on his heels. "No offense, big sister, but what the hell were you thinking?"

Her eyes filled and she turned and clung to him, shuddering. "It was the only way," she said. Her voice was nearly lost beneath the tumult of the battle, as the others fought to hold the *makol* line. But it was her voice. And that was her inside those eyes, for the first time in a long time. "I couldn't get them all the way here," she whispered against his neck. "I thought I could, but I lost the thread. And then I couldn't find you."

He held her tight. "That's okay. I found you. But why did you try it?"

"The serpent needs help."

"No!" Reese screamed. Strike's head jerked up as she slammed her fists into the serpent shield, face etched with horror. Inside the temple, Iago rose over Dez's motionless body with the serpent staff raised for a killing blow. "Dez!" she screamed. "*No!*"

# CHAPTER TWENTY-SEVEN

Bruised, battered, dizzy with blood loss, and close to dead, Dez thought he had crossed the boundary, that he was having a last sweet fantasy of Reese's amber-whiskey eyes locking on him, her hands reaching for him, her voice calling him.

Time seemed to slow for a second as he rasped through his bruised throat, "I'm sorry, sweetheart. So fucking sorry." Sorry he hadn't gotten it right the first time around for them, sorry this time had turned out to be too late. Sorry their timing always sucked.

Then he saw her mouth go round in a scream, time sped back up, and he knew it wasn't a dream. She was there, reaching for him. Screaming his name even as another part of him whispered: *Use me. I am and will always be a part of you.*

A last spurt of energy flared through him. He had lost his knife and his muscles were quivering, but as Iago swung down, he lunged up, jamming his fist into the Xibalban's solar plexus, holding the star demon so the pointed statuette protruded between his fingers. The statuette drove up and in as the serpent staff cracked into his shoulder. He felt sickening pain. But Iago, too, was hurt.

The Xibalban reeled back with a high, keening scream that was neither human nor *makol*. A wave of darkness rolled over Dez as he pulled the star demon out and stabbed his enemy, over and over, sticking him in the gut until the final blow when he left the bitch *inside* his enemy's abdominal cavity. Ichor ran over his arms, hot and acrid.

Iago went down hard, flat on his face. He began regenerating immediately, but not as fast as before; the star demon was slowing the process. The solstice thrummed in Dez's bones, and he was suddenly conscious of the ominous rattle of dark magic, just at the threshold of his serpent's hearing, coming from the stones that made up the temple itself. Which was a big "oh, shit" because it made him think he was going to be standing right on top of a hellmouth real soon. Or maybe a vulture's nest.

Time was running out. He couldn't stop now.

Dragging himself to his feet, he found his knife where it had skidded beneath the throne. He hefted it and looked at Reese, who still stood pressed up against the shield, watching him. He didn't know how she had gotten there, or what her presence meant for the two of them, but Jesus, gods, he didn't want to do this in front of her. Not again. Her lips moved; he couldn't read them, but it didn't really matter. He didn't have a choice. Feeling suddenly empty, he turned to where Iago lay facedown, halfway regenerated. Movements automatic, heart heavy, he got a hand across the Xibalban's forehead, pulled back his head, and carved a wicked slash across his throat.

Ichor fountained, mixed with blood. And he was back in the nightmare.

It was gruesome work. He clamped his teeth together and didn't look at her—couldn't bear it—as he sawed off the *ajaw-makol*'s head, then flipped him, cut away his body armor, and carved a deep furrow below his ribs, where the skin had started to knit around the earlier wound. Steeling himself, he punched through the diaphragm and jammed his hand up inside Iago's chest. Broken ribs scraped his knuckles as he felt for the beating fist of his enemy's heart, found it, and yanked it from its moorings.

He recited the banishment spell through gritted teeth.

Nothing happened.

"No!" he shouted as his heart plummeted. "Godsdamn it, no!" Darkness clouded his vision; rage suffused him. He lunged to his feet, ready to shout at the sky, to curse the gods to—

He saw Reese. She was just standing there with her palms pressed to the shield. And her eyes shone like they used to, with the look that said: *you're my hero, my cowboy.* It had to be an illusion, a delusion. But it pushed back the darkness far enough that he could see the light again.

"Motherfucker." He dove for Iago, jammed his hand back inside, fished around, and found the star demon. *You are the Triad mage,* she whispered the moment he made contact. *And he is a warrior of your bloodline. Take his powers and his knowledge as your own. His is yours. Everything is yours.*

Green washed his vision for a second and he could feel the powers buzzing just beyond his reach as the offer came clear. He was the Triad mage; he could take the talents from a dead mage of his bloodline, and Iago was certainly that. What was more, he could do so many things with the Xibalban's magic. He could open the intersection at El Rey; he could teleport; he could borrow the talent of any other mage he touched. And the Xibalban's skull harbored the demon's memories as well as his own; he knew spells the Nightkeepers didn't. With him as part of the Triad, Dez would be . . .

*The guy I don't want to be,* he thought, looking up at Reese and feeling his heart turn over and then settle with the good, solid weight of decision.

"She's mine." He gave a convulsive yank, pulled the statuette out of Iago's corpse, and sent it skittering away. "You're not."

Something wrenched inside him—a tearing pain in his heart and head, like his magic was being ripped away as the demon dug in her claws and fought. But he didn't give in to the pain; he wasn't going to let her fuck up his life this time. Gritting his teeth and forcing the words through the agony, he repeated the banishment spell.

Luminous green flashed like sheet lightning, the *ajaw-makol* crumbled to greasy ash, and thunder cracked in the temple, detonating a green-tinged shock wave that smashed away and down, tearing through the serpent shield. Reese cried out as she was thrown backward and slammed into the ground. The shock wave flattened the Nightkeepers, rolled through their shield, and plowed into the *makol* lines, rippling through them as luminous green winked out and the villagers collapsed, unconscious.

The pain vanished, leaving Dez hollowed out. But he didn't give a shit.

"Reese!" He grabbed his fallen knife, and bolted for her, all too aware that the dark-magic vibrations beneath his boots were getting steadily worse.

She lunged up off the ground as he reached down for her, and they slammed together, mouths fusing. He dragged his hands down her body to grip her hips, hold her to him, then back up to band his arms around her, lifting her up against his body. "You're here," he said between kisses. "Thank the gods you're here." He pulled away to look into her eyes. "You're my compass, Reese. My sanity. I promise you that—"

She clapped a hand across his mouth. "No promises. I don't need them, because I trust you. I believe in you. What's more, I believe in *us*."

The hollowness the star demon left behind began to fill back in with another kind of greed. He leaned into her. "Thank Christ. I thought I had lost you. I thought—"

A jolting shudder ran through the ground beneath his feet and the sound of grating stone suddenly surrounded them with a harsh rattle of magic, like the tail of a giant rattlesnake gearing up. Beneath that, he heard a terrible stone-on-stone screech that sounded like a giant bird. A vulture. Gods.

"Take the staff," an unfamiliar voice said. "Become the serpent king."

He spun to find Anna standing there. Only it wasn't the Anna he had known for the past year—instead of the fog he'd gotten all too used to seeing in her eyes, he saw clarity. Wisdom. Prescience.

"Where did you come from?" But before she could answer, her words sank in and his gut clutched. "*Shit.* Is Strike—" He broke off when he saw him standing strong and tall, with his arm around Leah's waist, looking better than he had in months.

"It's a long story that we don't have time for," Strike said. "But you still need to do this. You're the king we're going to need for this war."

Dez wasn't sure how his heart was still beating, given the ice in his veins. "I won't sacrifice you, damn it."

"You don't have to. You already killed your rival. I'm giving you this of my own free will, as demanded by the thirteenth prophecy." Tears gleamed in Strike's eyes. "There is no greater sacrifice for a king to make than to give up his throne on behalf of his bloodline. After today, the jaguars will no longer be the royal house." The ground shifted, trembled. "The serpents will."

Jesus gods. This wasn't happening. Dez closed his eyes for a moment, growing even colder when Reese moved away from him. He turned toward her. "Reese—"

She was holding out the star demon. The idol wasn't covered with ichor anymore; it had dematerialized along with the body. But it oozed with Iago's psychic stink.

For the first time, instead of being swamped with possessiveness, he was vaguely repulsed. "I don't want it."

A smile broke across her face like the dawn, though her eyes stayed serious. "I saw. You beat her just now. You used the demon to kill Iago, but you didn't let it use you. But . . ." She took his hand, flattened it out, and dropped the statuette in his palm. For the first time in a decade, it didn't feel like anything other than an artifact—cool, smooth, with a buzz of power. There were no whispers, no words. "She's part of the staff, just like shaking things up is part of being a good leader. She balances off the others. You can't have light without dark, or else it's all just one big twilight."

Like the twilight Lord Vulture would bring if he didn't take the serpent staff and fulfill both the thirteenth and serpent prophecies. The ground trembled with another birdlike shriek of stone-on-stone that had the others checking their weapons.

Reese closed his fingers around the idol. "I've over-reacted to so many things over the past couple of weeks because I was scared of what I was feeling, scared of how much more you could hurt me than you did before. And I was so busy being scared, I forgot to trust myself, especially when, deep down inside, I knew you weren't the guy who became the *de rey* anymore. You've beaten that part of yourself, just like you beat the star demon. I should've seen it, should've believed that sooner, but I didn't. Stupid of me."

"Not stupid." He covered her hand with his own, trapping the small statuette between them. "Brave and independent." He tugged her closer. "And the woman I love. My mate. My queen." He lifted his free hand to her cheek. "I love you. You have my heart, my soul, and my power. Please say you'll stay with me forever. Promise me." He held his breath when her eyes darkened and her lips turned down, and he could almost see her draw inward as she realized what he was asking—a bond, a promise, a commitment with no exit strategy. Maybe even, in her perceptions, a box to trap her.

Then her eyes filled, and she launched herself at him.

He caught her against him, his heart hammering when she said against his throat, "Forever. Because I love you. I love who you are right now, at this moment. And I'll love you tomorrow, and next year, and, gods willing, the year after that. You're it for me, you always have been. And I believe in you, in us. Whatever comes next, we'll make it through together. I promise."

She kissed him. Magic flared and his wrist warmed, and she gasped against his mouth. Shock hammered through him as he pulled away and they looked at their wrists, where they wore matching *jun tans*. *Holy crap*, he thought. *Holy, holy crap*. Suddenly, everything he had never dared want before was right at his fingertips. Doubt shivered through him for a second at the realization that the only other time he'd felt that way was when he was under the demon's influence.

But there were no whispers, no compulsion. There was only love and magic.

Reese grabbed him by the collar and dragged him down for a kiss. "We might not have been destined mates, but I'd say we more than earned these marks over the years."

Not years, he thought, because for him it had been love at first sight. Someday, he would tell her that. But not now. "I was lost," he said against her lips, holding her, hanging on to her. "Thanks for finding me." They kissed again, long and deep, sealing their promise and tapping into the core of the Triad's light magic within him. Power spun, coursing through him, charging the air as the ground shuddered beneath them.

"Go ahead," she said, stepping away. "Do it."

He faced the strange limestone throne as light magic raged within him and lightning lit the air above. Strike brought him the serpent staff, which seemed heavier than its weight when he took it. Aware that the others were gathered in a semicircle behind him, the sun god's firebird was perched atop the temple, and a thousand villagers lay beyond, waiting for a miracle, he started fitting the compass artifacts into the clever twists of the serpent staff, which was a puzzle without looking like one.

He started with north, the white wind god, bringing the light of truth and integrity to the reign of the serpents. South, the yellow two-faced mask, would bring balance and completion. East, the red skybearer, would help him inspire, lead, and spark new ideas. And then finally west, the black star demon, who carried the power of the shadows and transformation. He expected to feel a kick of new power when he fitted the last one into place. All he felt was the weight of new responsibility twining through him, interlocking with the fealty oaths. And maybe that was the way it was supposed to be, he thought.

Pausing, he turned toward Reese and mouthed, "I love you." Then, holding her eyes, he said the spell that Keban had beaten into him so long ago.

The four artifacts melted and swirled, running up against gravity to spread along the twisting staff, bleeding colors across a center of green. A sudden thunderclap came from the cloudless sky, and a roar of denial rose up from the ground. The air shimmered around the temple, and then turned dark. A tremor ran through him at the deep, ominous color, but then it shifted, becoming a pure glowing white, and then cycled through yellow, red, and dark again, before returning to white.

The rattle of dark magic disappeared. The ground stopped trembling, and deep in his gut, Dez knew that the prophecies had been fulfilled, the dark lord restrained. There would be no twilight for Lord Vulture this time.

For a second he thought it was all over. Then the white glow shimmered again, unfolding outward to reveal gray-green fog, and a figure within it: a *nahwal*, an ancestral being—this one with shining cobalt eyes and a ruby stud in one ear. Anna gasped.

"Father," Strike said, his voice a pained rasp, his face etched with grief over what he was giving up—

for himself, for his bloodline. But the *nahwal* smiled as he held up a stone scepter carved into the shape of a rampant, large-nosed god. Then he brought it over his knee. And broke it.

Pain tore into Dez's biceps, high up where the muscles intersected. He gritted his teeth, smelled burning flesh. *Sacrifice*, he thought, and held Strike's eyes, saw agony as the *hunab ku*, the king's mark, transferred from one to the other.

Something shifted in Dez's chest, then in his head and heart. And, suddenly, he felt the fealty oaths and responsibilities truly interconnect within him, felt the mark stabilize on his arm, felt the weight of generations past and future weighing him down and buoying him up. He locked eyes with Reese, with his mate and queen, as he became king. Lightning flashed and both the *nahwal* and the Manikin scepter disappeared in the brilliant flare of light. And the air went still.

Dez crossed to Reese, took her hands, raised them to his lips, and whispered, "Thank you for making it here in time."

She rose up on her tiptoes and returned the kiss, ramping the heat to a humming in his blood. "Thank you for turning down whatever the star demon offered you when you killed Iago."

He went still. "How did you know?"

"I know patterns. And I know you."

Yes, she did. Better than anyone ever had or would. And she still loved him, which was the fucking miracle. He drew her in, crushed his lips to hers, and took them under with a kiss.

Reese's thoughts raced almost as fast as her blood as they kissed, but there were no reservations, no regrets. He was arrogant and imperfect, yet perfect for her. And he was the only man she had ever loved, would ever love. And loving him wasn't a trap. She wouldn't let it be. That was what she put into her kiss, and what she took back from him.

"Look!" Anna cried softly, pointing upward.

High above the temple, the cloudless sky had begun to glow. The firebird screamed, launched itself from the highest pillar and took wing, spiraling joyously up into the sky, trailing flames from its wings.

Leah gasped and sagged, nearly hitting the ground before Strike could catch her. There was another flurry as Alexis lurched against Nate.

And then, as a clarion trumpet call sounded from far away, Leah and Strike laughed with joy, their faces lifted to the sky. "Kulkulkan!" she cried, reaching up as if to touch a flash of red, a slide of scales, a glimpse of the creator god she had been separated from for so long. Then, suddenly, the temple pillars brightened, becoming colors—not the compass points this time, but the full rainbow. The glows lifted, headed skyward, and then shot straight up to where the firebird circled, wheeling and dipping.

"Ixchel," Alexis whispered, her face alight as she was bathed in the rainbow light of her goddess.

"Look!" Sasha gasped. "More!" And it was true: high above, through the glowing gap in the sky, they could see a wing here, a flash of scales, clothing, jewels, and stones as the gods acknowledged their lost children.

Then, as the height of the solstice passed, the sky solidified, the glow disappeared, and even the firebird was gone, the sun shining brightly where it had last been.

Reese gripped Dez tightly, then sucked in an awed breath as the rainbow light drew back into itself, returning to the temple. As it hit the pillars, the stone shimmered and changed . . . and when the glimmer faded, where the undulating serpent had been, there were four columns, one at each compass point. Each of them was a jaguar, with Strike, Leah, Sasha, and Anna standing ranged in front of them, looking stunned.

In the center, a huge *chac-mool* altar arched over a linteled doorway that led into the earth. As they watched, the doorway shimmered and went solid, closing until the next cardinal day.

"Holy shit." Reese breathed, gripping Dez's hand tightly and getting a squeeze in return.

In sacrificing his kingship, Strike had won them a new intersection. The Nightkeepers had fulfilled the prophecies. And their luck had finally turned.

Dez whooped, lifted her, and spun her in a dizzying circle while cheers rose up into the sky. Tears glistened, crazy grins flared, kisses met and melded, and Sven's coyote tipped up his nose in a joyous howl. More, movement rippled in a concentric pattern moving outward from the temple as the villagers began to stir. Dez tugged Reese so they could look over the edge to where a clamor of noise was suddenly swelling. The villagers weren't *makol* anymore. But from the looks on their faces, they were sure as hell confused, headed toward terrified.

"I've got this," Rabbit said. He turned to Dez. "Cheech and his brothers are out there—I can feel his echo. They'll help me translate."

"And me." Myrinne put herself next to him.

Dez nodded. "Keep in touch, let us know if you need anything, blah, blah."

Rabbit's eyes widened almost imperceptibly. "That's it?"

"That's it." Dez lifted a shoulder. "I don't have the history with you that the others do. And"—he glanced down at Reese, eyes softening—"I'm learning to deal with the person standing in front of me, not the one I remember, or think I remember, from before. So, yeah. That's it. Try not to make me look like an idiot."

"Will do." Rabbit grabbed Myrinne's hand and headed into the milling crowd.

Reese watched them go, instincts pinching. "Are you sure about that?"

"No. But I can't blame him for what he might do." He watched Rabbit a moment longer, then turned to the others. "Time to head home." He looked at Strike. "Can you handle it?"

Strike grinned and held out his hand to Anna. "We've got this one. No more misfires. Promise."

Reese was laughing as she linked fingers with Dez, lifted up on her toes, and pressed her lips to his, so they were kissing while the world lurched sideways, went gray-green, and the Nightkeepers headed back to Skywatch.

# CHAPTER TWENTY-EIGHT

One month later
*Denver*

"I still can't believe it." Reese spun in a wide circle, hands outstretched, head tipped back so she could take in the transformation.

Warehouse Seventeen was being rehabbed into Sky-watch North.

Local crews and contractors crawled over the place, shouting questions and answers, and wielding power tools that sounded like *makol* buzz-swords, but creating rather than killing. The charred warehouse ruin had been stripped back to its girders and was being rebuilt, not just to its former questionable glory, but into an entirely new incarnation, with three tiers of offices and bedrooms surrounding a central atrium that was open to the sky through tinted glass panels. The Nightkeepers' ceremonial objects and armaments would be put in later. For now, it was all about bringing the building—and the neighborhood—up several notches.

Standing a few feet away with his hands in the pockets, Dez raised an eyebrow. "Can't believe I bought the place, can't believe how far the renovations have gotten, or can't believe that I did it on the sly?"

"All of the above." She stopped spinning and grinned at him, her heart catching at the sight of her man. Her mate.

Wearing jeans, combat boots, and a brown bomber that hid his marks and his .44, he looked as tough and capable as always, but there was more now. The heavy weight of his responsibilities had added new lines to his face, new tension in his jaw. But those were balanced by the glow that lit his eyes when he looked at her, crossed to her, and brushed his lips across hers.

She closed her eyes and leaned into him. He was warm and solid, someone she could depend on. Someone they could all depend on. Not that the two of them didn't argue—they fought like banshees, probably always would. But he listened to her now, and when he didn't, she was tough enough to beat her side of things into his thick skull.

They were making it work.

"This is a fabulous surprise," she said, still reeling from how quickly her morning had gone from his, "I've got something to show you," to a quick 'port hop that had landed them in the middle of Warehouse Seventeen—the place where they began. She shot him a quick look. "You're not worried about being recognized?"

He lifted a shoulder. "Nate and Carter took care of the paperwork, so the cops won't be able to find anything outstanding on me. Besides, it's been a few years, and people see what they expect. When they look at me, they'll see the latest city guy to jump on some grant money, not the very former—and very dead—*cobra de rey*." He paused and shifted, hunching his shoulders a little. A faint shadow crept into his eyes. "And, ah, this isn't the whole surprise."

The shadows—worry? nerves?—didn't trigger the *oh shit* they would have before. Now his expression just made Reese wonder what he was up to. "Am I going to like the rest of it?"

"I sure as hell hope so." He pulled his cell, checked the time. "You mind poking around on your own for a few minutes?"

She waved him off. "No problem. I'm sure I can find some trouble to get into." But as she watched him head off toward the east entrance, she murmured, "And you'd better not be getting *yourself* into any trouble." No matter how much she loved him, believed in him, she couldn't stop the skim of nerves. Something was up. Something big. And she couldn't see the pattern.

*Skywatch*

Sven hurled a fallen cacao branch, arching it high over the picnic area to bounce crazily on the packed dust. "Go get it!"

Mac yipped eagerly as he bounded after the toy, racing with a loose-limbed abandon that Sven could feel in his own bones. It stirred him up, making him feel restless. Or rather, *more* restless. He had been increasingly edgy ever since he had returned from helping out down at Skywatch South—aka Coatepec Mountain— where Anna, Lucius, and Natalie were excavating several ruins near the reborn jaguar palace, in the hopes of figuring out how their ancestors had used the site, and how it would fit into the coming war. Besides being an intersection, that is.

It had been dirty, backbreaking work, and right now he probably should be exhausted. Instead, he and Mac were walking the perimeter of the compound for the second time that morning.

The coyote brought the stick back to him, eyes dancing.

"Fine. But this is the last time." Shaking his head, Sven cocked his arm to throw it up by the pool—

And the long-range alarms went off with a high, unearthly shriek.

Seconds later, JT's voice came through his armband. "We have incoming. There's a baby Hummer in the front, followed by—shit, buses? What the fuck?"

Adrenaline kicked through Sven. "I'll be right there. Update the others."

He was the only mage on-property right then; the others were scattered on various assignments. But with two teleporters in action now, there would be backup on site within a few minutes. He just had to hold out that long. Mac stayed right beside him as he bolted up through the mansion, grabbed a shotgun off the rack of spares near the door, and burst out the front. Magic washed over him as JT opened up the ward to let him through, then again as the *winikin* closed it behind him.

There was a dust cloud hazing the horizon, growing larger and more distinct, then becoming the shadow of a vehicle. Several vehicles—an H3 with heavy tint on the windows, pimp-style, and two gray-painted buses that had probably hauled school kids in a former life.

What the fuck, indeed.

Sven cast a shield spell around him and Mac as the H3 rolled up too close to him, the driver and passenger visible only as silhouettes behind the tint. He made a show of checking the gun, figuring he'd hold the fireballs until he got a better idea of the situation, or his backup arrived.

The driver's door opened and a man got out—a late-thirties soldier type with a brush cut and shades, wearing jeans and a USMC sweatshirt. He wasn't real big, but he was plenty capable looking. And he didn't seem the slightest bit concerned about Sven, the shotgun, or the low, rumbling snarl coming from Mac. Instead, his lip curled as he gave them an up-and-down. "Oh, joy. A coyote."

Sven got the feeling he wasn't talking about Mac.

As the passenger door opened, he bristled and said, "Who the hell—" His words died as he got a look at the H3's other occupant. He got two syllables out: "Cara."

Mac yipped with joy and bounded over to her. She greeted him like an old friend, which might have struck Sven as being odd, if his brain hadn't just vapor locked. He hadn't seen her since that day on the dock, hadn't been able to find her thereafter. She had disappeared. Now, it seemed, she had reappeared. With friends.

She was wearing a long silver-gray coat that brushed around her ankles as she walked, parting to show dark pants and stiletto boots. Soldier Boy started forward but she waved him back, so she was alone when she faced Sven, hidden behind her dark shades. "We're here. Where do you want us?"

Sven looked beyond the H3 to the buses, saw the outlines of people in every row of seats. "Who are . . ." He trailed off, felt his jaw drop. Couldn't pick it up. "Those are JT's rebels?"

"Actually, they're my rebels now," she said, with a quiet thread of steel in her voice that had his attention snapping back to her, had him seeing that her red-painted mouth and the square set of her shoulders were nothing like those of the woman who had come down off that boat to talk to him.

"Glad you made it," Strike said unexpectedly. Sven glanced back to find Leah, Sasha, and Michael backing him up, shot Mac a dirty look for not warning him they were there.

Michael nodded to Cara. "Welcome back to Skywatch."

"We'll see," she said softly, then gestured to the main gate. "Can we come in?"

Sven didn't say a damn thing. He couldn't. He was too busy trying to figure out why he was the only one here who seemed to be surprised.

"Sorry, Cara," Strike said apologetically, "but we're

going to need to check out the others before we pass them through. New security protocols."

She nodded. "Understood. We'll wait."

"Actually," Strike said, "I think you should come with us."

"Where to?"

"Dez wants us all up north. You might as well meet him face-to-face."

Cara nodded and headed back to exchange a few words with Soldier Boy. When she started to follow the magi through the main gate, Sven caught her arm. "I've been looking all over for you. Why didn't you tell me what you were up to?"

"Dad knew. If he didn't tell you, then it must have slipped his mind."

"Bullshit. He doesn't forget anything."

"Then he decided not to tell you. That's between you two—leave me out of it." She met his eyes with a reserve he didn't recognize. "Look, let's get one thing real straight: This doesn't need to be weird. The past is in the past. Let's leave it there and move on, okay? I've got a job to do, you've got a job to do, and they probably won't intersect that much. I'd like to keep it that way. Deal?" She held out her hand.

He stared at her hand, at the unmarked forearm the move revealed. Then he blew out a breath that didn't do much to settle his suddenly revving system. "Fine. Whatever."

But when they all uplinked in the great room, the magic leaped through him with a wild surge that had Strike raising a brow in his direction. Instead of saying anything about it, Sven asked, "What does Dez want us in Denver for?"

"Beats the hell out of me." Strike's lips twitched. "But considering that he nearly killed me on the firing range at five this morning and walked away still looking gray around the edges, I think we can guarantee that whatever it is, it's big."

*Denver*

When Dez texted her to meet him back in the atrium, Reese had to tear herself away from the window perch she had found up near the roof, looking out over the neighborhood. She could see a handful of other construction projects, some new signs, different storefronts, a scattering of foot traffic, and only one surreptitious handoff of cash for illegals. The 'hood had come up in the world. Then again, so had she.

*On my way*, she texted back, and headed downlevel. Given where they were and what had happened the last time they had been there, she had a feeling Dez might've tried to arrange some sort of smooth-things-over meeting with Fallon. She wasn't sure if she hoped that was it or not—things felt over for her on that front, and she didn't think it would do them any good to pretend they were going to be friends, or even that he would forgive her. Unless he was seeing someone. That would make her smile. Especially if it was someone who didn't mind that he showed love by quietly fussing, overprotecting.

She had finally figured out that she liked love that

was expressed at top volume, usually mixed in with words like "pigheaded royal" and "stubborn ass of a king," and that spilled over into the newly redecorated royal suite—or rather, into the bedroom of the royal suite, where one whole wall was taken up by a painted mural of a Montana skyline. It was another of Dez's "surprises," and one that had already seen some major makeup sex. And nonmakeup sex. And lovemaking.

She was grinning when she came out of the stairwell and swung around the corner to the atrium. Then she stopped dead, her grin fading when she saw the crowd that was waiting for her.

The full complement of magi and *winikin* hadn't been in the same place since the battle atop Coatepec Mountain; for them all to be here now said there was something major going on. There were a couple of new faces, too—one was a vibrant young woman with a white skunk stripe. That would be Cara Liu, she knew. But the other guy—lean and red-cheeked, wearing a heavy coat and a scarf wrapped up past his mouth, with round glasses perched on his nose, was a stranger.

It wasn't a reunion with Fallon, then, which was a relief. But what the hell *was* it? Some sort of dedication ceremony? Yeah, that was it. Maybe. Nerves stirred. Then the group shifted, parted, and she saw Dez at the far end. He was looking at her expectantly, those wary shadows still in place.

She moved toward him almost without volition, her body drawn into his orbit by a gravitational pull of rightness that said: *there you are*. Destined mates or love at first sight—how much of a difference was there, really?

Joining him up at the front of the room, aware that they were the center of attention—though as the king's consort, she had gotten pretty used to that—she whispered, "What are we doing, naming this place or something?"

His lips curved up. "Or something." He dipped into an inner pocket of his bomber, pulled out a jeweler's box . . . and went down on one knee.

And Reese. Stopped. Breathing.

Time telescoped and a decade disappeared in an instant. They were standing almost exactly where they had been the last time, when everything had been so very wrong. But now, as he opened the box, everything was right. The ring was made of white gold, a serpent that curled around a central stone. But instead of a cobra guarding a black stone, this was a sleekly elegant serpent god that curved around a sparkling multicolored array of white diamond, red ruby, yellow chalcedony, and gleaming onyx arranged in a circle around an emerald that glowed, green and perfect, at the center.

Her eyes filmed, spilled over. And she didn't swipe the tears away, didn't mind being a girl. Because if she couldn't be a girl when the man of her teenaged dreams and woman's fantasies proposed to her, when could she?

"Oh, Dez . . ." she breathed. She wanted to tell him that it was beautiful, that it was perfect, the moment was perfect. But she couldn't get any of that out. She could only stare at the ring as the past and present merged, finally finding their balance, becoming the whole of her life, and the anticipation of their future. They would wait until after the end-date, she knew. Just as the magi were resolved not to bring children into the world prior to the war, they were holding off on human-style marriages, some because they believed more strongly in the mated marks, others so they would have something to look forward to. She wanted to be one of those looking forward.

He cleared his throat. "I promised myself I wouldn't fuck up proposing this time."

"The lack of bodies is a good start," she observed, then winced and bit her tongue when the guy standing beside Dez choked, his eyes going round behind his glasses.

But Dez's eyes gleamed, as if that had given him the answer he needed. Suddenly, she realized the shadows she had seen in him came from wariness. Nerves. Did he really think she would turn him down? "Fuck the speech," he said hoarsely. "I love you, Reese Montana. Marry me. Please marry me. By all that's holy, I don't want to do this without you at my side, wearing my ring."

"Yes." She caught his face between her hands and stepped into the lee of his legs to lean down and kiss him, feeling the stir of heat and magic they made together. "Of course I'll marry you," she said against his lips. "I love you. Oh, how I love you."

He rose up into the kiss, then stood, still kissing her, until they were wrapped together, the heat spinning around them. Then he broke the kiss and stepped away from her to take the serpent ring from the box, which he tucked back into his jacket. He didn't put the ring on her finger, though. Instead, he palmed it and took her hands in his, the ring forming a bump between their hands. Then he nodded to the stranger. "Go ahead."

The guy smiled faintly, took a piece of paper out of his pocket and unfolded it.

Reese stared at him, blood suddenly rushing so loud in her ears that she couldn't hear the guy when he started reading, could only see his lips moving. "Wait," she interrupted. "What?"

"You said you would marry me." Dez nodded to the others. "I've got witnesses."

She didn't look at them, couldn't. Her heart raced, making her muscles tremble with the need to move, though there was nothing to flee from, nothing to fight. Her voice shook. "I thought . . . Don't you want to wait until, you know. After?"

"That's the one thing I *don't* want to do. I waited too damn long before. I'm not making the same mistake again." He tightened his fingers on hers. "I want to marry you right now," he looked around, grinning, "and most definitely right here. I love you, and I don't want to wait another minute." A pause, a hint of wariness. "What do you say?"

They were standing in a half-rebuilt warehouse in near-frigid temperatures, both wearing jeans and leather, each with a knife in a pocket and a gun hidden somewhere within easy reach. There were no Barbie dresses and tuxes, no flowers, papier-mâché, or drippy music. And that made it exactly right. A smile split her face. "I say yes."

The shadows fled, leaving only love behind. "Thank the gods for that."

He tugged her into his arms and kissed her, long and deep, with an intensity that sent sweet heat roaring through her, turning the chill air suddenly tropical. She clutched him, clung to him, sank into him. They had made love in the shower that morning, twining slick and slippery together, but she wanted him again, here, now and—

"Ahem," Strike said drily from behind Dez. "You skipped a couple of steps. Including the 'I dos' and the cake."

She broke away. "There's cake?"

Dez groaned, then laughed along with the others. "Guess I know where I stand." But he was still chuckling as the stranger got going again, reading from a simple set of nondenominational vows and prompting them at the appropriate moments.

Her "I do" was a little shaky, his cracked as a single tear leaked down. Then he kissed her, and, as she leaned into him, trembling, he slipped the serpent ring onto the fourth finger of her left hand. It curled around her finger, warming against her skin and shimmering with a faint prickle of magic that said she was done wandering, done being lost. She and Dez had finally, after all these years, come home to each other.

# GLOSSARY

**Note:** Most of these words sound the way they're spelled, with two tricks: First, the letter "x" takes the "sh" sound. Second, the letter "i" should be read as the "ee" sound. Thus, for example, Xibalba becomes "Shee-bal-buh." Hope that helps!

## Entities

**Banol Kax**—The lords of the underworld, Xibalba. Driven from the earth by the many times great-ancestors of the modern Nightkeepers, the *Banol Kax* seek to conquer Earth on the foretold day: December 21, 2012.

**itza'at**—A female Nightkeeper with visionary powers; a seer. The *itza'at* talent is often associated with depression, mental instability, and suicide, because the seer can envision the future but not change it.

**nahwal**—Humanoid spirit entities that exist in the barrier and hold within them all of the accumulated wisdom of each Nightkeeper bloodline. They can be asked for information, but cannot always be trusted.

**Nightkeeper**—A member of an ancient race sworn to protect mankind from annihilation in the years leading up to December 21, 2012, when the barrier separating the earth and underworld will fall and the *Banol Kax* will seek to precipitate the apocalypse.

**makol**—These demon souls are capable of reaching through the barrier to possess evil-natured human hosts. Recognized by their luminous green eyes, a *makol*-bound human retains his own thoughts and actions in direct proportion to the amount of evil in his soul.

**Order of Xibalba**—Formed by renegade Nightkeepers around A.D. 600, the order was believed to have been destroyed in the 1520s. However, the order survives, and is now led by a powerful mage named Iago, who has bound his soul to that of the long-dead Aztec god-king, Moctezuma.

**winikin**—Descended from the conquered Sumerian warriors who served the Nightkeepers back in ancient Egypt, the traditionally raised *winikin* are blood-bound to act as the servants, protectors, and counselors of the magi. However, some *winikin*—rebels who mutinied against the king—escaped prior to the massacre. Now, their return threatens to upset the fragile balance of power at Skywatch.

**Places**

**Skywatch**—The Nightkeepers' training compound is located in a box canyon in the Chaco Canyon region of New Mexico, and is protected by magical wards.

**Xibalba**—The nine-layer underworld home of the *Banol Kax*, *boluntiku*, and *makol*. May be entered through a hellmouth located in the cloud forests of Ecuador, which Iago has hidden.

**Things (spells, glyphs, prophecies, etc.)**

**barrier**—A force field of psi energy that separates the earth, sky, and underworld, and powers the Nightkeepers' magic. The strength of the barrier is decreasing as the end-date approaches; the power of the magi becomes stronger as the barrier weakens.

**cardinal days**—The Nightkeepers' powers are strongest during the solstices and equinoxes . . . but so are those of their enemies.

**compass artifacts**—When assembled together by a mage of the proper bloodline, these artifacts become a powerful—and potentially deadly—force.

**hellmouth**— An underworld access point that opens only during the cardinal days.

**jun tan**—The "beloved" glyph that signifies a Nightkeeper's mated status.

**library**—Created by far-seeing Nightkeeper leaders, this repository contains all the ancient artifacts and information the magi need to arm themselves for the end-time war. Once hidden deep within the barrier, the library now resides on Earth, within Skywatch's box canyon.

**Solstice Massacre**—Following a series of prophetic dreams, the Nightkeepers' king led them to battle against the *Banol Kax* in 1984. The magi were slaughtered, with only a scant dozen children surviving to be raised in hiding by their *winikin*.

**skyroad**—The celestial avenue connecting the earth and sky planes, allowing contact between the Nightkeepers and the gods. Since Iago's destruction of the skyroad, the gods have been unable to influence anything happening on earth, giving the demons control.

**Triad**—The last three years prior to December 21, 2012, are known as the Triad years. During this time, the Nightkeepers are prophesied to need the help of the Triad, a trio of über-powerful magi created through powerful spell casting. However, Brandt is the only functional Triad mage, as Anna is comatose and Dez's ancestors used up the magic saving his soul.

**writs**—Written by the First Father, these delineate the duties and codes of the Nightkeepers. Not all of them translate well into modern times.

## The Nightkeepers and their winikin

**Coyote bloodline**—Coyote-Seven, known as Sven, can move objects with his mind and wears the warrior's mark, but is missing a part of himself. His *winikin* was the senior-statesman, Carlos, who turned over the responsibility to his daughter, Cara Liu. Cara didn't want to be anyone's servant, though, and soon left Skywatch.

**Eagle bloodline**—A bird bloodline, and therefore connected with the air and flight. The members of this bloodline include Brandt, his wife Patience (who has the talent of invisibility), and their twin sons, Harry and Braden, who are five years old. Patience's *winikin*, Hannah, and the former *winikin* leader, Jox, have taken the twins into hiding.

**Harvester bloodline**—Typically the holders of passive, healing magic. Jade is a spell caster and warrior, though she spends much of her time with her human mate, Lucius. Together with Natalie and JT, two of the rebel *winikin*, they form the core of the Nightkeepers' surveillance and intel capabilities.

**Hawk bloodline**—Also connected with air and flight, this bloodline can be aloof and unpredictable. Nate Blackhawk, the surviving member of this bloodline, was orphaned young and trusts few. He is a shapeshifter whose destructive power is kept in check by his love for his mate, Alexis.

**Jaguar bloodline**—The royal house of the Nightkeepers. The members of this bloodline tend to be loyal and fair-minded, but can be stubborn and often struggle between duty and their own personal desires. The current members of the jaguar bloodline include the Nightkeepers' king, Strike, and his sisters, Anna and Sasha. Strike is a teleporter; Anna is a seer who denies her talents and was struck into a coma by the Triad magic; and Sasha is the Nightkeepers' healer. Strike's mate and queen, Leah Daniels, is full human, a former Miami-Dade detective who now leads Strike's royal council.

**Peccary bloodline**—The boar bloodline is old and powerful; its members ruled the Nightkeepers before the jaguars came to power. Red-Boar was the only adult mage to survive the Solstice Massacre; he lost his wife and twin sons, and never forgave himself for living. He was killed soon after the Nightkeepers were reunited, giving his life for his king and queen. Red-Boar's teenage son, Rabbit, lives with the stigma of being a half blood, and commands wildly powerful magic. He is—more or less—kept in check by his love for his human girlfriend, Myrinne.

**Serpent bloodline**—The masters of trickery. Snake (Dez) Mendez is a bad actor who joined the Nightkeepers late and is only just beginning to win their trust. His *winikin*, Louis Keban, is dangerously unbalanced and knows far more than he should. Dez is a loner; his only real vulnerability is in his feelings for ex–bounty hunter, Reese Montana.

**Smoke bloodline**—They are often seers and prophets, but the surviving member of this bloodline, Alexis Gray, wielded the power of the goddess Ixchel, patron of weaving, fertility, and rainbows. With the destruction of the skyroad, she has lost her Godkeeper connection but remains a fierce warrior, strong in the power of her mated bond with Nate Blackhawk.

**Stone bloodline**—The keepers of secrets. Michael is a master of the protective shield spell as well as the killing silver magic called muk. His *winikin*, Tomas, and his mate, Sasha, combine to keep him balanced when the deadly magic threatens to tip him toward darkness.

**Earthly allies**

**Leah Ann Daniels**—The former detective is Strike's mate and the Nightkeepers' queen.

**Lucius Hunt**—Once a *makol*, now Lucius is the Nightkeepers' Prophet and head geek. Mated to Jade and a warrior in his own right, he is currently sidelined while healing from a near-fatal injury.

**Reese Montana**—Tough and self-reliant, with an outer shell hardened by past betrayal, this ex–bounty hunter has toned things down and gone private. But when she's offered a chance to get back in the action and help save the whole damn world, she jumps at the offer . . . even if it means working with the man who broke her heart a decade earlier.

**Myrinne**—Raised by a witch who told fortunes in the French Quarter and was sacrificed by Iago at the hellmouth, this young, ambitious beauty is Rabbit's lover.

**Earthly enemies**

**Iago**—The leader of the Order of Xibalba is a mage of extraordinary power, capable of "borrowing" the talents of other magi. Iago has gained additional power by allying himself with the bloodthirsty Aztec god-king, Moctezuma, and now seeks to take out the Nightkeepers by trickery.

The Jeep skidded in the turn, hit a bump that would've done a ski mogul proud, caught some air, and landed shuddering. There wasn't much dust—New Mex was in its rainy season just like the rain forests Sven, Mac, and JT had come from—but rocks clunked against the undercarriage and something mechanical thumped ominously. In the back, a bulky hammock swung wildly from side to side, its canine occupant emitting a low, annoyed growl.

Sven hung on to the holy-shit handle and jammed a knee against the door. "Jesus, JT, what's the fucking rush?"

Not that the irascible *winikin* didn't usually drive like a death bat out of hell, but this was something else. Or maybe it wasn't, and Sven just wanted it to be, because he was in zero hurry to get where they were going.

"One of us is getting laid tonight, and it ain't you." JT bared his teeth in a smile that held more than a bit of *nyah-nyah*, along with a solid dose of anticipation that had nothing to do with Sven and everything to do with Natalie, the pretty archaeologist who was waiting at the other end of the access road.

"Nice. Real nice." Sven scowled out the window. The tint reflected the bristle of his hair, which had bleached nearly white during the nine months the three of them had spent hunting *makol* in the Mayan highlands. "Watch it or I'll suddenly realize I 'forgot' something that we have to go back for."

And given that "back" was a solid three-day drive plus some magical shenanigans at the U.S.–Mexico border, that would put a serious crimp in the plans of Mr. I'm-getting-some-and-you're-not.

"Try it," JT suggested with a "you and what army?" sneer, but they both knew Sven wouldn't pull rank— first because there wasn't any rank to pull as far as he was concerned, and second because this was no random trip home.

Dez had called them back to Skywatch, which meant there was something going down. More, that "something" was big enough that the king hadn't been swayed by Sven's argument that he was *this* close to figuring out why hundreds of villagers who had been released from *makol* possession last winter had reverted and gone vampiric, attacking their friends and families and turning them into more of the green-eyed monsters. Instead, Dez had told him to get the hell home. And he'd had a definite "don't make me repeat myself" tone when he'd said it. So they were headed back to Skywatch, whether or not Sven liked the idea.

*Shit.*

At the sound of a soft whine coming from behind him, Sven scowled even harder at JT. "You might want to slow down before Mac makes you." His familiar had toughened up over the past year, getting over his adolescent spookiness, but the burly coyote still wasn't big on transportation, whether by wheels or teleport. He liked having his paws on the ground.

"Whoops. Sorry about that, big dog." JT eased up on the gas. He might be a stubborn ass and way too ready to pick a fight over the Nightkeepers versus *winikin* stuff, but he was a loyal son of a bitch, and Mac had saved both their lives down in the *makol*-infested Mexican highlands.

Even though the ride smoothed out, Mac kept whining low in his throat, sending off distress vibes that bumped up against the mental barrier Sven kept between the two of them. There was a canvas *rustle-thump* as the coyote lurched out of the hammock, and then his big head appeared between the men, his shoulders jamming the gap between the two front seats. The coyote's eyes—pale green, with an eerily human directness—locked on the road ahead, where Sky-watch was invisible behind a couple of sandy humps.

JT chucked him under the chin. "What's the matter, boy? Timmy fall in the well again?"

"You're a godsdamned riot," said Sven, who'd heard about a million variations on the theme since he and Mac had bonded. And, yeah, it had been funny the first hundred or so times, but the laughs were thinning out across the board as the countdown moved into the last month before the end-date.

The gods were holding the barrier so far, but with the *makol* spreading viruslike, the dark-magic threat was increasing daily. And with tension stringing everyone tight as shit, Sven and Mac had been getting on each other's nerves more and more, making the mental block between them a necessity and weakening the magic that came from their partnership. That wasn't good, but Sven didn't know how to fix it. Or, rather, he did, and it so wasn't happening. Thus, the mental barrier.

Now, though, something was getting through: *Danger*. The thought-glyph that came from the animal was faint, but recognizable. And when he raised an eyebrow in Mac's direction, the coyote chuffed a low bark. It wasn't his "emergency!" howl or even his "get your ass over here and deal with this" bark; it was more a signal of "I think there might be something wrong but I'm not sure." Mac's instincts had proven damn good, though, and Carlos had drilled it into Sven's head: *Never disrespect your familiar.*

He could bend the bond if he did it carefully . . . but if it snapped, he was screwed.

So, cursing under his breath, Sven lowered the mental block. As it fell, he muttered under his breath, "This better be for real and not just you jonesing to get out of the car."

Then the magic took hold, aligning his senses with those of his familiar, and for a moment he perceived the interior of the Jeep from Mac's point of view: the vehicle's shuddering bounciness; the two men in the front, one excited the other reluctant; and an intense hit of eau de dirty laundry with a chaser of stale Mickey D's. Then the connection locked in and he caught the mental stream the coyote was directing at him—not thought-glyphs but pure emotion: frustration, fear, and anxiety overlain with an image of a beautiful dark-eyed woman with a white skunk-stripe in her straight black hair.

*Cara Liu.*

"Son of a—" Sven broke the connection and glared, sending back a double-helping of the thought-glyph that meant "cold" in the tradition of the coyote blood-line, but for him and Mac had come to mean "chill out and knock it the fuck off."

JT glanced over. "Problem?"

"Nope." Sven faced forward, ignoring his familiar. He didn't block the coyote's mental stream all the way, though; it buzzed along his nerve endings and filled his mind with thought-pictures, one of which gelled. In it, Cara was standing at the edge of the training hall in the sleek gray military jacket that marked her as the leader of the *winikin*. With her dark eyes gleaming in challenge, her hair tied back in a slick ponytail and her hands behind her back in a parade rest that made her seem far taller than her fine-boned five three, she looked calm and capable, and nothing like the girl he'd grown up with. But then again, neither of them was the same as they had been back then, thank the gods.

"Guess I'm not the only one excited to get back," JT said as they crested the last hill and the coyote's whining got louder.

Sven didn't answer. He hadn't let on to JT that for

the past few months Mac had been nagging that they needed to get back to Skywatch, that Cara needed them. She was fine, though—he had checked and double-checked. Not to mention that if she needed someone, her second in command, Zane, had made it real clear that he was taking care of business in that department.

Mac growled low in his throat, his attention fixed on where the training compound spread out in front of them at the bottom of the incline.

The stone walls that blocked off the open end of the box canyon were a lighter shade than the red-rock canyon walls, the mansion beyond a study of earth tones and white trim. Behind the sprawling, multiwinged structure, a small grove of trees butted up against the huge steel training hall that the *winikin* had claimed as their territory, no magi need apply. Beyond that were cottages, the firing range and urban warfare setup, and at the back of the canyon, nearly lost in the distance, the entrance to the Nightkeepers' ancestral library. There were people scattered pretty much everywhere, reminding Sven how crowded things had gotten in the compound when Cara and her forty-some rebel *winikin* showed up, nearly tripling the population of Skywatch overnight. Granted, the Nightkeepers needed all the trained bodies they could get right now, but still.

Bracing himself for the close quarters and the feeling of being in the middle of a Nightkeeper-*winikin* stand-off, Sven used his magic to drop a section of the ward spell that guarded the compound. "Door's open."

"You going to be okay?" JT asked as they drove through.

The question surprised him, as did his fleeting impulse to let off some steam in the other man's direction. The *winikin* might be kind of a dick, but he always told it like it was, and Natalie loved him, which had to mean something. Problem was, JT was also one of the more outspoken voices among the rebel *winikin*, and Cara was trying to meld the traditionalists and rebels into a unified fighting force. The last thing she needed was a rumor linking her to the last bachelor full-blooded Nightkeeper. It wouldn't matter that the link came through his familiar, because half the time the damn coyote echoed his emotions. There was no way he'd be able to convince the others that Mac was on his own in this one. Presto, instant rumor, and hello, political nightmare.

So Sven gave the "no biggie" shrug that used to be his trademark but now felt strange and awkward. "I'll be fine once I'm not inhaling doggie breath up close and personal."

JT might've kept going at him, but as they rolled to a stop in front of the mansion, the door opened and Natalie came pelting out. And JT was a goner. Grinning and thoroughly distracted, he swung out of the Jeep and made a beeline for her.

Mac barked but held his place until Sven waved at the open door. "Go on. Go find her, for Christ's sake. Get your damned belly rub, and leave me the hell out of it."

But although the coyote lunged out and hit the ground running, he didn't take off. Instead, he made a wide circle around the Jeep, yapping like a freaking

Chihuahua. And as Sven dropped down out of the Jeep, JT bit off a curse and turned back to him, face set in hard, harsh lines. "Mac was right. There's a problem."

Sven looked beyond him to see that Natalie's face was pale, her eyes wide. And behind her, Anna, the compound's only *itza'at* seer, hovered in the doorway staring at him as if he were somehow her only hope. "What happened?" he grated as Mac slithered to a stop at his heels and stood there, quivering.

It was JT who said, "Cara's gone missing . . . and the teleporters can't lock on to her."

Which meant she was either belowground . . . or dead.